VEGAS HEAT

Books by Fern Michaels:

Up Close and Personal
Fool Me Once
Picture Perfect
About Face
The Future Scrolls
Kentucky Sunrise
Kentucky Heat
Kentucky Rich
Plain Jane
Charming Lily
What You Wish For
The Guest List
Listen to Your Heart
Celebration
Yesterday
Finders Keepers
Annie's Rainbow
Sara's Song
Vegas Sunrise
Vegas Heat
Vegas Rich
Whitefire
Wish List
Dear Emily

The Sisterhood Novels:

Final Justice
Collateral Damage
Fast Track
Hokus Pokus
Hide and Seek
Free Fall
Sweet Revenge
The Jury
Vendetta
Payback
Weekend Warriors

Anthologies:

Silver Bells
Comfort and Joy
Sugar and Spice
Let It Snow
A Gift of Joy
Five Golden Rings
Deck the Halls
Jingle All the Way

FERN MICHAELS

VEGAS HEAT

ZEBRA BOOKS
Kensington Publishing Corp.
http://www.kensingtonbooks.com

ZEBRA BOOKS are published by

Kensington Publishing Corp.
850 Third Avenue
New York, NY 10022

All Kensington titles, imprints and distributed lines are available at special quantity discounts for bulk purchases for sales promotion, premiums, fund-raising, educational or institutional use.

Special book excerpts or customized printings can also be created to fit specific needs. For details, write or phone the office of the Kensington Special Sales Manager: Kensington Publishing Corp., 850 Third Avenue, New York, NY 10022. Attn. Special Sales Department. Phone: 1-800-221-2647.

ISBN-13: 978-1-4201-0695-4
ISBN-10: 1-4201-0695-3

First Hardcover Printing: March 1997
First Trade Paperback Printing: March 2009
10 9 8 7 6 5 4 3 2 1

Printed in the United States of America

I'd like to dedicate this book to those nearest and dearest to my heart: Cynthia, Susy, Patty, Michael, David, Kelly and Billy. And for the four legged creatures who warm my heart, old and new; Fred, Gus, Harry, Maxie, Rosie, Lily and Lennie, Buck, Weenie, Spanky, Pete, Zack, Tinker, Einstein, Izzie and Bennie. I love each and every one of you.

Part One

1980

1

Those in the know said Babylon was a one-of-a-kind gambling casino. Those same people said the Thornton family, owners of the casino, had overextended themselves. The big question on the Big White Way was how Ash Thornton, a man confined to a wheelchair, a man whose body was racked with pain twenty-four hours a day, could hope to operate Babylon.

The windowless counting room, an inner sanctuary where the money washed through daily, bore testament to how well the wheelchair-bound man managed. For Ash the ultimate thrill was being immersed in the sight, smell, and touch of money—tons of money, stacks and bundles of coins so heavy he had been forced to buy a hydraulic lift to move it all around the counting room.

It was amazing to Fanny that rather than counting the money, Ash had the cash bundled according to denomination and *weighed*. Her daughter Sunny had told her a million dollars in $100 bills weighed 20 1/2 pounds; a million dollars in $20 bills weighed 102 pounds. A million dollars in $5 bills weighed 408 pounds.

There was even a name for the electronic coin-weighing scale, the Toledo Scale. Sunny had laughed, a tinge of hysteria in her voice, when she said a million dollars in quarters from the slots weighed twenty-one tons. A fortune passed through Babylon every day of the year, so much money that it had to be weighed instead of counted.

What *was* she doing here? *I'm trying to justify my mother-in-law's faith in my ability to safeguard the Thornton family fortune,* Fanny told herself. *I'm trying to help her family and to keep my own family intact.*

Fanny Thornton hated the opulent, decadent casino. Today, she should have called ahead to arrange a meeting someplace else, made a luncheon reservation as far away from this fool's paradise as possible. She knew that floor Security had announced her entrance the moment she walked through the door. Ash was probably watching her from one of his top-secret peepholes. Birch and Sage were probably on their way to intercept her while Sunny sat with her feet propped up on an open desk drawer, awaiting her arrival. She, too, would have been notified that Fanny Thornton was in the casino. The big question to all of them would be, why?

Knowing what was ahead of her, Fanny quickened her step, refusing to look at the acres of slot machines and banks of poker tables. Directly in her line of vision, striding toward her, were her handsome twin sons, dressed in dark suits and pristine white shirts. They could have posed as Wall Street bankers. They were smiling, but only Sage's smile reached his eyes.

"Mom! What brings you down here? Try and work up a smile or the customers will think Babylon hasn't been kind to you." Birch leaned over and kissed her lightly on the cheek.

"Mom, it's good to see you." Sage hugged her as he gave her a smacking loud kiss. "Do you have time for lunch or at least a cup of coffee?"

"I have the time. How's your father?" Her voice was polite, nothing more.

"Is that one of those questions that doesn't require an answer or is it one of those questions whose answer doesn't matter?" Birch asked as he cupped her elbow to lead her through the casino.

"Both."

Sage laughed, a sound of genuine merriment. Birch's features tightened.

Fanny looked from one of her sons to the other. The twins were like night and day. Sage was loving, open, warmhearted, and always the first one to ask "what can I do to help?" He was so much like her he scared her at times. Birch was cool, noncommittal except where his father was concerned, selfish, and arrogant, possessing all the same traits his father was known for.

Fanny shook off her son's hand, a motion that caused Birch's lips to tighten. She didn't care. She had every right to expect loyalty from her children. "If it's your intention to lead me to your father's office, forget it. This may surprise you, but I don't require an escort."

"Mom, why are you always so difficult when you come here?" Birch asked.

Fanny stopped in mid-stride. "That's a very amusing statement, Birch. I've been to this casino exactly twice in eighteen months. The first time was at the grand opening. The second was when Sunny fainted and Sage called me. The first time I was here I spent so much time smiling I thought I would end up with TMJ. My second visit was spent putting cool cloths on Sunny's forehead. Perhaps you have me mixed up with someone else."

"Mom, Birch didn't mean . . ."

"Yes, Birch means exactly what he says. I don't like this place. I have never liked it, even when it was on the drawing board. Those feelings have not changed. The only reason I'm here is because of business. Now, if you don't mind, I can find my way to Sunny's office by myself. Fetch your father, please."

"Mom . . ." Birch watched his mother walk away, her shoulders stiff, her ears closed to whatever he wanted to say.

"When was the last time you called her just to say hello, how are you?" Sage asked. "She hasn't forgiven us for choosing up sides two years ago. I can't say that I blame her. It was the worst kind of betrayal. You know it, and I know it. We're damn lucky she even talks to us."

"This is bullshit. We're running a business here. There's no room for 'he said, she said, I don't like this and I don't like that' crap. What's the point in calling, she's never home. She's always off somewhere with Simon."

"*Uncle* Simon, Birch. Show some respect. Mom can do whatever she pleases. She doesn't owe us explanations. She's fifty-four and she's independent. She makes more money than this casino does. Go ahead, defend that one."

"I don't have to defend anything. I don't kiss ass and take names later like you do, Sage."

"Where the hell did that come from? Mom walks in here and she has every right to do so and that invisible alarm goes off. Dad gets in a flap, Sunny goes white in the face, and you look so damn brittle it wouldn't surprise me to see your face split wide-open. Am I the only one who's normal around here? Scratch that, and add our sister Billie to the normal list. Don't forget for even one minute where the money came from for this fancy-dancy casino. Or is that what's eating you?"

"Let's not get into this now, Sage. I'll get Dad and meet you in Sunny's office. Where do you suppose *Uncle* Simon is? Dad calls him *her* shadow. He says they're joined at the hip. Actually, he didn't say hip."

"I know what he said. I was there. That crap is getting really old, Birch. Why can't you accept things for what they are? You're turning into Dad's clone. I just want you to know I hate what I see."

"Ah, the good son. Mom's good son. I'm the bad seed, is that it? Because I hate it that our uncle has taken over Mom's life? Dad hates it too. He still loves her."

"That's about the biggest crock I've ever heard. You're even more stupid if you believe it. You need to start lining up your ducks, Birch, before it's too late."

"Jesus, Sage, that almost sounds like a threat."

"It's whatever you want it to be," Sage said, turning on his heel. "I wouldn't make light of this to Dad. Whatever it is that brought Mom here must be serious. Hey, isn't that our little sister making her way in our direction?"

"What the hell! Is this a family reunion?" Birch demanded.

Sage grinned. "I think it's one of those things that's going to require a family vote. Billie, you're lookin' good!" He hugged his sister. Birch did, too, but not with the same enthusiasm.

"You handsome devil! You still beating the women off with a stick?" Billie teased as she tweaked Sage's cheek. "If you'd wipe that scowl off your face, Birch, you'd be just as handsome. What's up? Mom just said to be here at noon."

"Your guess is as good as ours."

"How's our little mother to be? I can't believe Sunny is going to have a baby."

"Dad can't believe it either," Sage said. "He's taking it personally. He thinks Sunny is having this baby to embarrass him. He won't allow her out on the floor."

"What?"

"You heard me. You wouldn't believe the crap that goes on here."

"Sure I would. Sunny takes it?" Billie said, her eyes wide with disbelief.

"She doesn't want to make waves. She says she learned her lesson that time when we all turned on Mom. In addition, I don't think she's feeling all that good. Tyler asked me to keep a close eye on her. I worry about her. If she doesn't shoot off her mouth, something is very wrong. Birch . . . Birch seems to take some kind of perverse pleasure in baiting her. It's taking a toll on her, Billie. So, enough about us, how are you doing? You still seeing that guy?"

"Yes, and don't ask me any more questions. My love life is my own. Tell me about yours."

"Her name is Iris. She said her mother named her after her favorite flower. She reminds me of Mom. Really down-to-earth, wants a family. She just got a professorship at the university. She's so smart she makes me look like a dummy." Billie hooted with laughter. "Sunny says Rainbow Babies is making so much money you guys can't count it fast enough."

"Kid clothing sells. We're doing well. Why does it have to be us guys versus you guys? I hate that, Sage."

"Because that's the way it is. This family has always been divided, and it will probably remain that way as long as Dad calls the shots around here. I don't see any changes on the horizon."

"Is there anything I can do?"

"Sure, have dinner with me and Iris over the weekend. I'd really like you to meet her. Bring along what's his name." Sage dropped his voice to a whisper as they approached the door to Sunny's office. "Billie, I want out of here. I gave it my best shot, but it isn't good enough. This was supposed to be a four-way operation, but Dad and Birch call the shots. Sunny and I are just their flunkies. I hate getting up in the morning knowing I have to come here."

"Then do something about it. The Dutch have a saying, Sage. If you can't whistle on your way to work, you don't belong in that job? Do you whistle?"

"Hell no, I don't."

"There you go. Is there anything I can do?"

"If there is, I'll call you. I just know this is going to be one of those spill-your-guts things. Everyone is going to say things they'll regret later on. The wedge will become wider. One of these days we're going to be strangers to one another. Wanna bet?"

"No thanks."

The door to Sunny's office opened. Billie said, "Mom, you look wonderful. Sunny, you look terrible. Are you taking your vitamins?"

"Of course I'm taking my vitamins. I'm married to a doctor. I just called down to the conference room to get it ready. We're going to need to spread out. The kitchen is sending up coffee and sandwiches. How's what's his name?" Sunny asked, leading the way out of her office.

"What's his name is just fine, thank you. So, Mom, what's this all about?" Billie asked as she linked her arm with her mother's.

"Family business. Serious business. I'm going to stop by the offices later. I haven't seen Bess in three weeks."

"Sunny's Togs and Rainbow Babies aren't the same without you. Bess misses you, Mom. She's just like you and Aunt Billie. You really are lucky to have such a good friend."

"I know that. We're like sisters. Actually, we're closer than sisters. I'm worried about Sunny, Billie. Has she said anything to you?"

"Only that she's taking her vitamins. Get her out of here, Mom. There aren't any windows, she's indoors all day, sometimes for twelve hours. It doesn't look to me like she gets any thanks for all her hard work either. Wouldn't it be something if she had twins?"

"Bite your tongue, Billie," Fanny said.

"Are you going to give us a clue as to what this meeting is all about, Mom?" Sunny asked. "Pop's smack in the middle of winding up all the details for the World Series Poker Championship. The emperor of Las Vegas as he's called these days, will view this meeting as a thorn in his side."

Fanny snorted. The World Series Championship was what Wimbledon was to tennis—the oldest and most prestigious of all the tournaments. Players came from all over the globe to compete. For three straight weeks, twenty-four hours a day, people would line up and play, right up to the main event, the $10,000 buy-in no-limit tournament that would last four days until a new champion was crowned.

"Fanny, what a pleasant surprise."

Fanny stared at the man in the wheelchair, the man who had once been her husband. She felt her shoulders straighten. There were no regrets. Not now, not ever.

He was impeccably dressed, manicured, and coifed. "Whatever this is about, Fanny, can we make it quick?" he said, not looking at her. "I'm up to my ears with the final details for the championship. There aren't enough hours in the day." His voice was syrupy, the way it always was when he thought he could charm her, wheedle her into doing what he wanted.

"Dad, I offered to help," Sunny said. "Sage . . ."

"Forget it, Sunny. The customers don't want to see your big belly. It's a turnoff. Men don't want reminders of home and hearth when they come to paradise."

Fanny sucked in her breath when her daughter's eyes filled with tears. "That was unnecessarily cruel, Ash, and you need to apologize to your daughter."

"It's okay, Mom." Sunny said.

"No. It is not okay. It wasn't okay when your father said the same things to me years ago and it's not okay now. This is not *your* casino, Ash. It belongs to the Thornton family enterprise. Sunny has a role here, and if you forgot what it is, I can have my attorneys refresh your memory. I also don't give a damn about your championship gambling tournament. Now, I came here to discuss something very important."

"You're really trying to stick it to me, aren't you, Fanny? Where's Simon? Shouldn't he be here?"

"Why is that, Ash? He doesn't belong to this immediate family even though he is your brother. But, to answer your question, I don't know where he is. Before we get down to the reason I'm here, outline what Sunny can do to take part of the burden off your shoulders. *Now*, Ash."

"Mom, it's okay. Really it is."

"Ash? Birch? Sage?" Fanny said. The three men stared at Fanny, blank looks on their faces. "I see, no one knows what's going on. Well, we'll change that right now. Sunny, you are in charge of the championship. You will report to Billie and me at the end of each workday. If it's too much for you, hire some help. Now that we've settled that little matter, let's get on with it."

"Just a goddamn minute, Fanny. You can't waltz in here and tell me how to run this business."

"I just did. We've moved on, Ash. What part didn't you understand?"

"You're deliberately screwing this up, Fanny. The minute you get your fingers on something it goes to hell."

"I made a decision, Ash. When I do that, I don't look back, and I don't back down. If I did, I wouldn't be in business, and you wouldn't be sitting here in this . . . this obscene den of opulence. As I said, I came here for a reason. I'm giving you all the courtesy of asking your opinion. I'll weigh what you have to say very carefully." Fanny drew a deep breath as she stared at the faces of her family.

"What is it, Mom?" Billie asked gently.

"Billie Coleman needs our help. As you know, your grandmother Sallie bought into Coleman Aviation years ago. The stock has been holding its own until now. Ash, I know Moss talked to you about the plans for his new plane before he died. I also heard you say you would help in any way you could. Simon also agreed. The Colemans are tapped out. They have nowhere else to turn. They've come too far now to let it all settle in the dust. I think we should do all we can to help Aunt Billie bring Moss's dream to life the way we all worked to make this dream possible for you, Ash. I'd like to hear your thoughts."

"Charity begins at home, Mom. What have the Colemans ever

done for us? Uncle Seth didn't give a damn about Grandma Sallie. His own *sister*. I don't plan on forgetting that," Birch said.

"What happens if they go belly up?" Ash asked. "Where does that leave us, Fanny? What exactly do you want from us? Our cash flow isn't that strong. Or are you saying you want to mortgage everything. That's it, isn't it? Jesus Christ, Fanny, we could lose everything on some cockamamie dream of Moss's."

Fanny's heart hammered in her chest. She waited.

"Aunt Billie is family. Families stick together. If this is a yes or no vote, then I vote yes," Sage said.

"Me too," Billie said without hesitation.

The score was two to two. If Sunny didn't vote, it would be up to Fanny to break the tie. The turmoil on her daughter's face tore at her heart. Once before Sunny had taken a stand and made a decision she couldn't live with.

"What are you waiting for, Sunny?" Ash demanded, his eyes boring into his daughter.

Fanny shivered at Ash's tone as she too waited for her daughter's response.

"I love Aunt Billie. I love all the Colemans. I say what's ours is theirs. I know in my heart Aunt Billie would do the same for us. I'm voting the way Grandma Sallie would want me to vote. I vote yes."

"That's just dandy. And when that plane doesn't get off the ground and we're hiding out from our creditors, where will you all be?" Ash snarled, his wheelchair burning rubber as he pressed the electric control.

"You're a jerk, Sunny," Birch said. He followed his father out into the hall.

"No, you are not a jerk," Billie said as she wrapped her arms around her sister. "I know what it took for you to do that." This last was said in a hushed whisper.

"So, what's the game plan?" Sage asked.

"I'm going to talk to Simon. He's our investment man. I don't think he's going to agree. This could go either way. Sage said it best. Families need to stick together. It's possible we could lose our shirts."

Billie's voice was flippant. "The sign on my door says I'm the head designer of Sunny's Togs and Rainbow Babies. If we lose our shirts, I'll design us new ones."

"Attagirl," Sage said, pounding her on the back. "C'mon, Sunny, sit down. You don't have any color. Are you sure you're okay?"

Fanny's head jerked upward at the concern in Sage's voice. "I'm taking all of us to lunch at Peridot. Billie, call Bess and ask her to meet us there. Sage, ask Birch if he wants to join us. There's no point in asking your father, but do it anyway. I'll meet you at the front door. I want to call Billie and tell her the good news."

The moment the door closed behind her children, the phone was in Fanny's hand. She would call Billie, but first she was calling Sunny's husband.

"Dr. Ford here."

"Tyler, it's Fanny."

"What's wrong?"

"That's what I want you to tell me. Sunny looks like death warmed over, and that's a kind statement. Aside from morning sickness, a pregnant woman usually has a wonderful sparkle in her eyes, color in her cheeks. She's a happy woman. This is not the case with Sunny. And another thing, she shouldn't be working twelve hours a day."

"You're right about everything, Fanny. Were you ever successful in changing Sunny's mind or getting her to do something she didn't want to do? I've spoken to her doctor, and he tells me she's fine. He said if she wants to work, she should work. She eats well, she exercises moderately, she takes her prenatal vitamins, and she sleeps through the night. She tells me she takes an hour nap in the middle of the afternoon. She makes sure she takes breaks and walks outside. She didn't have morning sickness. She's never been one to complain. My personal opinion is she's under a lot of stress at the casino with her father and brothers. Did something happen or did you just call to ask me questions? Whatever we say, Fanny, will go no farther."

"I know that, Tyler." Fanny told him about the brief meeting and Sunny's vote. "She looks so . . . fragile, so washed-out. She appeared a little wobbly to me. If she's willing to come up to Sunrise for a week or so, would you have any objections?"

"None at all. I've suggested the same thing to her, but she's married to that casino. I hate that goddamn place."

"Not as much as I do. Maybe I can work a little mother magic." She told him about the vote to help the Colemans. "How's everything going otherwise, Tyler?"

"Reconstructive surgery is not glamorous, but it is rewarding to make someone feel whole again. I love what I do as much as Sunny loves what she does. So, you see, I'm the last person who should even make suggestions where her job is concerned. I'm being paged, Fanny. Call me if you think there's something I can do. Not that my vote counts, but I think you're doing the right thing. Tell Billie I said hello when you talk to her."

"I'll do that, Tyler. She adores you, you know. She said you remind her of her son Riley."

"That's one of the nicest things anyone has ever said to me. Look, you do what you feel is right and don't let anyone make you back down. Families need to stick together. We'll talk again."

Fanny's fingers drummed on Sunny's desk. She should be feeling better after Tyler's reassuring words, but she didn't. Her motherly intuition was telling her something was wrong. She dialed Billie Coleman's number in Austin, Texas.

"Is everything okay?" Billie asked, breathless. She had picked up the phone on the first ring. "Every time I hear the phone the word disaster rings in my head. Before you can ask, we're facing a brick wall. Money just pours out of here. I don't know what to do. If I don't finish this project, then Riley's death and all those other boys who died in Coleman aircraft will have been in vain . . . how can I live with that? As sick as he was at the end, Moss worked tirelessly to perfect this plane. How can I do less?"

"You can't. The Thorntons are going to help, Billie. I'm at Babylon right now. We voted and the money will be on the way by the end of the week. If it isn't enough, we'll go back to the drawing board. Please, Billie, don't cry. Be thankful your granddaughter Sawyer is the aeronautical engineer on this project."

"We're all obsessed with this plane project, Sawyer more so. My own children . . . Fanny, how is it possible for a mother to be estranged from her two daughters? I never, ever thought such a thing would happen to me, how my daughters can fight me on this plane. All they want is the money they say we're wasting. They say a new plane won't bring Riley back, and they're right about that. He was their brother, and I know they loved him. On a more pleasant note, I just know Sawyer is going to explode when I tell her about your offer. That child has worked for months now, getting by on three hours' sleep a night. She eats, sleeps, and dreams about her grandfather's dream plane. She's going to get it off the ground too, thanks to you. Fanny, I wish there were words . . ."

"Words aren't necessary, Billie. We're family."

"We could lose our shirts."

"Well, guess what? Your namesake said if that happens, she would design us new ones. You can't beat an offer like that."

"No, you can't. How are things going on the Big White Way? How's Sunny? Is Birch still giving you heartache?"

"I'm in the conference room here at Babylon, Billie. I'll call you this evening. I'm taking the kids to lunch at Peridot."

"That place where you and Sallie got blitzed at your first meeting? When I told Thad how Devin took you two home in a hearse because no one had gas, he laughed until he cried."

"Drunk or not, that is one of my fondest memories of my mother-in-law. Oh, Billie, I miss her so much. She had such faith and trust in me. I hope I can live up to her expectations. I know in my heart she would approve of what we're doing. Family, Billie, is what life is all about. Sallie always said our families' destiny was in your hands and mine. Together, we'll work toward that end."

"We won't fail, Fanny. You can take that to the bank. Do I dare ask about Simon?"

"Tonight, Billie. Give everyone my love. Now, take a nap, okay?"

"At ten o'clock in the morning?"

"Why not? Aren't we independent women? If we are, then we can take a nap anytime we want. Actually, we can do *anything* we want. Both of us have earned that little perk. Talk to you tonight."

The Peridot restaurant was as old as Las Vegas itself. It was also Fanny's favorite restaurant for the very reason Billie Coleman had mentioned earlier.

"I love it when my brother finally acts like a grown-up and holds our chairs out for us," Billie said.

Sunny's voice was blunt yet sad when she said, "You're leaving, aren't you, Sage?"

"I want to. I'm willing to stay until you have the baby and get back into the swing of things. We're just flunkies, Sunny. You know it, and I know it. I glide around the floor trying to look important. I'm not sure what you do behind those closed doors. I don't know if you're aware of the latest developments. Is anyone interested?" The women nodded just as Bess Noble, Fanny's second-in-command, joined them.

"I heard that," Bess said as she kissed everyone before taking her seat. "Now, tell us what the latest development is."

"Dad and Birch want to buy riverboats in Biloxi, Mississippi, for gambling. He planned to apply for a mortgage, but you beat him to it, Mom. At least I think you did. Dad and Birch can be secretive at times. Those riverboats are a great big can of worms. I spoke up and said it had to be put to a vote, but they ignored me. At the risk of repeating myself, what the hell kind of family is this? Tell me, Mom, what you want us to do to help Aunt Billie."

"I'm going to call Simon this evening and discuss everything. We'll sell off all our shares of Rainbow Babies and Sunny's Togs. Simon never sold them. He fibbed to us about that transaction. Thank God he did. We're going to move our offices out of Sallie's Bingo Palace. It will go on the market tomorrow. It's prime real estate so it should fetch several million. I'm going to mortgage Babylon. By tomorrow the news will be on the Strip and the sharks will start to gather, so be prepared. I'll empty out that monster safe in Sunrise. I'll *mortgage* Sunrise. I'll sell all the jewelry Sallie left me. That's already in the works. I'll borrow what I can to make up the difference. The only monies we'll have coming in will go to make the mortgage payments. I did have a thought, though, and I'd like your opinions. Sallie never raised the rates for the other casinos to tie into her sewage and electrical systems. It's time for a hefty increase. Those fees, I believe, will keep our heads above water."

The sighs of relief could be heard around the table. "Good thinking, Mom," Sunny said.

"It's about time," Sage offered.

"This might be a good time to unveil my latest creation," Billie said as she dug into the voluminous bag she was never without and pulled out two soft dolls. "Meet Bernie and Blossom. I showed them to a few of our salespeople who took them on the road. Guess what! We already have orders for ten thousand. The big question is, how are we going to market them? The next question is, where do we get the money? Do we form a separate company or do we license them under Rainbow Babies or Sunny's Togs? I thought we could hire the Bernsteins to get our publicity started. We can have a million of these on the market by next Christmas."

Sage stared at his sister, his face full of awe. "Just like that! Where are you going to manufacture them?"

"Made in the good old U.S. of A. Forty bucks a pop or $39.95. People like to walk away with change even if it's only a nickel. We learned that in marketing class."

Fanny held the soft fabric doll in her hands. As always, she marveled at her younger daughter's abilities. "The scraps from Rainbow Babies, right?"

"Yes, but each face is different. I know eight people that come to mind who will be willing to work on the faces. The doll itself and the garment can be made for under a dollar if mass produced. The faces are what will cost, and labor of course. Sign on, Sage, we can use your expertise. You said you want out of Babylon. So, what do you all think?"

"I think this is one of your best ideas," Bess said, a calculator in hand.

"Billie, these dolls are priceless. I wish I had your talent. Can I have the first one off the line for my new baby, Bernie if he's a boy? If I have a girl, I'll take Blossom. They are so adorable. Raggedy Ann and Andy will be passé."

Billie reached into the bag again and withdrew two tissue-wrapped bundles. "I already made them for you. I wanted something special for you. That's where I got the idea. Think about it, Sunny, you have a clothing company named after you and now you're the inspiration behind these two dolls. I don't think we're headed to the poor house just yet."

"This calls for a celebration," Fanny said.

"Let's have some of that same wine you and Grandma Sallie had that famous day you first met. Tell us the story again, Mom," Sage said.

"It was wartime and I was meeting your grandmother for the first time . . ."

The moment the door closed behind Ash Thornton, he went into a rage. "Now, do you see what your mother is capable of? She undermines every single thing I do. If she'd keep her nose out of the casino business, things would be just fine. Do I interfere in her business? No, I do not. Your mother has to dabble in everything. She's not content to own two of the biggest clothing companies in the country, she has to make her presence felt in everything that concerns me. I'm not going to let that happen. We're going to go ahead with those riverboats. I want you in Mississippi tomorrow. Get everything under way. She won't stop us. If she does . . . I'll deal with it then and there. When Sunny comes back from lunch, send her in here. She's out of here until that kid arrives. I have enough problems without her jinxing me. Why are you looking at me that way, Birch? Business is business. We're on top, and I plan on staying there. So I already took a mortgage out, so what? I got a good interest rate and cut Granger's markers to half. That's how you do business in this town. I love bankers who gamble. Hell, the governor was in here two weeks ago, and he shot a load that made me blink. You suck up to these people and you can get anything you want. You have to know how to play the game. Your mother doesn't know the *name* of the game much less how to *play* it. I even know what her next move is going to be. She's going to raise the rates on the sewage and electric plants. That won't endear us to the rest of the owners. The dark stuff will start to fly. Anything can happen in this town and take my word for it, something will happen as soon as those rate hikes go into effect. Your mother talks a good game about tightening our belts and all that crap. Don't kid yourself, son, it's what Fanny wants when Fanny wants it. Thanks for sticking up for me. They'll eat our dust yet."

"Dad, this is all wrong. The past is past. Can't we let it die and make things better? I know you can't go back, but you can go forward and make it better than it was. Sage is going to walk. I could see it in his face."

"Sage is not a team player. Neither is Sunny. You and me now, we have the same goals. We'll make those goals, too."

Birch watched as his father swallowed a handful of pills. He could feel his shoulders slump. Sage was his twin, his other half. He never felt quite whole unless Sage was close by. He adored Sunny, always had. It was all getting away from him, just like the last time when they sided with their father against their mother.

"You can't tell Sunny she isn't needed right now. If we do that, Mom will shut this place down so fast we won't have time to blink. She'll do it, Dad. I'd hate to see you make the mistake of pushing her to the edge. She won't jump over the edge, she'll plow you right under. She takes her commitment to Grandma Sallie and this family very seriously. You're wrong about Sage, too. Sage has the charisma to make this place work. He works the floor like a pro. Any casino on this Strip would hire him and pay him five times what we pay him. He'd be worth every dollar, too. Don't mess with Sage, Dad."

Ash eyed his son, his one remaining ally. His mind was scrambled with the pills he'd just taken. His chaotic thoughts reeled back in time to when he was Birch's age. He'd been just as tall, just as good-looking, just as virile, just as mobile. He stared at the replica of himself and wanted to cry. "Sage is weak," he mumbled.

"You're wrong. Sage has more guts than the two of us put together. I'll walk out of here before I let you put Sage down."

Ash stared at his son and knew he meant every word. He waved him out of the room. When the door closed behind Birch, great wrenching sobs tore at his wasted body. "I hate your goddamn fucking guts, Fanny," he sobbed.

In his office, Birch sat down behind his desk. His head dropped to his hands. He wished he could turn back the hands of the clock to the day he and Sage left for college with Simon behind the wheel.

He knew the story behind his father and his Uncle Simon. He'd heard his father's version, his grandmother's version, Simon's version, and then his mother's version. Somewhere in between was the *real* story. Late at night in the college dorm, he and Sage had put their own spin on the story and came up with one they could both live with. Now, eighteen years later, history seemed to be repeating itself. He was his father and Sage was Simon. He remembered how his Uncle Simon had come out the winner in all the different stories, even their own. That meant Sage was a winner and he was . . . his father all over again.

It was three o'clock when Birch closed his briefcase. "Biloxi, Mississippi, here I come," he muttered. The knock on his door startled him. "Come in," he called.

"Nah. I don't think so," Sage said from the open doorway. "I stopped by Dad's office to drop this off, but he was asleep. He'd just tear it up anyway. You can do whatever you want with it. It's my resignation. You going somewhere? Let me guess. Biloxi, Mississippi, right? Big mistake, Birch."

"Come on, Sage, we go through this at least once a week. You always back down. This thing is going to blow over the way these things always blow over. This is our business. We need to pull together."

"That's really funny coming from you. I've had it. What we voted for was right for all the right reasons. I don't have any regrets. All I want is a life, and I'm damn well going to get one. Uncle Simon walked away and got his life. I've got the guts to do the same thing."

"Let's not forget that good old Uncle Simon walked off with the queen of this parade. Our mother."

"Mom's personal life is none of our business. Justify what happened with Sunny, Birch. Don't tell me nothing happened either. I know how you and Dad do things."

"Sunny belongs at home taking care of herself. Mom stayed home and took care of us. Why isn't that good enough for her?"

"The why of it doesn't matter. It's her choice. We made a pact early on. You can't blow Sunny off. You're gonna do it, aren't you? I refuse to be a party to anything that hurts one of us. What the hell happened to you, Birch? For months now we've been at opposite ends of the spectrum. I miss the old Birch, my buddy and my pal. Where'd he go?"

"Get your ass in here and stop telling the world our business. What about Dad?"

"Ah, the emperor's son has spoken. The queen's son is speaking now, the son who is his own man, and he says, fuck you, Birch." In a dramatic gesture, Sage threw his hands high in the air. "Jesus, do you have any idea of how good I feel right now? Because I'm in such a good mood, I'm going to give you some advice for free. Forget those riverboats, they're going to sink to the bottom of the Mississippi River. Give some thought to buying a gondola. Isn't that what emperors ride around in or sail in . . . ? Whatever. See you around."

"Sage, wait. We need to talk. Sage, get in here. What the hell is bugging you? Come on, we can talk this through and make it work."

"Sorry, Birch, not this time."

The sound of the door closing behind his brother sounded ominous, final. Birch cried then for what he'd allowed himself to become: the emperor's son.

2

Fanny waved good-bye to her children, then frowned as she watched Sage and Billie link arms with Sunny. She turned to Bess. "I'm worried."

"I know. Why don't we take a walk, just you and me, Fanny? Remember the old days when we traipsed around this town? Two young girls who never in their wildest dreams thought they would be where they are right now."

"I had such dreams back then. I thought I had a marriage made in heaven. Hell would be more like it. I tell myself there must have been some good years. If there were, why can't I remember them?"

"It's over. You can't look back. You told me that a thousand times or more."

"That's because Sallie always said it to me. I miss her so much, Bess. A day doesn't go by that I don't think about her. She was my best friend. The mother I never had. I try to do things the way I think she would want me to do them, but I'm never sure I'm succeeding."

"Maybe you need to stop doing that and do what *you* think is best. Sallie isn't here anymore. She trusted you. That means she trusted your judgment. Lay her to rest and live your own life. It's time for you to crawl out from under her shadow."

"Oh, Bess, it sounds so simple. I can't turn it off. I envy you and your nice normal family. You and John were meant for each other. Doctor and Mrs. Bess Noble. I love the way that sounds. You and John got the brass ring, my friend."

"We've had our ups and downs, Fanny. Every married couple does at one time or another."

"You came out stronger, though. We're to the half century mark, Bess. Actually, we're past the mark. I'm divorced. My family is divided. No one is happy. Sunny's ill, I feel it in my bones. My eyes see things I don't want to recognize. Yes, my businesses are successful. Yes, I provide jobs for a lot of people, including my children. When is it my time in the sun, Bess?"

"Whenever you decide to make a commitment to Simon. You could get married tomorrow at a Las Vegas wedding chapel if you wanted to. You could do it the minute you pick up Simon. It's a choice, Fanny. You have to get rid of all that guilt you're carrying around. So what if Simon is Ash's brother. So what, Fanny! You're divorced for God's sake. Ash no longer has a hold on you. His accident wasn't your fault. Let it die already." There was such exasperation in Bess's voice that Fanny laughed aloud.

"I think you care more than I do."

"That's a bald-faced lie if I ever heard one. You love Simon. He loves you. Carrying on an affair is what Sallie did. That's not who you are, Fanny. You're a home and hearth person. If you deliberately *choose* to pattern your life after Sallie's that's one thing. If you let circumstances dictate to you, that's something else. Sallie has a hold on you from the grave. You need to shake it loose."

Fanny stopped walking to stare at her friend. "Is that what I'm doing, Bess?"

"Yes." The single word was an explosion of sound from Bess's mouth. "I want to see some backbone. Starting right now!"

Fanny hugged her friend as people walked around them, smiles on their faces. "What would I do without you, Bess?"

Bess shrugged. "We need to start scrounging for money for the dolls. You can put John and me down for $75,000. I know the kids will kick in with their savings. Your kids, that is. Mine don't have any savings."

"Don't you have to ask John?"

"Nope. That's why we work so well together. He knows I wouldn't do anything to put our lives in jeopardy. We have other savings. If he knew the situation, he'd offer before I could get the words out of my mouth."

Fanny recognized the truth of the statement. "Isn't it strange, Bess, how Billie managed to save the day? She did it once before with Rainbow Babies. The truth, Bess, am I doing the right thing where Billie Coleman is concerned?"

"Absolutely. When it comes down to the wire, Fanny, when everything else is shot to hell, family is the only thing you can count on. In the end family always comes through for you. Trust me on this."

"My own family . . . Birch . . ."

"Birch is torn, Fanny. All you can do is be there for him when he finally comes to terms with his role in his father's life. Birch isn't a kid anymore. You always said because he was minutes older, he was the leader and Sage was the follower. That changed somewhere along the way. Sage is his own person and has been for a very long time. I think Birch knows that and doesn't know how to get back on even footing. He'll figure it out, and when he does, he'll come back to the fold and you'll be there because that's what mothers do."

"But, will I feel the same way about him? Right now I love him, but I don't like him. Does that make sense? He hates it that I'm considering marrying Simon."

"No, Ash is making him hate the idea. Birch always adored his uncle. He has to deal with that, too. He has a lot on his plate right now. The minute Sage is gone, he's going to start soul searching. We'll just have to wait and hope he sees the light. By the way, how is your ex?"

"His debonair self as far as I could see. If you're asking me if he's still taking all those drugs, my answer would be yes. His eyes appeared glassy to me, but he wears tinted glasses indoors. Sage told me once the fluorescent lighting bothers his eyes. I don't want to know, Bess. All I want is what Sallie wanted, a simple life with a man I love and who loves me. I want my family."

"Then tell Simon you'll marry him and don't change your mind this time. No matter how much he loves you, he won't wait forever. Neither one of you is getting any younger."

"I have loose ends in my life, Bess. I hate loose ends. I know life doesn't come in a tidy little box with a ribbon on top. I have the box and the ribbon, but I can't tie it into a bow. I still haven't found my mother. My instincts tell me she's out there somewhere. I'm ashamed that I didn't do more to find her. I could have half brothers and sisters, a whole other family I know nothing about. I need to do something about that. Then there's Jake and his money. I've borrowed on that money so many times I've lost count. I need to lay that to rest, too. It's been thirty years, Bess, since that bus holdup when Jake gave me his money to hold. I wanted to give the money back, but I could never find him. He must have a family somewhere. I never did tell Ash about that money. Simon invested it time and again. It's a small fortune."

"Fanny, with all the new technology out there today you can hire the best of the best. It might take a while, but I think you'll be able to lay those two matters to rest once and for all. Now, didn't we have a nice chat? Time for you to be getting ready for the drive to the airport. Isn't Simon due in soon?"

"How do you know he's coming in and that I'm picking him up?"

"Because you're wearing your yellow dress. You always wear yellow when you pick Simon up. Sometimes you are very transparent, Fanny."

"Obviously," Fanny sniffed. "I didn't lie back there at the meeting when I said I didn't know where Simon was. I didn't know *precisely* what city or town his plane was flying over at that moment." Fanny grinned and hugged her friend.

She would have known him anywhere, even in a dark room, this love of hers. She wanted to jump over the barrier and run to him. Instead she held out her arms and smiled. "I missed you. I thought about you every minute of every day. The moment I open my eyes in the morning my first thought is, is Simon awake yet?"

He kissed her while the world on the tarmac watched. Neither one cared. "It doesn't have to be this way," he said against her lips.

"I know," she whispered. "For now it is what it is. I do love you, more than I loved you yesterday and not as much as I will tomorrow. So there!"

"How's everything?"

"Some things are good, some things are bad, some things are indifferent. Nothing much changes around here. We'll talk later. Let's just enjoy each other. It's been two whole weeks, Simon!"

"Three hundred and thirty-six hours or twenty thousand one hundred and sixty minutes. Damn, I can't calculate the seconds in my head."

"Who cares? You're here and that's all that counts."

"Fanny, let's get married. Right now. I'm willing to keep it a secret if you don't want the family to know. I see something in your eyes I've never seen before and it scares me. *Now*, Fanny."

Fanny slid into the passenger side of her car. Simon always drove when they were together. Her heart started to flutter in her chest. Simon's words sounded like an ultimatum. The hard set of his jaw frightened her. Bess's words rang in her ears. "Simon won't wait forever."

Fanny's voice was squeaky, jittery-sounding when she said, "By now, do you mean on the way home or *soon?*" Simon's demand coupled with what had transpired earlier left her feeling drained. She needed to say something positive, something light and funny to take away the harsh look on her beloved's face. She couldn't find the words. Was it possible they weren't in her vocabulary? Was it possible she wasn't meant to marry Simon? The thought was so devastating she could feel her eyes start to burn.

"Fanny, did you hear what I said?"

"Yes, Simon, I did. I'm thinking."

The disbelief in Simon's voice was total. "You're *thinking?* That doesn't say very much for us, Fanny. What in the name of God do you have to think about?"

"Everything, Simon. Everything."

"That word sounds ominous. I don't think I care for that explanation. Would you mind explaining?"

"Can we have this discussion when we get to Sunrise?"

"It doesn't look like I have a choice. What's happening to us, Fanny?"

Fanny's voice was a tortured whisper. "I don't know."

"I thought what we felt for one another was rock solid. You and me against the world, that kind of thing. Am I wrong, Fanny?"

"No. I never thought I could love someone as much as I love you. I didn't know I could feel like this. I don't want to lose you like I did the last time, Simon. If you recall, I asked you to marry me and you turned me down flat. Those were the longest, the most miserable days of my life. We'll talk over cocoa, and a nice warm fire. It's still chilly on the mountain in the evenings."

"Okay, Fanny. So, how are the kids? They're always going to be kids to me no matter how old they are."

"We'll talk about that tonight, too. I am worried about Sunny. Tyler said he spoke to her obstetrician and he said she was fine. She is not fine. Something is wrong, but I don't know what it is."

Simon sighed. Maybe it wasn't him after all. Maybe Fanny's eyes were filled with sadness because of her children. The invisible load on his shoulders lightened. However, the wariness stayed in his eyes. "How's Ash?" His voice said he didn't care one way or the other. The expression in his eyes was a direct contradiction to his words.

"As arrogant as ever. I've only been to Babylon twice since the grand opening. I don't think I'll ever get used to seeing people gamble before breakfast. I wish we had never built that damn place." Fanny's voice was so vehement, Simon's eyebrows shot upward.

"It wasn't the answer you were looking for, was it?"

"It was the answer for Ash. He's breaking all the rules. All the agreements we had. He thinks I'm going to go along with his shenanigans because of the kids. He deliberately baits me, deliberately pushes me to the wall. I hate his defiance and it has nothing to do with his accident or with him being in a wheelchair. He hates my mobility and my feelings for you. He hates my father and my brothers for finishing *his* casino. They call him The Emperor on the Strip. Somehow he managed to get this poker tournament for Babylon. People have to pay ten thousand dollars to play. That just absolutely, totally, mystifies me. Ash says it's a real feather in his cap."

"I'd say so. He'll clear a few million for the Thornton coffers and it will only enhance his image in Vegas. The Emperor, huh?" A storm began to build in Simon's eyes that Fanny couldn't see. "What do you suppose that makes the rest of us?" Simon threw his head back against the headrest and laughed so hard tears rolled down his cheeks. Later, when he dried his eyes, Fanny was startled at how angry his eyes looked. The deep belly laugh sounded forced to her ears for some reason. She shrugged off the feeling. If Simon was angry, he had a right to be angry. She couldn't let little things like that mar her happiness.

Fanny didn't mean to laugh. Nothing her ex-husband did was funny. But they both started to laugh until they were giddy. The tense moments were over. For a little while.

They made the rest of the drive to Sunrise in comfortable, companionable silence. From time to time Simon squeezed her hand.

The moment he pulled the car into the courtyard, Fanny said, "Now I can *breathe*. I need my daily sagebrush fix. Smell it, Simon, isn't it wonderful? The air up here on the mountain is so clean and pure. Down in town I always feel like I'm fighting to breathe. Ten years from now Las Vegas is going to be as crowded as New York City. I'll be sixty-four then. Do you think I'll care, Simon?"

"I hope not. I want us to retire and go off together someplace. A new place because new beginnings should have new surroundings. Just you and me, Fanny. We're never going to need anyone else. I'm selling my brokerage house, my client base, the whole ball of wax. All my real estate is on the market. My plan was to put on a blindfold and stand in front of a map and stick a pin in it. Then I was going to have you do the same thing, at which point we'd pick somewhere in the middle. Whatcha think?"

"Oh, Simon, do you really want to do that? I've never lived anywhere but Pennsylvania and Nevada. I need to think about this, Simon. You're selling *everything?*"

"Everything. I'm ready for a new beginning. I've paid my dues."

"Is that another way of saying you're going to stick the pin in the map with or without me?" She wondered if the fear she felt showed in her face.

"I'm afraid so, Fanny." The intense angry expression was back in Simon's eyes.

Fanny felt her knees start to crumple. "That's . . . that's an ultimatum."

"No, Fanny, it's a statement of fact. I'm going to do this. I want *us* to do it together. It's what we said *we* both wanted for our lives. I'm doing my best to stick with the plan."

For the second time in one day, Fanny Thornton's world turned upside down. "Let's go down to the studio, Simon. I need to let Daisy out. She's going to be so happy to see you. Daisy is the nicest present anyone ever gave me. She's all the more precious because you picked her out."

Simon sucked in his breath. The studio was Fanny's place of refuge, her port in any storm that crashed into her life. They'd made love there so many times—wild, uninhibited love and sweet, gentle love. Only in that safe haven did either one of them feel free. He was starting to hate Sunrise and the mountain it sat on. He was even beginning to hate the studio, viewing it as a shackle tying Fanny to the mountain, to the house she'd shared with Ash. They wouldn't be coming back here again, he'd make sure of that. He shivered in the bright sunshine as Fanny inserted the key in the lock.

Daisy slammed her small body against Fanny's legs, yipping her pleasure now that her mistress was home. Fanny rolled on the floor with the little dog, her skirt hiked up past her thighs. "Join in, Simon," she gasped as she rolled over and over, Daisy hopping from her to Simon.

And then he was on top of her, staring down into her flushed face the minute Daisy scooted out the door. "I don't think there's another human being in this world who can tear at my heart the way you do, Fanny." His heart thundered in his chest as Fanny returned his ardent kisses and embraces. He thought he would choke on his own desire when her rich sound of pleasure curled around him.

How wonderful she smelled, a delicious womanly scent that was all her own. A warm, sunshiny smell mixed with flowers and sagebrush.

His lips left the sweetness of her mouth, seeking the softness beneath her chin where her throat pulsed and curled into her shoulder as he worked the straps of the yellow dress down over her shoulders. Fanny helped him, wiggling and sliding until she was naked beneath his hard body. Her own hands were feverish as she worked at the buttons of his shirt, the zipper of his trousers.

His hands traveled the length of her as he sought those places that gave her the most pleasure, a taut breast, a welcoming thigh. He fought to harness his growing desire as he waited for her own greedy passion to match his own.

A sound escaped his lips, a moan, a plea, as he crushed her mouth to his. When he at last broke free, he stared down at her, at the tawny luster of her breasts that summoned him, their rosy crests erect and tempting. Her slender waist curved into his hands, her rounded haunches grinding into his thighs.

Simon's lips touched her everywhere, his thirst for her deep and raw as he sought to quench it. He felt her body cry out to him as her slender legs wrapped themselves around him. She offered herself completely as their lusty passions met and were satisfied, again and again, until they lay back, their breathing ragged gasps, their slick bodies molded to one another.

A long time later, Simon said, "Can you even begin to imagine what it would have been like if we were doing this when we were *twenty?*"

There was something in his tone, something she should be picking up on. She'd worry about whatever it was later. "Absolutely wonderful," Fanny sighed. "I'm glad we didn't know each other when we were twenty. We wouldn't be here now, at this, the best time of our lives."

"Is it the best time, Fanny?"

Fanny sat up, oblivious to her nakedness. "It's supposed to be. I want it to be. I feel it is. There are some loose threads . . . I love you, Simon, more than I can ever put into words, and I know you love me in the same way."

Simon handed Fanny her clothing and watched as she struggled with her thoughts. "Then why do I feel like an old sleeve that's unraveling a little bit at a time?"

Fanny walked into the bathroom, her buttocks jiggling for his benefit. "Life isn't easy, is it, Simon? Life just gets in the way of so many things. I wish I knew how to deal with it."

Ten minutes later, Fanny was back in the living room sitting on one of the deep red chairs that she loved, Simon across from her in a matching chair. He handed her a cup of coffee.

"You were saying."

"That life gets in the way of so many plans. I think, Simon, that unknowingly, unwittingly, I have been trying to emulate your mother. I said I wouldn't do that, didn't plan to do it, but there it is. In my desperate desire to do what Sallie wanted, at least what I thought she wanted, I reacted. You know the old saying, for every action there is a reaction. Like now, with us. We're a reaction to something I did or said. Sallie was right about a lot of things and she was wrong about a lot of things, too. Bess said it best earlier today. She said I chose to pattern myself after Sallie because I loved her so much. I want to run away. What I *really* want to do is pick up my purse in one hand, Daisy in the other, and walk out the door and not look back. I want you to be waiting on the other side of the door when I make my grand exit."

"Then let's do it!" Simon said, rubbing his hands together, his face gleeful at the prospect of what Fanny had just said. The same look was back in his eyes. Fanny felt a chill race down her spine.

"I can't, Simon. Life got in the way this morning. I made promises and commitments and I have to honor them. That's what life is all about. At least my life. It's tearing me apart, Simon, but I have no other choice."

"One always has choices, Fanny. Tell me straight out what it is you're trying to say."

In a flat monotone, Fanny told him everything, starting with the Colemans, Sunny's health, young Billie's newest brainchild. "Then there's my mother to find and the old business of Jake that has to be brought to closure. You promised to put an investigator on finding Jake. I keep forgetting to ask you if you found out anything."

"The last report was a big zero. The man dropped off the face of the earth. I did try, Fanny. You need to chalk it up as one of those little mysteries in life that will never be solved. As far as I'm concerned, Jake's money is yours." Simon sucked in his breath and let it out with a loud *swoosh* of sound. "You're making a mistake, in my opinion, in regard to Billie Coleman."

"No, Simon, I'm not. Maybe this is something only a mother understands, then again, maybe not. Billie's son was flying a defective Coleman plane when he died. The Thorntons own the controlling interest in Coleman Aviation. What kind of person would I be if I turned my back on Billie now? Her son died! Other mothers' sons died in planes of ours that were defective. That has to be made right, and the only ones who can make it right are Billie, her granddaughter, and me. Sawyer is as committed as we are. It's almost as though God put Sawyer on this earth to finish Billie's husband's plane. Maybe it really is a mother thing. I know the monies I'll be giving her won't be enough, but we'll worry about that later. We're family, Simon. Sallie would want me to do what I'm doing. Me, Fanny Logan Thornton wants it, too. This is who I am, Simon, and I can't change. I will not turn my back on Billie. Right now I'm all she has, and I know what that feeling is like."

Fanny felt her insides cringe at the coldness she saw reflected in Simon's eyes. "Why do you ask my opinion on things if you have no intention of following my advice?" he asked. "You could lose everything, Fanny. Have you thought about that?"

"Yes. That's all I've been thinking about. We put it to a family vote this morning. Birch and Ash are against it, but then they have an ulterior motive, they want to buy riverboats in Biloxi, Mississippi, for gambling. Ash never liked Billie Coleman. He blamed her for my independence. I heard him tell Moss Coleman he would help in any way he could when it came to building this new plane. With Moss dead, he's reneging. I don't like that. In my eyes, a person is only as good as their word. I can, and I will, live with my decision. You're to sell everything off, Simon, and wire the monies to the Coleman account by the close of business on Friday."

"With all that you could still walk out the door. You can lose your shirt here or somewhere else, somewhere where we're together." His voice sounded too cool, too practiced to Fanny's ears. He was upset.

"My daughter is going to need me. I want to be here for her."

"Sunny could come and stay with us for a while. This isn't working for me, Fanny."

"Sunny wouldn't agree to that. She has a husband she loves and who adores her. We aren't talking about a rash or some hair loss. Whatever it is, it's serious. I'm the first to admit this is all in my head, but I know I'm not wrong. Ash is going to do . . . something. Birch is going way out on a limb. I need to be here when the limb comes down. I've made up my mind now that I will leave no stone unturned in finding my mother. I'm going to do this, Simon. You're being obstinate."

"Where does that leave me? I do not care for the word obstinate at all. Do you *ever* plan on marrying me?" His voice was icy cold when he said, "It always comes back to Ash."

"Oh, yes, Simon. Yes, yes, yes. I just can't give you a time or a place. What we have right now is working. Isn't it? You need to take Ash's name out of your vocabulary."

"Not for me. You made your decisions. I made my decisions, too. What we're faced with is a stalemate. You won't or can't budge and neither can I. *I don't like to lose, Fanny.*"

Simon's voice was so strange, Fanny started to cry. "You're making this sound like a . . . contest of some kind, you against me. Then you throw Ash into the same pot. Please, Simon, try to understand."

"Fanny, I do understand. I understand, but I can't accept it. I want a life. There's no point in rehashing this. I'll leave now, but I have to borrow your car. I'll call you and tell you where it is at the airport. I'll take care of your business before I leave."

"Simon, wait . . . we're grown adults, surely we can work this out and come to a decision we can both live with. It can't be your way all the time, Simon. It just can't. I need you."

"And I need you. I'm walking out that door, Fanny, and I'm going to close it. Daisy is right here. There's your purse on the table. Your choice, Fanny, your call."

Go! Go! Go! Fanny's mind shrieked when the door closed behind

Simon. Daisy was in her arms. She picked up her purse from the table, her eyes going to a framed picture of herself with her children under the cottonwoods. She stared at it for a long minute before her shoulders slumped. Daisy jumped from her arms the same moment her purse thudded to the floor.

Simon waited on the other side of the door, but not for long. She wasn't going to open that door. He turned and walked up the path to the courtyard where the car was parked.

Inside the studio, Fanny watched from behind the curtains. "Come back, Simon, please come back." The sound of the car's engine turning over drove her to one of the big red chairs. "Good-bye, Simon."

His shoulders rigid with anger, Simon floored the gas pedal as he started down the mountain. He found himself blinking as he tried to dispel the rage that was rivering through him. Where in the hell had he ever come up with the idea that Fanny would bow and bend to his will? For some reason he'd thought her pliable, with a sapling strength. She was proving to be a goddamn three-hundred-year-old oak that would outlast him and anyone who crossed her path.

Simon's foot pressed harder on the accelerator. He was being stupid, this mountain road was something he needed to respect. His foot eased up a little. He changed his mental gears. Ash and the kids. That's what it came down to. It would always be Ash and the kids versus him. Fanny didn't need to hit him over the head with a sledgehammer. Everything she said or did involved Ash in some way or the kids. "I can't and I won't accept that."

Simon rolled down the window before he turned on the radio. The music blasted through his head and on out the window to ricochet down the mountain. He flicked the radio off before he maneuvered the car around a murderous curve in the road.

"We'll just see about that. I told you the truth, Fanny, when I said I don't like to lose."

He set the controls to cruise, turned the radio back on, then lowered the sound. Soft, mellow music filtered through the car.

It was a game. It was always a game. The kind of game he and Ash used to play. As in all games, there was a winner and a loser. The secret was patience. *Wait it out, Simon,* he cautioned himself. *You'll win because you always win.*

Simon Thornton smiled. It was so true.

3

Simon Thornton stood, his eyes sweeping around the comfortable office where he'd spent the major part of his life. Months ago he'd separated his life into three stages; first, his years in the military, where he'd used someone else's identity just so he could get away from his parents and his brother Ash. The second part was heading for New York where, with his nose to the grindstone, he'd carved out a business that made him a millionaire a hundred times over. The third part was Fanny. His reason for getting up in the morning, for living, for *being*. The time was finally here when he could stick it to Ash once and for all. It was supposed to be the best day of his life. The day he'd separated his life he'd decided his pie was to be cut in thirds because Fanny was the final slice. Now all he had was a pie with no topping. There was no reason to get up in the morning, no goal to shoot for in the living department. As for being . . . well, he was tough, he could exist with the best of them. He knew how to go through the motions. If he wasn't happy who was going to notice? No one. Not one single person. Maybe Jerry.

He opened all the drawers in his desk, prolonging the moment when he would walk through the door and then close it. Jerry, his friend since childhood, along with all his employees, would have balloons, a cake, some champagne, and probably a present that everyone chipped in to buy. His eyes would burn when he shook hands, clapped others on the back, and then, finally, the bear hug for Jerry. Thirty minutes out of his life. After that he'd head uptown to his apartment to pick up his luggage, at which point he would be completely homeless for the first time in his life.

The urge to smash something, preferably Ash's handsome face, was so strong that Simon clenched his fists, then stuck his hands in his pockets. He was smart enough to know anger didn't solve anything. All he had to do was fall back and regroup. It wasn't supposed to be like this. Fanny was supposed to be here with him when he walked away for the last time to start their new life. His clenched fist hit the wall just as Jerry opened the door slightly and angled through it.

"That bad, huh?"

The pain in Simon's hand matched the pain on his face. "I suspect I'll get over it in about a hundred years."

"Is there anything I can do, Simon?"

"If there was, you'd be the first person I'd ask."

"I feel like I did the day we cooked up that scheme for you to use my cousin's identity. I bawled for days when I realized you were finally gone. Now I'm gonna bawl for weeks, maybe months or years. Simon, do you know what the hell you're doing? You waited this long for Fanny, what's the harm in waiting a little while longer? Ultimatums never work for the person issuing them. We both know that. What in the hell ever possessed you to do that?"

"I could see it all sliding away, little by little. I figured it was better to get on with it. I don't like parts of things, little bits of this or that. When two people love each other they should be able to work together to make a good life. Like you and your wife. Fanny had her mind made up before I got up to bat. I don't want to talk about this, Jerry."

"You still haven't told me where you're going. You're going to write and call, aren't you?"

"Sure."

"You really are going to stick a pin in the map. Jesus, Simon, that's not romantic at all. It's stupid. Why don't you just get in the truck and drive till you run out of gas? That makes a little more sense. Simon . . ."

"Don't fall apart on me, Jerry. Right now I feel like I was put together with spit and chewing gum. I need . . . I need to walk out of here all in one piece. We'll always be best buddies. We both know that. I'll be in touch. Finish up Fanny's business for her. All the wheels are in motion. She wanted it all done by the close of business today. Get rid of the damn map on the wall. Okay, buddy, let's get this show on the road."

The banners and streamers were colorful, his employees shouting, "bon voyage" as champagne corks popped. Shrill whistles and hoots of "You're going to hate retirement," rocked against the walls. "Speech, speech!"

"C'mon, I'm not a speech maker. Thanks for your loyalty and for the good job you've done all these years. I'm going to miss all of you. End of speech."

Someone said, "Jerry went to get something for you."

"It better fit in my Rover."

"Oh, it will fit," Jerry said, leading two small dogs into the room. "This is Tootsie and this is Slick. They've had all their shots. They're hale and hearty. Total weight is a little over six pounds. Slick's the heaviest. Tootsie, as you can see, is delicate. We were going to get you one of those man dogs so you could call him Duke or Spike, but these little beauties beckoned. They're called Teacup Yorkies. They're trained and both have been neutered. They understand one command; freeze! They're seven months old. Say something, Simon."

"I guess they'll fit in the Rover," Simon said as he nuzzled the tiny dogs under his chin. "This wasn't in my game plan."

"I know," Jerry said. "I put their gear in your truck. You might have to pile your stuff on the top. Listen, I gotta go," Jerry said with a catch in his voice.

Simon bit down on his lower lip. "Yeah, yeah. Thanks, everyone. I'll send a postcard."

The clock in the lobby said it was 1:10 when he walked toward the doors that led to the underground garage. At 2:20 he drove onto the New Jersey Turnpike, heading south, Tootsie and Slick nestled in his lap.

Fanny slipped from her bed, her eye on the digital clock on the nightstand. Her suitcase stared at her like a single malevolent eye. Last night she'd pulled it out and then replaced it in the closet seven times. Then she'd cried herself to sleep. She'd woken at 2:30 and called Bess and said, "I'm going. I'll be in touch." At 3:05 she'd called her again and said, "I changed my mind." It was now 4:25.

Fanny's eyes were wild as she looked around her studio. Her little corner of life. Empty. Daisy whimpered. "As much as I love you, Daisy, you aren't enough. Get your stuff and pile it up by the door. We're going to New York! I'm not giving up Simon for anyone."

She was a whirlwind then as she stripped off her clothes while dialing the airport to have the Thornton plane readied for her trip. "Don't even think about telling me it can't be done? You do it!" She showered, dressed, gulped a cup of yesterday's leftover coffee before she snatched Daisy's gear and stuffed it into a shopping bag. The last thing she did was scribble a note that she left on her drafting table.

Fanny burned rubber, something she'd never done in her life, as she careened down the mountain. An hour later she was running toward the Thornton plane, the shopping bag slapping against her leg, Daisy jostling up and down in her arms.

"Fanny!"

"Bess! Oh, Bess, this is the right thing, isn't it? How did you know? I called back and said I wasn't going. It feels right. Tell me it's right."

"It's right, Fanny. I'm glad you came to your senses. I know you better than you know yourself. You love Simon, and he loves you. Call me and let me know where you are and what I can do. Give Simon a big hug for me. I want to be your matron of honor, and I don't care if it's in Zamboranga. Promise."

"Oh, Bess, I promise. Thank you for . . . being you. Thank you, thank you, thank you. Gotta go. Life is wonderful," she called over her shoulder as she climbed the metal steps. She turned and waved and then blew her best friend a kiss.

In less than twelve minutes she was airborne. In just a few hours she would be in Simon's arms. In her bag she had a map and two pins. "I love him, Daisy, so much it hurts. They don't make bandages big enough to cover that kind of hurt." She leaned back into the depths of the cushioned seat.

The Thornton jet set down at 12:30 Eastern Standard Time. Fanny barreled down the steps and ran across the tarmac to the terminal where she looked around wildly for a sign that would direct her to the transportation area. She ran again, jostling people in her hurry to get to the taxi area. "Wall Street," she gasped as she tossed the shopping bag onto the backseat. "Soon, Daisy. Hurry, driver."

Fanny leaned back against the cracked leather seat. Why was she in such a hurry? Close of business meant five o'clock. The market closed at four. She had plenty of time before Simon walked out of his office building at five-twenty. Her breath exploded in a loud sigh. So close yet so far away. I'm coming, Simon, I'm coming.

Fanny thrust a twenty-dollar bill at the cab driver. She ran to the door, Daisy whimpering at these strange circumstances. She woofed once when she picked up Simon Thornton's scent near the elevator. "Shhh," Fanny said.

Fanny burst through the doors of Simon's offices, her hair in wild disarray, the dog yipping in her arms to see a sea of faces staring at her. She was aware instantly of the balloons, the cake that hadn't been cut, Jerry's tortured face. She could feel the scream starting to build in her throat. "Where is he, Jerry?"

"Fanny . . ."

"Jerry . . . did . . . is he gone, Jerry?"

"I'm sorry, Fanny. He left ten minutes ago. I know he was headed for his apartment to pick up his luggage. Then . . . he wouldn't tell me where he was going. He said he'd write . . . he said that once before and I got two letters in . . . maybe you can catch him. Try, Fanny."

"Call him, Jerry, tell him I'm on my way. Tell him to wait. Please, Jerry."

"I can't, Fanny. His phone was disconnected yesterday. He dumped all that stuff he used to carry around in a Dumpster and he ripped out his car phone."

Fanny started to cry.

"C'mon, we'll take the express elevator. I'll drive you, my car's in the garage. If he hit traffic or if he stops to say good-bye to the doorman or something, we might make it."

"Drive a hundred miles an hour. I'll pay for the tickets. Oh, God, this can't be happening to me. Pretend you're Mario Andretti, Jerry. Can't you go any faster?"

"Fanny, this is New York. It's impossible to . . . try and relax."

"What will I do if he isn't there? Are you sure you don't know where he's going?"

"I'm sure. I wish you had come yesterday. Yesterday he was lower than a snake's belly. I don't know what you'll do, Fanny. I guess you go on the way he's going to go on. Right now there don't seem to be many options for either one of you." His voice was strained and fretful-sounding.

Fanny started to cry again. Daisy curled deeper into her arms. "It's my fault. I'm turning out just like my mother-in-law, and Simon saw that. Can't you go any faster?"

"I'm trying, Fanny."

When at last Jerry pulled his car to the curb, his tires screeching, Fanny bolted from the car. "Simon Thornton, is he here?" Fanny demanded of the doorman.

"He's gone. He left about fifteen minutes ago."

"Did he say where he was going?" Fanny asked.

"All he said was good-bye and he was on his way to a new life. He had two little dogs with him. I'm sorry."

"I'm sorry, too," Fanny said, wiping at the tears dripping on Daisy's head. In the car, Fanny broke down completely. Jerry stared at her helplessly.

"What do you want me to do, Fanny?"

"Take me back to the airport. I can take a taxi if you have something to do."

"If you want the monies wired into the Texas National by the close of business, I'll have to hail you a taxi. Simon was adamant about everything being done by five o'clock today. I gave him my word it would be taken care of. He did everything you wanted, Fanny."

Fanny nodded miserably as she exited the car to wait for a taxi. "Thanks for everything, Jerry. You'll call if . . . ?"

"Of course."

"Tell him I came. Tell him . . ." Fanny opened her purse and pulled out the map and the two safety pins attached at the corner. "Tell him . . . I brought the map and the pins. He'll know what you're talking about."

"I'll tell him, Fanny. Here's your cab. You take care of yourself now, you hear."

"You too, Jerry. Simon is very lucky to have a friend like you."

Fanny was back on the mountain by midnight. She garaged the car and set Daisy down on the ground. Instead of going to her studio, she walked down the path to the small private cemetery. She raised her eyes heavenward. "It's me, Sallie. I screwed everything up. I hate this helpless feeling. I don't know what to do. I can't seem to think straight. I was so close. I missed him by minutes. I don't know how to handle this. How did you manage to go on when Devin died? How did you get through the hours and the minutes? How did you manage to smile? You just went through the motions. Inside you were as dead as Devin was. I think I knew that, but I didn't want to dwell on it. I don't want that to happen to me. I don't want to be like you. I just want to be Fanny Thornton. I want to feel, to love, to cry and laugh. I can handle this. You just watch me. I'll say good night, Sallie. You probably won't be hearing from me for a while, so give my regards to Devin." As an afterthought she said, "And to Philip, too."

Daisy woofed softly, begging to be picked up. The little dog in her arms, Fanny walked around the small cemetery. Overhead the heavens were star-spangled, the three-quarter moon casting a silvery glow over the ageless cottonwood in the middle of the cemetery. The sweet smell of sagebrush engulfed her as she made her way down the small path that led back to her studio.

Inside the studio, Fanny headed straight for her drafting table and the telephone. Bess picked it up on the first ring. "I missed him, Bess. By fifteen minutes. No one knows where he is or where he was going. I guess he stuck his pin in the map and didn't look back. I feel so empty and lost. Why didn't I listen to you that day in the parking lot? I didn't listen because I'm stupid. Stupid, stupid, stupid. I just wanted you to know I'm home. Good night, Bess, and thank you for being my friend."

The connection broken, Fanny changed her clothes and made a pot of coffee. Life was going to go on and there was nothing she could do about it. As of today, this very minute, Simon Thornton was somebody she used to know. Somebody she loved with every breath in her body. The sad part was, Simon didn't love her in the same way. She lifted her coffee cup high in the air in a toast. "Be happy, Simon." Daisy howled, an earsplitting, heart wrenching sound that matched the high-pitched keening wail that escaped her own lips.

The following morning Fanny was up, dressed and ready for whatever the day would bring before the sun climbed over the mountain. It was barely light when she let herself into the corporate headquarters of Sunny's Togs and Rainbow Babies—Sallie Thornton's old bingo palace.

Fanny was hard at work packing up the contents of the rooms when her children and Bess appeared at seven-thirty. "We're relocating to the mountain. It will cut down on our overhead. Chue's cousins, nephews, and nieces are ready to start on Bernie and Blossom tomorrow. Here's our schedule . . ."

"Attagirl, Fanny," Bess said, hugging her. "I didn't say anything to them. I wanted to wait to hear from you."

"Thanks, Bess. I don't think I could handle my children's pitying looks right now. We need to have some letters made up for our customers."

"I took care of that yesterday, Fanny."

"A truck to move this stuff up the mountain?"

"Taken care of yesterday, too. I knew the mountain was our only option. They'll be here by noon."

"The material for the dolls?"

"The mill is shipping it directly to the mountain. Delivery is scheduled for tomorrow. The scraps are on their way as we speak."

Fanny nodded. "Has anyone heard from Sunny?"

"I passed her on the way in this morning. I guess she's at Babylon. She likes to get up when Tyler does so they can have breakfast together, and she gets a few quiet hours in the casino before all hell breaks loose. She waved, so I guess she's okay," Sage said.

Fanny looked at her watch. "I'm going to the bank and I have a few other errands to run, so I probably won't be back till noon. If I have time, I want to stop and see Sunny. Carry on, troops," she said lightly.

Fanny walked through the Nevada Savings and Loan, the Thornton family's bank, down a short corridor where her personal banker, Bradford Tennison, sat behind a polished mahogany desk. They were old friends now, thanks to Sallie Thornton's intervention years ago. "Fanny, what brings you to the bank so early in the morning? Ah, I see, it's serious. Close the door. Can I offer you a cup of coffee?"

"No thanks, Brad. Has Simon been in touch with you?"

"Several times. There's a problem, Fanny. Your ex-husband applied for a mortgage on Babylon. The board approved it three days before I received Simon's call. The paperwork was in order. If this means anything, I voted no. Gambling boats on the Mississippi are risky ventures in my opinion."

"What are you saying, Brad? Ash can't . . . I have to approve any . . . Two signatures, Brad."

Tennison's faced turned pale. "We had two signatures, Fanny."

"You didn't have the one that counts. Mine. I sat here for three hours over a year ago when all this was settled. You and I talked about this. You even said it was a wise decision on my part. Did Simon know about this?"

Tennison's face went from pale to stark white. "I don't know, Fanny. I was in Carson City on bank business. I'm sure one of the bank officers told him. I'm sure we didn't do anything wrong."

"If you're so sure, why is your face so pale? I'll pull everything from this bank, right down to the last penny. I'm almost afraid to ask, how much did Ash . . ."

"Sixteen million dollars."

"Sixteen million dollars!" Fanny watched as the banker's forehead beaded with sweat. She could feel the moistness on her own forehead. She wiped at it with the back of her hand. "Tell me this is just in the works, tell me you didn't cut the check."

"I wish I could tell you that, Fanny, but I can't."

"Then you damn well better stop payment. If you tell me it's too late, I am personally going to wreck this bank. That's not a threat, that's a goddamn promise. Get your people in here, Brad. Now!"

Fanny was so furious she could barely focus on the furnishings in the room. How could this have happened? How dare Ash do this to her? Fanny stopped pacing long enough to place a call to Sage. Her voice was hoarse with rage when she questioned her son.

"Mom, I don't know anything about it. One of us has to sign along with you. That's all you ever told us. Nothing like this has ever come up before. Maybe Birch signed and . . . I don't know, Mom, I'm just speculating. For whatever this is worth, Dad is holding some very impressive markers that have Ryce Granger's name on them. He's second-in-command at ye olde bank. How did that get past Uncle Simon? I can be there in five minutes with all the account folders. Everything is spelled out. They gotta make good. Wait for me before you start wrecking the place."

Fanny's shoulders started to shake as she broke the connection without bothering to answer her son. Yes, how did it get past Simon? She needed to calm down, to get her thoughts in order. The bank was responsible if Ash pulled a fast one. She wondered what the word "impressive" meant to Sage. She had to admit she didn't know how much money the casino would hold in the way of markers. Obviously a lot.

"Fanny, come with me, we're going to one of the boardrooms where we won't be interrupted."

His face was still pale, Fanny noticed. She followed him, her back stiff. She thought her jaw was going to crack any second.

It was a windowless room with only a long conference table and a sideboard. A telephone and several manila folders sat on one end of the sideboard. Nine ashtrays and a silver service containing steaming coffee sat in the middle of the long table. The table was amazingly shiny, Fanny thought as she looked down to see the reflections of the white faces of the men standing at attention, yellow legal tablets in hand.

Fanny slammed her purse on the table just as a knock sounded on the door. The palm of her hand shot upward and then out. "I'll get it."

Sage stood in the open doorway to hand his mother a thick yellow folder. "Thanks, honey, I can handle this," she said in a low whisper.

"You sure?"

"I'm sure."

"Do what I do, kick some ass and take names later," Sage whispered. In spite of herself, Fanny smiled.

"I can do that."

"I know. I ain't your son for nothing. Good luck." He squeezed her shoulder reassuringly.

Fear, Fanny thought, had to be the single most debilitating emotion there was. It was everywhere in the room, swirling and circling her like a deadly fog.

"Someone explain to me what happened." Fanny's eyes swept the table and came to rest on Ryce Granger.

"It's like I said, Fanny. Ryce called the main office and was told he needed two signatures on the application. Ash and Birch signed all the forms. I was in Carson City, not that that makes a difference. Ryce had full authority to put the wheels in motion."

Fanny leaned into the table, her eyes unwaveringly still on Ryce Granger's face. "Was that before or after he cut a deal with my ex-husband to wash some, if not all, of his markers at Babylon? Don't insult me, Brad, by pretending Mr. Granger didn't know it was my signature that was required, not my husband's. The way I see it, this bank is out sixteen million dollars. You will return sixteen million dollars to the Thornton Family Partnership account within forty-eight hours. I have no interest in knowing how you will do this. You will do it or I'll have the banking commission down here so fast your heads will spin off your necks. It is not my responsibility to help you get your monies from Ash. Nor can you foreclose on the casino. If I were you, I think I might look into riverboat gambling. You own those boats now. You and Ash Thornton. You made a deal with the devil, gentlemen. Oh, and one other thing. The Thornton family will no longer be banking with this establishment. Good day, gentlemen. Remember, forty-eight hours from this minute, not one second longer."

Outside the bank, Fanny looked upward at the pale blue sky, a sky that looked more fragile than the finest porcelain. *Where are you, Simon? Did you know about this?*

Fanny drove to Babylon, her thoughts everywhere but on the matter at hand. What would Sallie have done? Did she handle things right? How was the move coming? *I'm going to kill you, Ash Thornton. Oh, Simon, I need you. Please, please, come back.*

Fanny parked in the underground parking lot in a reserved space next to Sunny's car. She exited through the emergency stairwell to come out on the second floor where Ash maintained his suite of offices.

Fanny burst into Ash's offices, slamming the door behind her. "You better hope these walls are soundproof, Ash!"

"Fanny, how the hell did you get in here!"

"I sneaked in. I took a page out of your book. Your surveillance stinks. I'm here, and that's all that matters. Where's Birch?"

"I don't have to account to you, Fanny. If you want to know where Birch is, you should call him. I'm busy."

"You're going to be a hell of a lot busier when you have to deal with the banking commission. They're going to get you on forgery, and I'm not stepping in on your behalf this time. You made Birch, your own son, a party to all of this. You got away with it, too. The big question is, how are you going to repay sixteen million dollars plus interest? Those riverboats belong to the bank now, and since you wiped Granger's markers, you're left holding the proverbial bag. How did you think you were going to get away with this? Do you think I'm really that stupid? Yes, I guess you do," Fanny said sadly.

"You screwed up my deal! Damn you, Fanny. Jesus, I hate your fucking guts. I must have been crazy out of my mind to marry you. This is a dog-eat-dog business and you know it. I'm a cripple, locked in this stinking chair, and all because of you. If you'd just die, we'd all be happy."

Fanny backed up a step, her face draining of all color. "It wasn't my fault that you fell off that girder."

"The hell it wasn't. If you'd given me the money, my own money, Thornton family money, I wouldn't have had to be up there to begin with, trying to keep my eye on things so costs would be down. Oh, no, you give it to me after. *AFTER* I'm sitting in this chair. It was your own guilty conscience that made you go ahead with Babylon. When it was too late, when I had nothing left. I sit in this chair twenty hours a day, full of painkillers while you're out there fucking my brother. The whole town knows about your affair. The kids know, too."

"I didn't try to keep it a secret, Ash. I can do whatever I want. I'm not your wife any longer. As for the town, do you think I care? I made a promise to your mother and I'm doing my best to keep it. I'm sorry you feel the way you do. I refuse to get into the name-calling and the backbiting. Family business behind closed doors is one thing. You've taken it public now. I have no control over the bank. In a week's time their doors will be closed, and you're responsible. All those people will be out of jobs. You have to take responsibility for that, too. The Gaming Commission won't let you work here any longer if you're convicted. This is about as serious as it gets, Ash. Were you ever going to tell me?"

"Shut up, Fanny."

"Is it that you don't want to hear my words, or is it my voice?" Fanny asked, looking around at the opulence of Ash's office. Top-of-the-line stereo system, hidden bar and refrigerator, private wall safe, recessed television, leather chairs and couch. Black-marble bathroom complete with Jacuzzi, priceless paintings on the walls, subdued lighting, perfect for those late-night assignations. All the trappings of the good life. She thought about her tiny studio with the faded red chairs, the fieldstone fireplace, and the narrow twin beds. There simply was no comparison.

Ash's voice was vitriolic, full of hatred when he said, "You wormed your way into my mother's life. You turned her against me and Simon, too. You got it all, the money, the land, the jewelry, the gold, the stock. You stole what was Simon's and mine. My father told me you would do it, too. He knew what was going on. My mother the whore. You're just like her, Fanny. She wheedled that money out of Cotton Easter just the way you wheedled it out of her. You're a cheat and a thief masquerading in a mother's body."

Fanny grew light-headed at the ugly words. He was getting to her, pushing her buttons, jerking her strings. If only Sallie hadn't put her in this position. If only she hadn't agreed to take care of the Thornton monies. If only . . . if only.

Fanny's voice was colder than ice. "My conscience is clear. I will never forgive you for the position you've put Birch in. The headlines will probably read EMPEROR AND SON INDICTED IN BANK FRAUD."

"Then help me, goddamn it."

"Not this time, Ash. Not this time."

"What about Birch?"

"Like father like son," Fanny said.

"You'll help Billie Coleman, but you won't help your husband and son? I hope you rot in hell, Fanny."

"Billie is taking responsibility and trying to correct a terrible wrong. If I were in her place, I'd do the same thing. Birch knows right from wrong just the way you know right from wrong. What's that saying, you play you pay?"

Fanny's legs felt like wet noodles as she made her way to Sunny's office.

Sunny looked up from her cluttered desk. "Mom! Twice in one week? No one told me you were on the floor. Is something wrong?"

"I came in through the garage. I wanted to . . . surprise your father. Do you happen to know where Birch is?"

"Biloxi, Mississippi. Mom, what's wrong?"

Fanny told her.

"Mom, they could go to jail. You can't let that happen. You can do something, can't you?"

"No. If Birch is in Mississippi, it's a done deal. Ash wired the money. I don't know the ins and outs of that, but it has something to do with federal regulations, state lines, and things like that."

"Pay the money back."

"It isn't that simple. The owners of the riverboats are already spending their money. I suppose it's possible for your father to cut some kind of deal with the bank. Forty-eight hours from now we will no longer be banking at Nevada Savings and Loan. The Nevada National Trust bank will be handling the Thornton accounts."

"Mom, the bank will shut down if you pull out."

"There is that possibility."

"I hate to say this, Mom, but Grandma Sallie wouldn't let all those people lose their jobs."

"That's your father's responsibility. Your father should have thought ahead to what could happen down the road. Pure and simple, he did not think he'd get caught. If I hadn't agreed to help Billie Coleman, we still wouldn't know what he'd done. I'm not Sallie, Sunny. I have to do what's right, for us, for me."

"Dad and Birch won't be able to work in the gaming business if . . ."

"I know. How are you feeling, Sunny?"

"Tired at times, other times I feel like scrubbing walls and floors. Mom, aside from all of this, is there something else bothering you? You don't look right to me."

"Your father said some very ugly things. I just have to come to terms with it all. I guess I'm tired, too. I have a hundred things I have to do. Why don't you and Tyler come up to Sunrise over the weekend?"

"Can't. I have a mountain of things to do before the championship. With Birch gone, Dad piled it all on me. I'm not complaining. I'd rather be busy than just sitting here. Is there anything I can do?"

"If there is, I'll call you. You might want to take Birch aside when he comes back and present a clear, concise account of what's going on. Your father's version won't . . . be as accurate. It's up to you, though. If you don't want to get involved, I understand."

"I'll talk to him. I think he'll be back in the morning."

When the door closed behind her mother, Sunny sighed deeply. Who was that cold-eyed person who just walked out of her office? Certainly not the mother she knew and loved. Did she dare walk down the hall to her father's offices? And say what? Hey, I heard you're going to jail. She rummaged through the mess of papers and schedules on her desk for the number Birch had given her when he left. In case of an emergency. What could be more of an emergency than this? She dialed the operator and placed a person-to-person call. Birch's harried voice came over the wire. Sunny started to babble the moment she heard her brother.

"Jail, Birch. Bars, striped suits, the whole works. Did you hear what I just said?"

"Mom won't let that happen," Birch said.

"Perchance are you talking about the mom you turned your back on? You could never take that one to the bank. In the old days it might have been true. Not this time, Birch. You need to come back. What's the point in staying there? It's all falling apart anyway. This is going to be one of those snowball things," Sunny said in a jittery-sounding voice.

Not this time. Sage had said those same words to him just days ago. "Okay, I'll get the next plane out."

It was six-thirty when Sunny cleared her desk in preparation to leaving the casino. She sensed him before she actually saw him. "Lock the door," she ordered.

Birch locked the door, his face full of questions. "He's acting like a one-man Gestapo unit. He's fired seven people in the past few hours. Twenty others have threatened to quit. The kitchen is in an uproar. The pool overflowed around three o'clock and five ceilings are ruined. Some high roller out of Cincinnati and his retinue says he's pulling out of the tournament and he wants his money back because we didn't come through with the satin sheets his girlfriend requested. The phones aren't working on the seventh floor. There's some shady parasite hanging out in the garage who insists on talking to Dad, and Dad won't go to the garage. The gears on the hydraulic lift in the counting room are stuck. Some guy walked out of here with $96,000 of our money. A pretty routine day if you ask me. What the hell were you thinking of to sign those loan applications, Birch? You know Mom has to sign off on everything."

"Dad said things switched up. I just figured she was so caught up in Uncle Simon she didn't want to be bothered with the casino since it was doing so well. Maybe I should have questioned it, but I didn't. Jesus, it never occurred to me that Dad would lie about something so important. I swear to God, Sunny, I didn't know."

"If Dad backs up your story, then I guess you don't have anything to worry about."

"What do you mean, *if?* I'm telling you the truth. Where is he?"

"Today he's like a spook. He's everywhere. I'm going home. This isn't my problem."

"I could use a little help here, Sunny."

Sunny ignored the pleading tone in her brother's voice. "From me and my big belly? When I could have used a little brotherly intervention with *him*, a few kind words, where the hell were you? Not this time, big brother."

"Sunny, it wasn't like that."

"The hell it wasn't. What you need right now is a Popsicle. The only problem is, Mom isn't here to give you the magic cure-all. I bet she installs those iron gates at Sunrise again to keep us out. See you tomorrow."

Rage, unlike anything he'd ever experienced, coursed through Birch. The moment his body ceased to shake, he headed for his office, where he sucked down two long swallows of his father's favorite whiskey. His eyes murderous, he then headed for the floor, his eyes raking the happy throngs of people parting with their money. The moment he spotted his father, he weaved his way through the narrow lanes of slot machines and the merry sound of coins dropping into the trays.

A tight smile on his face for the benefit of the customers, Birch leaned over and whispered in his father's ear. "Put the goddamn thing in gear or they'll be peeling you off the ceiling."

In Ash's office with the door closed and locked, Birch swung the wheelchair around until his father was facing him. He snorted in disgust at his father's glassy eyes. "You fucking lied to me. You said things switched up. I should have checked, but I didn't think my own father would lie to me. Damn you, why?"

"Why? That's a pretty stupid question. I'm sick of the way your mother handles things. She doesn't know anything about this business. We could make a fortune off those riverboats. She's not going to do anything. Fanny's all talk. She's got this thing about families sticking together. Do you think for one minute she'll let our asses go to jail? Come on, Birch, get real."

"Yeah, that's exactly what she's going to do. Guess what, I'm not going to jail, not for you, not for anyone. I believed you, I trusted you because you're my father, and you fucking screwed me over the way you screw everyone over. It will be up to Mom who she believes, and I don't think it's going to be you. If I were you, I'd give some real serious thought to what you're going to do."

Ash stared at his son. "Come on, Birch, we're talking business here. You gotta do a lot of things that are stomach-turning, but in the end it works out. We can pull this off. I know how to deal with Fanny. I'm counting on you, Birch."

"Not this time."

Ash stared at the door for a long time before he swallowed his second handful of pills in an hour. When his body grew lax, he slipped from his chair, whimpering and mewling like a kitten.

4

Fanny stared at the stack of legal documents piled up next to one of the big red chairs in her study. Her gaze swept sideways to the family picture on the table between the red chairs. Tears puddled in her eyes. A family divided.

Four months of legal hassles, bills, ugly phone calls from her ex-husband, and pleas from her son Birch to make it all come out right. As if she had magic in her fingertips. Legally, Birch was out of the woods, but Ash was swinging in the wind, cutting his own deals with the bank and the Gaming Commission. The money had been put back into her account and then transferred to her new bank. It was business as usual now. She absolutely refused to think about where Ash had managed to get another sixteen million dollars.

Fanny sighed. She had her own business problems to contend with, plus worrying about Sunny. And always, her thoughts were on Simon. Where was he? What was he doing? Did he think of her the way she thought of him? Had he been in touch with Jerry? Fanny shifted her thoughts to her corporate books. A headache started to hammer behind her eyes. With money so tight, everyone was jittery. They were overextended at the bank, their mortgage payments were late, and no one was drawing a salary. Even Bess had agreed, saying, when it's there, you'll pay me. I can wait. They were all waiting for Billie Coleman to make a payment on the monies that had been loaned to Coleman Aviation.

She would never, ever, believe she'd made a mistake in lending Billie the money. Somehow, she'd find a way to keep the businesses going. If she had to sell Sunrise, she'd do it. Sunrise was a place—wood, brick, mortar. People, family, meant more than a structure. If she sold the Thornton family home, she could stay afloat a little while longer. Perhaps the new owner would lease space to her. If not, they had to set up operations in Bess's three-car garage. "I'm sorry, Sallie, I have no other choice," she muttered. Fanny dropped her head into her hands. She really had to stop talking to her mother-in-law as though she were alive.

The phone rang just as she was about to dial the real estate agent's number. "Billie, Billie, slow down. What do you mean you're in Japan? Why? You have a grandson! A grandson you never knew about! Slow, Billie, slow down, the connection is bad as it is. Yes, yes, Moss knew about your grandson but because he was half-Japanese, he never told you? My God, what kind of man would do a thing like that? And a daughter-in-law! I'm sure she's wonderful if your son married her. I am so happy for you, Billie. Who's giving you all the money you need? Ah, I see." Fanny listened, her heart thundering in her chest when Billie told her a payment would be on the way to Nevada the minute she returned to Texas.

"I'm bringing my grandson back with me for a visit. His mother Otami, too, if she's willing to come. Sawyer wants to move everything over here. It's just so hard for me to believe my granddaughter is this *wunderkind* aeronautical engineer. Moss would be so proud of her even though he didn't have much use for women. She's going to get his dream plane off the ground and flying. To say she's the marvel in marvelous is an understatement. We're contemplating the move here to Japan and weighing the cost. Fanny, we could never have gotten this far if it wasn't for you. We all owe you our lives for your kindness and generosity. You are the only one who understood what getting Moss's plane in the air means to me. I'll never be able to thank you. Would you listen to me babble on? I'm sorry I didn't tell you I was leaving, it happened so suddenly. Tell me what's going on. Have you heard from Simon?"

They talked for a long time, two old friends who shared the same values, the same commitment to family. "Say hello to your family, Fanny. Never give up, Fanny, never. When things are the darkest, when all the doors seemed closed, you'll find a light. I'm the living proof."

Fanny smiled. She wanted to say she'd just seen the light with Billie's promise of a payback. Instead she said, "I can't wait to meet your new grandson and daughter-in-law. Call me as soon as you get back to Texas."

Fanny took a deep breath as she gathered up the corporate books and stack of bills. She stared at Daisy for a full minute before she tossed the papers in the air. "C'mon, Daisy, we're going for a walk. I need to say a few thank-yous."

She was a pretty young woman, plainly but neatly dressed. She could have been anybody; no one paid attention to her as she walked about the casino floor, her eyes taking in the furious whirring of the slot machines, the drink girls, the money changers with their carts, and the excited squeals of winning customers and the groans and moans of the losers. Suddenly she felt conspicuous and didn't know why. Maybe if she put some money in the machines, she'd feel like she had a right to be here. She dropped a dollar in the slot and pulled the handle. Twenty silver dollars dropped into the tray at the bottom of the machine. She blinked as she dropped in a second dollar. Fifteen silver dollars dropped to the tray. She blinked again.

"Would you like to trade in the silver for paper money, Miss?" one of the money changers asked.

"Yes, thank you. Can you tell me where the office is or where I can find Mrs. Thornton?"

"We don't have a Mrs. Thornton. We have a Mr. Thornton senior and a Mr. Thornton junior. You can't go to the offices, but I can call and have someone come out here to talk to you."

"Would you do that please?"

"Which one do you want, the older or younger one? Who should I say wants to see him?"

"My name is Lily Bell and I think I'd like to speak with . . . the young Mr. Thornton."

"You wait right here, Miss. It might take ten minutes or so."

In his office, Birch picked up the phone. "Did you tell her my mother doesn't work here? Did she say what she wanted? Where is she exactly? Okay, I'll be out in five minutes." He finished what he was doing, buzzed Sunny to tell her he was going out to the floor.

He saw her from a distance and knew in his gut that she wasn't a customer. He stared a moment longer. She was dressed simply in a plum-colored dress with a matching handbag. Her hair was a cluster of dark curls that capped a face almost devoid of makeup. He could see small pearls in her ears but no rings on her fingers. He drew a deep breath when he saw her smile at someone who spoke to her. In the time it took his heart to beat twice, Birch Thornton knew he wanted to get to know this young woman better.

Up close, he was surprised to see how tall she was. Incredible dark eyes behind heavily fringed lashes stared at him. He was right about the makeup. She didn't need it. "I'm Birch Thornton, can I help you?"

"I hope so, Mr. Thornton. I'm Lily Bell," she said extending her hand. "Is there somewhere we could talk? What I want to discuss is a personal matter."

Birch hesitated for a bare second. Her serious expression said this is important. "How about some coffee in our private dining room? No one will bother us there."

Lily nodded as she walked alongside the tall, immaculately dressed man. He smiled at her as he ushered her into the small, elegant dining room reserved for family and the chosen few who were invited from time to time. "Please, sit down. I'll call the kitchen for the coffee. It won't take long. I also have to let my sister know where I am so I can be paged if necessary.

"It's very good coffee," Birch said, his tone light, his eyes twinkling.

"I'm sure it is. I'm just nervous. I'm not sure I should be here. Sometimes I do things without thinking them through. What that means is, I reacted to . . . something. I was sure I had thought it through, but maybe I didn't. I really wanted to see Mrs. Thornton."

"Mrs. Thornton is my mother. She rarely comes to the casino. Can you tell me what this is about? We can always call her."

"I would rather see her in person."

"You're making this sound very mysterious. Why don't you start at the beginning? I'm a very good listener."

Lily rummaged in her purse and withdrew a snapshot. She slid it across the table toward Birch. "Do you recognize the woman in the picture? Study it very carefully."

Birch reached for the picture and studied it as Lily requested. "She looks familiar, but no, I don't know her. I don't think I've ever seen her."

"Does she remind you of anyone?"

"Sort of. Who is she?"

"My father's second wife. My . . . stepmother. She's very ill."

"I'm sorry, but what does that have to do with my mother? Do you think she knows her?"

"I think she's your grandmother, your mother's mother. Look at the picture again and tell me if that's who she reminds you of now."

"There seems to be a resemblance. My mother's mother abandoned her family. My grandfather raised my mother and her brothers all by himself. He did a good job of it, too. No one ever heard from her. My mother tried to find her, she hired detectives, but she was unable to locate her. What kind of woman does something like that? What is it that you want exactly?"

"To reunite mother and daughter. I told you I don't know if coming here was right or wrong. I did what I felt was right. If this is your grandmother, your mother is the one who has to make the decision. I saw a picture of your mother and your other grandmother a long time ago, in one of those Sunday family sections. I just happened to be watching my stepmother when she saw it, and she burst into tears. It said your mother's maiden name was Logan and she came from Shamrock, Pennsylvania. That's where my stepmother was from. We live in Bakersfield, California. She was very good to me. I have a half brother and sister, Paul and Anna. And before you can ask, we don't want anything from your family. Paul and Anna didn't want me to come here. They wanted to let things be. I'm not like that. I think families should stick together. When my own mother died, my father really was mother and father to me. When Harriet came along, she treated me like her own child."

Birch leaned back in his chair, his eyes speculative. "What do you want me to do?"

"Arrange a meeting with your mother. I want to talk to her. In the end, Mr. Thornton, it will be her decision. She has a right to know. If for some reason you don't want to arrange a meeting, I'll have to find another way to meet her. I've come too far now to back down."

"Do you want to go now or will later on or tomorrow do?"

"Time is of the essence. Harriet doesn't have long."

"Let me clear my decks. Drink your coffee, have another cup, and we'll leave. There's a lavatory at the end of the room in the corner in case you want to use it. I won't be long. It's a forty-five-minute ride up the mountain. I think, Miss Bell, you did the right thing."

"Do you really, Mr. Thornton?" Lily smiled. It was a smile that wrapped itself around Birch, the kind of smile that tugged at his heart.

"Yes, I do." He returned her smile. Lily grew light-headed and thought about things like moonlight, stardust, and then more earthy things like holding hands and walking through flower-scented meadows. With someone like Birch Thornton.

His stomach churning, Birch strode through the casino, unaware of the admiring glances following him. Somebody was watching over him. Lily Bell had given him the reason he needed to go to Sunrise to see his mother. He'd apologized for the fiasco at the bank, grateful to his father for backing up his denial. He'd taken his lumps by accepting his mother's stern, cold attitude, somehow managing to slink off with his head bowed, his heart quivering in his chest. Now, he had the one thing his mother craved more than anything in the world: entrance into his grandmother's world, a world denied his mother since birth.

Birch slowed his footsteps as he approached the door to his sister's office. He loved Sunny. From the time they were little he'd been her staunchest supporter. He hated seeing the disappointment in her eyes where he was concerned. He'd apologized to her, too, and all she'd done was nod her head. She'd cut herself off from him and his father, doing her job, staying out of sight, crying quietly when she thought no one was around. Sunny had the same kind of guts Sage had, the kind that counted. He listened for a moment before he tapped lightly on the door. The faint sound of the computer keys stopped. "Come in."

"Sunny, do you have a minute?"

"I have lots of minutes, Birch. Sit down."

"How are you feeling?"

"Is that one of those polite questions to make conversation or do you care?"

"Jesus, Sunny, every time I talk to you you have a burr in your undies. I care, or I wouldn't have asked."

"I feel like a pregnant woman. You didn't stop in here to ask me how I am. What's up?"

Birch told her.

"Wow! Where is she?"

"In the private dining room. Do you want to meet her?"

"Surely you jest. One minute you want me to stay hidden because of my big belly and the next you want me to walk out on the floor where customers can actually *SEE* me. Or do you want me to go down through the garage and come up by the service elevator? If Dad sees me on the floor in the monitor, this place will be in flux for three days." This last was said so bitterly, Birch cringed. He pretended not to see the tears in his sister's eyes.

"I want you to walk with me. That means at my side. I don't much care what Dad does or says these days. I'm doing my job just the way you're doing yours. God, Sunny, how did you handle your estrangement from Mom when you two went at it? It's killing me."

"You were wrong, Birch, just the way I was wrong. Mom taught us to take responsibility for our actions. That was the hardest lesson I ever learned. I chipped away a part of her heart. I don't think I can ever repair the damage I did to her. I hold back now because I don't ever want to see that awful look in her eyes again. You sold out, Birch."

"I didn't know, Sunny. Dad lied to me."

"That was my excuse, too. It isn't good enough. Have you spoken to Sage or Billie?"

"I call, but they don't call back. I'm not going to force myself on them."

"Do what I do, get in their face and go on from there. Refuse to accept their attitude, and if that doesn't work, beat the shit out of Sage."

Birch snorted. "Jesus, Sunny, you have to stop talking like a truck driver. Sage would deck me. Billie would kick my ass all the way down the mountain."

"You deserve both. Betrayal is a serious business, and no, I will not intervene."

"I didn't ask you to."

"You were thinking about it. I know you, Birch. Do you ever think we'll be a real family again?" Sunny's voice was so wistful, Birch put his arm around her shoulders.

"I like to think so, but I wouldn't bet the rent on it."

"What's *he* been doing?"

"I have no idea. I try and stay out of his way. He's up to something, though. He's got more schemes than a wizard. I gotta tell you something, Sunny. I'm scared shitless about that sixteen million dollars. I think we both know where he got it. When the other shoe falls I hope I'm not around. I pray to God every day that he can keep all those deals he cut straight in his mind. Another thing, he's got everyone in the world looking for Uncle Simon. It's like he dropped off the face of the earth. Guess he had it with this family, too."

"He's part of this family. Don't think for one minute Uncle Simon isn't hurting. He's out there somewhere thinking of us every hour of the day. That's the way he is. I don't know what happened between him and Mom. If ever two people were meant for each other . . ."

"Dad said . . ."

Sunny was a whirlwind. She was out of her chair and across the room, backing her brother up against the wall, her face almost touching Birch's face, her eyes spewing sparks. "When in the damn hell are you going to learn you can't believe anything *he* says? When, Birch?"

Undaunted, Birch blustered, "Uncle Simon had all the right breaks. He's not in a wheelchair."

"Uncle Simon made his own breaks. All he ever did was give. He never took."

"Except Mom."

"Yeah, Mom. Not until it was all over between her and Dad, though. You have a long way to go, Birch, before you belong in my little circle. I've had enough of this crap. All we do is spin our wheels. Let's go meet the charming Lily Bell. Let's see what she has up her sleeve. Everyone wants something."

"And you have the nerve to say I'm cynical!" Birch snorted. "She said she doesn't want anything."

"If I told you that, would you believe me?"

"Coming from you, yeah, I would."

Sunny smiled. Her grip on her brother's arm tightened. It was her way of showing approval.

"What's she like?"

"She kind of reminds me of Mom. The way I remember Mom when we were growing up. She's pretty. Her smile is . . . nice. I liked her."

"Aahhh."

"Get off it, Sunny. Smile. We're on camera."

Sunny stuck out her tongue as she let go of her brother's arm to do a deliberate duck walk, her stomach protruding for all the world to see. In spite of himself, Birch laughed aloud. He reached for Sunny's arm and for the benefit of the customers watching, said, "We're getting married this afternoon." Sunny howled with laughter.

"That's going to make *him* nuts for a whole week. I'm glad to see you haven't lost your sense of humor."

"Okay, we're here. Try not to be obnoxious, Sunny."

In his office, his eyes on the monitors, Ash seethed with rage. He buzzed Security, barking his order, "Bring my daughter and son here. Now! They're headed for the private dining room. I want to know who they're meeting."

The head of Security raced down the hall toward the private dining room, reaching it just as Birch was about to open the door. "Sunny, Birch, hold on. Your father wants to see you right away." The head of Security's voice was flat. His eyes looked worried.

"Tell my father we're both too busy to join him right now." For the benefit of the security camera, and Neal Tortalow's job, Birch jabbed a finger in the man's chest to make his point.

"He isn't going to like this, Birch."

"Ask me if I care, Neal."

Birch closed the door behind Sunny, and locked it. In the blink of an eye he had his jacket off. He tossed it over the security camera attached to the wall overhead.

"Well-done, big brother."

"I'm Sunny Thornton Ford, Birch's sister," Sunny said, holding out her hand. Lily Bell's handshake was every bit as firm as Sunny's.

"It's nice to meet you, Mrs. Ford. Do you want me to tell you why I came here?"

"Birch told me. I'd like to see the picture. Growing up we only knew one grandmother. Oh, yes, I can see the resemblance. I don't know how Mom is going to take this, Miss Bell. It's been so long and she never knew . . . her brothers, my uncles might remember."

"Brothers?"

"Uncle Daniel and Uncle Brad. My grandfather is still alive, too, but in frail health. I don't understand, didn't she tell you any of this?"

"No. She doesn't know I'm here. I made up my own scenario and checked it out as much as I could. I don't know this for sure, but I suspect, from things she said from time to time, that she didn't feel she had any right to appear in your mother's life. During her last operation she did a lot of muttering when she was coming out from under the anesthetic. That's how I was able to piece things together. There was this article in the paper about your mother and the elder Mrs. Thornton. Harriet kept it, and I saw her reading it many times. She almost wore out the paper. It didn't say anything about your uncles." Her voice was fretful now, the cornflower blue eyes sad, tears gathering in the corners of her eyes.

"Let's have some lunch!" Sunny said. She pressed a buzzer and spoke quietly. "A double pastrami on rye, two pickles, a glass of milk and a side order of potato salad. Birch? Make that two. Miss Bell?" She nodded. "Three of everything. Hurry up. I'm starving. Oh, bring it in from the side door."

"Are you hoping for a boy or a girl?" Lily Bell asked politely.

"It doesn't matter."

"Your baby will make Harriet a great-grandmother."

"What's she like?" Sunny asked.

"She treated me like a daughter. She was there for me when I needed someone. My father loved her, and she loved him. My own mother died shortly after I was born. Together, my father and Harriet had a son and daughter. They didn't want me to come here. Maybe I shouldn't have, I don't know. I was at the hospital sitting there for my shift with Harriet, and I thought about all the nice things she'd done for me, and I decided maybe, just maybe, I could . . ."

"What will you do if my mother and uncles don't want to . . . meet her?"

"I'll go home and put this behind me. I'll know I tried. I'll tell Harriet about the visit. She hates lies, so I'll tell her the truth. I wish I could tell you why she left her family, but I can't."

"Leaving three little kids for a man to raise is pretty shitty in my opinion," the outspoken Sunny said. Birch nodded in agreement.

"I agree with you," Lily Bell said.

Their lunch arrived at the same moment Ash Thornton banged on the dining room door. "Open the goddamn door, Birch!"

Birch bit into his sandwich as did Sunny. Both pretended they heard nothing. Following their cue, Lily crunched on a pickle. "Let's not mention this to you know who," Birch said as he gulped at his milk.

"I'm way ahead of you," Sunny replied as she trundled over to the service door to lock it. "This is a good sandwich. I'm going to have heartburn all afternoon."

"That means your baby is going to have a lot of hair," Lily said. "What's your mother like?"

"One of a kind," Birch said.

"The best," Sunny said.

"I'm looking forward to meeting her. I'd like to know all about her in case she decides not to go with me to California. I want to be able to tell Harriet what a wonderful daughter she has."

"No thanks to her," Sunny blurted. "I believe she's the person she is because my grandfather Logan and my uncles raised her. If your Harriet had a hand in it, I doubt she'd be who she is today."

Birch kissed the top of Sunny's head. "You don't know that, Sunny. Stop being such a hard-ass."

"Your sister is probably right, Mr. Thornton. Harriet often said she wasn't the same person she was in her youth. But then, who is? Isn't that what maturity is all about? I'm also certain Harriet shouldered all the blame. If it were otherwise, she would have gone back to her family in the later years in an attempt to make things right."

"I'll have Security break down this door if you don't open it this damn minute," Ash Thornton bellowed from the other side of the door.

"I think, Miss Bell, this might be a good time for us to leave."

"If you aren't going to finish that sandwich, can I have it, Birch?"

"Take it with you, Sunny. You look tired. I'll give you a ride home."

"Very good idea. Tyler can drop me off tomorrow morning."

"If I were you, I'd take a few days off. With pay of course."

"I like that idea, too."

Lily Bell's face flushed at the ripe curses filtering through the door. She allowed herself to be ushered out the service door and didn't question why they were going through the kitchen to an alley leading to Birch's reserved parking space.

"I'd say that was a very clean getaway," Lily said.

"I'd say so," Birch said, volunteering no other information.

"I'll take care of things, make a few calls," Sunny said as she got out of the car in front of her apartment building ten minutes later. "Take as much time as you need, Birch. It was nice meeting you, Miss Bell."

"You too, Mrs. Ford. I hope you have a little girl that looks just like you."

"That's what my husband said. With my luck it's going to look like Birch. He's quite good-looking when he's spiffed up. He's a twin, you know."

"You can go in anytime now, Sunny. Don't you have to take a nap or something?"

"Birch, give Mom a hug. A really big one. I know for a fact she has a whole box of cherry Popsicles in the freezer. She's dying for us to ask for one."

"No kidding! How do you know that?"

Sunny smirked. "I was with her when she bought them. She said she was getting in practice again for when this little guy of mine makes his entrance. Ask for one, Birch."

"My dad always gave me a licorice stick. It made all the bad things go away," Lily volunteered.

Birch smiled from ear to ear. He was starting to like this young woman.

"Nice meeting you, Miss Bell," Sunny said. She offered up a jaunty salute in her brother's direction.

The ride up the mountain was made in companionable silence. From time to time one or the other would say something that brought a smile to the other's face.

Birch thought he was being devious when he blurted, "Are you and your half sister and brother married with families?"

"No. I came close once, but he wanted different things from life than I did. My sister is engaged. Paul says he's going to remain a bachelor. He's a forest ranger, and he loves the outdoors. Young women want bright lights and people. Anna will probably marry in a year or so. They want to save money so they can buy a house and not have to pay rent. I have a good job, and I inherited my father's house. We all have a nice life. I want you to know that so you understand we don't want anything from your family. How about you, are you married? Your sister said you had a twin. Are you look-alikes?"

She wasn't married. She had a good job. The urge to reach out and touch her hand was so strong, Birch's knuckles grew white on the steering wheel. "You're going to like my mother." The words blurted out of his mouth so fast, Lily smiled.

"I'm sure I will."

"Thanks for not asking about that ruckus back at the casino."

"Do you want to talk about it? I'm a stranger, and I never betray confidences. Sometimes it helps to talk."

He wanted to unload, to confide, more than anything in the world, knowing instinctively this young woman wouldn't judge him. "It's one of those family things that doesn't bear repeating. That's just another way of saying this, too, will pass. Tell me about you."

"I live in a world of books. Growing up there were no children my age in the neighborhood, so I read a lot. Books became my best friends. I was a librarian for a few years until I opened my own bookstore. There's a small café attached to it. No one was more surprised than I when I made a profit. Not right away, of course. I like being independent and not having to account to anyone. Do you know what type book sells the most?"

"Thrillers?"

"Yes. Mysteries, high-tech thrillers. I read them all. They're my favorites. Do you read?"

"When I have the time. Sage, my brother, is the real reader in the family. When do you plan on returning to California?"

"Tomorrow morning."

"If my mother decides to go with you, I can fly you in the company plane. I think I might like to meet my grandmother. I wish I could tell you Mom will go, but I really don't know. If she decides not to go, I will."

"That's very nice of you, Mr. Thornton."

"Can we be Birch and Lily?"

"Sure. What do you do at the casino? I had no idea what a gambling casino was like. I just don't understand how people can gamble away their money. I could never do that. I work for my money."

"You sound just like my mother. She feels like you do. We grew up in the gaming profession. To us it's like any other business. Some days it gets away from you, but it works out in the end. We have thousands of employees who make sure things run smoothly."

"I don't know if I could work in a room with canned air all day. I like to look out a window. I read somewhere that people who handle money all day get sick a lot. Is that true?"

Birch laughed. "I'll have to check that one out. Off the top of my head I'd say our absentee level is about normal. We're almost there." Again, he had the urge to reach out for her hand. "Will you have dinner with me this evening?"

"Well . . . I didn't plan . . ."

"You have to eat."

"I didn't bring any . . . I just brought my overnight case. I don't have anything fancy to wear."

"I'm not into fancy myself. What you have on is beautiful, and it will fit in anywhere I take you. I like to go to out-of-the-way places where the food is good. Places the tourists don't know about. Are you a meat or fish person?"

"I like everything. Yes, I would like to have dinner with you. It doesn't matter where. I adapt."

"Ah, a girl after my own heart," Birch said lightly. This time he did reach out to touch her hand. He withdrew it quickly, a huge smile on his face.

"That's Chue's house on the right. My grandmother Sallie brought him and his sister up to the mountain when they were children. Chue looks after things here and is responsible for the hanging gardens at the casino. Su Li, his sister, is a famous doctor. She's retired now, though. We consider them family." Birch slowed the car at the bend in the road so his passenger could admire the gardens Chue had planted.

"It's lovely."

"My grandmother lived in a little house right in the middle of the garden. She had it built specially so she could take care of my grandfather. When she died, my mother burned it down. At my grandmother's request. Her ashes are scattered over the mountain. Look. There's Daisy." Birch slowed the car again and opened the door. Daisy hopped in and snuggled in Birch's lap. "Here comes Mom!" He turned in time to see a startled expression on Lily's face.

"She looks just like Harriet." Her breath exploded in a loud sigh of relief.

"Mom, I brought someone to see you." He hugged her and whispered in her ear. "Hear her out, Mom, this isn't as crazy as it sounds. Mom, this is Lily Bell. She came from California to see you." His whispered voice dropped even lower. "I like this girl, Mom."

"Miss Bell," Fanny said, offering her hand to the young woman. "It's a pleasure to meet you. Why don't we go into the studio and have some coffee?"

"Why don't I make the coffee while you and Lily talk?"

Puzzled, Fanny agreed as she led the way to her studio.

While Birch clanged and banged in the kitchen, Fanny listened to Lily's story. From time to time he poked his head out of the tiny area to see his mother's expression. Her face was whiter than chalk. Her hands trembled as she held the small photograph at different angles to view it.

"I don't know what to say."

"I imagine it's a terrible shock. I don't blame you if you don't want to see her. I didn't know you had brothers until your son told me. I wish I had more to tell you, but Harriet didn't talk about her old life. I'm so sorry."

"Birch?"

"I can see the resemblance in the picture, Mom. Why don't you call Uncle Daniel and Uncle Brad and see what they say? I can fly you up there in the morning, Mom. It will be a day out of your life. If you don't go, you'll always wonder if you made the right decision."

"I'll call my brothers and see what they say. Birch is right—if I don't go, I'll always wonder. I need to think for a minute. Birch, show Miss Bell around. Introduce her to Sage and Billie. I hear Bess's car. Would you ask her to come over to the studio?"

When the door closed behind her son, Fanny let her emotions loose. Her clenched fists banged at the arms of the red chair. Tears trickled down her cheeks as she tried to see the numbers on the phone to call her brothers. Somehow she managed to blurt out Lily Bell's story. "I'm going, Daniel. You and Brad have to make up your own minds. Miss Bell said time is of the essence. You could take the red-eye and be there before me. We can meet in the hospital lobby. I don't know if you should tell Daddy or not. I'll leave that up to you. Do you think this is some kind of omen, Daniel? Why now after all these years? We have a brother and a sister we never knew about. That has to mean something to us. I'm going! You will? All right, Daniel. Give Daddy my love, and I'll see you in the morning."

Fanny turned. "Did you get all that, Bess?"

"You found your mother. That's wonderful, Fanny. It is, isn't it?"

"Yes and no. Why don't I feel something?"

"You will. I see the resemblance," Bess said as she held the picture up to the light.

"I see Daniel and Brad more than myself. I look more like my father. I know it's her. I just know it. What in the world will I say to her? She's dying. What if I say the wrong thing?"

"I don't think you need to worry about right or wrong. You say what you feel. Stay as long as you need to stay. We can handle things here. I picked up the mail, and the good news is Billie Coleman sent us another check."

"Bless her heart. I need to call her tonight. I keep forgetting about the time difference in Japan. Was there any other mail?"

"If that's your way of asking me if there's a letter from Simon Thornton, the answer is no. Fanny, why don't you just write him a letter and pray the post office forwards it? I'm sure Simon has personal mail. If it isn't forwarded, where does it go? He has no home. He sold the business. Mail goes somewhere. Just do it."

Fanny bent over to pull a shoe box out from under one of the red chairs. "Should I mail all 120 of them? I've written one every day since I got back. I used to write to Ash like that. Every single day. Look what it got me."

"Four great kids, a wonderful business, one-of-a-kind friends, this lovely mountaintop home, and now your mother. If you hadn't met and married Ash, you could be clerking in a dimestore and I'd still be serving egg salad sandwiches at the counter in my father's drugstore. You and I might never have met. Everything happens for a reason. We both know that. I say mail the damn letters. I'll take them down the mountain tonight when I go home."

"Okay."

"I love it when one of us makes the right decision."

"Oh, Bess, I'm finally going to see my mother. I swear, I never thought it would happen. Say a prayer that I feel something when I see her. I don't want her to die without knowing us. We had so much love to give her, the boys and me. How could she just up and leave us like that? I need to know why. I want to know what it was that made her walk away. Maybe if she tells me something I can believe, I'll feel something. Oh Bess, what if she says she never thought about us, never wondered how we turned out?"

"She isn't going to say that, Fanny."

"But what if she does?"

"Then you'll tell her you're sorry she felt like that. You'll tell her you and your brothers thought about her every day of your lives. Stop worrying, mothers don't say things like that. Is there anything I can do, Fanny?"

"No."

Bess let herself out the door. She looked through the window to see Fanny curled up in the red chair, the picture of her mother in her hand.

"Oh, Mom, I have so much to tell you," Fanny whispered to the picture.

5

The hospital had a hushed quietness in the early hours of the morning. The sickening smell of flowers waiting to be delivered permeated the small lobby. Fanny gagged at the overpowering scent. Flowers and hospitals led to funerals and more flowers, eulogies and tears.

She saw them then, her two older brothers. They looked like tired little boys as they paced between the gray plastic-and-chrome chairs, their hands jammed into their pockets. The relief in their eyes when they saw her brought tears to her eyes. "I'm so glad you came," Fanny said.

"Dad insisted. We would have come anyway, Fanny. I don't know what I'm supposed to feel or what I should say," Daniel, the oldest, said in a weary voice.

"I think we'll know when we get there. If it's any consolation, I feel the same way. I'd like you to meet the young lady who . . . Lily, this is Daniel and Brad."

Lily acknowledged the introduction. "I'll go up first, and if Harriet is awake, prepare her. I'll come back for you. The coffee shop is open and the coffee is quite good." Fanny nodded.

Birch ordered coffee that no one drank.

"I think I wish this wasn't happening. Our lives are going to change now," Daniel said. "I don't think I want another brother or sister. You guys and your families are all I need or want."

"I agree," Brad said.

The bitterness in both her brothers' faces tugged at Fanny's heart. "We need some closure to this part of our lives. Our children have a right to know about our side of the family. Everything happens for a reason. Sometimes the timing isn't quite what we would like, but you have to deal with it. Right now, it's the only game in town. If it wasn't for Miss Bell, we still wouldn't know. We have the right to know the whys of it all. I want to know. Please, let's try not to be bitter. We all have good lives, wonderful children, and our families are intact. More or less."

"As usual, Fanny, you're right," Brad said squeezing her shoulders.

Birch watched the interaction between his mother and uncles, his heart thumping in his chest. The more or less pertained to him and his father. It always came down to family. Would he be as charitable as these two giants towering over him if he was in their position. They'd come here with bitterness in their hearts because a member of their family asked them to. And now, that member, his mother, had somehow managed to wipe away the bitterness. All he could see in their faces was sadness.

Lily Bell walked over to their table. "She's awake. It's difficult for her to talk, but she wants to see all of you. She . . . she wanted the nurse to fix her hair and put one of her own gowns on her. Another five minutes and we can go up. Anna and Paul are on the way. Is there anything you want to ask me?" The question was directed at Fanny's brothers. Both men shook their heads.

They waited.

The door to the coffee shop opened suddenly. Fanny was aware of movement, of hushed whispers. She looked up to see Sunny, Sage, and Billie. She cried then as her children circled around her. Out of the corner of her eye she saw Sage draw Birch into the tight little circle. "You belong here too, big brother. Sunny took up two seats." It brought the desired smiles Sage was looking for.

"We can go up now," Lily said, her eyes on her watch.

If the frail woman in the bed had ever been pretty, it wasn't evident now, but there was an alertness in her eyes Fanny hadn't expected. They circled the bed, uncertainty on their features.

"I'm Fanny, Mom. This is Daniel and this is Brad. My children are here too, Birch and Sage, they're twins. This is Sunny, who's going to make you a great-grandmother, and this is Billie. I want to be honest and tell you none of us knows what to do or say. I think we want to know why you left us. We have a right to know that. We can go on from there."

"Your father was a good man. Solid, dependable, hardworking. I wanted something different. I tried to tell him that, but he didn't *hear* me. When you were born something happened to me. All I did was cry. I couldn't eat or sleep. Three children in diapers overwhelmed me. I tried, but I couldn't make it work. I left knowing in my heart your father would do a better job of raising you three than I ever could. I was right. Many times I wanted to call or write, but I told myself I gave up that right. I have no excuses, and I don't ask your forgiveness because I'm dying. I'm grateful that you came. I always wondered how you turned out."

"Pretty damn good," the outspoken Sunny blurted.

"I want you to leave now. Go back to your families and lead your own lives. Mine is over, and I take full responsibility for all the things I should have done and all the things I shouldn't have done. I have two children who will mourn for me. I don't know if I have a right to say this or not, but I'll say it anyway. I'm very proud of the way your father raised you."

"Just a damn minute here," Sunny said.

"Hush, Sunny," Fanny said.

"What will you name the child?" Harriet asked, her voice little more than a raspy whisper.

"It's not going to be Harriet, that's for sure."

Strangled sounds came from the frail figure. "I like that. There's one in every family. Brad was like that as a little boy."

"He still is, Mom," Fanny said. "Is there anything we can do for you?"

"Say a prayer once in a while. Not for me, for your father. Goodbye."

There was nothing for them to do but leave.

More strangled sounds came from the bed. "What did she say?" Fanny asked Lily.

"She said you weren't to stay for the funeral."

Sunny waddled back to the bed and leaned over. "Well, guess what, *Grandmother*, we aren't staying. We all came here because of our mother, not because of you. You're right, you don't deserve us. When you get to your final destination say hello to our *other* grandmother." She leaned closer and kissed the dry sunken cheeks. "That's for my mother."

"Take care of her."

"You bet we will. You have a good trip now, you hear."

The old woman's tortured laughter followed them from the room.

"If you weren't pregnant, I'd lay you out right here," Sage said. "What the hell got into you? Have a good trip? Jesus."

"She laughed, didn't she? I didn't want her to think we're like her. I wasn't being mean-spirited, Sage, I was trying to lighten the moment. She knew that, I saw it in her eyes."

"It's a damn good thing Mom didn't hear all of that."

"Is that a threat you're going to hold over my head?" Sunny asked.

"If I thought it would get me anywhere, I would. Just shut the hell up and let's go. This family is going to breakfast *to talk.*"

"About what? I am hungry. I'm always hungry. I eat all day long. I'm actually starving."

"Miss Bell is going to bring . . . what do I call them, aunt, uncle, what? Anna and Paul, I guess," he said answering his own question. "After we talk I assume we'll leave. It was a good idea of yours, Sunny, to come here. I thought Mom was going to faint dead away. Are you okay?"

"If you feed me, I will be. Now do you understand about family, Sage? This is all so sad. Mom must be devastated. I don't know what to say to her or if I should say anything. Sometimes I think this family is jinxed. I saw that little thing with Birch. You're a nice guy, Sage, and if I say so, it must be true."

"So, how are you *really* feeling?"

"Real shitty. I think there's something wrong with me aside from my pregnancy. I've had every test in the book and nothing shows up. It's something I feel, something I just know, if that makes sense."

Sage felt his stomach lurch. He wanted to say a prayer right then and there for his sister and didn't know why. He closed his eyes for a second, trying to imagine life without Sunny in it. "I'll tell you what. If you don't feel better after you deliver, we'll go to New York. They're supposed to have the finest hospitals and the best doctors. I'll go with you. I think it's your pregnancy, though."

Sunny stopped. "No. It's something else. I'm afraid, Sage."

He was afraid too. "Don't go spooking me now, Sunny. I bet you're having twins and that's why you feel like you do."

"I hope you're right, Sage."

To Sage, his sister's voice had an ominous ring. "You know me, I'm always right. Hey, did'ya see that guy driving by? He looked just like Uncle Simon."

"What guy?" Sunny asked as she looked up and down the road.

"He's gone now. It looked just like him. I guess today isn't the best of days. Maybe I wanted to see him to make sense out of all of this. Uncle Simon always had the answers to everything. If Mom ever needed Uncle Simon, it's now."

"Dad ruined that. He's at the bottom of it all," Sunny said. "God, can't we talk about something pleasant once in a while? I think Birch likes Lily Bell. I think he likes her a lot. So there."

"Long-distance romances never work. So there yourself."

"Birch can fly here every other day if he wants to. I see something brewing right under our noses."

"You need to mind your own business. Try and keep that mouth of yours shut over breakfast. This is Mom's gig, so don't go screwing it up. We're here. Behave yourself and don't embarrass us."

"Up yours, Sage."

Sage grinned. Sunny was never going to curb her tongue or her actions. Sunny was a what-you-see-is-what-you-get girl. His eyes were worried, though, as he held the door open so his family could enter the restaurant.

Lily Bell declined breakfast, saying she would wait outside for her half brother and half sister. Birch joined her. Sunny smirked in Sage's direction as she ordered a breakfast large enough for three people.

"We have to do what she wants, and she wants us to leave," Fanny said.

"I don't have any problem with that," Daniel said. Brad seconded his brother's words.

"It's sad. She was our mother. I wanted to feel something, I really did, but she was a stranger. I watched her eyes and I don't think she felt anything either. Do we just leave and not look back? That seems cruel. She said nice things about Daddy. Miss Bell said she was a nice person."

"Let it go, Fanny," Daniel said. "We have our closure now. Oops, here come our new siblings." He stood to extend his hand and introduce himself. Brad and Sage did the same.

"Please, sit down. Would you like some coffee?" Fanny asked.

Anna and Paul sat down but declined the coffee. An uncomfortable silence fell around the table. Fanny waited until Anna spoke. "I think things should be left as they are. We'll go on with our lives and you'll go on with yours. We have nothing in common even though we share the same mother. Paul and I are glad you got to see Mom for your sake. I don't know what happened before, and neither Paul nor I want to know now. It goes without saying that we won't make any demands on your family. Now, if you'll excuse us, we want to go to the hospital."

Fanny nodded. The men stood again, but this time there were no handshakes.

"Cold-hearted bitch," Sunny said. She bit into a blueberry muffin slathered with soft butter.

"My life won't be torn asunder if I never see those two again," Billie said.

"They're holding themselves in tight control. They lost their father, and now they're going to lose their mother. I don't think they knew what to do. We have no other choice but to abide by their wishes and respect their grief. Daniel? Brad? Do you have anything to say?"

"You're right, Fanny. It's behind us now."

"I want to thank whoever's paying for this wonderful breakfast," Brad said as he looked pointedly at Sage. "There's an eleven o'clock flight to Pittsburgh, and we'll make it if we leave now. I'm sorry things didn't turn out better, Fanny."

"I'm okay with this, Brad. I got to see my mother. I never thought that would happen. The truth is, I gave up a long time ago. I'm just sorry it's under these circumstances. Give Daddy a big kiss and hug for me."

"Birch and Lily are driving them to the airport. We'll meet up with them there," Sage volunteered.

"That's nice," Fanny said.

"You okay, Mom?" Billie asked.

"I think so. I feel like I should have . . . said something meaningful or . . . something. I didn't even kiss her or touch her hand."

"Mom, if you were meant to do those things, you would have done them. She didn't expect it, and I don't think she wanted it. If you want the truth, I think we interrupted her dying schedule. That's my opinion." To the waitress she said, "I'll have an orange and a blueberry muffin to go."

Fanny smiled at her daughter. "I think you might be right. *Exactly* how much weight have you gained, Sunny?"

"You don't want to know, Mom."

"Tyler calls her two-ton Lizzie." Sage guffawed. "I'm telling you, she's having twins."

"If I do, I'm naming them Daniel and Brad. If I have a girl, I'm calling her Polly."

"Really, Sunny. That's wonderful. They'll be so pleased if it comes to pass."

"Sure, those guys are so generous I know they'll cough up a really good trust fund for their namesakes. They're such mushy pushovers. I just love them to death. Pay the check and let's get out of this town. It's depressing," Sunny said.

Across the street from the restaurant a tall man dressed in khaki slacks and rumpled tee shirt climbed from his car and entered a small market attached to the gas station. The two little dogs hopped up on the shelf behind the backseat to stare out the window. On the other side of the street the Thornton family climbed into Sage's rental car.

In her struggle to get comfortable, Sunny found herself staring across the street at the small black car. "Did you see those two cute little dogs? I think I'm going to ask Tyler to get me one. I always wanted a dog. That's the same guy, Sage, the one I told you looked like Uncle Simon. Shoot, he's going the other way. I'll tell you, he was the spitting image of our uncle."

"She's always seeing strange things," Sage said to his mother, who was busy craning her neck to look where Sunny was pointing.

"I do not *see things*. The man looked *exactly* like Uncle Simon. He was even wearing khaki pants and a tee shirt. It's the same guy we saw before. I'm not making this up, Mom."

"Turn around, Sage, go back to the gas station," Fanny ordered. Sage slammed on the brakes and made a U-turn in the middle of the road. The moment the car stopped in front of the little market, Fanny was out of the car, running inside. She fumbled with her wallet and withdrew a picture of Simon. She held it up to the young clerk. "Was this man just in here?"

"Yes, ma'am, not five minutes ago. He bought some dog food, dog treats, newspapers, and cigarettes."

"Has he ever been in here before?" Fanny thought her heart would thunder right out of her chest.

"I've never seen him."

Fanny ran back to the car. "It was Simon. Sage, take this road and see if you can overtake him. It was Simon!"

"Mom, he could have turned off anywhere. He's got ten minutes on us. I'm doing it, I'm doing it," he said at the anguish on his mother's face.

"No one ever pays any attention to me," Sunny said, biting into the muffin she'd taken to go.

"Can't you drive faster, Sage?" Fanny demanded, her head out the window as she tried to scan the highway.

"Mom, I'm going eighty now. Get your head in here before someone going ninety clips it off. He could be anywhere, Mom. There were five turnoffs and all those side streets he could have turned on. Let's stop at a gas station and see if he's listed in the phone book. We can check with the utility company, too."

"Just keep driving, Sage. It was him. I can't believe this."

"I can," Sunny chirped from the backseat. "Things like this happen in the movies all the time. Picture this, we find him and I go into labor and deliver twins. Everyone lives happily ever after."

"I wouldn't blame Tyler one bit if he divorced you. You need a muzzle."

"You're just ticked off because I saw him twice, and you didn't believe me either time. I bet he's living on some mountaintop. All by himself with those two little dogs. He only comes down off the mountain for dog food, cigarettes, and newspapers. He's probably living off the land, thin as a rail, unhappy, wondering where it all went wrong."

"That's enough, Sunny," Fanny said. Her voice was as shaky as her insides.

"The interstate is up ahead. What do you want me to do, Mom?"

"Pull over to the side of the road. I need to think."

The occupants of the car remained silent as Fanny squeezed her eyes shut. So close and yet so far away. Sage was right, he could be anywhere. Better to go back and hire a private detective to locate Simon. At least now she knew the general area he was in. Sunny was probably right about Simon living on a mountaintop. Simon loved the mountains. How like Simon to get two dogs.

"Go back to the airport, Sage. Birch will be waiting for us. I can always come back here when we aren't so pressed for time."

"Are you sure, Mom?" Sage asked.

"I'm sure. None of us needs this today on top of everything else."

"Mom, can I say something?" Sunny asked.

"Of course, Sunny."

"I remember Uncle Simon talking about a place called Stallion Springs one time. I think it's somewhere in the Tehachapi Mountains. He said he owned some land there and one day he was going to build a cabin. We were little when he said that. I don't even know why I remember it."

"He never mentioned it to me. It's a place to start. We'll find him."

"Only if he wants to be found," Sunny muttered under her breath.

Simon Thornton threw down the newspaper he'd been reading. The two little dogs at his feet immediately dragged it off. In ten minutes it would be in shreds and then one or the other would poop in the middle. Normally he'd just shake his head and laugh. Not today. Today he was out of sorts. Today he was seeing his nieces and nephews everywhere. He'd had his usual nightmare about Ash three times in the past week. He was thinking too much, and he hadn't slept well since the day he walked out of his New York office.

"Cabin fever," he muttered to the dogs who ignored him. They were on the financial page now, growling playfully at one another. Maybe it was time to move on. The question was, where? "I always wanted to see Oregon," he muttered again. He hated it when he muttered to himself. If he didn't watch it, he'd become a wilderness recluse. Like he wasn't one already. What he should do was go into town and call Malcom and maybe Ash and maybe Fanny. Just to say hello. Then again, maybe he wouldn't do that. What would be the point?

The point was . . . he was tired of fishing, tired of hunting, tired of sitting here on the front porch of someone else's cabin doing nothing. Actually, he was goddamn sick and tired of things not going his way. He should be building his own cabin so he could freeze his ass off in the winter. He was drinking too much, too. Drinking so he could sleep. When he did sleep all he did was dream about Fanny and Ash. When he wasn't dreaming about them he was dreaming about his mother and his youth.

One phone call. What was the harm in making one phone call. Enough time had gone by so it wouldn't seem like he was backwatering. Who should he call, though? Fanny, Malcom, Fanny, Ash, Fanny. It wasn't right that he wasn't staying in touch. Things could be happening, things he should know about. Ash's condition could worsen and the boys wouldn't know where to locate him. *That* he needed to know about. Fanny could be sick, Sunny could be having her baby. Malcom could be in trouble at the company.

Five minutes later he had himself convinced he needed to go back to town. He piled the dogs in the car, his shoulders lighter. He whistled because Slick liked to join in by howling at the top of his lungs. Tootsie usually slept through the whole ordeal.

Simon drove steadily, the miles ticking off slowly as he ran different conversations over and over in his mind. He'd call Fanny first. He'd say whatever came into his mind. Then he'd call Malcom. Ash would be last on his list.

Two hours later, Simon pulled into a Mobil station, where he asked the attendant for ten dollars in change. He was breathing like a long-distance runner when he placed the call to Fanny and got her answering machine. He hung up. His second call was to Malcom whose secretary said he was out of town. He felt his shoulders start to slump. What the hell, Ash was better than nothing. Instead, he placed a second call to Fanny and told the operator to stay on the line, that he wanted to leave a message. He listened to her sweet voice say, "I'm not here, please leave a message and the time you called."

Simon cleared his throat twice before he could speak, his heart jumping crazily inside his chest. "Fanny, this is Simon. It's around two o'clock. I just wanted to call to say hello and to let you know I'm fine. I've been moving around quite a bit and will probably grease up my sneakers and move again by tomorrow. I think about us all the time and what we had and what we could be having now. You know how much I love you, but I need to tell you again. Perhaps someday when things are right . . . will that day ever come, Fanny? I feel sort of foolish talking to a machine. I guess I'll say good-bye. I think about us every single day. Oh, I got two dogs. Tootise and Slick. They're great company. Daisy would love them. I'll call again when the loneliness gets too unbearable. Good-bye, Fanny."

Ash's voice boomed over the wire. "Simon, is that really you? I've got everyone in the world looking for you. Listen, I got myself into a bit of a mess. I need some help here. Fanny put the squeeze on me, and I'm lucky my ass isn't in jail. Where the hell are you?"

"Does it matter, Ash? I'm talking to you now. What is it you think I can do for you?"

"You can loan me about fourteen million dollars is what you can do for me."

Simon threw his head back and roared with laughter. "Ash, if I had fourteen million dollars, I wouldn't be standing here in a phone booth talking to you. What did you do this time?"

"I told you, I didn't do anything. Fanny squeezed me out. I bought these riverboats in Biloxi, Mississippi. She went through the roof because the bank gave me the money on my signature without hers. She threw a fit and the damn bank had to close down. A whole bunch of other shit went down, too. I was swinging in the wind, little brother, so I had to cut some deals, and I can't make good. How much can you loan me?"

"Zip. Squat. *Nada.* How could you do such a stupid thing? Did you involve the kids? You did, didn't you?"

"Birch went along with it." Ash's voice was whiny, full of self-pity. "Are you refusing to help me? You owe me, Simon."

"Where's Fanny, Ash?"

"Jesus, you aren't going to believe this one. Some chick waltzes in here saying she knows where Fanny's mother is and they all took off and left me here to run things. Ungrateful snots. Do they give a shit about me? No they do not. Birch just up and took the damn plane and didn't even ask my permission. This is not a considerate family."

"Fanny finally found her mother," Simon said, his voice full of awe. So that's where she'd gone.

"Yeah, the old lady is dying. It's just like Fanny to rush there to hold her hand."

"Yeah, Ash, that's just like Fanny," Simon said softly.

"Where the hell are you, Simon? I need a little help here. I thought we were brothers. Hell, you're marrying my ex-wife. That has to count for something."

"Who told you that?"

"Get off it, Simon. Everyone in Las Vegas knows. What I don't understand is why you left. Did Fanny pull one of her famous stunts on you, too? If she did, you know what I've had to put up with. I'm desperate here, and you aren't making it any easier. Do you want me to beg?"

"Ash, what's the money for?"

"To pay back the loan. The interest is killing me. They'll kill me next. You know what those people are like. Do you want my death on your conscience? Mom wouldn't like this, Simon."

"Ash, you aren't a stupid man. Why did you go to those thugs?"

"It wasn't like I had other choices, Simon. In my condition prison was not an alternative. You know they'll kill me. You have the money; I know that, too."

"You know what, Ash, no matter what this family does where you're concerned, it's never enough. All you do is demand. We give and give and give and all you do is take and take and take. I will not give you fourteen million dollars to pay to gangsters and thugs. If you needed it for your own well-being, I wouldn't hesitate. If you needed a kidney, an eye or a lung, I'd be the first in line." That had to be the biggest lie he'd ever told in his life, he thought smugly. "Sell the goddamn riverboats to someone else and get your money back. I'm surprised you didn't sink them to collect on the insurance. Oh, Jesus, don't do that, Ash. Insurance companies are like cops—they can and will find out you did it and you'll get into some really big trouble. You're on your own this time."

The curses were so ugly Simon could only smile in satisfaction. He hung up the phone and got into his car. Tootsie and Slick were all over him, sensing his unhappiness. He shifted gears, his thoughts far away. "I hope meeting your mother was everything you wanted it to be." Tootsie snuggled in his lap while Slick leaped up to wiggle around on the back of the headrest.

The ride back to the cabin was made in silence.

Cuddling with Daisy, Fanny listened to Simon's message over and over again. Each time his voice sounded more dear, more wonderful. She thought she was playing it for the ninety-ninth time when the phone rang. She recognized her ex-husband's irate voice immediately. She knew she should hang up, but even Ash couldn't bother her today. Today Simon called and said he would call again. Her world was right side up.

"Okay, Fanny, I'm going to cut right through to the quick of it. God help me, but I need your help. I'm only going to say this once. If you don't help me now, you'll be attending my funeral in a few days. Are you listening to me, Fanny?"

"You're screaming in my ear, Ash. Of course I can hear you. Aren't you going to ask me about my mother?"

"No. I don't care about your mother, and I'd be a hypocrite if I said I did. Why you care about someone who left you as a baby is something I don't even want to pretend I understand. I need fourteen million dollars in three days or they'll be delivering my body parts to your front door. That's the sum total of why I'm calling you. Simon refuses to help me. He called a few hours ago and flat out turned me down. There's nowhere else to turn. You have to help me."

"No, Ash, I don't. Aren't you being a little dramatic?"

"Maybe you should read the newspapers more often in that ivory tower you live in, Fanny. I am not being dramatic. I admit I made a mistake. Put yourself in my position. I wouldn't have done well in prison in my condition. You hung me out to dry, Fanny, and we both know it. Do you want my death on your conscience?"

"Of course not."

"Then give me the money. I'll find a way to make it up to you. Those riverboats are going to make a fortune."

"Sell them, Ash."

"I don't have time to sell them. I have three days. It was pure dumb luck that Simon called today. I've been trying to find him for months. He owes me his life, and this is how he repays me. I hate his fucking guts."

Fanny swayed dizzily. "Ash, I don't have fourteen million dollars. Everything we own is mortgaged to the hilt. And before you can bring it up, Billie Coleman has already paid two installments on the money she borrowed. We're just getting by."

"Then tap the kids' trust funds. You have the power to do that. Fanny, I'm desperate."

"They've been tapped already, Ash. Get it through your head, there's no money. I'm not a magician, I can't pull it out of a hat. This is your own doing, Ash. You got yourself in this mess because of your greed. Stop and think now, what would an emperor do in your position?"

"Will you be serious? I'm scared, Fanny. I don't think I've ever been scared in my life except when I had the accident. I'm totally helpless now. Please, you have to find a way to help me."

"Ash, I don't know what to say. I don't know how to help you. I would if I could. You know that. That's the reason you called me. I need to think. I'll call you back in the morning."

"In the morning! That cuts my time down to two days. I'm sitting on a ticking time bomb, and you tell me you'll call me in the morning! Jesus Christ, Fanny, that's not what I need to hear right now."

"It's the best I can do at the moment. Are you going to be at the casino this evening?"

"It's the only place I'm safe. All right, I'll wait for your call."

Fanny didn't think she had the strength to hang up the phone. She felt the beginnings of a headache as her stomach started to churn. She'd wanted to go out to the cemetery and talk. She needed to look upward and speak to Sallie so she could try and understand her feelings. Now, she couldn't do that. Now, she had to think about Ash and his impending dismemberment. She wished she could cry, for her mother, for Simon, for Ash. She knew if she gave in to that particular weakness, her strength would be gone.

She had to do something, but what? What would Sallie have done? Forget Sallie. Sallie had lived in a make-believe world for too long at the end. As sweet and as wonderful as she was, she wouldn't have been able to handle this either. Or would she?

Fannie dropped to her knees and pulled out the jewelry box that had once belonged to Sallie. Helter-skelter she dumped everything on the floor until the false bottom fell out. Thank God the folded piece of paper was still there. What was it Sallie had said so long ago? If you're ever in trouble, call this number and speak to the person who answers the phone. Just tell them who you are. No name, no address, just a phone number. Fanny sucked in her breath. Should she call now or should she wait? Maybe she should play Simon's message again. Maybe she should go out to the cemetery. Maybe she should read a book on dismemberment.

Fanny stared at the phone for twenty long minutes before she could gather up the courage to pick up the receiver. Her hand trembled so badly she could barely dial the numbers from the paper.

The phone was picked up on the second ring. The voice was harsh and cold. "State your business quickly."

Fanny flinched. "This is Fanny Thornton and I need to speak with you and I need to do it now. Not later, not tomorrow. I can be in town in forty-five minutes, and I can meet you at Sophie's Cafe. Yes or no?"

"One hour, Mrs. Thornton."

Fanny stared at the pinging phone in her hand. To calm herself she played Simon's message five more times.

Fanny walked into Sophie's Cafe with three minutes to spare. She sat down at a table in the corner and ordered a cup of coffee. Her gaze settled on the door. She waited. When the door finally opened, the two people sitting at separate tables got up and left. The waitress disappeared. She heard the snick of the lock and then the shades over the door being rolled down. It was like a scene in a bad movie. *I can do this. I really can do this.*

He looked so normal, so clean and pressed, that Fanny relaxed. He wasn't a youngster, but he wasn't that old either. *It's the white hair that makes him look older,* Fanny thought. *He's waiting for me to say something.* "I don't know who you are but my mother-in-law left me your phone number and said if I ever found myself in trouble, I should call and speak to whoever answered the phone. I, myself am not in trouble, but . . . I . . ."

"I'm aware of your problem."

"I rather thought you would be. I need your people to reduce the interest on my ex-husband's loan. Bank rates will do nicely. Will you agree to that?"

"Impossible."

"Then let's try this on for size. Tonight, I shut off the power and the city goes black. After I do that, I turn my water valve and your people don't flush. I can keep the electricity and water on at Babylon. You lose. We win. All night. Tomorrow night and the night after. Is it still impossible?"

"Yes."

"That's a very foolish response. In one night your casinos will lose millions. We pick up millions, but we do have an occupancy problem. Shall we try it for one night? By the way, who are you?"

"Just someone who was indebted to Sallie. My name isn't important. Wait here, Mrs. Thornton. I'll return in one hour. They serve a very good goulash. By the time you finish I'll be back with your answer." He snapped his fingers and a bowl of spicy goulash was set in front of Fanny. She barely heard the door close.

Fanny looked around for the door to the ladies' room. Inside, she leaned against the door, her body shaking uncontrollably. She struggled to take long, deep breaths that exploded out of her mouth like gunshots. When she felt calm enough to walk, she returned to her table. She stared at the goulash and then at her watch. The minutes ticked by. She nibbled on a piece of French bread and thought about her mother. Was she still alive? "I need a phone."

Fanny dialed the operator and placed a call to the hospital. She asked for the floor nurse on Harriet's floor and was told her mother had passed away at twelve minutes past noon. She placed a second call to Shamrock, Pennsylvania, and spoke to her brother Daniel. "Tell Brad and Daddy. We'll talk tomorrow, Daniel."

Fanny's third and fourth calls were to the water company and the electric company. To both she said, "Stand by for my call. I'll call you either way once I've made my decision."

More minutes crept by. Fanny placed money next to the phone for her long-distance calls. The money and phone were whisked away so fast, Fanny barely saw them disappear.

Her headache was alive now, banging inside her skull. She needed to be hard and strong and not let these people intimidate her.

Five minutes to go.

The goulash was cold now, the French bread dry and hard.

Three minutes to go.

"I need a telephone."

Two minutes to go. One minute.

Fanny stared at the doors of the café, at the green shades drawn to the bottom of the glass.

One minute past the hour.

Two minutes past the hour.

Fanny picked up the phone, her back stiff, her jaw tight. Water or power? Power of course. She dialed the number, announced herself just as the door opened. "Six points above the bank rate."

"No deal."

"In five minutes, Mr. Secore, turn off the power. You understand the power is to stay on at Babylon. I'll stay on the line."

"Five points."

"Four minutes, sir. The answer is no."

"Four points."

"My answer is the same."

"Three and that's as low as I'm authorized to go."

"I'm sorry. Bank rates. It's dark outside. Aren't the lights pretty? I don't think there's another place in this country that has as many lights as this town. *Thirty seconds.*"

Fanny watched sweat bead on the chiseled features. He was scared.

"Pull the switch, Mr. Secore."

"Wait."

"Too late, Mr. whatever your name is." Fanny dialed again.

"Mr. Quincy, this is Fanny Thornton. Turn the valve. Make sure there's water at Babylon. Thank you."

"Mrs. Thornton . . . please, wait."

"Why?"

"Let me go back to my people. Four points isn't that unreasonable."

"To me it's very unreasonable. Bank rates. The power and water stay off all night. Another thing, Mr. whatever your name is, nothing had better happen to my ex-husband. If it does, I will call in the FBI and they'll be all over your people . . . what's that expression that's used so much these days? Oh, yes, like fleas on a dog. Sallie would be very disappointed that you didn't come through for her. I think she honestly thought you people had a code of honor. Obviously she was wrong. Another thing, if anything happens to any member of my family, and that includes me, there will be no water or power until everything is probated, and our affairs are so complex it could take *years.* Think about that when you go back to report to your people. I'll call you tomorrow morning at nine o'clock."

Fanny walked out the door, her back stiff, her eyes watering with the headache pounding inside her head. She had to drive to Babylon now through the dark city. God in heaven, what had she just done?

Twenty minutes later, Fanny walked into her ex-husband's office. Birch was standing next to his father, his face ashen. Ash's face was gleeful.

"By God, you did it, Fanny! You shut down this town! You

brought them to their knees. I'll kiss your feet, Fanny, if you want me to. You came through for me. I knew you would."

"At what cost to the rest of us, Ash? At what cost?" Fanny whispered as her son wrapped his arms around her.

6

His arm tightening on his mother's shoulder, Birch said, "I don't think it's a good idea for you to drive up the mountain tonight, Mom. I'll call the desk and get you a room."

"He's right, Fanny. The dark stuff is going to hit the fan in about thirty minutes. Forget what I just said, it's happening now," Ash said, his eyes on the monitors. His excitement was palpable.

"Stay here, Mom. Keep the door locked. Dad, are you going out to the floor?"

"Damn right I am."

The moment the door closed, Birch said, "Turning off the power and water is about the stupidest thing we've ever done. What the hell got into Mom?"

"I didn't tell her to do it if that's what you're thinking. I asked her to bail us out and she said we're tapped out. You heard what I heard. Jesus, we're over occupancy. We have to do something."

"You do it, Dad. I have to get Mom a room."

"Take a look at the registration desk. We were probably sold out five minutes after she had the switch pulled. We need more help. Start calling around. Give Sage a call. Billie, too. Everyone we know. This is a golden opportunity, and we can take in some serious money this evening. Don't just stand there, Birch, get to work!"

"What about Mom?"

"She can stay in the penthouse with me. There are two bedrooms, you know."

Birch raced back to the office. "No rooms, Mom. You'll have to stay in the penthouse. Don't worry. He'll be on the floor all night. It's jamming out there. I have to get some help here."

"Can I do anything, Birch? I'm willing."

"I think it would be better if you went upstairs. I don't want to have to worry about you." He buzzed the head of Security. "Neal, come around to the office and take my mother up to the penthouse. If you can spare anyone, have them hang out in the hall. After you do that, call in everyone who's off tonight. Cut whatever deal you have to to get them in here."

"She really pulled the switch, huh?"

"That's not the half of it. They can't flush either."

"I didn't know your mother had that kind of guts. I don't mean that in a . . ."

"I know what you mean. I never thought she'd do it either. I think she's in shock that she did it. Keep checking on her all night, okay?"

"Sure, Birch."

Birch walked over to a secluded alcove and picked up one of the phones to ask for an outside line. He dialed, the breath rushing from his mouth when he heard Sage's voice. "Sage, Mom pulled the switch and turned off the valve. The town is pitch-dark. I need you to come in and help. Call Billie and anyone else you can think of. This is going to be one very long night."

"Why?" Sage gasped.

"Because those . . . hoods have Dad on the ropes. I've got her safe in the penthouse, and Neal is watching out for her. Listen. I don't have time to chat. Call Sunny, but tell her to stay home. She could get hurt if she's on the floor. Some of these people can act like animals when things get out of control, and, trust me, things are out of control. Tell Tyler to come over if he's free. Bess, too, and John if he isn't at the hospital."

"I'm on my way. I'll call from the car. What's The Emperor doing?"

"Holding court. What the hell do you think he's doing?"

"For some reason I thought he'd be counting his money. I'll see you in a bit."

Birch trotted out to the floor, his eyes raking the room for a sign of his father. Every table, every slot machine was filled to capacity. The noise was deafening. He thought about calling the police when he saw the guards at the huge front doors. He'd never seen people clamor and bang on plate glass to get into an establishment to gamble away their money. In another hour or so it was going to turn ugly.

"Mr. Thornton, the switchboard is going berserk. We can't handle the calls coming in. These messages seem like the most important. I thought you might want to see them right away as some of them sound . . . disturbing."

Birch shoved the stack of yellow slips into his jacket pocket. He could just imagine who the calls were from and what they said.

It took Birch thirty-five minutes to cross the room. On the way he broke up two tussles with patrons fighting over slot machines. "Do it again and you're out of here, and you won't be permitted back in. This is the only game in town so think carefully."

Smiling and jostling his way through the packed room, Birch finally reached his father, who was speaking with a reporter from the *Nevada Sun*. "Dad, I need to talk to you." Ash excused himself, turned his chair around to follow Birch.

"This is what I like, a full house. The tournament was nothing compared to this. So, what's your problem, Birch? Aside from wall-to-wall people, things are running okay. I saw Sage a moment ago, and Billie was handling drinks. Bess is changing monies. That's Tyler over there with Neal, so I guess he'll be handling the money, too. I called Wells Fargo and they're going to pick up money on the hour. I haven't seen any of the other owners, have you?"

"I haven't seen them, but I heard from them." Sage pulled the stack of crumpled messages from his pocket. He rifled through them. "All present and accounted for. What's your next question?"

Ash's eyes were so gleeful Birch felt sick to his stomach. "If your mother hangs tight on this, I'm home free in three days. It's time those sharks took a hit. Not only will they be willing to give me bank rates, they'll pay us to turn the power and water back on. I can either go with the bank rates and pay the loan off the way I wanted, or I can pay it off and walk away. I also have the option of banking all this money we're raking in to get those riverboats operational. Three days, Birch. Customers will be bouncing off the walls and hanging from the ceiling to give me their money."

Birch's stomach rumbled. "What about Mom?"

"One of a kind. She always comes through," Ash said magnanimously.

"That's not what I meant. They'll meet her demands tomorrow and she'll turn everything back on. She'll never go for three days."

"She will if they threaten her. That's the next step. Intimidation is how they get to you. Fanny won't tolerate it. She'll extend the days each time they do or say something she doesn't like. Your mother is a woman of principle. I'm counting on her staying that way, too. She won't let me down."

"That's funny as hell coming from you, Dad."

An ear-piercing whistle sounded across the room. Birch craned his neck to see Sage motioning to him. "Enjoy it while it lasts," Birch said to his father.

"I am. This is my night, kiddo. I can't wait to see the morning papers. I can see it now, three-inch headlines." Ash waved his arms expansively. "EMPEROR TAKES OVER CITY!" He shrugged at Birch's retreating back.

Tonight, Las Vegas was his alone.

"This is a zoo. We better start clearing out some of these people before the fire marshal shuts us down."

"If you think that's going to happen, you're nuts. No one in this town is going to mess with Mom. The threat was always there, right out in the open, but no one, and that includes me, ever thought this night would come to pass. Mom is the most powerful woman in this town, probably this state. If you were the fire marshal, would you take her on?"

"Probably not, but there's danger here. I say we go to the stockroom and pull out all those portable fire extinguishers and keep them handy. You have to keep all the exit doors clear. We need some more people, Birch. Hell, I'm willing to go out on the street and recruit if necessary. I guess you know the switchboard is jammed."

Birch waved the stack of messages under his brother's nose. "And, on top of these, let me tell you what our father's thinking is on all of this . . ."

"I hate this goddamn business," Sage muttered as he struggled through the crowds of gamblers.

Upstairs in the penthouse, Fanny stood in the dark staring out at the town that was just as dark. She shivered. She wanted to go home and play Simon's message again. She needed to hear his calm, sane voice. Needed to hear him say he loved her, needed to hear him say he would call again. She wanted to sit in her big red chair with Daisy in her lap.

"I'm going home." She scribbled off a note and left it on the dining-room table.

Thirty minutes later, wearing Ash's jeans, windbreaker, and baseball cap, Fanny slid behind wheel of the junk car Sunny kept in the garage for emergencies. She gunned the motor and then roared up the ramp and out to the main road. She didn't take a deep breath until she was out of town and on her way up the mountain, her high-beam lights leading the way.

A long time later, after disconnecting the phone, when she was ensconced in the depths of the old red chair, coffee cup in hand, Daisy in her lap, she burst into tears. "Oh, Simon, I need you." Fanny fell asleep, Simon's name on her lips, his message playing over and over until Daisy, too, drifted into slumber.

Simon woke, showered, shaved, and brewed a pot of coffee he carried out to the porch. He propped his feet on the railing, staring off into the distance. His left hand dropped to the portable radio next to his chair. From long years of habit he listened to the early-morning news and the late news. He adjusted the volume and waited to see what had gone on in the world overnight. He listened, his thoughts far away until he heard the commentator say, *"Last night just as darkness fell, the Big White Way in Las Vegas turned black and dry. Stories, none of which can be confirmed, range from Russian spies blowing up the electric company to squirrels chewing up the circuitry. One has to wonder how and why squirrels would turn off the water, though. The smart money is saying the man known as The Emperor of Las Vegas turned off the power and water in a fit of pique. Ashford Thornton, the owner of Babylon, couldn't be reached for comment. Babylon is the only casino to have power and water in the town of Las Vegas. We invite any listeners who have additional information to call us here in the news room. This is Sam Le Roy signing off. Stay tuned for Maxwell Minton and the latest Top 40 hits to start off your day."*

The legs on Simon's chair hit the porch with a thud. Tootsie and Slick woke up, stared at him, then went back to sleep. Simon cursed his lack of a phone, civilization and anything else that came to mind. "C'mon, you guys, gather up your gear. We're going to Las Vegas."

Simon didn't bother to pack. He gathered up his clothes and possessions, making nine trips to his car throwing everything in the trunk any old way. He emptied out the coffeepot and carried a cup to the car, where he set it on the console. "Hop in." Tootsie and Slick climbed into the backseat, their chews, toys, and blankets spread around them. If he was lucky, he could make Las Vegas by eleven o'clock and Sunrise by noon.

It wasn't until Simon stopped for gas at the halfway point that he realized Ash didn't have the authority to turn off the power and water in Las Vegas. Only Fanny could do that. "Son of a bitch!" He threw money in the general direction of the gas station attendant, slid into his car and peeled rubber, his tires leaving long black skid lines on the concrete.

Fanny connected the phone at one minute to nine. It rang almost immediately.

"Mom, where have you been? We've been calling all over the place. There was a busy signal at Sunrise. We thought someone snatched you and forced you to leave that note. Are you okay?"

"I'm fine. Tell me what happened."

"It would be easier to tell you what didn't happen. We made a barrel of money. Sage, Billie, Bess, and Tyler came to help out. Sage went out on the street and recruited bouncers. We needed to keep the exits clear in case anything went wrong. We were seriously over our occupancy rate. The cops and fire department were out in force, but nothing serious went awry. The casino is still jamming. Wells Fargo takes money out on the hour. Dad just took about ninety pills and is sleeping. Sage is eating breakfast, Billie is catnapping, and Tyler went to the hospital. Sunny just walked in a minute ago. Our rooms are booked solid, and Dad raised the rates by a hundred percent. Nobody complained if you can believe that. All the headliners from the other casinos left town this morning. At least that's what the news said. This stuff is going to make a hell of a scrapbook. Mom, why'd you do it?"

"Your father said those people would kill him. He was frightened out of his wits. I had to do something. Where could I possibly come up with fourteen million dollars in three days? I had to do what I did. I gave them a choice, they chose not to take it. All I asked for was bank rates on the loan. They came down to three above the bank, and I said no. Three percent of fourteen million dollars compounded daily is a lot of money. We played hardball. They blinked. Did I say that right, Birch?"

His mother the hardball player. His mother going up against gangsters. It boggled his mind. "I couldn't have said it any better. What are you going to do now?"

"I told them I'd call them at nine o'clock. It's after nine. I don't want to seem eager. Maybe I won't call them."

"Dad wants three days. Can you handle it, Mom?"

Three days. Fanny's stomach started to gurgle. "I'm just going to . . . what I'm going to do is . . . wing it. I want to hear what those people have to say."

"Every single one of them called the casino last night. The switch-board finally blew out around four this morning. It's being fixed as we speak. I'm calling you from a phone booth out on the street. We didn't return any of the calls. I'm going to try and grab some sleep. Sunny is going to watch the monitors. Call me when you know something. Mom, be careful."

"I will. I have Daisy right here."

"I don't think that powder puff is going to be much protection if anyone comes looking for you."

"They won't do that, Birch. They know the alternative if they do. Get some sleep, honey. I'll talk to you later."

Fanny replaced the phone and reached for her coffee cup.

The phone rang again just as Fanny poured more coffee. She let it ring five times before she picked it up. "Mrs. Thornton? You said you would call at nine o'clock. I waited for your call."

Fanny sucked in her breath. She would recognize that voice if she was in a cave full of screaming bats. "I was washing my hair at nine o'clock," Fanny lied.

"Washing your hair?" Fanny could just imagine the stupid look on the man's face.

"Uh-huh. What can I do for you this morning?"

"Two above the bank rate."

"Be serious. This is not negotiable. I have things to do today so I need to know if you're going to be calling me back."

"We're not your husband's personal bankers, Mrs. Thornton. We made the loan in good faith and your husband signed the necessary papers."

"Ex-husband. Ash was heavily medicated when he signed those papers. I told you, the matter is not negotiable. I have to roll my hair now or it will frizz up. Good-bye."

Fanny gulped at the coffee in the heavy mug. "Either you're stupid, Fanny Thornton, or you have no brains," she muttered to herself.

When the phone rang again, Fanny let it ring eight times before she picked it up. She listened to the cold, angry voice, a voice she matched perfectly when she said, "I told you this is not negotiable. You know my terms. You're starting to irritate me. Either you agree now or just for pure orneriness on my part I'll leave the switch and valve off a whole day as punishment when we do come to terms. You can't win, Mr. whatever your name is. Tell that to your people. Now, get the hell off my line. Someone important might be trying to call me."

"Mrs. Thornton, you're being very foolish. I cannot control my employers. Things happen in this town that are never spoken of again. Please, you need to reconsider and allow my people to save face here. In addition you are restricting the rights of my employers to earn a living. They can sue you."

"You just threatened me. I will not tolerate that kind of behavior. Is it your intention to cut me up in pieces and stuff me in a paper bag? The switch and valve stay off for two days. Each time you call me I'll add another day. Sue me. The case will be in the courts for years. All your dirty laundry will be aired. The Feds will take over this town, and we both know it. One hundred percent interest is ludicrous. What I will negotiate are the monies you pay me to turn the switch and valve back on. You're dark for two more days. Don't . . ." Fanny grappled for a word her daughter Sunny would use under the circumstances to make her point. "Don't *piss* me off." She wasn't sure, but she thought she heard a chuckle on the other end of the phone as she was hanging it up.

Fanny looked around her small, comfortable studio. Would they kill her? She needed to do something. Scrub the kitchen floor. The small bathroom needed to be cleaned. The windows should be washed.

Fanny looked down at herself. She was still dressed in Ash's clothing, the jeans rolled up six times around her ankles. The tattered sweatshirt that said U.S. Navy on the front, Ash's prize possession, seemed fit attire for the work at hand. A red bandanna tied around her hair completed her outfit.

Fanny was hard at work, the kitchen floor covered with soapy water when Chue burst through the front door. "Miss Fanny, a parade is coming up the mountain. Five long black cars like . . . the ones at Miss Sallie's funeral. Another blue car is behind them. What do you want me to do? Is this trouble?"

"Oh, yeah." Fanny could feel bile rise in her throat. "When they get here, escort them in and then go to your house and call the boys at the casino."

"I will stay. I know jujitsu."

"It's all right, Chue. This is going to be a verbal battle."

"They are here."

"Let them in, Chue."

Fanny dipped her rag into the soapsuds and was industriously scrubbing the tile floor when she noticed two rows of shiny black shoes out of the corner of her eye. She leaned back against the cabinet on her haunches. "Welcome to Sunrise, gentlemen. Humph," she snorted. "Where are your chain saws? That's how you do it, isn't it?" When her heart exploded would her chest cavity just burst or would her heart tear itself loose and come up and out through her throat?

"Do what, Mrs. Thornton?" a soft cultured voice asked.

"You know, slice and dice, rip apart my joints, that kind of thing. I'm not afraid of you," she blustered.

"You have no reason to be afraid. Concerned, yes. I think perhaps you watch too many movies. We're legitimate businessmen. These gentlemen, myself included, are here to conduct business."

"You mean you're here to negotiate. Let's tell it like it is." Fanny ignored the outstretched hand. Through the sea of shiny black shoes she saw a pair of worn sneakers with frayed shoelaces, the kind of laces dogs chew on. Suddenly her cozy kitchen was lighter, brighter. The sun seemed warmer as it sliced through the venetian blinds and across her neck. She jerked her head. The rows of shiny black shoes faded before her eyes until the worn sneakers found their way front and center. "Move!" she said irritably. "Simon! Oh, Simon, is it really you? Move, move," Fanny yelled as she scrambled to her knees on the wet floor to get to her feet. "Oh, Simon, you're here. How did you know? Sit, sit," she said to the men. "Make some coffee, finish the floor, do whatever you want. I'll be back in a little while."

She was in the air swirling about the small room, her lips pressed against Simon's as he tried to whirl both of them out the door, three yapping dogs at their feet. "Oh, Simon, you came back. I followed you that day and missed you by fifteen minutes. Fifteen minutes. I wanted to die. Where were you? Sunny saw you in Bakersfield and we tried to follow you. Oh, Simon, I have so much to tell you. I found my mother. I actually saw her. Kiss me, hold me tight and don't you ever let me go again. God, I love you, Simon. I want to get married. Today."

"You came after me! I didn't know, Fanny. I never should have left. It was stupid of me. I heard the news this morning. I'm ready to get married right now," Simon said, kissing her eyes, her nose, her ears.

"I have to finish scrubbing the floor first and find a dress to wear. What color, Simon?"

"That blue flowered one. All my clothes are in the trunk and they're wrinkled."

"I'll iron them for you. I love you, Simon. So much I ache. I want to carry lilies of the valley. I love the way they smell. Should it be private or should we invite people? That's all nonsense, all I want is you. I can carry plastic flowers."

"Whatever you want, Fanny. What the hell is going on? Are those men the other casino owners? Why are they here, Fanny? Do you have any idea of how much danger you're in?"

"I don't want to talk about that. I want to talk about us. We're finally getting married. Introduce me, Simon." Fanny dropped to her knees to fondle the little dogs' ears. "Oh, look, they like Daisy. This is so wonderful. We're a family, Simon. Us and the dogs."

"Forever and ever. Let's get rid of these guys. Can you get rid of them or are they . . . ?"

"I have to make some deals here. How much should I ask for?"

"Push them to the wall." Simon's words left him giddy when he saw the smile on Fanny's face.

Fanny cleared her throat. "Gentlemen, sit down. When a man stands over a woman, it's for the purposes of intimidation. Fine. This is fine. Now, have you agreed to bank rates? You have. All right, now we have some place to start. The town is dark and waterless for two more days. You had a choice and you chose not to exercise that choice. Last night I did some calculating on my adding machine and the numbers were so high they ran off the roll of paper. That tells me you want to return to business as quickly as possible. This is what I propose. Forgive the debt to my ex-husband and we'll lease the riverboats in Biloxi, Mississippi, to you at the same rates you were charging him. What is power and water worth to you for the next two days? Tomorrow and the day after it will be worth more than it's worth today. While you huddle, I'm going to finish my kitchen floor because I'm getting married today, and I have to get ready. Even though I'm in a wonderful mood right now, that could change if your numbers aren't . . . acceptable."

Inside the studio with the door closed, Fanny hissed, "I think I finally figured out who that one guy is, the one I met last night at the café in town. Do you remember your mother's friend Jeb? She gave him a job and took care of his family? There were four boys and they all looked like Jeb. Sallie bought him a house and sent his boys to college. She paid all the bills when Jeb's wife got sick, and then she paid the medical bills for Jeb after he passed away. Sallie said Jeb used to feed her and Cotton and the other miners when they were broke. I'm almost positive the man I met last night is one of Jeb's boys, and if you look really closely at three of the others, they look like him, too. I don't know if it means anything or not."

"Fanny, what the hell are you talking about?"

"I'm just trying to make sense of all this. I want out of here, Simon. We can talk driving down the mountain. There are no words to tell you how happy I am to see you. The perfect ending to a nightmare. Ash . . . I don't want to talk about him either. There, the floor is dry. Let's take a shower together." She was babbling, but she didn't care.

"Fanny!"

"I just wanted to see what you would say. Hold the fort so I can get dressed. I was so afraid, Simon."

Simon followed Fanny into the tiny bathroom. "I don't know what's going on and *I'm* afraid. You have the edge on me by knowing. Hurry up, Fanny, I want out of here."

In the tiny kitchen Simon filled to overflowing with his presence, he poured himself a cup of cold coffee, his eyes on the men in dark suits outside the window. What were they saying? What were they agreeing to? Would they buckle under to Fanny? *Ash, you son of a bitch, I'd like to strangle you for putting Fanny in this position.* If he was lucky maybe they'd still kill Ash to make a point. He wouldn't grieve.

"Simon."

Simon turned at the sound of his whispered name. She was more beautiful than he remembered. He stood still, certain he was dreaming. If he didn't move or speak, he could preserve the dream.

"Simon?"

"Fanny," he said in a strangled voice.

"I'm ready to get married now. I'm wearing something old, something new, something borrowed and blue. I think that's the way it goes."

"I love this dream," Simon said.

"I thought it was a dream, too. Should we pinch each other?"

"I'd rather hold you and kiss you till you yell for mercy. I really like this dream."

"I do, too," Fanny said, advancing one step, then another until she was standing nose to nose with Simon. "I can feel your breath on my cheek and feel your heart beating next to mine. We aren't dreaming, Simon. I'm going to need a ring."

"We'll get one in town."

"Just a plain gold band. Thick, a little wide. Very plain. I love you so much. Oh, Simon, don't start something we can't finish here and now." Fanny nibbled on his lip, his ear, the side of his neck.

"Mrs. Thornton."

"Hmmmm," Fanny said.

"My associates would like to speak with you. Outside if you don't mind."

"I don't mind at all. Do you mind, Simon?"

"Yes, I mind. Get rid of them, Fanny. They're cluttering up our dream."

Fanny giggled. Simon loved the sound. He said so.

"I'm not a bit afraid. I thought they'd come here with guns and . . . you know, chain saws and . . . suitcases full of money to try and . . . bribe me. I didn't pack anything."

"Good idea. We'll buy everything. I have a feeling you're going to be very rich when you walk out of here."

"I don't want their money, Simon. I wouldn't take it if they gave it to me."

"That's a pretty stupid attitude, Fanny. Then what is this all about?"

"It's about Ash paying out one hundred percent in interest. He can only handle a legitimate bank loan with regulated interest rates. All that stuff I said before, those were just words. I wanted them to be on the receiving end of things for a change. They were bleeding him, threatening and intimidating him. I will not tolerate that. They said they were legitimate businessmen. Legitimate businessmen don't charge one hundred percent interest. Get Daisy's stuff, and I'll meet you by the car. Lock the door, Simon."

Simon's gay mood changed suddenly. "It sounds to me, Fanny, like you're still shackled to Ash. I don't want him in our lives. Cut him loose."

Fanny stared at Simon. "I can't do that, Simon. I told you once before there is a small part of my life that will always belong to Ash. It's the way it is. You have to accept it." She watched as a veil dropped over Simon's eyes. He nodded curtly before he turned his back on her.

"When will the power and water be turned on, Mrs. Thornton?" the spokesperson asked.

"When we come to terms. What have you decided?"

"We've decided you drive a very hard bargain. We aren't fools as you must realize. Every day our casinos are shut down we lose millions of dollars. We have no wish to repeat last night's disaster. As it stands now even though you turn on the power and water, we are still losing money. Our headliners left last night and early this morning. Contractually, we still have to pay them. Our food spoiled, our sewage system backed up. We also had several serious accidents because of the darkness. Many of our customers relocated to your casino and will undoubtedly stay there for the length of their visit. It's a domino effect. What all this means to you is, we agree to your terms." Fanny thought she saw grudging respect in the man's eyes.

"In writing, sir, in town, at my attorney's office." Fanny looked at her watch. "In ninety minutes. You might want to think about wearing gray flannel. Black is ominous. Then again, if that's your intent . . . gray is so much more business-like." Fanny smiled wickedly. Power was wonderful. She wondered if she would become addicted to it. Never.

The moment Fanny settled herself she heaved a mighty sigh. "Simon, if Ash wasn't wheelchair-bound, do you think he would have done the same thing?"

"Yes, but it would be worse. Ash marches to his own drummer." Fanny blanched at the coolness in Simon's voice.

A second later, Fanny was asleep. Simon smiled as he stretched out his arm to gather her close to him. The release of fear was better than any sleeping pill.

He was getting married. Finally. All because of Ash and his damn riverboats. The big question was, where should they go? What should they do with their lives? By agreeing to marry him, Fanny must be willing to do whatever he wanted. The only thing he knew for certain right now was he didn't want to spend one second longer in Las Vegas than he had to. He had to get Fanny away from her damn family. Fanny always had ideas. Maybe they could travel, see the world together. Maybe Fanny would want to buy a farm or move to a small town like the one she grew up in. He would agree to anything Fanny wanted to do as long as she didn't allow Ash and her family to invade their lives.

A prickle of fear rippled up Simon's back. Would Fanny leave her children and move away? Now that Sunny was about to deliver, would Fanny walk away from her first grandchild? Did he have the right to expect her to say good-bye to her family? She would be giving up her businesses, too. It wasn't going to be simple after all. Why couldn't two people just fall in love and live happily ever after? Because life gets in the way, he answered himself.

He drove on, Fanny's head on his shoulder. She didn't wake until he pulled into Babylon's underground garage. "Are we here already,

Simon? I fell asleep. I'm so sorry. I think it was all that anxiety and then the outcome. Simon, I played your message over a hundred times. What should we do first?"

"Fanny, I don't want to get married until this is over and done with. When we drive away from here I don't want to have to worry about Ash's enemies. Make no mistake, they are his enemies. No man is a law unto himself in this town even if his wife can turn switches and valves."

"You're scaring me, Simon."

"That's good, Fanny, because I don't want you thinking those hoodlums in their three-piece suits were telling you the truth when they said they were legitimate businessmen. They aren't. They caved in because you had them by the short hairs. They aren't going to forget it. They won't mess with you, but they will mess with Ash. Perhaps not right now. They'll wait until things quiet down, and it's business as usual. That's when they'll do something. Just be aware. I think we both need to talk to Ash. He won't listen to either one of us, but I want to know I did everything I could to warn him. First it was the poker tournament. He aced them out on that. There was this little episode. That makes two. Three will not be Ash's lucky number. I don't know, maybe we can get through to him."

"Don't count on it, Simon. Ash doesn't listen to anyone. I don't want him to spoil this for us. Are we going to tell anyone, or are we just going to *do it*?"

"I say we just go off and do it. We'll call when it's a done deed."

"Okay, Mr. Thornton. We have time to go upstairs to the office and tell everyone what's going on before we walk to the attorney's office. I'm sure the kids are worried."

"Lead the way, Mrs. Thornton."

"Talk about red letter days," Ash's voice boomed when Fanny and Simon walked through the door, his anger at his brother forgotten. His mood was expansive as he waved his arms about, his smile affable.

His eyes were so glassy Fanny could see herself in their depths. She could feel her insides start to churn. "Relax, Ash. Everything isn't over yet. I'm on my way to the lawyer's office to finalize everything. At that time I'll have the water and power restored. I made a deal, Ash. Me. Not you. And you damn well better live up to it. You have bank rates on your loan. I suggest any monies above the norm last night and today go toward an up-front payment of your loan. Your riverboats in Mississippi are going to be leased to those people at an appropriate rate of interest. You're ahead of the game, Ash. You're alive. If you want, give them the riverboats and we'll make it a wash and you won't have that tremendous debt staring you in the face every day. I think I can make a deal on that. It's your decision."

"Fanny, Fanny, Fanny, you brought them to their knees. You cut deals like a pro. They have to respect that. I told you I wanted the power and water off for two more days. You don't listen to me. Now, why is that, Fanny?"

"Because, Ash, you never say anything that makes sense. It's always me, me, me. You never think about anyone else. Did you for one minute think about all those people who aren't working because I shut the town down? Everything has its own ripple effect. I did what I did for you because I believed you would be killed. That's what you told me. I will not do it again. This advice is free, Ash. Stay where there are people and don't go anywhere alone. I have just enough time to get to the lawyer's and then I'm leaving town for an indefinite period of time. I'll say good-bye to the kids on the way out."

"Wait just a damn minute, Fanny. What do you mean you're going out of town? What if I need you?"

"What part didn't you understand, Ash? I did what you wanted. You're alive and well. You have the business to occupy you night and day."

"You gave away my damn riverboats. You just up and gave them away. That's just like you, Fanny. Your way or no way. Go ahead, take your lover and get out of my casino. Who needs you anyway?"

Fanny's shoulders sagged. "Have a nice day, Ash." *I will not cry. I absolutely will not cry. I refuse to cry. He cannot make me cry. He's to be pitied.*

"If crying makes you feel better then cry, honey," Simon said. "Ash was always a greedy horse's patoot. Come on, it's getting on toward ninety minutes. Are you comfortable with all your decisions?"

"Yes."

"Then, say your good-byes so we can take care of business and get married."

"I don't think I've ever heard anything that sounds more wonderful. Do you think the dogs are okay in the car?"

"They're sleeping like babies curled up together. They know we're coming back. The windows are partially open and the garage is cool, not to mention the fact that the attendant is keeping his eye on them."

Fanny's children hugged her and Simon both. "You're getting married, aren't you?" Sunny whispered.

"Uh-huh. *I'll call every day*," Fanny promised. "Take care of yourself, Sunny, and keep those boys in line."

"Be happy, Mom," Birch said, a catch in his voice. "We'll all miss you."

"Call Lily Bell and invite her for the weekend."

"He already did that," Sage said. "Have a good trip wherever it is you're going."

Fanny waved good-bye. "Why do I feel like I'm deserting them?"

"Because you've never gone away from them before, and the trip to Hong Kong doesn't count. They know you aren't coming back, and you know it, too. They have their lives and you have yours. I've waited all my life for this day, Fanny, and I want to get on with it before it's over. I'm giving you fifteen minutes in that lawyer's office and that's it."

"Okay, Mr. Thornton."

"Wait, Mrs. Thornton, I don't understand. What you're saying brings things to a wash. What about the . . . ?"

"You're Jeb's son, aren't you?" At the man's slight nod, Fanny said, "I thought so. The power and water are being turned on as we speak." She eyed the metal suitcases on top of the desk. She knew they were full of money. Money they thought she wanted. "I hope I never have to do this again. I want you to know I meant every word I said back on the mountain. What's it going to be?"

"We'll lease the boats. We'll pay three points above the bank rate. Is that satisfactory?"

"Yes." To the lawyer she said, "Whatever those three points amount to moneywise, give it to the Thornton Medical Center and the Thornton Pediatric Unit every month." Fanny scribbled her signature in six different places. She dusted her hands dramatically. "Done."

The man from the diner extended his hand. Fanny looked at it for a long moment before she held out her own hand. "I think Sallie and Jeb would approve," she said quietly. Fanny raised her eyes to see a smile tug at the corners of the man's mouth.

Fanny had to strain to hear the words, "You have nothing to fear from my people, Mrs. Thornton."

Fanny smiled. "I can't say the same thing . . . sir. Stay on your toes and you'll probably never see or hear from me again. There is every possibility that sometime in the future you might . . . *need* my help. I'm going to give you a number to call if that should happen. We'll use the name Sallie as a reference." The man nodded slightly.

Outside in the fresh air, Fanny took several deep breaths. "I'm ready, Simon."

"Where are we going to do it?"

"At the first wedding chapel we come to. They sell rings and flowers and everything. I want a veil. I can't get married without a veil. Oh, Simon, I forgot about you. What are you going to wear? Simon, Sage whispered something in my ear I want to share with you. He said, and this is a direct quote, 'Mom, *I think* Uncle Simon is the wind beneath your sails.' You are, my darling, Simon."

Simon's throat closed tight. In the whole of his life no one had ever said anything to him as wonderful-sounding as those few words. He smiled from ear to ear. He finally managed to say, "I don't care what I wear. Does it matter to you?"

"No, Simon, it doesn't matter in the least. I love you just the way you are and I'd marry you in your skivvies."

PART TWO

1983–1984

7

Fanny stood on the front porch doing what she did every day at this hour: she surveyed her domain. She looked at the lush green grass in front of the house. At the straggly shrubbery, at the wilted pots of flowers. In the early morning, just as the sun was coming up, the lawn looked like a carpet of emeralds sprinkled with diamonds, thanks to the morning dew. She loved sitting on the front steps with her cup of coffee when the weather permitted. Simon preferred to sit at the kitchen table in his bathrobe.

A frown built between her brows. Once, in the early days of her marriage, she'd thought they were alike, preferring the same things. She'd been so wrong then. They didn't even like the same food. Every day, seven days a week, she prepared two separate dinners, one for Simon and one for her. In the beginning it was fun, a challenge. Now, with the business going full steam, it was work. Everything was work. What she needed was a housekeeper, but Simon didn't want anyone living in the house with them. She'd given in on that point. The truth was, she always gave in.

Fanny finished her coffee. Today was their anniversary. She'd washed her fine china, polished the candlesticks, had Ash send her a magnificent bottle of fine wine that was supposed to be a surprise, ironed her best linen tablecloth. Tonight she would make only one meal, Simon's favorite, rare prime rib. She liked her meat well done. She would eat the ends.

Fanny set her empty cup on the steps. Her shoulders felt tense. A walk around the small yard might ease the tightness a little. She walked slowly, aware of the silence. It was so quiet here in Stallion Springs. She had no neighbors, no friends. Simon said they didn't need any, they had each other and the dogs. Days were spent with the dogs they bred and her evenings were spent sewing, since Simon monopolized the television set.

I'm not happy. I haven't been happy for a long time. She knew Simon was aware that something was wrong. So many times she tried to talk to him, to explain that she wanted to go to town, back to Nevada for a visit. His excuse was always the same: When you have your own business, you're married to that business. This business, he would go on to say, deals with flesh-and-blood animals. When we take a vacation, we'll take it together. In three years they hadn't had a vacation. This morning for the first time she realized she was a *prisoner*. She wasn't under lock and key, but she was a prisoner nonetheless. Getting permission from Simon to go into town was a major ordeal. There's no gas, I can't find the keys, there's something wrong with the tires. The list of excuses was endless.

The first months had been idyllic as the house and barns were being finished. Decorating had been such fun. And when the first batch of dogs arrived she had been ecstatic. She loved the tiny Yorkies they bred, and she hated giving them up. She was the one who cleaned the pens, fed them, and assigned them to the different buyers. Simon took care of the paperwork.

She longed for people, for her friends. During the second year she spent a great deal of time on the phone with Billie and Bess until Simon said the bills were too high. He'd sulked for seven straight days when she said she would pay the bill with her own money. She wasn't sure, but she thought he listened in on her phone conversations. He'd sulked for two straight weeks the day Bess showed up unexpectedly yelling "SURPRISE!" at the top of her lungs. He'd been cold but civil. Bess had never come back to visit, nor had Billie.

Fanny stood back to look at the spacious log cabin that was her home. At best it was Spartan. Simon didn't like what he called clutter while she loved knickknacks, family pictures, collectibles. All her treasures were still in the packing boxes. She shaded her eyes from the late-afternoon sun to look around the eleven acres that was now her home.

It was a far cry from Sunrise. Trees were trees, but somehow the trees at Sunrise seemed like they belonged while these trees just stood there, straggly, ugly, barren-looking in the winter. She'd made an effort in the beginning to prune the bushes, to plant flowers, to clear away the brush, but Simon had ridiculed her efforts. Rather than see that cold, blank look in her husband's eyes, she'd given up her gardening efforts. Everything now was overgrown and stragglylooking. The urge to cry was so strong, Fanny bit down on her lower lip.

"Fanny! Fanny!" Fanny looked at the cabin, then at the barn. If she went to the barn, there was every chance her roast would be overdone and her anniversary dinner would be spoiled. "Just a minute, Simon."

"Now, Fanny."

Fanny ran to the barn. "Cissie's ahead of schedule. You need to calm her. Where were you? Don't tell me. You were talking on the phone to Sunny again. How the hell many times did she call today? I thought you were going to tell her to stop calling so much."

"I wasn't talking to Sunny. I was cooking dinner. Just to keep the record clear, my daughter didn't call today."

"It's still early, she will. With a kid and a new baby to take care of, you have to wonder where she gets the time to call you six times a day."

"She never calls more than twice a day. I'm her mother, Simon. I like talking to my daughter. Especially when you don't listen to our conversations," Fanny snapped. She dropped to her knees to stroke Cissie's head. "There are times, Simon, when I think you are trying to drive a wedge between me and my family."

"That's the most ridiculous thing I ever heard come out of your mouth."

"Really. Then why did you object to me putting pictures of my family in the living room?"

"Because they're *your* family, not *our* family. We have our own life now. If you weren't so tight-assed about things, we could have a wonderful life."

Fanny tried to keep her voice on a conversational level so Cissie wouldn't get excited. "You knew I had a family when I married you. My children are your nieces and nephews, so they are your family, too."

"They're Ash's kids, not mine."

"What do you want me to say, Simon?"

"I'd like it if you wouldn't let them infringe on our life. It was fine in the beginning, then that daughter of yours started calling every two minutes because she misses her mommy. For God's sake, Fanny, they're grown men and women."

"I wonder why you married me, Simon. I never pretended to be anything but what I am. What I am is what you said you loved about me. You really should go see about the roast if you want me to stay here."

"I have to get Flossie and Flicker ready and their paperwork done because the Albertsons are coming to pick them up at six o'clock.

That's a thousand dollars, Fanny, and I think it's a little more important than your roast."

"Simon, did you forget, it's our anniversary? I was making a special dinner."

"Did you whine like this with Ash?"

"Why is it everything I do has to tie in with Ash in your mind? I hate it when you do this, Simon. I really hate it. Another thing, the Albertsons called to say they told you yesterday they wouldn't be picking up the dogs till nine tomorrow morning. Mrs. Albertson said she spoke to you. She was just calling today to remind us. So, are you going to look at the roast or not? Personally, I don't care one way or the other."

"If you don't care, then why should I do it?"

Fanny could feel her eyes start to burn. "Suit yourself."

"You aren't happy, are you, Fanny?"

Fanny was tempted to lie. "No, Simon, I'm not happy."

"You compare this marriage to the one you had with Ash, right?"

"Wrong." Fanny felt herself flush with the lie.

"Maybe we should invite him for the weekend."

"Maybe we should," Fanny said through clenched teeth.

"You'll see him at the christening. It's a one-day thing, Fanny. I'm not staying."

"Suit yourself. I'm staying longer. I want to see Billie and Thad. I want to do some shopping with Bess, and I want to visit with my children. I want to get to know my grandchildren."

Simon's steely gaze pierced her. "When were you going to tell me your plans?"

"When it was time to leave. I hate fighting with you. Why should I make myself miserable two days in advance? Simon, what has happened to us? It's all going wrong."

"If you would spend a little more time with me and a little less with your kids, we wouldn't squabble so much."

"I'm really sorry you feel like this. I've given one hundred percent to this marriage to the exclusion of all else. When I go up to the house, since there's no point in trying to save dinner, I'm going to unpack my boxes and I'm going to put out my pictures. I'm going to town tomorrow and buy frames for Jake's pictures. I think you might have given maybe 10 percent. Those aren't very good numbers, Simon." Fanny continued stroking Cissie's head.

"Fanny, what are you talking about? You're making me sound like some kind of . . . an ogre. I just don't see why we need pictures everywhere. I don't like clutter. You knew that when you married me."

"Maybe you don't need pictures, but I do, and I don't think my family should be considered as clutter. I'm sorry I didn't bring this up a long time ago. I hate fighting with you, Simon."

"We aren't fighting. We're having a discussion. Fighting is what you used to do with Ash. I think you have us mixed up."

"You see, Simon, that's where you're wrong. I know exactly who it is that's mixed up, and it isn't me. I've had it. I'm sick and tired of your attitude. I'm sick and tired of hearing Ash's name in every conversation we have. Three's a crowd, Simon, in case you haven't noticed. I was hoping today, because it's our anniversary, that we could have a nice dinner and try to get back to where we were. Our marriage is in trouble, Simon."

"If you'd stop seeing problems where there are no problems, if you'd do as I ask you to do, you wouldn't be causing yourself so many problems."

"For three years, Simon, you've been trying to make me into someone I'm not. I allowed it because I loved you so much. I desperately wanted this marriage to work. I would have stood on my head if that's what you wanted. Nothing I do is good enough for you. I'm sorry. This simply is not working for me."

"What the hell does that mean, Fanny?"

"It's not working. I'm not happy. I'm tired of trying. The only thing I want right now is to pack for my trip back home. I'm counting the hours. Actually, Simon, I'm counting the minutes. Now, be quiet. The pups are coming."

Two hours later, mother and six pups were resting comfortably. Fanny washed her hands, dried them, and left the barn. In the kitchen she removed the overdone roast from the oven and dumped it in the sink along with the pared vegetables and salad. The garbage disposal struggled to grind the voluminous amount of food. She returned the candlesticks and candles to the china cabinet. The last thing she did was to fold her linen tablecloth and put away her good china. The wine bottle stood on the counter in full view. Retail it would have cost close to $200. Ash had told her to consider it an anniversary present even though she'd asked him to send it to her.

Fanny saw Simon's shadow in the doorway before he opened the screen door. She sucked in her breath. Where had it all gone awry? What did she do that was so wrong? How much more could she do? Her eyes sparked as she reached for the wine bottle.

"Where did that come from?"

"Nevada. Surely you realize the liquor stores around here don't stock this kind of wine. I wanted it to be special because I mistakenly thought today was a special day. In a way it was, Cissie had six beautiful pups."

"Did Ash send this wine?"

"Yes, he did. At my request. You can either join me or you can drink your orange, grapefruit, lemon juice. I really don't care, Simon."

Simon snatched the wine from her hands and poured it down the drain.

Fanny stared at her husband for a full five minutes before she got up from her chair. She walked upstairs, tossed her makeup into a small bag along with a nightshirt. She looked around for her purse. She reached for it along with her jacket.

"What are you doing, Fanny? Where are you going?"

"Back where I belong. Get out of my way, Simon." His arm stretched across the open doorway. Fanny ducked under it and ran down the steps. Simon followed her, taking the steps two at a time.

Simon's voice was outraged when he shouted, "You're walking out on me on our anniversary? Isn't that what Ash used to do to you?"

"Shut the hell up, Simon." Fanny turned the key in the ignition. "I'm going to Sunrise. We were both invited. If you want to join me on Sunday, do so. If you don't, that's okay, too. Now get the hell out of my way before I run over you. Oh, yes, happy anniversary."

Simon stared at the back of the Jeep Cherokee as it roared down the driveway. His eyes were cold and calculating when he returned to the fragrant kitchen to pour himself a glass of juice. "This is all your fault, Ash," he muttered as he downed the juice. "Everything that's ever gone wrong in my life is your fault, you son of a bitch."

Sunny Thornton Ford rocked quietly in the comfortable rocking chair, her eyes on the toddler playing with a basket of colorful blocks, her arms warm and full with seven-week-old Polly. She leaned her head back into the softness of the rocker to allow the fear she always felt to take over her body. Fear she always felt when things were too quiet, too serene. She had to do something. Very soon.

Her gaze dropped to the basket of mail at the side of the rocker. She could pull it off if she really tried. Tyler would never stop her from going to her college reunion and she knew for a fact he wouldn't be able to go with her. She had capable household help and her sister Billie said she'd stop by twice a day to play with little Jake and Polly. She could do it. She'd attend the reunion, get her picture taken, take a roll of film herself, sign all the old yearbooks, get hers signed, gather up all the handout materials and stuff everything in one envelope to show Tyler on her return. The moment she was free she would head for Boston and the Leahy Clinic. Three days of intensive testing would tell her what was wrong and if it was possible to correct her condition. She would pay for the tests with cash, so nothing would show up on her health insurance.

Damn, she hated keeping secrets from her husband and her family. She shouldn't even be contemplating this.

Polly squirmed, her face puckering as she prepared to burp. The sound was loud in the quiet room. Jake laughed and Sunny smiled. Her family.

Today was going to be her true test. The family would be here for Polly's christening. She had to get into her cheerful mode, schmooze with family members, pretend not to see the concern on her husband's face, and see that everyone had a good time. How she was going to do that while sitting was still a mystery to her. She heaved a mighty sigh. She was tired of covering up, tired of not feeling well, tired of lying, and tired of the fear that consumed her twenty-four hours a day. Maybe Sage was right and she had a screw loose inside her brain.

Sage was her confidant and she didn't know why that was. She wished now, for the thousandth time, that she'd made more of an effort to socialize with Iris, Sage's wife, and Lily Bell, Birch's long time fiancée. She adored both young women. By her own choice she'd given up her job at the casino, elected to stay home with her children. She was safe here from inquisitive eyes and callous questions. At home she could control her wobbly gait. At home she could drop things and cover up her little accidents more easily. If she bumped into things, the help just smiled when she'd say, "Oops, I'm so clumsy."

Today, though, her mother and Simon would be here. She'd never been able to hide anything from her mother. Her mother would notice. Then again, if Sage could occupy her, maybe not. Fanny would be busy with Jake and Polly. She could plead weariness and sit as much as she could. Although Sage hadn't said, she was certain he'd confided in Iris. Iris would take up some of the slack, too. *What the hell is wrong with me?*

She cried then, her tears dropping on Polly's downy head. What if she had a terminal disease and she never lived to see her children grow up? Now she knew how her father felt, trapped in his wheelchair. Would he show up for Polly's christening?

Jake stopped building his bridge, scrambled to his feet, and ran to the French doors leading to the small balcony. "Pop Pop's here, Mommy. Me go push his chair."

Sunny looked at her watch. "Go ahead, Jake. Bring Pop Pop here, okay?" Her father was three hours early. What did *that* mean?

She heard the sound of the whirring chair before she saw it. She worked a smile onto her face as she shifted Polly so her father could get a better look at the infant.

"She looks like you did when you were born. My God, that was so long ago. We miss you at the casino, Sunny."

"I bet. You couldn't wait for me to leave when I was pregnant with Jake."

"Image is everything, Sunny. Right now I suspect you're more of a pro in regard to image making than I am. I came up here early because . . . look, I know I've been a lousy father, but that doesn't mean I don't care. I do. Sometimes I get so full of self-pity I can't see beyond my own needs. I have a keen eye, though. I know something's wrong. I know you're trying to hide it. I want to know why. You're too young to be going through something like this. I want the truth. I won't betray you, Sunny. I'm not that big a louse."

Sunny could feel the tears start to build behind her eyelids. "I don't know what's wrong with me. I came up with this plan . . . I don't know why I'm fighting it, fear I guess. I didn't want anyone to know. Tyler . . . everyone is worried about me. Hell, I'm worried myself. That's a lie. I'm scared to death. I'm afraid to find out."

"Sunny, hiding from something isn't the answer. You have to look it square in the face, deal with it, and go on from there. I know what I'm talking about. Whatever it is you can deal with it. You have more guts than anyone in this family."

"Had. I have two children now. I came up with this plan. Tell me what you think."

Ash listened, his eyes on his daughter. He stared intently as though seeing her for the first time.

"It sounds like a roundabout way of doing things. There are very good doctors here, and we can bring in specialists. What do you *think* is wrong?"

"I think I have a muscle or nerve disease. I read up on everything I could find and I think it's multiple sclerosis. That means eventually I'll be in a wheelchair like you. I won't be able to take care of my own kids. People . . . *die* with the disease."

"How long have you known?"

"About a year before I got pregnant with Jake. I blamed everything under the sun and refused to see a doctor. I had tests. Nothing showed up. I figured if they couldn't find anything whatever, it would go away. It didn't. I never said I was the smart one in the family."

"No, that spot is reserved for your mother. Does she know?"

"She hasn't been here since Jake was christened. He's three now. We talk almost every day. Actually, we used to talk every day. Weeks go by, and we don't talk. She's too busy with her new life. I think she thinks of me as an intrusion. Sage knows. Birch . . . Birch doesn't say anything. Everyone has their own lives. Billie is so busy with the business we don't see each other that often. I see the worry on her face. I guess they all figure I'm married to a doctor, and I'm old enough to take care of myself. I haven't done a very good job of it."

"Do you want me to go with you, Sunny? It's time for me to get an evaluation myself. But, before we do that, why don't I do some checking and see if there's a specialist a little closer to home. It would be better to start with one doctor and stick with him. If you need treatments, you'll be near home. That's important."

"That's very funny coming from you, Dad."

"I know. Do you want some advice, Sunny? You don't have to follow it."

"Sure."

"Everyone is going to be here today. Let me tell them. Or, you tell them yourself. They all care about you. None of them will turn their backs on you. It's going to take some guts, but you have those by the bushel. Your mother is going to be devastated."

"Hardly. She's so wrapped up in her new life with her new husband there's no time for visits, or . . . anything. I'm the one who does the calling. She does call once a month. I could die in a month, and she wouldn't know. Mom and Uncle Simon with a breeding kennel. From Wall Street to scooping up poop. It's an eye-opener, all right. They're making a fortune and love what they do. I suppose that's half the battle. I'm jealous."

"I understand the feeling, Sunny. I've envied Simon for years. Then he up and marries my ex-wife. It didn't go down real easy. So, what's your answer? I'm here for you. A little late, but I'm here."

Sunny's shoulders drooped. She started to cry.

Ash stared at his daughter, a helpless look on his face. Suddenly he wanted to make things right for this girl of his that he'd wronged for so many years. He maneuvered his chair until he was alongside her. He reached for her hand and smiled. "Hey, we can do anything, we're Thorntons, kiddo. I'm going to be here for you, and that's a promise you can take to the bank. Things are running so smooth at the casino I can take off whole blocks of time. We'll do whatever we have to do, Sunny."

Sunny leaned over to lay Polly in the cradle next to her chair. She slid from the rocker to sit at her father's feet, her head in his lap. She cried silently as her father patted her head.

Ash's heart filled with something he'd never experienced before. He found himself choking up as he talked to his daughter. He knew he had to say the right words or it would all get away from him. "Listen to me, Sunny. I know you're scared. I know what that's like. What's worse is the realization that things might not get better but stay as they are or even worsen. You have to handle the cards that are dealt to you because it's the only game in town, kiddo. You don't even want to think about the alternative. I went down that road, too. I can't begin to tell you how many times I thought about ending it all. I'd start thinking about how I screwed things up, about the mistakes I made. I'd think about Simon and how much I hated him. Then I'd think about your mother and you kids. Every damn night I'd vow to make things better the next day. I never did though. I let other things get in the way. I love life and I know you do, too. That's why I'm still hanging around. Yeah, I take pills and smoke stuff I shouldn't. It's the only way I can cope so that I can be around. Like I said, the alternative doesn't bear thinking about.

"What we're going to do is get a diagnosis. We'll get the best of the best and you will do whatever it takes to get you on the road to recovery. You can handle this, Sunny, because you have two little kids to think about. This isn't just about you anymore. It's about Jake and Polly and your husband and the rest of us. We're going to get you some full-time house help. I know a thing or two about that. Your mother was worn to a frazzle with the twins and my mother stepped in and made things right. We'll lick this together."

"Dad, what if I end up in a wheelchair? I can't walk a straight line anymore, and I bump into things. Tyler won't . . . how's he going to feel about me if that happens? What kind of wife and mother will I be?"

"The best. The same kind of wife and mother you are now. For

starters you have to stop thinking so negatively. The first step is dealing with it. After you tell the rest of the family, we'll go on from there.
Is it a deal, Sunny?"

"It's a deal."

Fanny backed away from the doorway, her vision blurred. She
motioned for Simon to be quiet and to back up and return to the
foyer.

"What's wrong?" Simon asked.

"Ash is in the room with Sunny." She told him what she'd over-
heard. "I should be the one doing this, Simon. Why did Ash have
to . . . ? Why Ash? I was so damn busy leading this life you and I
made for ourselves I ignored my daughter when I knew something
was wrong. I pretended things were all right. In my heart I knew they
weren't. My God, what have I become? How could I become so selfish? I'm sorry I ever listened to you. This, Simon, is the result."

"For heaven's sake, Fanny, Sunny is a grown woman, and she's
married to a doctor. It's her health, her body. What could you have
done? Dragged her to a doctor? Forced her to do something she
wasn't ready to do? We both know Sunny. If you had done that, she
would have told you to mind your own business and we both know
it. So what if Ash is the one who is finally getting her to do something? He's succeeding, and that's the only thing that matters. If you
stop and think about it, Fanny, he is the right person."

"I find that very strange coming from you. Ash must have an
ulterior motive then. He never does anything without a reason.
He's probably still after Sunny's trust fund. I know he could get
Birch's with a snap of his fingers. I bet you that's what this is all
about."

"Maybe this time it's different. Maybe this time Ash is acting like
a real father. I think you want to believe that. Let it be, Fanny. Let
Sunny handle things her way. If that includes her father helping her
through this, accept it. It's got to be what's best for Sunny. Right now
she's relating to Ash. We have our own lives."

"I should have called more often. You always got so upset when
my children called, Simon. I hated seeing that angry look on your
face. I should have visited. You didn't want me to visit. I'm sorry I
listened to you. Sunny kept saying she was fine. I actually started to
believe I was mistaken. I feel so guilty. What if she isn't fine? What
if this is really serious? How do I deal with that?"

"One day at a time. That has to be Birch. He's the only one who blares his horn all the way up the mountain. Looks like Sage is right behind him. In about an hour this house is going to rock right off the mountain. When do you expect Billie Coleman and Thad Kingsley?"

"Momentarily. I'm so happy for Billie. She's loved Thad for so long. It's strange though, isn't it? Thad was Moss's best friend. They went through the war together and remained friends until the day Moss died. Thad loved Moss like a brother. Thad loves politics, but Billie hates it. Senator Thad Kingsley. It has a nice ring to it. I don't think Billie will like living in the Washington fishbowl when they marry? What will that make Billie?"

Simon smirked. "A senator's wife. Don't you think it a little strange that Billie is contemplating marrying her husband's best friend? How long have they been fooling around?"

Fanny stared at her husband. "No more strange than me marrying you. No, Billie was not fooling around. I resent you even thinking such a thing. There are days, Simon, when I don't know who you are anymore. There are days when I don't even like you."

"I'm the same old me. Being anywhere near Ash brings out the worst in me. Sorry." Fanny didn't think he sounded sorry at all.

"The senator from Vermont. Billie told me how wonderful Thad's farm is. She loves it there. She loves it as much as I love Sunrise. Wait till she finds out how many pups we have. Isn't it strange, Simon, how life has come full circle for us? This should be the most wonderful time of our lives and it isn't wonderful at all. Now this problem with Sunny. I'm feeling cheated and angry, and I don't know what to do about it."

"I don't want to hear that kind of talk. Let's go outside and welcome the young people."

"Why does what you just said make me feel very old? And why isn't there any warmth in your voice?"

"Because we are old. As usual you're imagining things."

Fanny stared at her husband's cold features. Fanny frowned. He was switching up again and acting like the old Simon.

The greeting was everything a family greeting should be. There were hugs and kisses, good-natured hisses and boos because there weren't enough letters and phone calls, more hugs and kisses when young Billie and Bess arrived.

"Where are the presents?" Bess shouted. "We have ours. I don't see any gaily wrapped packages for Miss Polly."

They played the game because, as Ash said, it was the only game

in town. The concern and worry in her children's eyes matched
Fanny's. It didn't need to be said with words, they all knew that
today was a turning point of sorts for one of their own.

"Presents! You want presents! Well take a look at this," Sage said,
popping his trunk open. He pulled out a bright red tricycle. "Complete with horn and a banana seat!"

"I can top that," Birch said, opening his trunk. "Roller skates with
a key, a scooter with a bell on each handle."

"Ha!" Billie said. "Take a look at this red wagon! Complete with
a family of dolls!"

"What did you bring, Mom?" they asked in unison.

"Well I . . . I didn't know . . . I thought . . ."

"This is Dolly," Simon said, taking a basket out of the car. "She's
seven weeks old. Polly and Dolly. A savings bond, too," Simon said.

"Dad's here," Billie said. "Wonder what he brought. Sneak a look
in the van and see if there's a package, Birch?"

"Yep, a big one too. Where is he?"

"He's with Sunny," Fanny said quietly.

"How's our new little mother?" Billie asked.

"I imagine she's fine," Fanny said. "I haven't seen Tyler."

"He makes rounds early on Sundays. He'll be here soon."

"Let's go inside," Fanny said, "and see what we can do to help."

"This is how we're going to do it. You're going to wash your face
and then you're going to get behind my chair and push me out into
the family room. After the greetings, you're going to . . . what,
Sunny?"

"Tell them everything. What if Tyler isn't there, Dad?"

"Then we'll wait for Tyler. He'll be here any minute. You can do
this, Sunny. I'll be right beside you. You made a commitment and
now you have to follow through. You have no idea how good you're
going to feel once you open up."

"Dad, what made you come up here early? What made you . . ."

"I heard Birch talking to Sage several days ago. You gave up too
easy, kiddo, that's how I knew for certain something was wrong. I
know how much you loved working at the casino. The bright lights,
the noise, the moans and groans get into your bloodstream after a
while. I want you to come back. I *need* you, Sunny. Christ, is that a
confession or what? I want it to be your goal. If, and this is a big if,
you feel it's a worthy goal. This is the eighties, the working woman's
decade."

"What if . . . what if . . . I end up in a chair like yours? Will you still want me?"

"Don't you ever ask me a stupid question like that again. Of course I'll want you. After a while the chair becomes invisible to other people. His and hers. Father and daughter. It has a nice ring to it. I know you have ideas, Sunny, and I want us to act on those ideas. I want Babylon to be Uno forever. Together we can do it. You game?"

"Yeah. I really am. Okay, I'm going to wash my face and we'll get this show on the road."

"Daddy's home," Jake said, running from the room, his chubby legs pumping furiously. A moment later Tyler was standing in the middle of the room, Jake on his shoulders.

"Ash, nice to see you. Where's Sunny?" he boomed. Then in a whisper he said, "Did you talk to her?"

"You know women. She's splashing perfume or something." Ash nodded and whispered in return, "It's under control."

In the family room there were more hugs and kisses, more oohs and aahs, as Tyler showed off his new daughter.

"She looks so much like Sunny it's uncanny. Do you agree, Ash?" Fanny said as she reached for her granddaughter.

"It was my first thought when I saw Sunny holding her. I brought a present. Will you get it, Birch? I want you to know I sweated this present, kiddo, but I managed to track it down. It's used, secondhand if you will, but I thought you'd like it."

There was a mild scurry as brothers and sister ran to the courtyard to bring in Polly's gifts. They laughed over the tricycle and scooter. Sunny openly frowned at the puppy in the basket. "I don't think so, Mom. Not now. Jake might hurt it without meaning to and I don't have the time to train a dog. Please don't be offended, but you'll have to take her back. I appreciate the bond. Thanks, Mom and Uncle Simon."

"C'mon, c'mon, open mine," Ash said.

"It's almost too pretty to open," Sunny said breathlessly. "Okay, here goes." She removed the large red bow and the silver foil paper. Nestled inside the large box, amid mounds of tissue paper, was a complete layette.

"Your mother made you one just like this when you were born. I convinced her to make another one for the fund-raiser at the medical center. It fetched the most money in the raffle. A doctor's wife bought it. She saved it all these years. I tracked her down through the medical center and got her to agree to part with it. This layette is what convinced your mom to go into business. Sunny's Togs are the result. The woman said it's in mint condition. Do you like it?"

"Oh, Dad, this is super. What an absolutely wonderful gift. Mom, it's exquisite. I'll save it for Polly's first baby."

Fanny stared at Ash, her mouth dropping open. The urge to put her fist to her ex-husband's face was so strong, she clutched at the puppy until it squealed.

Simon leaned over to take the puppy and whispered, "Easy does it, Fanny."

"Thank you all for the wonderful presents. Listen, there's something I want to tell all of you before the minister gets here. Please, let me say what I have to say and when I'm finished, let's not beat it to death. I don't want any discussions, any advice, or any of that stuff."

Sunny reached for her husband's hand. Ash reached out to take her other hand. He squeezed it.

Sunny talked steadily, her eyes on Bess, who was holding Polly. "So, that's the way it is. Dad's going to go with me. He's going to be my . . . backbone until mine stiffens up a little more. I'll deal with it, and I'll handle it the best way I can. I have the best husband in the world, and I know he's going to be there for me. When whatever it is I have is under control I'm going to go back to work at the casino. I guess that's it and in the nick of time. I hear Reverend Gillespie so let's get Polly christened so we can enjoy the party and just being together. Is everyone okay with this?" Sunny beamed at the smiles and nods.

Fanny could feel her insides start to quiver. All she wanted to do was run from the room and cry. Everyone had to be as aware as she was that her daughter had difficulty looking her in the eye. Her hug had been a mere touching of the shoulders and there had been no kiss, or smooch, as Sunny referred to a real kiss. *She hates it that I got married and moved away,* Fanny thought.

Baby Polly voiced her opinion of the christening with one long, loud wail. She was asleep in Billie's arms a moment later.

For the first time in her life, Fanny felt like an outsider. It showed in the stiffness of her shoulders and the grim set of her jaw.

After the ceremony, the young people moved off toward the kitchen and the patio, Ash and Simon headed for the cemetery. Fanny looked at Bess.

"It's going to be okay, Fanny. All you need to think about now is the end result. It doesn't matter how or why Sunny gets there. Let Ash do the father thing. I saw something in his eyes, Fanny, when Sunny was talking. It was good. Usually you, me, the world, can read Ash Thornton. Today was unlike anything I've ever seen where he's concerned. Maybe that's what's bothering you. This time he might come through all the way for Sunny."

"I refuse to believe that. I know Ash."

"You *used* to know Ash. The puppy wasn't a good idea, but then I guess you know that. If Sunny is feeling deserted, the puppy was just a reminder of that desertion. You cut the strings, Fanny. Don't attempt to tie a knot now to make things better. It is what it is. You're entitled to a life of your own. You paid your dues, and it's your turn now. You are happy, aren't you, Fanny?"

"Actually, I'm not happy at all, Bess. My marriage is . . . was . . . a mistake. I think I'm finally ready to talk about it. I feel like I don't belong here."

"You don't. You're damn right we'll talk about it later. Your kids get their own lives, you get yours, if you're lucky, and everyone gets on with the business of living. Or, moving on if you prefer that term. I like to think of it as my time in the sun."

"Bess, the last time I saw Jake was at his christening. He's three years old. I can't tell you where those three years went. They're gone, and I can't get them back. I don't even know that little boy. What's worse, he doesn't know me. I know in my heart Sunny left him with a sitter when Sage and Iris got married just to keep him from me. Sunny looked right through me. All those calls, every single day. They meant something to her. I . . . oh, Bess, I thought of them as interruptions because that's how Simon viewed it. More often than not I'd hurry her off the phone. My God, what did I do in the name of love that's now sour?"

"You had the audacity to reach out for some happiness with a new life. We'll talk about that new life when you're ready. Stop being so hard on yourself. Mother-daughter love is something that can never be destroyed, no matter what."

"You're wrong, Bess. I feel it here," Fanny said, thumping her chest. "Maybe I'll stay on for a little while. Simon can handle things back at the ranch. I'm not sure I even want to go back there. With him."

"Were you invited?" Bess asked bluntly.

"No. I should . . . don't I . . . I need an invitation?"

"Absolutely. You never take anything for granted where kids are concerned, and it doesn't make any difference how old those kids are."

"This is my house," Fanny said defensively.

"Was your house. Another family lives here now."

"Are you saying I'm not welcome?"

"Fanny, I don't know. So much is going on right now. You could *offer* to stay. Sunny would probably view it as after the fact. That's just my personal opinion. If it were me, I don't think I would even offer. You need to go back home and settle your own life. If Sunny needs you, she knows where to find you."

"You make it sound like I'm forcing myself on my daughter. I don't much care for this conversation. My children are like yo-yos, Bess. They keep switching sides and that shouldn't be. A parent's love is unconditional. A child's isn't. Someday I hope I'm wise enough to understand it all. I'd leave right now if Billie and Thad weren't coming."

"That's something Ash would do, not something Fanny does. Shift into neutral and . . . what is it Ash says? Oh, yes, play the game, it's the only one in town. Go join your daughters and daughter-in-law in the kitchen. Just be Fanny."

Fanny walked into her old kitchen. It was Sunny's kitchen now, warm and light with plants and herbs on the windowsill and shiny copper pots hanging from the beams. A colorful rag rug sat beneath the huge claw-footed table. There were baskets of flowers on the hearth and a new red plaid cushion on her old rocker. Bess was right, this wasn't her kitchen any more than the rest of the house was hers.

At some point during her scrutiny of the kitchen she'd become aware of a change in the tone and the conversation.

"Am I interrupting anything serious?"

"Of course not, Mom," Billie said. "We were trying to figure out what it will take to get Birch to the altar with Lily. Bachelorhood isn't *that* wonderful."

Fanny had never been able to warm up to Lily Bell. Secretly she thought Birch could do much better, but she would have cut out her tongue before she voiced such an opinion.

"Birch was always a slow starter. He builds up to things," Fanny said lightly. "How's your family, Iris?"

"Mom and Dad went on a cruise. When they make a port of call

Dad golfs and Mom shops. They're bringing Sage and me grass skirts and Sage swears he'll dance for all of us wearing his. It should be interesting because he has two left feet."

"I would like to see that. He has rhythm though," Fanny smiled. "Do you use the studio much, Sunny?"

"I haven't been in it since the day we moved in. It's not locked if you want to go down there."

"No. I was just curious. It seems a shame to waste the space now that we've moved the offices back to town."

"We can't disturb the shrine," Sunny said as she nestled small baby carrots next to thin slivers of cucumber on a silver tray.

Shrine? She wasn't going to touch that one. Because she was the closest, Fanny reached out to take the tray from Sunny's hands just as Jake charged through the kitchen door, his father in pursuit. The tray fell and skidded across the floor.

"I'm sorry, it was my fault," Fanny said, dropping to her knees to pick up the vegetables. "It wasn't your fault, Sunny."

"If you hadn't dropped it, I would have. I drop everything. Tyler, you need to stand Jake in the corner. He knows better than to charge through the door like that."

"Honey. He's only three. Three-year-olds have the attention span of a gnat." The moment the words were out of her mouth, Fanny regretted them.

"Then why was it good enough for us and not for him? Some of my earliest memories are of 'don't run, walk or you'll get your fanny paddled.' Getting paddled when I didn't listen is another unforgettable memory. Long-distance grandmothering doesn't work these days, Mom."

"I see that," Fanny said as she put the vegetables in the disposal. "I think I'll go outside. If there's anything you want me to do, call me."

"Sure, Mom," Billie said.

"Where's *that* dog?" Sunny asked.

"Simon put her back in her basket in the car. I'm sorry about the dog. I guess neither Simon nor I thought it through." Fanny's tone was apologetic, defensive. The urge to reach for her daughter and shake her made her quicken her pace.

Outside in the bright sunshine, Fanny wandered aimlessly through the garden, stopping to pick a flower from time to time. How many hours she'd spent in this very garden. Once it had been a comforting place to sit and think, a place where she found solace in her troubled marriage. More than once she and Ash had made love on the springy green grass. It was silent now. She looked overhead to see if there were any birds nestled in the trees.

Fanny sat down and reached for a long blade of grass. She placed it between her fingers and brought it to her lips. An earsplitting sound echoed around the garden. Once she'd had a contest with her mother-in-law. She couldn't remember who had won. The little contest had been one of her nicest memories, and now she barely remembered it.

"A penny for your thoughts, Fanny."

"Tyler. I'm afraid they aren't worth even a penny. Where's Jake?"

"Napping. He plays hard and falls asleep on his feet. How are you, Fanny?"

"I thought I was fine until I got here. The truth is I can't wait to leave. I don't feel like I belong here, and I also don't feel welcome."

"I live here, thanks to your generosity, and I feel just the way you do sometimes. These last two years have not been easy."

"Why didn't you say something?"

"Why didn't you ask, Fanny? Sunny's your daughter. We talked about her several times. If there was anyone in the world she'd listen to, it was you. You didn't take the time. I guess I'm blaming you. It isn't right, but it's how I feel."

"Honesty is always good. A person would be a fool not to respect an honest statement of fact. Are you asking me if I'm going to defend myself for the last three years?"

"Only if you feel the need to explain. At this point I really don't care where you've been or what you've been doing. My only concern is my stubborn wife and my two children. Is that honest enough for you?"

Fanny stared at her son-in-law. She saw the torment and anger in his eyes, noticed his clenched fists. She adored this young man with the magical hands, hands that could reconstruct a person's face after a bad accident and make that person whole again. She knew he was a good husband and father. "Of course. Let me make sure I understand this. What you're saying is you're holding me responsible for Sunny's condition. You're her husband, Tyler. You live with her every day. Why couldn't you get her to a doctor? Surely you must have watched her deteriorate. I wasn't here."

"My point exactly. A psychiatrist I spoke with told me women, Sunny in particular, want to be perfect for their husbands. That means no warts, no nothing. When deformities, real or imaginary, show up, the wart holder feels inferior and starts to go into a shell. Confiding in a mother who loves unconditionally, accepts everything unconditionally, is the way to go. That mother gives emotional support. To Sunny you were her cherry Popsicle but you didn't show up to hand it to her. I know she calls you every day because I see the phone bills. What in the goddamn hell did you think, Fanny?"

Fanny felt her insides start to crumple. "I think I thought she wasn't happy. I swear to you, each time she called I asked how she was and asked if there was anything I could do. I invited her to the ranch, but she declined, said she didn't want to come without you and you were too busy. She never once asked me to come here. If she had asked, I would have come. I think you know that, Tyler."

Tyler shrugged. His voice was frosty when he said, "I went to Ash. I have to say he was already on top of it. You have to give the devil his due, Fanny. He came, saw, and did what you should have done."

"That's so cruel, Tyler."

"It's a fact. You can't dispute a fact. I came here to tell you Billie and Thad have arrived and they're on the patio."

Fanny nodded because she didn't trust herself to speak. She watched her son-in-law walk away. She wished she could cry, but her eyes felt dry and hot. The rest of her body felt icy cold.

Fanny straightened her shoulders and strode up the path to the patio. Her smile was warm and all-encompassing when she hugged Billie and Thad.

"Fanny, this baby is so beautiful I never want to let her go. She looks like Sunny. Sit, sit, and tell me what's going on and then I'll tell you horror stories about Washington. I can't wait till we get married. Keeping two residences is ridiculous," she whispered. "I heard about the pup and Thad and I are going to take her if you don't object. He's got her inside his shirt. He's some guy. I didn't think I could ever be this happy, Fanny. You aren't exactly blooming. Do you want to go for a walk and talk?"

"I'd like that. Let me check first to see if there's anything I can do to help."

"Not a thing, Fanny," Bess said. "Be back in an hour. John's barbecuing, and he wants to hear compliments."

"Are you sure?"

"Absolutely."

"That's good because we have to leave right after dinner. Thad rented a plane to make the trip. He has to be back in Washington at the crack of dawn. We'll make it with the time difference. God, I hate politics."

Billie linked her arm with Fanny's. "Now, tell me what's wrong."

Fanny told her. "I want to cry," she said. "I need to cry, but I can't."

They talked, these two old friends who understood family, and who had shared more tragedy in their lives than most people experienced in a lifetime.

"When is it my turn, Billie? Why is this my fault? They're all blaming me. I can see it in their faces. Ash . . . Ash has taken my place. I swear on my children, Billie, I don't begrudge what he's doing as long as his motives are pure. I don't believe they are, and I hope I'm wrong. I'd give up my life for any one of my children just the way you would.

"I was sitting in the garden before and I started to think about Sallie. She knew her children would break her heart. She talked about it so often. It has to be me, Billie. My children keep switching up. One minute they side with me, the next it's with their father. Why can't it just be all of us? They have every right to love their father. That doesn't mean they have to like all the things he does. The same goes for me. They constantly choose sides and smack in the middle of all of this is Simon. If I had married anyone but Simon, things would be just fine. I don't know what to do."

"What did Sallie always tell us? When you don't know what to do, do nothing. That's my advice, Fanny. You want to stay here now, don't you?"

"Part of me does, but as Bess pointed out, I wasn't invited. Simon and I will be right behind you when you leave. Ash will be here for Sunny. If I believed in my heart that there was something I could do, nothing in this world could make me leave. It's a terrible feeling not to be needed or wanted by your own children."

"At this point in time, Fanny, your children love you as much as you love them. This is one of those crises that pop up from time to time when everyone goes off the deep end. Things always right themselves later on. Do whatever feels right to you, Fanny. You can call me any time of the day or night. You know that. When you have more of a grip on things, we can take a vacation together. We could go back to that little house in Arizona that belonged to Sallie and Devin. Or if you feel the need to get away to lick your wounds, you could go alone. Did you ever tell Simon about that little house?"

"No. I don't know why I didn't. Probably because of something Sallie said. You know, never share everything. Some things need to be kept private. When I felt the urge to bolt, I thought about that little house. We probably should be getting back. Bess's husband is a cranky cook. A good one, but feisty. I don't think I can eat anything anyway. Do me a favor, Billie. Eat and run so I can leave. I never thought I'd live to see the day I would say something like that."

Billie laughed. "Next time I get to unload. My granddaughter and my daughter are at it, too. Sawyer absolutely refuses to acknowledge Maggie as her mother. It's eating Maggie alive, and there's nothing she can do about it. It seems to me like we just move from one crisis to the next with barely a breather in between. Take a deep breath now. You can handle this, Fanny."

The next two hours were pleasant enough. Everyone smiled, joked, ate, drank, and cleaned up. Fanny watched Ash closely, her thoughts in a turmoil. As Billie and Thad said their good-byes, Fanny walked over to Ash's chair, leaned over and whispered, "If I ever find out you have an ulterior motive for what you promised today, I swear, I'll make you regret the day you were born. Better yet, I'll shut down Babylon. For good. I have the power to do that. I think it's wonderful that you got Sunny to agree to seek help. Don't let her swing in the wind, Ash." She leaned even closer, her voice more hushed, "You fuck with our kids, and it's all over for you. That's a threat *and* a promise. I apologize for my language. Unfortunately it's the only kind you understand. Did I make myself clear?"

"Absolutely."

"Then I'll say good-bye."

"Leaving so soon, Mom?" young Billie said.

"Yes. You young people can visit. Is there anything I can do before I leave?"

"Not a thing," Sunny said as she hugged her mother. "You're upset with me, aren't you?"

"A little, but it's okay. I understand, Sunny. If you need me or if I can do anything, call me. I can be here in a few hours. Polly is just as beautiful as you were when you were born. Take good care of her. Hug Jake for me and give him a big kiss."

"Okay, Mom."

The chorus of good-byes rang across the mountain as Simon slipped the car in gear.

Fanny was silent for so long, Simon reached over and chucked her under the chin. "Tell me *exactly* what's wrong. How can I help you? What can I do? If my opinion counts for anything, I want you to know that I believe Ash will come through. We had a long talk at

the cemetery. For the first time in his life he cares about someone besides himself. In his condition that says a lot."

"Simon, I want to stay here for a few days. I'd like it if you
dropped me off in town and went back to the ranch yourself. Just
for a few days. I think I need to be by myself for a little while."

"If that's what you want, Fanny. My thinking is you shouldn't be
alone."

Fanny thought her husband's voice was whiny and threatening
at the same time. She felt her insides start to crunch.

"I *need* to be alone. If you don't or can't understand that, then I'm
sorry."

"I do, and I don't. Will you at least call me?"

"No. Alone means alone."

"If you had married anyone but me, this wouldn't be happening,
would it?"

"I don't know. What I do know is I cannot allow my children to
dictate my life. I would not do that to them, and I will not tolerate
it from any child of mine. Just drop me off at Babylon. I want to locate the most strategic places in the casino in case I have to torch it."

"Jesus, Fanny, do you know what you just said?"

"I told Ash I would do it if he didn't follow through with Sunny.
I will, too. Yes, drop me off at Babylon."

"Fanny, do you see this developing into a problem between the
two of us?"

"We already have a problem, Simon. My family that you're so intent on keeping away from me is now right before me. I will deal
with it, and I don't want any interference from you. Now, tell me, is
Polly the most beautiful baby you've ever seen?"

"You were probably just as pretty when you were born. I know a
secret."

There was such tight control in Simon's voice, Fanny felt her insides start to shrivel. "You can't keep a secret, Simon. Tell me."

"Okay. Thad isn't taking Billie back to Washington. He's taking
her to Hawaii!"

"Oh, how wonderful for Billie. When is he going to tell her?"

"When she realizes they aren't landing at Washington National
on time. Are we going to be okay, Fanny? I need to know."

"I'll be fine, Simon. I don't know about you. I think I still love you,
Simon."

"You *think!*"

"Yes, think. I haven't been happy for a long time. You know that, and you don't seem to care. You are much too controlling, and I do not like the way you try to keep me from my family. I'm having a hard time believing I capitulated where you're concerned. I won't do that again, so be so advised."

"That sounds like a threat."

"Call it whatever you want. It's the way it is."

"Obviously we need to have a long talk."

"We had three years to talk, and it didn't work. Do you know why it didn't work? It didn't work, Simon, because you were too busy listening to yourself instead of hearing what I had to say. I don't care to discuss this anymore."

"Fine," Simon snapped.

"We should be leaving, Tyler. It's after nine and Sunny looks tired."

"It's a good kind of tired, Sage. She loves it when you all come up here and she gets to show off the kids and her homemaking skills. Birch looks like he's had a few too many. Perhaps you should drive him down the mountain."

"I already thought about that and mentioned it to Lily. She's agreeable. We'll say good night then. Guess I'll take the lead. Is Dad staying over?"

"He didn't say anything to me. I don't think so. He said something about wanting to be in town first thing in the morning to get things moving."

"Guess he'll bring up the rear then."

"Time to go, Sage. You're last in line and blocking my car," Birch said.

"Get in my car, Birch, you've had too much to drink. Tyler will move your car to the garage and drive it into town tomorrow. I'll bring him back up the mountain in the evening."

"Telling me what to do again, Sage?"

"You're drunk, Birch."

"Want to see me walk a straight line?"

"Sage is right, Birch," Ash said quietly.

"Am I drunk, Lily? Are you afraid to drive with me?"

"Why don't I drive?"

"Does that mean you think I'm drunk, too?"

"I don't know if you're drunk, but yes, I think you had too much to drink," Lily said.

"Well I don't think any such thing. If you're coming with me, get in the car."

"I'm going first, Birch. Stay behind me and don't even think about passing me on the road. You ride my bumper," Sage said.

"Yes, sir!" Birch said, offering up a sloppy salute.

"Listen, Birch, it's been a long time since I drove this road in the dark. My reflexes aren't what they used to be. Ride with me," Ash said.

"C'mon, Dad, you can do anything. Isn't that what you always told us? Hell, you were a fighting ace during the war. You're single-handedly going to get Sunny on the mend and ride off into the sunset. Get in the car, Lily."

"Ride his ass, Dad," Sage said before he climbed into his own car. "Don't give him any maneuvering room."

"Okay, son."

Sage climbed into his car, fastened his seat belt. He turned to his wife and said, "That's the first time in my life that my father ever called me son. I hope it's not an omen of some kind."

In the few short minutes it took Sage to back up his car and swing it around, Birch roared past him in reverse, swinging his car around in the middle of the road. He blew his horn one, long blast as he careened down the dark mountain road.

"Son of a bitch!" Sage swore.

"Go after him, son. I'm right behind you," Ash said.

Sage needed no second urging. "He's going to do something stupid. I feel it in my gut. I always know when he's . . ."

"Be careful, Sage," Iris said. "He's not that far ahead, and he's not driving that fast. We can see his lights. Lily will talk to him. She said he's afraid to get married because of what happened to your mom and dad. Your dad is right behind us. Please, Sage, don't drive so fast. God, I hate this road. With all the money your family has, why didn't they ever install guardrails?"

"We rarely drive this mountain at night. To answer your question, I don't know. Birch has never been a fast driver. We've always been a cautious bunch. You learn to respect the mountain. It's the curves that worry me. Dad was right, he's been drinking, and when you drink your reflexes aren't what they should be. My father is an expert on things like that."

"I can't see his lights! I can't see his lights! Oh, Jesus! Oh God!"

8

Simon watched his wife drive away in her rental car. He should have pressed harder to find out where she was going. Goddamn it, he should have *demanded* Fanny tell him where she was going. He was her husband for God's sake. His eyes felt moist, which was strange in itself since he was in the desert. He could understand his dry throat and how difficult it was to swallow. He turned to get back in his car when Fanny's vehicle was no longer in sight. His stomach started to rumble and his chest was tight. He couldn't ever remember being this angry. Except maybe when he was a kid and he and Ash were going at it.

Where to go? What to do? Fanny told him to go back to the ranch. As he put the car into gear, he thought he could feel his life slipping away from him. Would Fanny come back? He desperately wanted to believe she would, but would the pull of her family allow her to continue with her own life—her life with him? He simply didn't know. His anger started to build.

Simon made a U-turn in the middle of the road. Just because Fanny said he should go back to the ranch didn't mean he had to do it. If he went back to the ranch without Fanny, it would mean he lost and Ash won. He could stay here, hang out by the car rental agency until her return. So what if the employees thought him a lovesick fool. He knew he wasn't a lovesick fool. He was hanging out to protect his investment. He drove three blocks, made a second U-turn, and headed back the way he'd come. He'd always been a man of his word. Five blocks farther down the road, Simon pulled to the curb. The urge to put his foot through the floorboard was so strong he removed his foot from the brake pedal and turned off the ignition. Where the hell was Fanny going? Maybe what he should do was forget about going to the ranch and drive to his friend Jerry's house. Jerry seemed to have a handle on why women did the things they did. Perhaps he would share his knowledge and offer comforting words. His mood lightened considerably at the thought of spending time with his old school friend who was now retired.

Thirty minutes later, Simon climbed from his car but not before he gave the horn three sharp blasts.

Jerry afforded Simon the first genuine laugh he'd had in weeks when he ran down the driveway dressed in purple-and-yellow lightning-striped shorts, green socks, and red tee shirt. "Yeah, yeah, yeah. I'm painting the kitchen. These are my work duds. You're just in time, Simon. If you help, we can zip it off and drink beer the rest of the day. Later you can tell me what's bothering you. I know something's bothering you because you're standing here. I am in-tu-it-tive as you well know. The best part is we'll have the house to ourselves. Carol went to Georgia to see her sister, who had her gall bladder taken out a few days ago." It was all said with the speed of an out-of-control locomotive. Before Simon knew what was happening he had on a shirt three sizes too big that was smeared with pea green paint.

"Carol said pea green is a restful color for a kitchen. Let me tell you, it's so damn restful she won't cook or clean. I myself almost fell asleep twice while I was painting the ceiling. You take the woodwork and baseboards and I'll finish the walls. How's life in the mountains? Want a beer now, or should we wait till the sun's over the yardarm? Maybe we should eat first. What do you think, Simon?"

Simon pried open a can of semigloss paint. "Fanny went off somewhere to think. She didn't want me along. I'm having trouble dealing with that. I watched her drive off and didn't try to stop her. You've been married a lot longer than I have. Did Carol ever do anything like that?"

"She does it all the time. She goes into the bathroom and locks the door. She stays in there for hours. Once she stayed in there for a whole day. She can't afford to go off to a hotel. Women do things like that when life starts to overwhelm them. To this day I have never found out why she does what she does. When she finally comes out, we don't discuss it. What that means is she came to terms with whatever was bothering her in the first place. You need to stir that paint with gusto."

"I thought you knew everything there was to know about women since you've been married so long."

"No one knows everything about women. I seriously doubt if anyone knows *anything* about women. Maybe if you told me what happened prior to Fanny going off, I might be able to offer some small measure of insight, but don't count on it."

Simon told him. Jerry rocked back on his heels. "That's a motherhood thing. You don't ever, as in ever, mess with motherhood. Listen, let's forget this kitchen and go outside. I have *three* cases of beer and two hammocks. What'ya say?"

Simon slapped the lid on the paint can. He sealed it by bringing his heel down on the top of it. "I'm your man."

"Here we go," Jerry said, climbing into one hammock and indicating that Simon should climb into the other one. "If you want to lie down, you need to position your head just right on the pillow or the beer will dribble down your chin. Watch me so you don't screw up."

"Gotcha. Are you telling me there's nothing I can do or say?"

"The kids are off-limits and sacred. They aren't your kids. The fact is they aren't kids anymore at all. They're grown adults. For some reason that doesn't seem to matter to a mother. Fathers are different."

"Fanny is feeling guilty. Her family has always been her number one priority. She's had to be both mother and father to them all these years because Ash is . . . Ash."

"How is your brother, Simon?" Jerry uncapped two beers and passed one to Simon. "I think we can finish this off before the sun goes down. What's your opinion?"

"Do you have an outside bathroom?"

"Nope. Just aim for the bushes."

"Ash has taken over where Sunny is concerned. If there's anyone who knows about disabilities, it's Ash. I saw his face, Jerry, and this time I think he's on the level. I really think he wants to help his daughter. I want to believe he's being a genuine father this time around, and until someone can prove me wrong, I'll stick with my belief. Fanny is certain Ash is trying to get Sunny's trust monies. Sunny has always blown hot and cold where her father is concerned. She does love him, though, and that's how he got her to agree to seek help. He's going to be right at her side. My feeling, Jerry, is, what does it matter who gets her to go as long as she goes. I think Fanny is seeing it as a betrayal of some kind. The kids resent their mother marrying me on the one hand; the other hand is glad, or was glad that finally Fanny seemed happy. It's all screwed up." His voice was so weary, Jerry handed over another beer that Simon swigged from, almost emptying the bottle with one long gulp.

"Are you afraid Fanny will want to come back here to . . . you know, do that mother thing?"

"I'm not afraid. Hell, I understand that this might be very serious. Sunny doesn't want her here. That's what's bothering Fanny. These past three years we've been so locked into ourselves we didn't go back to Sunrise. Fanny only saw Jake when he was christened. Sunny pointed that out to her. Ash on the other hand has seen the kid a lot, and he genuinely likes the little guy. He did a number on Fanny when he gave Sunny a gift from long ago. I thought Fanny was going to bawl her head off."

"It's wrong to have competition between parents," Jerry singsonged. "If we were painting, we'd be done by now."

"Ask me if I care?" Simon tossed his empty beer bottle in the general direction of the bushes. He held out his hand for a refill.

"What are you going to do next?"

"Stay here with you. Fanny told me to go home. It's not home without her. Everything's under control. I'll buy the next load of beer, okay?"

"Sounds good to me. Carol won't be back till next week. We can throw our wet towels on the floor, not make our beds, leave dishes in the sink and . . . whatever else we want to do. We have to finish the kitchen before she gets back, though."

"Let's call someone to do that. My birthday present to you."

"I accept."

"Jer, who do you think she'll pick, me or the kids?"

"I keep telling you. They aren't kids. Wherever she is, she's probably thinking about how she can combine the two things. She's not going to make choices. Didn't you learn anything about hanging around with me when we were younger? You saw how my mother did things. When Fanny comes back, it will be just like Carol coming out of the bathroom. It will all be under control."

Simon's eyes rolled back in his head. "You must be some kind of saint. I want answers, explanations. How do you stand it?"

"It drives me damn near nuts. I have to stand it because if I don't, she goes back into the bathroom. She honest to God put a dead bolt on the inside and cemented the pins in the hinges so I couldn't take the door off. We have wire mesh on the bathroom window, too. What'ya think of that?"

"Jesus."

"Yeah. I love her though. It will work out, Simon."

"Do you really think so?"

"Yeah, I do. Fanny loves you. You love her."

"Jerry, remember when my father had his stroke and my mother . . ."

"That was different, Simon. Devin and your mother weren't married. You and Fanny are married. Your dad was no kid. It's not the same thing at all."

"I wonder where Fanny is right this minute?"

"She's someplace safe and sound, someplace normal, someplace where she can sit and think. All you have to remember is Fanny loves you. When she does come back, remember the bathroom and keep quiet."

"Okay, Jerry."

Fanny Thornton removed the key from the ignition. She sat for a long moment staring at the cottage nestled in the cottonwoods. The Devin and Sallie house of happiness. Sallie and Devin's retreat from the world—given to Fanny just weeks before her mother-in-law passed on. What was it Sallie had said? "Everyone needs a sanctuary at some time in their life. This will be yours. No one but Billie Coleman and Bess are to know you have this little house. Promise me, Fanny." And she had promised.

Many times over the past years she had come to this tranquil spot on the Arizona border to lick her wounds.

Fanny climbed from the car and knew instantly that Chue or one of his sons had been here recently to prune back the shrubbery and to mow the lawn. She found herself staring intently at the diamond-shaped windows. For one wild, crazy moment she thought she saw Sallie Thornton reflected in the shiny glass panes. A headache started to pound at the base of her skull as she pulled her overnight case and bag of groceries from the trunk of the car. All she wanted was to have a cup of coffee and sit on one of the wicker chairs on the small front porch.

The cottage was immaculate, as though someone had just recently cleaned it. One of Chue's sons had probably done the outside work while a daughter had cleaned inside. Fanny ran the tap water for a few minutes until the residue was gone and the water ran clean and pure.

While the coffee perked, Fanny carried her bag to the bedroom on the second floor that ran the entire length of the house. She sniffed, recognizing the faint scent of sagebrush. She lifted the heirloom spread to see crisply ironed sheets. One of Chue's daughters had definitely been here. Early on, Sallie had expressed a liking for ironed sheets, and Chue's family had obliged.

The small blue-and-white-tiled bathroom sparkled. Fanny washed her face and hands, irritated that she dropped water on the vanity, angry that she was using the pretty cornflower-colored towels. Right now she was angry with the world, with herself. The question was, what was she going to do about it? "I'm going to drink my damn coffee and sit on my front porch. After I do that I'm going to bed and sleep for twenty-four straight hours, at which point I will wake, make more coffee, and sit on the porch again." She burst into tears as she walked down the stairs. As she poured her coffee, she wondered where Simon was and what he was doing. They'd only been apart a few hours, and already she missed him. How lost and lonely he'd looked when she drove away. She knew in her gut it was a *pretend* lost-and-lonely look. She knew her husband too well these days. Was it a mistake to come here to a place with no telephone, television, or radio?

The headache continued to pound inside her head as she made her way to the front porch, kicking off her shoes as she went.

Her feet propped up on the banister, Fanny leaned back into the padded cushions. Now she could think about her family and Simon. And Ash.

"Please, God, in this tranquil setting, help me figure out where I went wrong." A moment later, the intense hammering inside her skull lessened and then was gone. Fanny heaved a sigh of relief as she sipped at the scalding hot coffee. Her thoughts traveled back in time as she gave in to the serenity that was all about her.

Surely in a week's time she would find the answers she was searching for.

"Iris, go back up the hill and call for an ambulance. Hurry! I'm going down the cliff."

Iris needed no second urging. She floored the gas pedal and roared up the steep grade.

Sage yanked at his jacket, tossing it on the ground as he prepared to make his descent down the steep mountainside to where his brother's car smoldered.

Chue's excited Chinese jabbering turned to English when he arrived on the scene. "I brought a rope as soon as I saw what happened. Is it Birch?"

"Yeah, it's Birch. He cut around me and took off. Tie the end of the rope to the tree. I can't see a thing."

"My wife called for an ambulance. It will take some time for it to get here. Go, go, you do not have much time. I will follow you as soon as I secure the rope," Chue said.

Sage was already halfway down the rope, barely feeling the rope burns to his hands. He prayed and he cursed. When his feet hit the ground, he ran to the car and managed to drag Birch away from the smoldering vehicle. There was no sign of Lily. The absence of glass in the windshield told him all he needed to know. How soon would the car explode? He had no idea. In the movies it always took a few minutes.

"Lily must have gone through the windshield on impact. She's not in the car!" he shouted to Chue. "Birch always wore his seat belt. I unbuckled him. Stay clear, it's going to blow."

When the explosion occurred, Sage covered his brother's body with his own. "If you aren't dead, Birch, I swear to God I'll kill you myself for pulling a stunt like that," he sobbed. He looked upward to see his family outlined in the eerie orange light at the top of the road. He could hear their excited voices but couldn't make out their words.

"I can't find a pulse, Chue. You try. I'm too . . . I'm too . . . find his pulse, Chue. Did you find Lily?"

"She's dead, Sage. I do not know this for a fact, but I think she died on impact. I pulled her as far away as I could. He's alive, but barely. His pulse is very weak."

"Tyler!" Sage roared, his voice carrying up the mountain.

"I'm here, Sage. I had to go to my car to get my medical bag. Please, stand back and let me do what I have to do."

"Lily's dead," Sage said.

"Then there's nothing we can do for her. Your brother is my concern right now. Don't go to pieces on me. Your family needs you up there," Tyler said, jerking his head upward. "You need to think about calling your mother and Simon."

"Yeah, yeah. Is he going to live, Tyler? That's all I want to know. Well, is he?"

"I don't know at this time. Let me do what I'm trained to do." A moment later he looked up and said, "I gave you a goddamn order. Obey it! Your family needs you. I'll stay with Birch until the ambulance gets here."

Sage did his best to scramble up the mountain, his leather-soled shoes slipping and sliding as he grappled with the rope for leverage, Chue behind him. The eerie sound of the far-off ambulance rang in his ears as it carried over the mountain.

They were all talking at once, their voices shrill with fear. Sage wanted to cry at the stricken look on his father's face. "I don't know anything. Birch is alive, but he's unconscious. Lily Bell is dead."

"I called the hospital the moment I heard the crash. John will have every specialist in town waiting. They're all standing by. It's going to be all right, Sage," Bess said, putting a comforting hand on his shoulder. In a whispered voice she said, "Your father needs you right now."

"He knows this mountain. I thought he respected it like the rest of us do. How could he have misjudged it?" Ash asked brokenly. "Will he make it, Sage?"

"Dad, I don't know. Tyler is not a man of many words. We need to be grateful a doctor is on the scene."

"Someone has to call Fanny. They should be back at the ranch by now."

"I tried. One of the workers picked up the phone in the kennel and said your mother and Simon aren't there and has no idea when to expect them. I tried calling Billie Coleman, but there was no answer in Washington or at the farmhouse in Vermont. I'll keep trying," Bess said

Sage nodded, his eyes on his two sisters. This wasn't real. He always did dream in color, horrible dreams that woke him up in the middle of the night. During childhood his mother had always comforted him and sat by his bed until he fell asleep. Now, Iris did the same thing. She had the same comforting touch, the same warm smile and gentle eyes as his mother. He wondered if he'd fallen in love with her because she reminded him so much of his mother. *This isn't real. This is just a bad dream and I'm going to wake up and Birch is going to say, "Ha, I fooled you, didn't I?"*

"You aren't dreaming, Sage. This is as real as it gets," Iris said as she reached for his hand. "Thank God Tyler was here."

"Lily's dead. They were going to get married. How's Birch supposed to handle that?"

"One day at a time. Here comes the ambulance. Honey, wheel your father away from the edge. Talk to him. He needs you right now."

Sage didn't know what frightened him more, the white-clad figures carrying their medical equipment or the flashing lights.

"Come on, Dad, we have to get out of the way. Birch is in good hands. All we can do now is pray. Do you know how to do that, Dad?"

The sadness in his father's voice drove shivers of fear up Sage's spine. "I don't know if God will listen to someone like me. He listens to people like your mother. Did anyone reach her?"

"Not yet, Dad. Mom always said God listens to all his children. I think the trick is not to ask for something for yourself. Always pray for others. You can't say things like, if You do this for me, I'll do that for You. I never thought about it too much, but I bet that's why Mom is who she is. She never asks for herself. She always puts other people first. That has to mean something."

"If you call the Highway Patrol and explain the circumstances, they should be able to get Simon's license plate number and put it out on the air. It's possible they stopped along the way. Your mother likes to take scenic routes when she's traveling. Do that, Sage. Fanny will be devastated when she finds out."

"Okay, Dad, I'll get on it as soon as they bring Birch up. I want . . . need to be here for my brother. Are you okay?"

"Christ no. How's Sunny holding up?"

"Billie's with her. Sunny's tough."

"It's all going wrong, Sage."

"You're reacting to the moment, Dad. This family is always embroiled in one crisis or another. Birch is as tough as Sunny. He's going to be okay. Hey, I'm his twin. I'd feel something if . . . you know."

"That's about the biggest bunch of bullshit I ever heard. This is me you're talking to, Sage."

"Do you want me to say I'm piss-assed scared? Okay, I am. That doesn't mean things won't be okay. All I keep thinking about is how Birch and I drifted apart these past years. We used to be joined at the hip. I guess life does that to you."

"Cut the crap, Sage. I'm the reason, and we both know it."

"Why are we having this conversation, Dad?"

"Because you're blaming yourself. I will not tolerate that, son. Birch isn't a kid. When you go out on the road or up in the air you take responsibility for yourself and those around you. If you learned that lesson, why didn't Birch? He liked to hotdog the roads, and now Lily is dead and he's . . ."

The lump Sage felt growing in his throat seemed to be getting bigger by the moment. He nodded, his eyes miserable.

"They're bringing him up! They're bringing him up!" Sunny screamed, her arms flapping every which way. She ran, her knees knocking together, to where her husband was standing. "How is he, Tyler? Is he okay? He isn't going to die, is he, Tyler? I hugged him, but I didn't kiss him good-bye. Say something, Tyler."

"Take your family back to the house, Sunny. It isn't good, okay. Don't upset your father. I'm going with the ambulance."

"We're all going. We'll follow you."

"I want you to stay here, Sunny."

"Do you really think I'm going to do that? That's my brother on the stretcher. We all have a right to know what's wrong. We want to be there, to be close. We can't find Mom, Tyler. What exactly does not good mean?"

"Internal injuries. He took a hell of a blow to the head. He's in shock, and he's unconscious. We'll do the best we can. Trauma units are standing by. I'll see you at the hospital."

They gathered close in a circle as Sunny relayed Tyler's words. "I'll go with Dad. Sage, take Bess and Billie with you and Iris. They're in no shape to drive."

"And you think Dad is? Let's all go in the van, and I'll drive."

"That's good. I'll tell Dad. He has a built-in phone so we can keep trying to call Mom while we go down the mountain."

"I'll go back to the house. Everyone tell me what you need, so we can leave right away. Purses, sweaters, anything else? I'll wake your housekeeper, Sunny, and tell her to sleep in the kids' rooms," Billie said.

"Hurry, Billie."

"Five minutes, Sunny. Get Dad in the van, and I'll be back by the time everyone is settled. Try Mom and Aunt Billie again."

Ten minutes later, Sage started up the van.

Sunny groped for her father's hand. Ash squeezed it reassuringly. "He's going to be okay, isn't he, Dad?"

"Of course he is. Birch is a Thornton. We're hardy stock. He's going to get the best care in the world. Whatever he needs we'll provide. We all need to think positively. We're together, and we're going to stay that way. I don't want to hear a negative word from anyone. Is that understood?"

"That's something Mom would say," Billie said, inching closer to her father. Ash's fingers closed around Billie's. A tear splashed on his hand. He wasn't sure if it was from Billie or himself.

"Your mother still isn't home. I've alerted the Highway Patrol and the local police. They'll alert every police department within a two-hundred-mile radius. We'll find her," Bess said. Under her breath she muttered, "When, I don't know."

"I don't understand Mom anymore. In the old days she never went anywhere without leaving a note or calling someone to say where she'd be in case of an emergency. They should have been home two hours ago. This new life of hers . . . I hate it. I just hate it."

Ash's voice was weary when he replied. "Everyone deserves a life, Sunny. You kids had your mother at your side all your life. Cut her some slack, for heaven's sake."

"That sounds very weird coming out of your mouth, Dad," Sunny said. "She doesn't have time for us anymore. That's what bothers me."

"You aren't children anymore. You're young adults and young adults are supposed to have their own lives and make their own decisions. I don't want to hear any negative talk when it comes to your mother. Wherever she is or whatever she's doing, I'm sure there's a reason for it. Your mother never does anything without a reason."

Sunny's voice turned stubborn and obstinate. "She should be here. If her plans changed, how much time would it have taken to inform someone? She doesn't want to be bothered with us anymore."

"That's not fair, Sunny, and you know it," Bess said. "I think I'll carry that one step farther and ask you why, when your mother and my husband asked you what was wrong with your health, you denied having any problems and told everyone to mind their own business. When a person hears that often enough they back off and don't keep asking. You were the one who didn't want to be bothered. You told your mother more than once that she was stepping over the line where your life was concerned. She did what you wanted, and you still aren't happy."

"It's not the same thing. This is Birch we're talking about."

"If your mother knew about your brother's accident, she would move heaven and earth to get here," Bess snapped.

"Bess is right, Sunny," Ash said. "Your mother is going to be found, and she'll come here as soon as she can."

"What if . . ."

"There are no what ifs. It will be just the way I said it will be. The only thing I cannot give you is the time and the place when it will happen."

"What if something happens to Birch?"

"Shut up, Sunny," Sage yelled from the driver's seat of the van.

"Don't tell me to shut up. Can't you see? It's all falling apart? First it was me. Now it's Birch and . . . Mom. Who's next? What's next, is more like it?"

"Enough!" Sage roared. "One more word, and I'm pulling this van to the side of the road. The next thing I'll do is muzzle you or dump you out. I mean it, Sunny, one more word and that's it." Sunny clamped her lips shut as her nails dug into her father's hand.

They drove the rest of the way in silence.

Sage drove the van to the front entrance of the Thornton Medical Center. He engaged the lift that would lower his father's wheelchair to the ground before the others exited. "The rest of you go in. Iris and I will park the van. We'll meet you inside."

"Smart-ass bastard," Sunny muttered.

"Dumb-ass bitch," Sage muttered in return. He held out his arms and Sunny stepped into them.

"I'm sorry. I'm worried sick. You know me and my mouth. What do you feel, Sage?"

"I don't feel anything. That's because Birch is in a place I can't reach. You gave us too much credit when we were kids. We weren't *that* tuned to one another. We just said we were to get on your nerves, and you bought into it."

"You're telling me this *now!*"

"Timing is everything," Sage said as he drove off.

Sunny straightened her shoulders before she took her position behind her father's chair. "Okay, everyone, it's going to be a long night. I suggest we get some coffee and settle in. First though, I'd like us all to go to the chapel for a few minutes. We need to . . . to make arrangements for . . . Lily. The police are notifying her half brother and sister. Is everyone okay with this?" The others nodded.

Hour after weary hour passed with only one update two hours after Birch was admitted. John Noble offered it on the run: Birch was critical and everything humanly possible was being done to save his life.

Sage paced. Ash dozed, either from weariness or the handful of pills he swallowed. Sunny, Billie, and Bess huddled on a blue-striped sofa that smelled of lemons and mothballs. From time to time Bess used the pay phone in the lobby to try and reach Fanny, with no success.

Time crawled by. Eventually the first violet shadows of dawn could be seen through the windows. "Why is it that terrible things always seem to happen at night when it's pitch-black outside?" Billie whispered. She continued to whisper. "When the sun is out and it's a bright day I feel like I can handle anything. It's been so long. Someone should have come out by now to tell us Birch's condition. God, I wish Mom was here. Lily had no family except her half sister and brother. They were such cold, unfeeling people. Don't pay attention to me, I'm just talking to hear my own voice because I'm so scared."

"We're all scared, honey," Bess said. "If talking helps you, go right ahead."

"I don't want to hear you babble," Sunny said.

"That's too bad. Maybe if you listened to the people around you, you wouldn't be in the position you're in right now," Billie said.

"What's that supposed to mean? That I'm stupid?"

"If the shoe fits, wear it. I don't want to fight with you, Sunny. I guess you had your reasons for playing stupid where your life is concerned, but I fail to see what they could possibly be. Another thing, I'd appreciate it if you'd leave Mom out of your fits of anger and remorse. Everyone in life who has half a brain has to take responsibility for their own actions, and that includes you."

Ash jolted awake. "This is not the time or the place for family bickering. There's no need to pick each other apart out of frustration."

"Dad's right," Sage said.

They heard the tap of John Noble's shoes before they saw him. His eyes were bloodshot, his hair stood on end. His jaw was grim and he needed a shave. He cleared his throat twice before he could speak. "We've managed to stop the internal bleeding. Birch was in surgery for four hours. Right now he's in the Intensive Care Unit. He's being monitored minute by minute. That's the good news. The bad news is he's lapsed into a coma. This happens sometimes. It could be temporary or it could be . . . a while. There is the possibility he won't come out of it. For now that's all I can tell you. I'm not going to lie to you. Birch is in critical condition. It can go either way. I know you want to see him, so you can follow me and look through the glass. Five minutes. Not one second longer. Then I want you all to go home. Get some sleep, eat something, shower, and then you can come back. That's the way we do things here. If there's anything you don't understand, tell me now. Good, follow me."

Bess lagged behind to stand next to her husband as the others pressed their hands against the glass partition. "Is that all of it, John?"

"That's all of it. You have to find Fanny, Bess."

"Is it that bad, John?"

"It's that bad. Right now his chances look like zip. He's young, he's healthy, he could fool all of us. Lily was D.O.A. They've taken her body to the morgue. I don't suppose you know if her half brother and sister are going to claim the body."

"I don't know. The police said they would notify them. I'll check with them later. They say when you go into a coma you go to a deep, dark place. I read that somewhere, John. The article said if you talk to the person you stand a good chance of bringing them out of it. We could take turns doing that. Sunny can talk for hours and hours. Should we do that?"

"Bess . . . everybody has a theory about comas. I'm a medical man. When the time comes . . . if it comes, and you want to talk to Birch, I certainly wouldn't stop you. I've read those same articles. Prayer is good. Concentrate on that right now, and finding Fanny."

"Fanny was so upset when she left. Simon probably suggested something on a whim and they probably followed that whim. What if . . ."

John kissed his wife on the cheek. "Time's up," he said quietly.

"They don't hear you," Bess whispered. "Can't you see? They're all inside that room with Birch? Those kids have always been tighter than feathers on a duck. Each one of them has taken on Birch's pain. Sage is dying inside. That's his big brother by seconds."

"We have to go," Ash said quietly.

"He's going to die. He is, isn't he? Doctors never tell you the truth." A second later Sunny broke formation and entered the room. She flung herself across the bed, sobbing heartbrokenly. "Wake up, Birch. Please, you have to wake up. They're going to yank me out of here any minute. I don't care. I had to talk to you. Both of us can't go down. What will the others do if we both die? This is just a silly old accident. My stuff is worse, I know it is. You know Sage, he pretends to be tough, but he's all mush. He needs you. Billie needs you. Dad can't run the casino without you. Mom won't be able to handle it. Are you listening to me, Birch? Wake up. I want you to wake up right now. Please, Birch, do it for me. I swear I'll never say a cussword again. I'll do everything you say. Damn you, Birch, wake up! Everybody here is pulling for you. You can do it. We need you. Listen to me, Birch, if I go, and I know I have something really bad so that means I'm going to . . . you need to be here for the others. They all think I'm stupid for not going to the doctors earlier. I knew way back then. I know now. You're the lucky one because the doctors can fix you up. People recover from car crashes all the time. What I have can't be fixed. Are you listening to me, Birch?"

"He can't hear you, Sunny," John said as he gently led her from the room.

Sunny shook off his arm. "You don't know that. You can't crawl inside his head. I don't want to hear that. This place is supposed to be a medical marvel. Guess what, you better start doing some marvelous things. Don't you dare let my brother die. Do you hear me?"

"I hear you, Sunny. Now, I want you to hear me. If you ever pull another stunt like that, I'll bar you from this entire floor."

Sunny turned around. "You don't understand. I had to talk to him. I had to. I know you don't understand, and I don't care that you don't understand. I didn't jeopardize my brother's health. I know he heard me. I felt it deep inside me. I don't expect you to understand that either. No, you won't bar me from this floor. I won't allow it. I know you mean well and I mean well, so we're going to have to meet somewhere in between. I own one quarter of this medical center." She raised a shaky finger to point to Sage and Billie and then at Birch's room. "That's the other three quarters. Four quarters make a whole. If it comes to a vote. I know you think your way is best, but you could be wrong. Maybe my way is best because I love Birch, and he knows I love him. That has to count somewhere. That's my brother in there. Just so you know, Dr. Noble. Come on, guys, time to take Dad home. We'll come back later."

"Guess she told you, huh? Would you really bar her from the floor?" Bess whispered.

John Noble looked uncomfortable. "Let me put it this way. I'd try to reason with her."

Bess smiled wanly. "The four of them would shut this place down in a heartbeat just the way Fanny shut down Las Vegas. They are their mother's children, and that's their brother lying in there." John cringed at the reminder. "What in the name of God was she saying in there?"

"You don't want to know, Bess. Take them home and bring me some clean clothes. Toss in an egg salad sandwich, too. Put those little seeds in it, okay?"

"Take care of him, John."

John nodded. "Find Fanny and find her quick. Bess, you know those prayers you say every night on your knees by the bed, say some extra ones, okay?"

Bess nodded as she blew her husband a kiss. "I'll do my best."

9

Simon groaned when he saw the flashing lights of the police cruiser in his rearview mirror. "Shit!" Instead of slowing down, his right foot pressed harder on the gas pedal. He knew it was a stupid thing to do, but he did it anyway. Like he could outrun a police car in his drunken condition. He cursed Jerry for talking him into going to the market for more beer. He knew better than to get into a car when he was drunk. He was about to get out of the car when he heard one of the officers bark an order. "Stay in your vehicle, sir, and roll down your window."

Sir? Simon fumbled in his pocket for his wallet before he realized he'd just taken a twenty-dollar bill off the kitchen counter, change from their last Chinese delivery order. Drunk and driving without a license and vehicle registration. They'd lock him up and throw away the key.

Simon saw himself reflected in the officer's polished sunglasses. He looked like death warmed over, his hair was on end, and he hadn't shaved or showered in four days. He knew he smelled like a distillery

The first officer reached inside the car door and placed both his hands on Simon's shoulders. "Mr. Thornton, there's been an accident and you're wanted at the medical center. Get cleaned up and we'll drive you there."

"Oh, not Fanny. Tell me it isn't Fanny. What . . . who . . . how?"

"It's your nephew, Birch. He was in a serious automobile accident. Do you know how we can locate his mother?"

"I don't know where she is. She said . . . she was going somewhere

to think about some . . . family matters. That's why I'm here. I'm waiting. She didn't want me around when she was doing her thinking.
How bad is Birch?"

"You need to talk to his doctors. Follow us, Mr. Thornton, while
I radio this in."

Simon grappled with his drunkenness as his mind registered the
fact that Fanny was safe but her son was injured and in critical condition. He drove carefully, his eyes on the cops' taillights.

At the medical center, the family descended on him like a swarm
of locusts. "Where's Mom? Where's Fanny?"

"I don't know. Is there any change?"

"What do you mean you don't know?" Ash snarled. "How can
you not know where your wife is, for God's sake?"

Simon's insides started to rumble. "She said she was going off to
think, and she wanted to be alone. Do you really think I could have
stopped her? She wanted me to go back to the ranch, but I elected
to stay here and wait for her because she was so devastated when
we started down the mountain. It was what she wanted, Ash, what
she needed to do."

"And this is the result," Ash snarled again. "Birch could die,
Simon. What's that going to do to Fanny if she isn't here?"

"Ash, you can't blame Fanny. Sage put her rental car plate out on
the wire. Someone will see it, and she'll be here before you know it."

"What in the goddamn hell did she have to think about? That's
all she ever does, think, think, think. Don't even think about giving
me that crap about me getting Sunny to a doctor either. If she was
the mother she always claimed to be, she would have dragged Sunny
off three years ago. Oh, no, she ups and marries you and forgets all
about her children. I'm sorry, Simon. I'm all wound up. Forget all
that stuff I just said, okay? Wait just a minute here. If Fanny went off
to think, that means there's a problem between you and her. Aha,
now it makes sense. So, there's trouble in Paradise, eh?"

"If you weren't in a wheelchair, I'd flatten you right here and now.
Once an asshole always an asshole," Simon grated as he walked
away.

In the coffee shop, with a steaming cup of coffee that tasted like
real coffee, Simon fought the urge to cry. His shoulders started to
shake when he felt a gentle hand. "Simon, is it really you?"

"Bess. God, a normal person. Please, sit down. Talk to me in that
sane, sensible voice of yours. I just had a go-round with Ash."

"Is Fanny upstairs?"

"I don't know where Fanny is." He repeated his story for Bess's benefit. "Where would she go, Bess? For all I know she could be holed up in any one of the hotels in town. Or, she could be in the mountains sleeping in the car. Sage put her plate out on the wire. I have no clue. You know her, where would she go?"

Bess shrugged as she stared into Simon's eyes. They were so blank she felt afraid. "I've called everywhere. Billie and Thad didn't go back to Washington. I thought the four of you went off somewhere. This is like Fanny, but at the same time it's unlike her. The kids are right, though, Fanny never goes anywhere without telling someone where she can be reached. So, I guess her getting away must have something to do with the two of you."

"Until she married me. Her going away was because of Sunny. Don't make a federal case out of nothing, Bess. Thad took Billie to Hawaii. It was a last minute trip and a surprise."

"Yes, until she married you. Wait a minute! I think I have an idea. I might be wrong, but I don't think so. You wait here, Simon."

Simon stared at Bess's back as she raced from the coffee shop. Five minutes later he saw and heard her car screech out onto the main road. He gulped at the lukewarm coffee, his hands trembling so badly he could barely hold the cup. Had Fanny confided her unhappiness to Bess, to Billie Coleman?

Fanny stared at the bird's nest in the cottonwood. For days now she'd been mentally willing the mother bird to leave the nest. She'd even tried whispering to the mother bird, who stared at her, which was strange in itself. The bird wasn't afraid of her. Maybe it had something to do with the plate of worms she'd dug in the soft earth under the overhang. She thought the babies were ready to fly, but then, what did she know about birds?

"What I do know is if you coddle them too long, they'll never be independent and they'll hang on your tail feathers forever. Just do it and they'll follow you. They trust you. That's what motherhood is all about, you know. Trust is a two-way street where children are concerned. Children trust you to raise them right, to do right by them to the best of your ability, and a parent has the right to expect love and respect and trust, in that order. It's not that way with husbands and wives, though, and I don't know why that is. Another thing, that nest isn't big enough for all of you. Go on, fly. I'll tell you what, I'll go down off the porch and if it looks like they're in trouble, I'll catch them." Fanny didn't feel silly at all for talking to a bird or walking down the steps to see if her intuition was correct. She waited patiently as the mother bird finally perched on the edge of the nest, her wings rustling anxiously in the quiet morning air.

"Do it," Fanny whispered. She watched, hardly daring to breathe as the mother bird fanned her wings over the nest, lifting each little bird with the tip of her wing. Fanny felt the moistness in her eyes as each baby bird took wing. She laughed aloud as the mother bird took to the air, her right wing dipping slightly. Fanny offered up a snappy salute. "Anytime. Your job isn't over yet," she called. "You need to watch over them even if it's from a distance." Would they come back? Probably not. "It's supposed to be this way," Fanny murmured.

Fanny sat for hours on the porch, her eyes scanning the blue sky for a sign of the birds. A wave of sadness swept over her. They didn't need her or the worms she'd dug for them. They were off on their own, soaring high above the trees.

Maybe it was time to go back. Time to join the real world again. Time to call her children to tell them she loved them, time to make decisions where Simon was concerned. It was time.

She could be on the road in thirty minutes once she packed her bag, cleaned out the refrigerator, and gathered up her trash. She could stop at the first convenience store she came to and call Simon to tell him she was on her way. If she hurried and drove the speed limit, she could be back at the ranch by dark.

She heard the car, the sound of the horn, and then she saw a spiral of dust swirl upward. Company? Chue? Who?

"Bess! What are you doing here? How did you know I was here? Something's wrong. Tell me. What, Bess, what happened?"

"Fanny, sit down. We've been looking for you for four days. The police found Simon. He's been staying at Jerry's house. He didn't go back to the ranch the way you asked him to. He waited for you. It's Birch, Fanny. His car went off the mountain the night of the christening. Lily died in the accident and . . . Birch . . . Birch is in a coma. My suggestion would be to leave your car and have Chue and one of his boys come for it."

"Let me get my purse and key to lock the door."

Bess's breath exploded in a loud sigh. Had she expected tears? She knew a thing or two about glazed eyes and shock.

Fanny locked the door. "There were these birds, Bess, a mother and her babies . . ."

Bess listened until Fanny wound down. "Listen to me. Everyone is . . . upset. That's understandable. They're angry with you because you didn't say where you were going. Simon and Ash had words this morning. It isn't going to be easy, Fanny. Even if you'd been there, there was nothing you could do. There's nothing anyone can do. Everything medically that could be done has been done. Birch is in other hands now. Do you understand what I'm saying, Fanny?"

"Yes. How did it happen?"

Bess told her. "Sage pulled him out. Tyler was on the scene within minutes. I'm not going to lie to you, Fanny. It isn't good."

"They're all blaming me, aren't they?"

"In a manner of speaking. They're upset. You can see the terror on their faces. Ash is . . . inconsolable. Sunny flips out on the hour. Billie seems to be holding up fairly well. Sage is just angry. He's so stiff he looks brittle. He's not saying much. He just sits there and I know he's roll-calling every minute of his and Birch's life. You have to be strong, Fanny, and pull your family together before they destroy each other."

"What is John saying, Bess? Were specialists called in?"

"Of course. The best of the best, from all parts of the country. They've all concurred and they've all agreed, nothing more can be done. Your son is in other hands now, Fanny."

"A coma isn't good."

"People come out of comas all the time. Everyone, including John, thought Birch would come out of his after seventy-two hours, but he didn't. He's being monitored minute by minute. Pneumonia looms on the horizon so they're trying to guard against that. It could be turning around as we speak. Medical marvels happen every day of the week."

"I don't think I could bear it if something happened to Birch. How did Billie Coleman handle Riley's death? He was her only son. She told me once that a part of her heart, the part that was reserved for Riley, was missing. Can't you drive any faster, Bess?"

"Of course I can drive faster, but I'm not going to."

Fanny's voice was a low, hushed whisper when she said, "Bess, do you ever wonder, ever question God as to why certain people seem to get so much pain and grief in their lives and other people just go about their business and never experience a moment of anxiety? I've never understood why it's like that."

"Fanny, let's not get into that right now. Let's just say God acts in mysterious ways and let it go at that. My mother always said you never question God nor do you make bargains with Him."

"I find myself wondering what I did wrong. First Ash, then Sunny, and now Birch. Maybe I wasn't supposed to marry Simon. Maybe I'm not supposed to be happy. Why can't I cry, Bess?"

"Because you're numb. Crying just makes your eyes red and ugly. Remember how my mother used to tell us that all the time? It's true."

"I don't feel anything. It's as if someone took away my insides and the rest of me is just a shell. I can walk and I can talk, but I can't feel."

"Why did you go to the cottage, Fanny?"

"I had to do some hard thinking. Mostly about Sunny. I knew if I didn't get it all straight in my head, I would start to cover myself in guilt. I don't want to live with guilt. I had to do some thinking about Simon, too. We didn't have that talk, did we, Bess? I know now I was wrong. I never should have allowed Simon to dictate to me. I stepped over the line where Sunny was concerned. I have to find a way to make it right. At one point, early on, Tyler more or less, without actually coming out and saying the words, implied that Sunny was playacting to get attention. He worked long hours and she was alone a lot and there was trouble with Ash. Three doctors said they couldn't find anything wrong with her. John felt as I did, but we couldn't drag her wherever we thought she should go. Did John ever tell you Sunny told him if he didn't get out of her life she'd get her brothers and sister to agree to remove him from the staff?"

"No, he never told me that."

"Well she did. John backed off just the way I did. I wish you had a phone in this car so I could call the center. Does . . . Birch have a lot of tubes in him?"

"Uh-huh. He's hooked up to a lot of machines. It's frightening at first when you see them until you realize they're keeping him alive. Like John says, Birch is young, he's healthy, and he's a fighter."

"And he's in a coma."

There didn't seem to be any comment to Fanny's statement. Bess drove on in silence.

A long time later, Bess said, "I'll drop you off in front and park the car. ICU is on the fifth floor."

Fanny pressed the elevator button. *Your firstborn son will break your heart.* Fanny whirled around, certain she'd heard Sallie's voice. *You need to be strong, Fanny. Not for the others, for yourself.*

Inside the elevator, Fanny pushed the number 5. When the door closed, she whispered, "Are you here, Sallie? You are. I can feel your presence. Does that mean you're here to take . . . my son? Tell me, please." When there was no response to her plea, Fanny's shoulders slumped, then squared immediately when the doors of the elevator slid open to reveal her family in the small waiting area. No one rose to their feet, no one greeted her except Simon, who held out his hand. *You need to be strong, Fanny. Not for the others, for yourself.*

"Where is he, Simon? I want to see him."

"Ten minutes on the hour, Fanny. It's the rule."

"Then break the damn rule. I want to see my son."

"The second door on the right," Simon said.

Fanny heard the whirring sound of Ash's wheelchair. She turned in time to hear him hiss, "What the hell makes you so damn special? You abide by the rules, that's what makes this place work. We've been sitting here for four days with two and a quarter minutes each every hour. Suddenly the Queen of the Mountain decides to show up and claim the time for herself. It doesn't work that way, Fanny. Sit down."

"You're absolutely right, Ash. I'm sorry. Will they let me look through the glass?"

"No."

"Can I get you something to drink, Fanny?" Simon asked, his hand tight on her arm.

"No. Have you seen him, Simon?"

"For a few minutes. I didn't want to take the time away from the kids and Ash. He looks like he's sleeping. Ash is in charge, Fanny. From what I've seen, it's not a bad thing. I'll go get us some coffee while you talk to him. He needs to talk to you."

Fanny walked over to Ash. "It's twenty minutes to the hour. That gives us twenty minutes. Can we talk? Someplace other than here. The end of the hall looks empty."

Fanny walked alongside the whirring wheelchair. "Ash, I'm sorry about before. I just wanted to see him right away. I want you to tell me the truth. How is he? Has there been any change since the first day?"

"Absolutely no change at all. I don't know how he is, Fanny. The doctors don't say much. You know how doctors are. Tyler and John keep us updated hourly. It's as though he's in a deep sleep. Birch was always a deep, sound sleeper. Remember that time we rang a bell in his ear and he didn't move a muscle?" Ash's voice cracked then. Fanny placed a comforting hand on his shoulder.

"I remember. So many memories. All of them good with the exception of a few, and they don't matter."

"What will we do, Fanny, if he doesn't make it?"

"I don't know, Ash. I guess you go on because you don't have a choice. Just pray that doesn't happen."

"Do you seriously think God's going to listen to me? Give me a break."

"You don't know that He won't. Let's go to the chapel. It's just around the corner."

"I can't remember the words. It's been so long since I prayed."

"I know the words. I'll say them aloud and you can repeat them after me. When it's down to the wire, it's all that's left to any of us." Fanny reached for Ash's hand. He grasped it gratefully.

"Fanny, the kids . . . I want you to know I didn't say a word to them. I told them you'd be here. I tried to do what you would have done if you'd been here. I admit I'm a pretty poor substitute, but I did my best. We pulled together. Sunny went off the deep end for a little while, but she's back on track now. I don't want to see you trying to cuddle up to them. They'll turn on you. You have a right to your life, and I told them so. If they don't understand that or if they refuse to accept it, it's their problem."

Fanny nodded as she guided Ash into the small chapel. She lowered her voice "Ash, about Sunny, I want to thank you for getting through to her. It stung a little at first, but I'm okay with it. I did desert her, and I did neglect her. I'll find a way to try and make it right. I want you to know that."

"Do you think I don't know that? We got down and dirty and pulled it all out. Do you know what her defense is?"

"I can't even begin to imagine."

Ash cleared his throat. "Sunny said she wanted to be perfect like you. She refused to believe her symptoms were anything but, as she put it, pregnancy and new mother pains. Ignore it and it will go away was her philosophy. I don't want you to have regrets, Fanny. You were and still are a wonderful mother. I was and probably still am a lousy father. You can cry in here. Everyone does. I see them when they come out. I come in here once a day and just sit."

"She said that?" Fanny wailed. "Do you cry, Ash?"

"Yeah. Yeah, I do. There was some guy in here the other day bawling his head off. I tried to offer him some comfort. I told him about my accident and about Birch. Turns out he's the top surgeon here. He operated on a ten-year-old boy and lost him on the operating table. When he was leaving, he said something Mom always used to say, God never gives you more than you can handle. I'm ready to pray if you are."

"Our father who art . . ."

Simon quietly withdrew from the doorway. His features were so tormented he didn't see Bess until he bumped into her. "I don't think it means what you think it means, Simon. Parents tend to stick together in situations like this."

Simon nodded. "Do they hold hands and pray together? I'm asking because I've never been in a situation like this before. Maybe I should leave. I feel like I'm in the way."

"Do whatever feels right. There's no protocol in matters like this. I'll take that coffee if you aren't going to drink it." Simon handed over the plastic cup. Out of the corner of his eye he saw Ash and Fanny coming down the hallway.

"You can have my time, Fanny. I'll sit here and talk to Simon and Bess." Fanny flew down the hall.

Inside the dim, cool room, Fanny was only aware of her son. The machines, the tubes, the beeping sounds didn't exist. She reached out to touch Birch's hand, certain the words she was searching for would be forthcoming. Her mouth was dry, her tongue felt as if it were two sizes too big for her mouth. She realized then that there were no special words. In the end all she could do was let the tears roll down her cheeks and whisper, "I'm here, Birch."

"I know. I smelled your perfume when you walked in."

Fanny threw her head back as she bit down on her lower lip. Her tears continued to flow. *Thank you, God.*

"Oh, Birch, you're talking. How long have you been awake?"

"I don't know. Is it important?"

"Probably not."

"I had this bad dream that I was in a deep, dark hole, like a well of some kind and Sunny kept yelling and yelling. She wouldn't stop. Dad and Billie started to pull me out, and I kept slipping back. Then I smelled your perfume so I knew they must have pulled me out and I was okay." A second later he was asleep.

Fanny ran from the room and was almost run over by the team of doctors and nurses. "He's awake. He talked to me. Birch talked to me. He fell asleep again, but he's okay. Oh, Ash, Birch is going to be okay. I know it. I feel it."

"What did he say? Mom, tell us everything," Sunny squealed.

Fanny told them, word for word. "He smelled my perfume. Can you imagine?"

"See! See! I told you if you talk to coma patients they hear you. That's all I did. I yelled at him. I did and said everything I could think of. Sage did the same thing. Birch thought he was dreaming, but he wasn't—he was struggling to come out of that dark place. It worked. Did you believe me? No, you did not. From now on you will all listen when I tell you something. He didn't say anything else, did he?" Sunny asked.

"Only what I told you."

"I think those prayers worked," Ash said as he reached for Fanny's hand. Fanny clasped it tightly in both her hands. Simon left quietly and walked down the corridor to the elevator. He wished he was a kid again so he could crawl into a corner and suck his thumb. For the first time in his life he felt truly displaced.

10

Fanny looked at the kitchen clock and then at the calendar. It was hard to believe thirty days had passed since Birch's accident. Today he was coming home and tomorrow she was going back to the ranch, back to Simon. Her adrenaline started to flow at the thought of what would happen when she saw her husband again. Struggling to keep the conversation going on the phone twice a day was something she didn't want to think about. She wondered again, and not for the first time, how she'd managed to survive in this chrome-and-glass modern penthouse apartment that was Ash's home. She sipped at her coffee as she looked around. There wasn't one single thing in the kitchen that said anyone actually lived here. There wasn't a fingerprint anywhere on the shiny glass and chrome. There were no colorful chair cushions, no green plants, there wasn't even a window to decorate with curtains. She hated it, hated the bouncy chrome chair and the glass-topped table that tilted if you propped your elbows on it. Nor did she like looking at her feet through the glass tabletop.

Fanny heaved a mighty sigh. Tomorrow she'd be back at the ranch, back in her cozy kitchen with the red-checkered curtains and matching cushions on the worn, scarred oak chairs she'd found in an antique store. She wondered if Simon had watered the plants in the kitchen, the plants that she nurtured so tenderly. Of course he hadn't. Simon never did anything unless it affected him in some way. There would be mounds of dirty dishes in the sink. Her plants would be yellow and wilted. There would be dust on all the furniture. The same sheets would probably still be on the bed.

Right now, this very second, she knew Simon was sitting in his rocker by the fieldstone fireplace with his feet propped on the hearth, reading the paper, the small kitchen television set on the counter turned low. He'd be listening with one ear, muttering about excessively cheerful people at six in the morning.

Today was the most important day of her long stay. Ash and Sunny would be back from Johns Hopkins, Birch would be home, and she'd finally get to pack her bags in preparation to going home. Maybe, if things went well, she could leave later in the day and surprise Simon. Would he be surprised? She dreaded the trip because it was time to make decisions. Time to take charge of her life. Time to tell Simon the way it was going to be from now on.

Fanny wandered into the living room and turned on the television set. She watched an early-morning rerun of *Mannix*. All problems solved in sixty minutes allowing for commercial breaks. Life should be so simple and wonderful.

She hated this place. Truly hated it. She would shrivel up and die if she had to live in this shiny, forever-light place. She snorted when she remembered asking Ash if the windows could be opened. He'd stared at her as if she'd sprouted a second head and said, "Why would you want to open the windows when you have air conditioning?" Maybe the word hate wasn't strong enough. She needed to think of other things.

Her eye fell on the stack of mail on the glass-topped table. A funeral home thank-you card from Lily Bell's half sister and brother. "We appreciate your family's kindness during our bereavement." Signed, Anna and Paul Bell. How sad that there was no warmth, no smiles, no anything. They'd all gone to the funeral, paying for it as well. Sage had ordered the stone, closed the bookstore, and filed all the necessary papers. All Lily's assets would eventually be turned over to Anna and Paul. It had been a bad time for all of them. Birch had been stone-faced when he listened to the details. It was only later that Sage had told his mother what happened the night of the accident. Shy, quiet Lily had instigated a fight the moment they got into the car because Birch had told her he was having second thoughts about marriage and wanted to cool their relationship until he could get a better perspective on his feelings. Lily had grabbed the wheel and told Birch to pull over so they could settle it right then and there. He lost control and the car went over the side.

Birch, Sage said, would carry his guilt for a very long time. He would require several months of therapy, fresh air, and good food. He would mend. Would he ever be the same old Birch? Fanny simply didn't know. What she did know was she'd been there for her son, twenty-four hours a day once he came out of his coma. Not because of some misguided sense of guilt, but because she wanted to be with her son, to encourage him, to be there for him. It had taken its toll on her, though. She was hollow-eyed, and she'd lost eight pounds. Birch was on the road to recovery. She said a prayer that Sunny would be as fortunate. In just a few hours she'd know the outcome of all of Sunny's testing. In one hour the results would be in and then Ash and Sunny would fly home. A celebratory luncheon at Sage and Iris's house was scheduled for noon.

How was she to while away the hours until noon? Maybe she should go shopping and fix this place up. Ash would probably throw a fit if she tried to create a homey atmosphere in the penthouse. She shuddered when she thought of the shimmery, quilted black bedspread. She'd ripped the black satin sheets off in the blink of an eye and added cornflower blue flannel ones because Ash kept the temperature at 60 degrees and threatened to cut off her fingers if she played with the thermostat.

Fanny scratched the whole idea of changing the apartment and opted for a bubble bath instead. She could bring in the portable phone and have a risqué conversation with Simon while she soaked. Provided Simon was in the mood for a risqué conversation, which he probably wasn't.

Fanny walked into Sage's house at ten minutes of twelve. "It's good to see you, Fanny," Iris said, hugging her. Sage kissed her lightly on the cheek.

"Where's Birch?" Fanny asked.

"Drinking a cold beer on the patio. He wants to sit in the sun and get some of his color back. Iris is going to fatten him up in no time. He's a little jittery, and he isn't talking too much. I guess that's normal considering what he's gone through. Can I get you a soft drink?"

"Sure, honey. Iris, can I help?"

"It's under control. I'm just so happy I have the day off. Later I'm going to scrub the kitchen and bathroom. I miss doing all those things, believe it or not. I guess underneath it all I'm just a home-body like my mother. I can't wait to have a baby. Sage and I want a whole houseful of kids," she blurted. Fanny laughed.

"You're sure there's nothing I can do?"

"I'm positive. I'm trying to show off a little for my husband. He thinks of me as a bookworm."

"Then I guess I'll keep my son company for a little while."

Fanny sat down across from Birch. "It's a beautiful day, isn't it?"

"There were days when I didn't think I'd make it. I think I . . . no, I know I now have a healthy respect for what Dad endures every day. I have a long road ahead of me, but I'll make it. I have this guilt about Lily. Everything was fine that day until Sunny said something, and for the life of me I can't even remember what it was she said, and suddenly, everything changed for me. Lily knew it, too, because she got really quiet. What does that make me, Mom?"

"It makes you human. It was a tragic accident with tragic consequences."

"How was the funeral?"

"It was a funeral, Birch. You have to put it behind you and go on."

"I guess so. Mom, I've been thinking about something. Promise me you won't laugh when I tell you, okay?"

"I promise."

"I want to leave here when the doctors discharge me. I need to find my own way. I'm sick of the casino business, sick of never see-ing sunlight. Sage found his niche, and now it's time for me to find mine. One of the therapists told me about this place in Oregon where I could commune with nature, and from there work into a trail guide. I think I need to do something like that. At least for a little while. Sage and I drifted apart these last few years. I always thought we'd be in-separable forever. I've learned nothing is forever. I don't think I'll ever take anything for granted again."

"It sounds like you've learned a lot in the past thirty days, Birch."

Birch threw his head back and laughed, a pure sound of magical mirth. Fanny smiled. "Life is just full of surprises."

"How do you think Dad will take it when I tell him?"

"I don't know. You can't worry about that, Birch. Each of us has to find our own way, and each of us has to do whatever it takes to find the right path. I think he'll understand."

"I hope so. I want to thank you, Mom, for staying on. Do you know you gave me twenty-seven pep talks in one day? I counted." It was Fanny's turn to laugh.

Iris set a tray of cheese puffs on the patio table. "Your dad and Sunny just drove up. More glasses and more cheese puffs coming up."

"She's perfect for Sage. I've never seen him so happy and content. He can't wait to become a father. You like Iris, don't you, Mom?"

"I adore her. You're right. She's perfect for Sage."

"Wanna hear something funny, Mom? I never . . . I don't like Tyler. I have a feeling that if Sunny's news isn't good, he's going to bail out on her. Sunny and I talked about it once. She said before that happens, she'd beat him to it. When I wasn't worrying about myself, I was worrying about her. She's going to need a real strong guiding hand. I might go back to school and take some forestry courses."

Fanny looked up at the sound of Ash's chair making its way to the patio. *He looks exhausted,* she thought. She could feel her heart jump up into her throat when he reached for one of the cheese puffs. "Where's Sunny?"

"In the kitchen with Iris and Billie. She pulled up right behind us. She's telling them her version. I'll tell you mine. We have a diagnosis as of seven o'clock this morning. Sunny has multiple sclerosis. They tested her out the kazoo. The doctors arrived at their diagnosis by a process of elimination. Right up front I want to tell you it is not good when a young person gets the disease. For some reason it hits them harder than it would if they were struck down later in life. I believe the confirming factor was the elevation of her gamma globulin. As I said, they gave her every neurological test there was. She has a thinning of the myelin sheath covering the nerves. They thought that was very conclusive. When that happens you don't get flexibility. As I said, the disease is very progressive in young people."

"What . . . what's the treatment?"

"There is no treatment, Fanny. They're working on it, but they haven't got it yet. Dietary changes, fresh air, moderate exercise, that kind of thing. She could go along for years the way she is right now. Each attack seems to last longer and take more of a toll. Eventually she'll be in a wheelchair. She'll be able to do things for herself for now. When that is no longer possible, there's a facility in Texas that helps the more severe patients. The doctors were very blunt because Sunny was very blunt. She wanted everything spelled out, all the T's crossed, all the I's dotted. She handled it very well, so well in fact, she called Tyler and told him she wanted a divorce."

"Ash, don't say that," Fanny gasped.

Ash snorted. "That was the good part. The bad part was Tyler said okay."

"I don't believe this! Tyler was probably just humoring her."

"No, Fanny, he wasn't humoring her. She said they haven't shared the same bed since she got pregnant this last time. She said he's never home, doesn't call, and she told me yesterday he had an offer of a job in New York. He didn't tell her. She went through his mail."

"Didn't I tell you, Mom? If I was in better shape, I'd kill the son of a bitch!" Birch growled. "Sage, you need to have a talk with our brother-in-law, and if you feel the need to beat the shit out of him, give him a jab for me."

"To what end? Isn't it better if she gets rid of him now? Iris said it's important for women to do the dumping. With Sunny's condition, I can understand what she's doing. I will have a talk with him, though. When he walks away, I want him to know that we all know what a shit he is. What about the kids?"

"I don't think they got that far in the discussion," Ash said.

"I don't believe this," Fanny said.

"You keep saying that, Fanny. Why is it so hard to believe Tyler is a son of a bitch?"

"Because I thought you were the only son of a bitch in these parts," Fanny snapped. "Tyler was so good with Sallie when she was sick. He loves Sunny. He told me so."

"Guess he loves his career more. Why are you so surprised, Fanny? Didn't you do the same thing to me in a manner of speaking?"

"No, Ash, I did not. You have no right to even think such a thing much less say it, and you know it. Our marriage was over long before your accident. I did everything I could for you."

"Yes, you did, Fanny, and I'm sorry for shooting off my mouth. You did more than I had any right to expect. I've gotta tell you, Sunny's holding up better than I could have under the circumstances."

"I'm concerned about the children."

"He'll give them up. Trust me on that one," Birch said.

"My God, what's happening to this family?" Fanny said through clenched teeth.

"Hi, everybody! Did Dad tell you everything?"

"Yes. Yes, he did. Is there anything we can do?"

"Not a thing. It's such a relief to finally know what it is. I can handle this. As Dad said, I'm fortunate to be in a position where I can hire help and oversee them. If and when I have to go to Texas for periods of time, I can afford it. Most people can't. I'm blessed in that respect. C'mon, c'mon, this is a good day. Birch is home, he's recovering, we have a handle on me and we're together. Ah, I see Dad told you about Tyler. What can I say? It's better for both of us. He has his career to think about, and I do not want to be a burden to him or anyone else. I am really okay with this. I want you to believe me. Tyler and I have not . . . most of the pain is gone. I'm adjusted to life alone. You guys aren't going to stew and fret about me, are you?"

"Of course we are," Fanny said.

"Then you'll be spinning your wheels for nothing. Give me some credit, Mom, I'm not exactly stupid. So I didn't try to find out what it was earlier. It was my choice. It wouldn't have made one bit of difference. It is what it is."

"That's the right attitude, Sunny," Ash said, reaching for her hand.

"Dad had his tests, too. Unfortunately, his won't be back for another week. Iris is calling us, which means it's time to eat. Eat fast, Dad, I want to get home to see the kids."

"I can drive you home, Sunny. Your dad looks tired," Fanny said.

"No, no, that's okay. I can wait. Maybe you should shower and take a nap before we leave. It might be a good idea for me to do the same thing. Thanks for offering, Mom," Sunny said as an afterthought.

Fanny wanted to cry. She would have if Sage hadn't squeezed her arm. "Sunny's right, it is what it is. Just let it be."

Fanny drew a deep breath. "Okay."

"Sage, hold on a minute," Birch said as he struggled out of his chair. "If you have a minute, I'd like to talk to you." Fanny lingered inside the doorway as Sage walked back to his brother.

"I have as many minutes as you need. What's up?"

"I never thanked you for saving my life. I want to do that now."

"You would have done the same thing."

"Yeah, but you need to say things like that out loud. It kind of cements it if you know what I mean. Jesus, I can't tell you how happy I am that you and Iris found each other. We've had some differences the past few years, but my feelings for you never changed."

"I know that, Birch. All of a sudden we found out we were allowed to think and plan separately. We bought into that myth that

twins are supposed to think alike for too long. Spit it out right now.
Ah, hell, I know exactly what you're going to say. When you recover
you're taking off for the wilds of somewhere, probably to hunt big
game or some such shit."

"Close. You okay with that? Can you handle things alone?"

"You know better than to ask. I want whatever is best for you. If
it takes you ten years to get your shit together in one sock, so be it.
Don't go thinking you're *that* important."

Fanny moved on into the dining room the moment she knew
Sage put his arm around his brother's shoulders. All was right in her
sons' world.

The luncheon festivities broke up at three o'clock. Fanny and Ash
said their good-byes and headed for the door. "I'll pick you up at
seven, Sunny."

"Okay, Dad."

"Sunny, I'm proud of you. If you need me or if there's anything . . ."

"Sure, Mom. I'll call," Sunny said interrupting her. "I have to go
and do my share of cleaning up, or Billie will do it for me. Drive carefully."

Hot tears pricked at Fanny's eyelids. "I think," Fanny said, "that
was one of the neatest brush-offs I've ever gotten. She's better than
you ever were, Ash."

"Listen, Fanny, I know you're in a hurry to get back to the ranch,
but I'd like to ask a favor. Would you mind sticking around for a few
hours? Let me get a couple of hours' sleep and a shower. I need to
talk to you about something. I wouldn't ask, but it's very important.
I'm dead on my ass. I'd say feet but my feet don't work these days.
What do you say?"

"All right, Ash. I'll go shopping. Six o'clock, no later. I don't like
driving at night."

"Stay till morning."

"No. I'm packed and ready to go. I want to be around my own
things, in my own house. That's where my life is. Drop me off here
on the corner. Is there anything I can get for you?"

"Not a thing. I'll see you at six o'clock." Fanny nodded.

Instead of going shopping, Fanny stopped at the first drugstore
she came to and called Simon. When the machine came on, she left
her name and said she'd call back later. She meandered through the
drugstore looking at the array of cosmetics. She stifled a laugh when
she recalled how Bess had snitched almost all of her cosmetics from

her father's drugstore. It was strange how she remembered things from the past, pleasant things. Memories. So many of them. In the end, she settled for a paperback novel about murder and mayhem and went to the park to read it.

By the end of chapter two she'd figured out the murderer so she tossed the book into the trash barrel next to the bench. She concentrated on watching a group of plump pigeons squabble over a child's spilled popcorn. She sat for a very long time staring off into space. When a toddler's ball rolled against her shoe, she kicked it toward the little boy, who squealed his pleasure. She thought about her grandson, Jake. She wondered if he had a bright red ball. Sunny was partial to yellow and blue. She should know what color his ball was. She'd never heard him call her grandma. Her eyes started to burn. Guilty! Guilty! Guilty of being a lousy grandmother. She sat bolt upright on the wooden bench. What if Tyler tried to take the children from Sunny because of her condition? "Over my dead body," she seethed. She was certain it would happen unless he signed away his parental rights. *Don't think about that, Fanny. If it happens, you'll deal with it then. All the worrying in the world won't change things if they're meant to happen.*

Fanny looked at her watch. Time to head back to Babylon. In the lobby she stopped at the florist and bought two dozen yellow roses with assorted greenery. When she paid for them, she realized how stupid it was. Ash was going to the mountain and she was leaving. Who would enjoy the flowers? She was doing a lot of stupid things of late.

Ash was waiting for her, his hair still damp from the shower. She handed him the flowers. He sniffed them and smiled. "I don't think anyone ever gave me flowers before. Thanks, Fanny."

"What do you want to talk about, Ash?"

"Everything in the world. Fanny, look at me. Tell me what you see, and be honest."

"I see a tired, weary, bitter man."

"You're right. I'm also a man who's lost his edge. I can't do this anymore. I need to get out while I can still wheel my chair. I got the results from my tests yesterday. I didn't tell Sunny because she has enough on her plate right now. The doctors were kind, but truthful. I have two years, Fanny, three if I'm lucky. One of the more outspoken doctors said a year. I guess it's a crapshoot. There's nothing they can do for me, just like there's nothing they can do for Sunny. I bawled, Fanny. I just sat there and I goddamn bawled my head off.

Some cockamamie part of me really believed I could live forever."

Fanny blinked. She felt like someone had taken a sledgehammer to the middle of her stomach. "Ash, there are other doctors. They make new discoveries every day in the medical field. You can't give up. A positive attitude is half the battle."

"Fanny, I had the best of the best. Tests don't lie. To show you what a bastard I am, I made them run those tests three times because I refused to believe the results. My liver is almost gone, and so are my kidneys. I'm over the worst of the shock now so I can think clearly. Birch is leaving. I think we both knew that was going to happen. He hates this business just the way Sage hates it. Sunny loves it. Go figure."

"Ash, what are you trying to say?" Fanny felt naked with fear.

"I want to move to the mountain and leave this behind me. I want to know I'm leaving it in good hands—*your hands*. It's the only solution, Fanny. Sunny needs me. The truth is, I need her just as much. If you stop and think about the whole picture, it makes sense. You and Simon can handle this casino. Billie and Sage can handle your clothing business. You don't work at it anymore anyway."

"No, Ash, no, no, no. I hate this town. I hate this business."

"You hate it because of me. Be fair."

"Sell it, bank the money."

"Fanny, it's a gold mine. Only a fool would sell a gold mine."

"Hire people to run it. No, Ash, I can't do it. How can you ask me to give up my life? Simon hates this business, too. *NO!* Besides, he would never agree."

"It's for the family, Fanny. I'm going to die. You aren't doing it for me. Sunny is going to be incapacitated sooner than you think. You know what, it was her idea to ask you. She said . . . never mind. It's not important what she said."

"What did she say, Ash?"

"She said exactly what you just said. She said you would never give up your new life for any of us. She told me to ask you what Jake's middle name is? What is it, Fanny?"

"It's . . . it's . . . damn you, Ash, that child's middle name has nothing to do with this."

"It has everything to do with it, Fanny. How old was Jake when he started to walk? How old was he when he cut his first tooth? When did he get his first black eye? How come, bastard that I am, I know those things and you don't? Just for the record, those were questions Sunny asked first. I'm waiting for your answers, Fanny."

"I'm not going to let you throw a guilt trip on me, Ash."

"This is family, Fanny. When it's family, you pick up the slack. Isn't that what you always said? Where's all that family bullshit you doled out like cod liver oil? It *was* bullshit, wasn't it? Family is important when it's convenient for you. You got what you want so fuck the rest of us, right?"

"No, that's not right."

"Sure it is. Jesus Christ, we couldn't even find you for four days when Birch had his accident. You were off thinking. Thinking about this family and what was wrong with it. What the hell happened to motherhood, apple pie, and all that good stuff you used to jam down our throats?"

"I'm never going to forgive you for this, Ash."

"Like I give a good rat's ass about your forgiveness. When you're looking at what I'm looking at, it hardly seems important. Your blissful life doesn't seem too important to me either. Yeah, I have bushel baskets full of regrets. This is my one chance; hell, it's my only chance to make things right. I'm looking it right in the face, Fanny, and I'm not denying any of my misdeeds. My mother came to this state and made it what it is today. Babylon was built for my mother and father. It was my living monument to them. It's staying in this family, one way or the other. What that means to you is it's an either or answer."

"What's the or?"

"You don't want to know."

"Yes. I want to know."

Ash's voice was so low she had to strain to hear the words. "Sunny said she'd give the kids up to Tyler and come back here and run the casino. Before you jump down my throat, I told her it was out of the question. She would do it to show you up, Fanny. You committed the cardinal sin. You fucked with her kids. You know, Fanny, it's that motherhood thing. Lioness protecting her cubs. You should recognize the drill."

"I'd never have given up my children. Not under any circumstances. I would have cleaned toilets in dirty gas stations before I did that. Don't threaten me, Ash. No daughter of mine would do such a thing. Sunny loves those children. She's a wonderful mother."

"How would you know? Cut the bullshit, Fanny, this is me you're talking to. Yeah, Sunny loves the kids, but guess what. Tyler loves them, too, and he's going to fight for them at some point in time. Sunny is going to fight for what she wants just the way you're fighting for that wonderful new life you have. Surely you understand where she's coming from. That girl is never going to forgive you, Fanny, for not being there for her children. I know that hurts you right down to your soul. I see it in your face. Jesus Christ, Fanny, I didn't want to tell you that. You left me no choice. You're the last to know. You probably think I'm lying. Check it out, talk to the kids, with Bess, they'll tell you. Just don't tell Sunny I told you. The fact that you think I'm lying is pretty goddamn sad if you want my opinion.

"Fanny, I want you to know something. In my own way I loved you as much as I was capable of loving anyone. I'm sorry for what I put you through, sorry I couldn't love you the way you wanted to be loved. I'm sorry I wasn't a better husband and father. I guess when it comes right down to it, I'm sorry about everything."

"Ash, what's Jake's middle name?" Fanny whispered.

"Matthew. At first she was going to name him after Birch or Sage but changed her mind at the church. She didn't want to show favoritism. He walked when he was ten months. He cut his first tooth at seven months. He crawled backwards for a little while. Sunny was really concerned about that, but the doctor said it was okay. He's allergic to penicillin and he has this monster strawberry birthmark on his rump. He gave up his bottle at eleven months, said his first word at a year. He called me Pop Pop the day he turned one. I got such a kick out of that. He knows who you are because Sunny showed him pictures of you and talks about you to him. You should have seen his last birthday party, Fanny. We laughed ourselves silly over that kid. He has friends on the mountain. Chue's grandkids come over to play all the time. You wouldn't believe Christmas. I honest to God had fun."

"Ash, don't tell me any more."

"Why, Fanny? Aren't you the one who always said look it in the face and go on from there? Time's up, I gotta pick up Sunny. Stay as long as you like or leave if that's what you want to do."

"Aren't you coming back?"

"Nope."

"Ash, you can't do this!"

"Watch me."

"Simon won't agree to this. I don't know how to run this casino. I'm not saying I'm not going to do it . . . Ash, come back here."

"I bet you could turn this place into something spectacular without even trying. Just look what those flowers do for the table."

Fanny ran after the wheelchair. She dropped to her knees. "Ash, would she give those babies of hers up?"

Tears blurred Ash's eyes. "I'd try to stop her, Fanny. I don't know what she'll do after I'm gone."

"I hate your guts, Ash Thornton," Fanny screamed.

"I used to hate yours. I don't anymore. See you around, Fanny."

Fanny beat at the thick carpeting with her clenched fists until her hands were numb. Sobbing, she crawled on her hands and knees to the coffee table. She reached for the vase of roses and threw it at the double teakwood doors. "Do you hear me, Ash Thornton, I hate you? I hate you for doing this to me. All you do is take and take and take."

Exhausted, Fanny crawled up onto the deep sofa. She needed to call Simon. No, she needed to call Bess to verify Ash's cruel words. She dialed her friend's number and spoke haltingly. "Bess, I'm going to ask you a question. If you know the answer just say yes or no. When I hear your answer, I'm going to hang up. No, I'm not all right. I will probably never be all right again. In the scheme of things I don't suppose it matters very much. Did Sunny tell you and my children that she would never forgive me . . . for not being there for Jake?" Fanny sucked in her breath as she waited for Bess's response. "Your answer is yes?"

Fanny hung up the phone and drew a second deep breath.

Now it was time to call Simon.

11

~

Fanny stared at the ringing phone in her hand. She broke the connection as tears dripped down her cheeks. Her life was slipping away, and she was helpless to stop it. She picked up the phone again. She slapped the receiver back into the cradle. How in the world was she going to tell Simon what had just transpired with Ash?

Jackson Matthew Ford. A blue-eyed, blond cherub nicknamed little Jake. Fanny's thoughts whirled back in time to the holdup on the bus where a man named Jake had asked her to hold his money and then disappeared. Now there was a little Jake in her life. A grandson. Her daughter's firstborn child. How could she have been so stupid? She thought about the first three years when all the brown envelopes arrived at the ranch with huge scrawled letters across the front, PHOTOGRAPHS—DO NOT BEND. She remembered looking at them, remembered smiling at the infant's chubby cheeks and commenting to Simon that Jake looked like Tyler. Simon's cold-eyed stare forced her to shove the pictures in a drawer. She had all good intentions of framing them at some point in time. She never had. What was it Ash said? You're a piss-poor excuse for a mother and a bigger piss-poor excuse as a grandmother. Guilty as charged.

Fanny looked at the clock. She closed her eyes and envisioned Simon sitting on the front porch waiting with a bottle of wine in an ice bucket. He'd be sitting on the glider with a clear view of the road. The moment he saw her headlights, he'd run to the road and sweep her in his arms as she stepped from the car. It wasn't going to happen. At best it wasn't even a good dream. If anything it was a nightmare.

Fanny felt a surge of panic. Her mind screamed, *Run.* Don't let Ash do this to you. Too late; he'd already done it, and she was here, the living proof that once again Ash called the shots. She looked around, her face contorting in rage.

She moved then, upending the glass-topped coffee table. Stark alabaster figures sailed through the air, shattering the mirrored walls. She kicked and gouged at the leather furniture with a gold letter opener. Stuffing spilled everywhere. Pushing and shoving, she managed to topple the chrome shelving that held stereo equipment and a monster television set. When the glass remained intact on the television, she slammed a crystal lamp into the middle. Glass scattered everywhere. The portable bar on wheels with every liquor known to man along with crystal glasses skidded across the room to topple over in a pile of broken glass. The window treatments puffed and billowed as she yanked and ripped. The neon night outside the building glared at her.

Hate and despair drove her to the phone. She dialed from memory. "This is Fanny Logan. Turn the power off at Babylon. Do it *NOW!*" She yanked at the phone wire, the phone spiraling across the room to land in a pool of brandy.

Fanny squeezed her eyes shut. When she opened them a second later, she was standing in darkness. She made her way across the room before she crumpled to the floor, her outstretched hand grappling for the phone. She plucked at the receiver. There was no dial tone. She cried then because she didn't know what else to do.

What seemed like a long time later, Fanny wiped at her tears when she heard someone hammer on the double doors. Her head high, she smoothed back her hair and straightened her dress. Slipping and sliding in the broken glass, she made her way to the door. A circle of light slapped her in the face. She turned her head. "Yes, what can I do for you?"

"The power went off in the casino. Is Mr. Thornton here? He's needed on the floor."

"Mr. Thornton doesn't live here anymore," Fanny said.

The beam of the flashlight arched around the interior of the room. "Mrs. Thornton, did something happen here? Are you all right?"

"I guess you could say something happened. Do I look all right to you?"

"Yes, ma'am. What should I tell the staff? No one knows how to work the generators except Mr. Thornton."

"Is that so? You are of course referring to those three-million-dollar generators?"

"Yes, ma'am. What should we do?"

"Go home and go to bed. That's what I'm going to do. Don't disturb me again tonight." Fanny slammed the door shut in the man's face.

Fanny made her way to the bedroom, where she fell across the bed. She was asleep in the time it took her head to touch the pillow.

Fanny bolted from the bed when she heard sharp banging on the door. She was appalled at her reflection in the floor-length mirror. She'd slept in her clothes. What was worse, she *looked* like she'd slept in her clothes.

Fanny opened the door. Ash's heavy hitters. The second, third, and fourth string in the chain of command. "Yes?" She stood aside for the men to enter the apartment. She offered no explanations or apologies for the condition of the room.

"Mrs. Thornton, we need to speak with your . . . with Mr. Thornton," the second string said. The third and fourth string bobbed their heads in agreement.

"Mr. Thornton vacated the premises yesterday."

"Is there a way to reach him?" the second string queried.

"No."

"The power's off in the entire building. We're losing money, Mrs. Thornton. We're the only casino with a power loss. By any chance, did you turn the power off?"

"As a matter of fact I did. I was making a statement."

"A statement," the first, second, third, and fourth strings said in unison.

"Uh-huh. When I'm ready to make my coffee I'll turn the power back on. Is there anything else this morning?"

"Well . . . do you want housekeeping to, ah . . . ?"

"Not at this time. You can send a telephone repair man up here immediately. Have all the employees assembled in the ballroom at noon for a company meeting."

"Is Mr. Thornton coming back?" the fourth string asked.

"No. Good day, gentlemen."

Fanny finished showering and dressing just as her telephone was repaired. "It must have been some party," the man quipped as she signed her name to the work order.

"I was having a bad hair day," Fanny said.

"Uh-huh," the man said, backing out the door.

Fanny picked up the phone and dialed the power company. "This is Fanny Logan." She gave her password and said, "You can turn the power back on."

You need to call Simon now and explain why you're still here.

The phone in her hand started to ring. She waited till it grew silent before she picked up the receiver. "Bess, I know it's early, but could you come over to the penthouse and have coffee with me? I really need to talk to you. Fine. I'll be waiting."

Call Simon. By now he knows something is wrong. Call him.

The phone rang again. Fanny ignored it as she measured coffee into the wire basket. She chain-smoked until she heard the last plop-plop and the electric pot shut itself off.

The phone continued to ring. Fanny continued to ignore it. When she couldn't stand the continual jangling a moment longer, she took the receiver off the hook and disconnected the answering machine.

Now, if she could just remember where her purse was, she could make her second call. It was on the kitchen counter, right where she'd left it. Fanny rummaged until she found her address book. She flipped through the pages, memorized the number as she spieled it off to the operator.

The receiver was picked up in a faraway place by a sleepy voice. The sleepy voice became wide-awake the moment Fanny identified herself and apologized for the early-morning time difference. "I can be there by four o'clock your time, possibly sooner. Reschedule your meeting for five o'clock. With Bess, you, and me, we can handle anything. Take a deep breath and call Simon."

On the other side of the Pacific Ocean, Billie Coleman turned to Thad. "Fanny needs me, Thad."

He asked no questions. "Then we better get cracking so I'm first off the runway."

As Billie and Thad packed their bags, Bess Noble was ringing the doorbell at the penthouse apartment in Babylon Towers. She linked her arm with Fanny's as she pretended not to see the destruction all about her.

In the kitchen, Bess listened to her longtime friend until she stopped speaking, breathless with the effort. "And you haven't called Simon? Fanny, that's not like you. Regardless of what's going on in your life, you have to be fair to him. You can't know Simon won't agree to come here."

"There are some things in life that are a given, Bess, and this is one of those givens. Simon left this town when he was sixteen. He hates it with a passion. He told me once nothing in the world could make him live here. I think Simon is lost to me now. We've come to the end of our particular road, Bess. I know it in my heart. You know it too, so don't pretend with me. You and I always used to say we had choices and options. Mine all ran out yesterday."

"Fanny, I am so sorry. I know you don't want to hear this, but Ash is right about Sunny. As for Ash himself, he's doing what he has to do. It sounds like he's finally . . . What's that tired old cliché, seen the light?"

"And once again he's left it up to me to carry on. I'm tired, Bess, I can't keep doing this. What about my life? Somewhere, someplace, somehow, I must have earned some small measure of happiness. Is that all I get, a few lousy years? I could count the happy days on both hands during those years."

"I think you might be selling Simon short. He won't let you get away from him. He loves you too much. When you find people you can trust you can have them take over the casino."

"It's not that kind of business, Bess. Owner-operated means owner-operated. The Strip is full of sharks and barracudas. Right now the word is out, and they're gathering. The smart money is saying I can't do this and the dumb money . . . well, there isn't any dumb money. That's the bottom line. I want you to help me run this casino.

I called Billie, and she'll be here by four this afternoon. Which reminds me, I have to reschedule the meeting. Are you in, Bess? Do you have to talk to John first? It's going to be different from Sunny's Togs and Rainbow Babies."

"I'm in, Fanny. No, I do not have to talk to John, but I will. ST and RB run so smoothly it bothers me to take a paycheck. Now why don't you call Simon, and I'll start cleaning up the living room?"

"I don't want you cleaning up the living room. I need to live with that mess for a while so I don't ever forget the rage that attacked me last night. I never thought it was possible for me to . . . go berserk like that. Who knows, I may never clean it up."

Bess made a fresh pot of coffee while Fanny called downstairs to the office to reschedule the meeting.

"Sunny will never forgive me, will she, Bess?"

"At some point she will. A mother-daughter bond is very strong, Fanny. She's going through a lot right now. Time heals all wounds. We both know that."

"The scars never go away. Both of us know that, too. How could I have been so stupid? Do you know the middle names of your grandchildren?"

"It's not the same thing, Fanny."

"Don't try and make me feel better. Ash was right. All I was concerned about was my happiness. That's a laugh in itself. I had to work at pretending to be happy. Look what those years have gotten me. Yesterday I wanted to take a handful of Ash's pills and end it all, but I was too much of a coward. Ash is going to die. Sunny's prognosis isn't good, but she's handling it in true Sunny fashion. She's close to Ash now and he needs her as much as she needs him. I'm grateful for that. Birch is going away to . . . contemplate his life. Billie is so wrapped up in the business half the time she doesn't know what day it is. Sage is polite to me. I feel like a stranger in my own family."

"Think of it as temporary, Fanny. There's light at the end of the tunnel. You just haven't gotten far enough into the tunnel to see it."

"If I had one wish, do you know what it would be, Bess?"

"That Simon would pop up on the doorstep saying he's always wanted to live in a penthouse."

"Not even close. I don't even think Simon loves me. He plays a good game of pretend, but that's what it is, a pretend game. I feel so stupid. I'd wish Sunny would bring Jake here so I could get to know him. I think Ash loves that little guy more than he loved his own kids when they were little. He knows everything about him. He must have gone to Sunrise a lot. I never knew that. No one ever told me. Ash isn't the same anymore. It's not just the death sentence he's living under either. The change must have started when Jake was born. If only I could unring the bell."

"You can't, so stop torturing yourself. Go in the bedroom and call Simon. I'll make us some pancakes."

In the bedroom, Fanny kicked off her shoes before she snuggled between the periwinkle-colored sheets. Her hand trembled as she dialed the operator to place the call. She wasn't surprised when it was picked up on the first ring. "Simon, it's Fanny."

"Fanny! Thank God. Are you okay? Did you break down along the way? I've been chewing my nails here. I planned to give it one more hour and then I was going to start out to look for you. We need to get a phone for your car. Damn, I keep forgetting you're driving a rental. Why didn't you call, Fanny? I waited up all night for you. I didn't think it was possible to miss someone so much. Where are you? When will you get here?"

Fanny clenched her teeth. He *sounded* like the old Simon, the Simon she'd fallen in love with. Underneath, though, she could hear the anger.

"Simon. Oh, Simon . . . Ash is dying. He doesn't have long. A year, maybe a little longer. Ash puts his own spin on everything including his death. Sunny . . . oh, Simon, I've made such a mess of things because I let you dictate to me where my family is concerned. It's not all your fault, I went along with it. What I'm trying to say is, Ash dumped the casino on me. I had no other choice. I need to hear you tell me you understand."

"I can't do that because I don't understand. What in the world are you talking about? Ash wouldn't dump his casino on anybody. He thinks it's his. How do you know this isn't just another one of Ash's schemes?" Fanny shuddered at her husband's frosty voice.

"Give me some credit, Simon. I know."

"What are you trying to tell me, Fanny?"

"I'm trying . . . what I'm trying to say is . . . I can't come back to the ranch. If I do, I won't be able to leave. You had too much of a hold on me. I can't allow that to happen again. I have to stay here. I have to take over for Ash. He's doing what has to be done for Sunny. I have to respect that. If he doesn't have that much time left, I need to do what I can. Please tell me you understand. It's my family, Simon. I turned my back on them once. I'll never do it again."

"Fanny, you don't know the first thing about running a casino. Ash can hire qualified people. He's jerking your strings, and you're allowing it. I didn't sign on for this, Fanny. At the risk of repeating myself, your children aren't kids anymore."

"No, Simon, this time he is not jerking my strings. A family business cannot be run by outsiders. I didn't know anything about the clothing business in the beginning either. I can learn because I have to learn. Don't you see, I have to try and make it right for everyone?"

"Fanny, listen to me. Sell the damn casino. If you don't, it's going to destroy us. Jesus, you know how much I hate that business and that town."

"I can't do that either. I am so sorry. I think I always knew this was going to happen at some point. Is there anything I can say to make you want to come here and run the casino with me?"

"Not if you paid me my weight in gold."

Fanny's voice was a bare whisper. "I know. You always knew my family would come first. You tried to rob me of them, Simon. I'm having trouble dealing with that."

Simon's whisper matched her own. "Yes, I knew. We both gambled. Something both of us said we would never do. This is the result. What if you fail, Fanny? Then will you come crawling back to me?"

"That's an awful thing to say to me, Simon. I'll know I gave it my best shot. All any of us can do is our best. If I fail, it won't be for lack of trying. I can't turn my back on my family. I did it once when I married you. Do you realize, Simon, that I don't know my grandson? I never framed his pictures. I didn't hear my own daughter's pleas. Ash, of all people, knew those things. I didn't. I'm having a really hard time with that, Simon. Ash has stepped in and taken my place with Sunny. That alone is eating me alive. It's a good thing, so I can live with it. Right now they need each other. The only thing left for me to do is what I'm doing now. I wish it were different."

Simon's voice was so angry and choked, Fanny had trouble distinguishing the words. "I would do anything in the world for you. Except move to that hellhole. Inside of a week they'd have to lock me up."

"I know. That's why I'm not asking you to come here. I love you, Simon."

"Not enough to turn your back on that damn casino."

"The casino is only part of it. I cannot, I will not turn my back on my family."

"Ash isn't your family anymore."

"He's the father of my children and he's dying. This is tearing me up inside, Simon. We can talk it to death, but in the end we'll be back at our starting point. The day we left to come here you knew I wasn't happy with the way things were between us. We need to talk about us very soon. Will you send Daisy here? Her crate is in the garage."

"What am I supposed to do now? We had a life up until a month ago. Do you want a divorce? Are we separating? I need to know."

"I . . . I didn't think that far ahead, Simon. I'll do whatever you want. Perhaps in time things will change. I'm in no position right now to make promises."

"Aren't you coming back for your things?"

"I can't. If I see you, if I see the dogs and the ranch, I won't leave. I'll hunker in and be miserable. You'll find a way to keep me there. I can't allow that to happen. I have to begin over right here. I have such rage and anger inside me. Last night I smashed up this apartment and had the electric company turn off the power in the casino. Does that give you some idea of the state I'm in?"

"Fanny—"

"It is what it is. I love you, Simon." Fanny waited for Simon to repeat the words she'd just uttered.

"The way you say a part of you will always love Ash? That's not good enough for me, Fanny." What she heard next was the connection being broken. She knuckled her burning eyes.

Bess had said something about pancakes. Fanny climbed from the bed and straightened the sheets. Ash Thornton's credo; never look back. She needed to subscribe to that credo starting right now.

In the kitchen she sat down at the table. "Simon doesn't want to live here. He asked me if we were getting divorced."

"He just needs a little time, Fanny. When he starts to miss you so much he can't stand it, he'll show up. He needs you too much to walk away."

"He's not doing the walking, I am. You're wrong. Nothing in this world could make Simon come here to live. Absolutely nothing. He's going to send Daisy down by air. I'll have to pick her up at the airport."

"Eat, Fanny."

Fanny mashed the pancakes on her plate. "What do I do now, Bess?"

"You take it one day at a time. What's meant to be will be."

"We're home, Dad. Five bucks says Jake is here in"—Sunny looked at her watch—"forty-five seconds."

"That's a sucker bet," Ash said, engaging the lift device in the van. "However, I'll take it and say he gets here in thirty-nine seconds. Here he comes, chocolate ice-cream cone in hand, two fat kittens on his trail. Thirty-eight seconds! Fork it over, young lady."

Sunny fished in the pocket of her jeans and handed over a five-dollar bill.

"Here you go, sport. Tell Pop Pop where it goes."

"Jake's bank?" the little boy giggled.

"How much do you have in your bank?"

"A fortune."

"Attaboy. Climb on and we'll ride into the house." The little boy climbed onto Ash's lap, his chubby arms circling his grandfather's neck.

"Luv you, luv you, luv you," Jake said, smothering Ash's face with kisses.

"What about Mommy?"

"Luvs her, too."

"Man, you'd think we went away for two months instead of an hour at the grocery store. You kids never greeted me like this when I came home. Or, did you and I just can't remember?"

"Sometimes we did. Sometimes we didn't. Mom always waited to gauge your mood and then told us if it was okay. Most times it was. Go inside. I'll carry the groceries in."

"I can carry something. Just dump it in my lap."

"Dad, stop babying me. I can do it. I want to do it. I want to do everything I can while I can. Let's have some lemonade in the garden."

"Make that beer and it's a deal. God, I can't tell you what a relief it is since the elevator was installed. That was good thinking on your part to have it done while we were at Johns Hopkins. No mess, no bother."

"I did it as much for me as for you. Tyler and I had an unholy row about it. He said it was an asshole thing to do."

"Guess what? Tyler's an asshole," Ash said. "We shouldn't be talking like this in front of Jake."

"No, we shouldn't. It slipped out. He's heard worse when Tyler and I went at it. Come on, slumber bunny, time to take a nap. You need to tell me how your sister did while I was at the store with Pop Pop. Did she cry?"

"Lots and lots. Hers sleeping now."

"That's good. Run to the bathroom the way Daddy showed you. Lift the seat, okay?"

"Where's Daddy?"

"Daddy went away."

"Him come back?"

"Sometime. Pop Pop is here now. He's going to sleep in the room next to yours. Won't that be nice?"

"Uh-huh. Him eat eggs with me."

"You bet. Give me a kiss. Sleep tight."

"Don't let the bed bugs bite," the little boy giggled.

Sunny checked on the sleeping baby. How beautiful she was. *Please, God,* she prayed, *let me stay here long enough to see them both grow up.*

The garden was in full bloom, the colorful chaise longues vying for attention with the rainbow of flowers. Ash slipped from his chair to the thick padding and stretched out his legs. "Take a load off, kiddo, and let's talk. I say we start with Tyler and get that out of the way."

"I'm okay with it. I've had a whole year to get used to the idea that the marriage wasn't working. It's better we split up now than later. He's young. He has a wonderful career ahead of him. He needs a wife who can do that social thing. I can't do that. Sooner or later he'd cheat on me, and I'd be devastated. He can see the kids when he wants, he's promised to send support money. We'll alternate holidays, that kind of thing. He loves Jake. He's hardly had time to get to know Polly. If he starts to make demands, well, isn't that why there are so many lawyers? I don't think he'll mess with this family. Now that's out of the way what else do you want to talk about?"

"Your mother."

"How about something else? How about those test results you say you didn't get?"

Ash shrugged. "Let's talk about both things. Your mother first. She loves you very much. I know that for a fact. Can't you ease up a little?"

"What did I do wrong?"

"You didn't do anything wrong. You were polite, you kissed her hello, and you kissed her good-bye. You two used to be so close. How can you negate that?"

Sunny shrugged. "Mom had other things on her mind. I was so miserable I'd call her two or three times a day. One day she snapped at me over the phone. She said 'what do you want this time?' I didn't want anything, I just wanted to talk to her because I missed her. I was going to tell her that, too. I didn't call after that. She called once a month, you know, duty calls. I didn't want that. I made sure I was never around between one and three on the first Sunday of every month. It was the same with Sage, Birch, and Billie. They started doing the same thing I did. They weren't available. They let the machine take the message. You know what, Mom never even noticed. She made the call. We weren't there, our tough luck. This family has gone to hell."

"She's going to take over the casino. What do you have to say to that?"

"Whoopee," Sunny said snidely. "What did Uncle Simon have to say about it?"

"I don't imagine he likes it at all. He'll probably stay in California and Fanny will stay in town and they'll visit on weekends."

"That won't last. Mom is one of those touchy-feely people. She'll want him with her. I don't think she can do it, Dad. Do you want me to give her a hand? I could do mornings."

"I think she can handle it. Let's give her a chance. We can take the kids down in a few weeks. We could even do a picnic if you're up to it."

"No. That is not a good idea. It won't work, Dad. Sage, Billie, and Iris are coming up next weekend. Sage is going to barbecue if you can believe that."

"Are you inviting your mother?"

"No, and don't keep asking me to do things like that. She had her chance, and she blew it. I have one last thing to say, and then we aren't going to talk about Mom anymore. I heard Bess tell Billie that when she went to the ranch to see Mom, there were no pictures of any of us in the house. I sent dozens of pictures of Jake. Mom got married, moved away and that was the end of us. It didn't just sting a little. It stung a lot. So, what did your tests show?"

"Well, the good news is they said I have three pretty good years ahead and the bad news is the rest of the years are downhill. I look at it this way, three is better than zip. After that, who knows, maybe someone will come up with something that will work for my condition. Attitude is everything."

"Aren't you going to miss Babylon? You don't have to stay here with me."

"I want to. I love Jake. I want to watch him grow up. I want to be a part of his life, and I want to be around in case Tyler starts getting strange ideas. The noise, the crowds, the late hours, the drinking, the cigarette smoke, it started to get to me. We built it, got it off the ground, and it's taken off. They said it couldn't be done, but by God, we all pulled together and did it. Now, it's time for me to rest on my laurels. For the first time in my life I'm looking forward to doing absolutely nothing."

"There's plenty of nothing up here. What would you like for supper?"

"How about some good old pan gravy, pork chops, and those seasoned potatoes?"

"Sounds good to me. Mitzi made fresh bread today."

"Ah, soft butter, strawberry jam, and a good cup of coffee. Better than any dessert. And before we go to bed one of your peanut butter and banana sandwiches."

"Absolutely. Take a nap, Dad. Polly is due to wake up, and I don't want her waking Jake. I'll put your supper order in and see you later."

"I think I will take a nap."

The moment Sunny was out of sight, Ash squeezed his eyes shut. "I tried, Fanny. I'll keep at it. It's the least I can do for you," he muttered as he drifted into sleep.

12

"Listen," Fanny said, a desperate tone to her voice, "this isn't necessary. Why do I need this ritzy outfit and fancy hairdo? This is not who I am. I'm a simple person with simple wants and tastes. I feel like I'm playing dress-up."

"You *were* a simple person," Billie Coleman said. "The key word is were. Image is everything. I am so glad I had this dress with me. If you don't make any sudden movements, the pins will stay intact and you'll be fine. You could pass for a Wall Street banker in this outfit. First appearances are everything."

"Your hair and makeup are perfect. You march into that room like you're in control. We'll be right behind you," Bess said.

"And say what?" Fanny demanded.

"You say what we just discussed. You say things will remain as they are. Then you say, for now. You emphasize the words 'for now.' That alone will keep everyone on their toes. Remember, you are not stepping into Ash's shoes, you're stepping into Sallie Thornton's. That's how your staff, the casino owners on the Strip, as well as the media are going to view you. It's not a bad thing, Fanny. Sallie was a legend in her own time. Even if you don't think you can wear her shoes, pretend they fit. The way I see it, men don't like taking orders from a woman. That's going to be your biggest hurdle. You speak once, you speak softly, and you carry a big stick. If it worked for Teddy Roosevelt, it will work for you," Billie said.

"I don't answer any questions, especially where Ash is concerned," Fanny said. "I have that down. For now, it's business as usual. After the meeting we're bringing all the personnel files up here to go over them. Then, over the next few days, we'll conduct one-on-one meetings with all the key players."

Bess clapped her hands. "See. You got it. Practice that look where you stare right through a person. Power is the most powerful aphrodisiac in the world, and right now the word is out and everyone in this town is frightened out of their wits. Turning off the power last night was a stroke of genius. All the owners on the Strip are wondering why. The fact that you did it to your own casino has them all in a tizzy. They're just waiting for your next move. Tonight we have to decide that next move. You're the star of this meeting, Fanny. Bess and I are just observers. It's five minutes to five. Time to go downstairs. Before we go, Fanny, did you really tell those guys you turned the power back on so you could make coffee?"

"Yes. I imagine the word is out on the street about that little tidbit by now."

"Always keep 'em guessing," Billie said as she held the door open for Bess and Fanny.

"Remember now, Fanny, you aren't a Girl Scout leader. March in there like you own the place."

I can do this. I know I can do this. I will do this. I will do this because I have to do this. Fanny opened the door to the grand ballroom. She almost faltered at the sea of faces staring at her. She walked across the room and up the four steps to the bandstand. She held her hand up for silence and wondered why she bothered. If a pin dropped, she could have heard it.

"Ladies and gentlemen, thank you for coming. I'll make this as brief as possible. As of today I will be in control of this casino. You will take your orders from me and you will answer to me and no one else. If this is going to be a problem for any of you, you should leave now." Fanny waited several minutes to see if anyone was going to walk toward the door. "It's business as usual. *For now.* One last thing. Babylon business stays in Babylon. I don't think I need to spell out what that means to any of you. Oh, one other thing, always be aware that I have friends on the *other side of the street.* That's all, ladies and gentlemen. You may resume your duties."

When the door closed behind the employees, Bess did a jig and Billie clapped her hands. "You handled that just right. The other side of the street? I saw two people turn white when you said that."

"Let's have dinner in the private dining room. We'll work the floor and make our presence known afterward. I'm so nervous I need to sit down," Fanny said.

"Dinner's good," Bess said. Billie nodded.

Over potato-crusted salmon and a crisp garden salad that Fanny only picked at, she said, "I hoped . . . all day I was . . . I wanted to believe Simon would come. My brain knew he wouldn't, but some small part of me wanted to believe he would. How do I turn that part of my life off? What kind of person am I that I can do something like this? I need a goal, something to strive toward. Like . . . in two years, maybe three, I can go back to Simon and he'll be the way he was when we first got married. I don't know if I can handle two bad marriages. To brothers, no less. When Ash is . . . when . . . Long-distance marriages never work. If I have to stay here for the rest of my life, I'll go out of my mind. The words, *for now,* mean this is a temporary situation. This is a lifetime commitment, so who's fooling who here? I know in my heart Simon won't wait for me. I hate it. I just hate it."

"Fanny, give it a chance. Give Simon a chance, too. This is only day one. You could turn out to be so good at this business you might not want to give it up. A week from now, a month from now, Simon can have a change of heart. Sometimes the things you hate most in life are the very things you end up loving the most. It's strange but true. I wasn't going to bring this up, but this might be a good time to offer you a goal. This casino makes tons of money. Why not think about building one of those centers like they have in Texas for people with multiple sclerosis? Think about this, too. Maybe you could build a separate facility where a patient's children can come for periods of time. Think in terms of Sunny. Think about how much good you can do. It's what Sallie did, Fanny," Billie said.

Fanny's eyes glistened. "I don't want to be like Sallie. I just want to be me, Fanny Thornton. You're right, though, I could do that. I'll look into it." She lost some of the glazed look in her eyes at Billie's suggestion.

"Fanny, you *are* you. I didn't say you should turn into Sallie. Sallie did thousands of wonderful things for the people of this town. Her private life had nothing to do with her philanthropic goodness. Use the money from this casino to do good things. Maybe you won't hate it so much if you have worthy goals and you achieve them."

"I think Billie's right, Fanny. I'll pick John's brains and see what he says. You can set up a foundation. I think, and this is just a thought, but I'll bet my wedding ring Chue's sister Su Li will come back and oversee it for you. Oh, Fanny, it's a wonderful idea."

"It will take a fortune," Fanny said.

"It will take several fortunes. I'll see to it that the Colemans contribute half. We could make it a family foundation. We'll be helping Sunny and hundreds of people like her. I vote yes," Billie said.

"I don't have any money to give, but I can give my time. If my vote counts, then mine is yes, too. You need to cast your vote, Fanny," Bess said.

"Oh, yes. Yes, yes, yes. Maybe some good will come of this after all. Thank you both for coming here today. Let's eat our dessert and then work the floor for a while. After that, we'll go upstairs and brainstorm like we used to do in the old days."

"Hear, hear!" Billie said.

Across the street in a windowless room, men, impeccably clad, took their seats at a highly polished table. An elaborate centerpiece of fresh orchids sat in the middle of the table. To the left of the floral arrangement was a sterling silver coffee service. To the right, an identical sterling silver tray with crystal decanters containing one-of-a-kind cordials and old brandy. Crystal ashtrays and fresh packages of cigarettes were at each place setting.

The man at the head of the table, a Harvard graduate, opened the meeting simply by raising his hand for silence. His voice was cultured and resonant. "If my information is correct, The Emperor of Las Vegas is no longer with us. Do you see a problem, gentlemen?" The men shrugged as one. "How did it happen?" was the second question. Again, the men shrugged.

The man at the head of the table poured coffee. "The incident that occurred last night did not affect any of us. Business-wise, we made money. I understand that the explanation for the incident was that Mrs. Thornton was making a statement. I think we would all be wise to take that particular statement at face value. Mrs. Thornton is in total control of Babylon. I do not believe Mrs. Thornton has any desire to cross over to your side of the street.

"Mrs. Thornton has a sterling reputation, as did her mentor, Sallie Thornton. The Strip, this town, needs her. As long as your gentlemen stay on your side of the street she gives all of you respectability. The lady has class, power, and wealth. To my knowledge, that power and wealth have never been abused except once. All of you felt that abuse because some of you tried to cross the line and pull an unsavory business deal."

"A deal is a deal. We buckled under to a woman," a voice at the end of the table snarled.

"You conducted a business deal. Your tone of voice is not appreciated, nor will it be tolerated. You are not hoods, you're businessmen. You knew the ground rules when you hired me. Remember that."

"Mrs. Thornton is in the rag business. What does she know about the gambling business?" someone asked.

"I would imagine you'll find out very soon. Mrs. Thornton is a lady . . . of her word, as you all know. You might be wise to work behind the scenes to aid her endeavors if those endeavors turn out to pertain to something other than the gaming business."

"That would be aiding the enemy. Ash Thornton was the enemy."

The man at the head of the table sighed. "Ash Thornton was your competitor, not your enemy. All of you here need to recognize that the old days are gone forever. There's a new game in town called 'the legitimate way.' Are there any questions, gentlemen?"

"With The Emperor gone, what do we call Mrs. Thornton?"

"Mrs. Thornton sounds appropriate." The voice at the head of the table held a rich chuckle. A hint of a smile tugged at the corners of his mouth.

"If there are no questions, we're adjourned."

Marcus Reed stood to shake the hand of each man filing past him. His job here was done.

Fanny sat down at a small table in the Harem Lounge. She wished she could kick off her shoes and remove her hose so she could wiggle her toes. How in the world did Ash do this, night after night, week after week? She couldn't ever remember being this tired. She reached out to accept a glass of ginger ale from the bartender.

"It gets to you after a while, doesn't it?" a man at the next table said. Fanny watched as he unbuttoned the top button of his shirt and yanked at his tie.

He looked like a contented customer. She needed to smile and make polite conversation even though it was doubtful the man knew who she was. "It's these shoes. I'd give anything if I could take them off and wade in one of the pools."

The man smiled. "What's stopping you?" The tie was in his hands and then stuffed into his pocket. "I feel about ties the way you feel about your shoes."

"I think I'll just get lower heels. It was a lovely tie." *He was flirting with her.* Fanny felt her face grow warm. He was handsome, middle fifties, dark hair tinged with gray at the temples, classic features, winsome smile. *Winsome?* He was wearing a magnificent suit, custom-tailored. She knew a thing or two about fabric.

"I like the idea of wading in the pool better. I wonder if anyone has ever done that."

It was Fanny's turn to smile. "I rather doubt it. Did you win or lose tonight?"

"Actually, I broke even."

"That's not good for the house."

"Do you work here?"

"In a manner of speaking," Fanny said. She tried wiggling her toes inside her shoes. A corn was forming on her little toe, she could feel it start to burn. Three more hours to go. How *did* Ash do it?

"What does in a manner of speaking mean? Marcus Reed," he said, extending his hand.

"Fanny Thornton," Fanny said, reaching for his hand. When she didn't see any acknowledgment of her name, she said, "I more or less watch over things on the floor. It's an education in itself. I might enjoy it more if my feet didn't hurt so much."

"That does it." The man was off his chair in the blink of an eye.

In the time it took her heart to beat twice, Fanny found herself slung over the man's shoulder and whisked out of the Harem Lounge to the stunned surprise of the bartender. "One pool coming up."

"You need to put me down, Mr. Reed. People are staring and gawking at us. This is not funny. What if someone takes a picture. My rear end is in your face," Fanny said, her head bobbing up and down.

"So it is, now that you mention it. Here we are. As someone who once wanted to be an architect, I can appreciate the work and beauty of this pool. There you go, Fanny Thornton. Doesn't it feel good?" he said, standing her up inside the pool. "I'll hold your shoes until your feet cool off. Nylons dry in seconds according to my sisters."

"People are staring," Fanny hissed.

"Then let's give them something to *really* stare at." Marcus stepped into the pool. "Good lord, there's fish in here."

Fanny doubled over laughing. When she raised her head, Marcus splashed her. She splashed back. A crowd gathered, Billie and Bess in the front line. Fanny laughed harder at their startled faces. "I'm, ah . . . what I'm doing is . . ."

"Having fun," Marcus Reed laughed. "Well, as much as I'm enjoying this, I really have to leave. I have a plane to catch. It was nice meeting you, Mrs. Thornton."

"I'm sorry about your shoes and pants."

"Don't be. I haven't had this much fun in a long time."

Fanny watched Marcus walk away. She was suddenly aware of the people staring at her, of her friends Billie and Bess. It took her a second to realize she was seeing spots in front of her eyes. *Flash bulbs.*

"Did you have fun?" Bess asked.

"Actually, Bess, I did. My feet feel better, too. I don't think I've ever done anything quite so public before," Fanny said, stepping from the pool.

"I say we call it a night," Billie said.

Fanny picked up her shoes to follow her friends. She waved to the onlookers and grinned.

"Who *was* that man?" Bess asked in the elevator.

"He said his name was Marcus Reed. I met him in the Harem Lounge when I went in to rest my feet. He seemed like a real gentleman."

"Well, his three-hundred-dollar shoes and thousand-dollar suit are ruined. He didn't seem to mind," Billie said, a thoughtful look on her face.

"I have a feeling I'm going to be in the morning papers," Fanny said.

"Do you care?" Bess asked.

"Too late now," Fanny said. "They'll probably call me the Mermaid of Babylon or something equally silly. Ash will throw a fit."

"Life goes on," Billie said, the same thoughtful look still on her face.

"Okay, let's have some coffee while we go through the personnel files. Tomorrow is another long day."

Fanny snuggled beneath the flannel sheets. It dawned on her, just as she was drifting off to sleep, that she could get up out of bed and turn the air conditioning higher. She adjusted the thermostat and climbed back into bed just as the telephone rang. *Please, God, let it be Simon. Please.* But it was her ex-husband's voice on the other end of the phone.

"Ash, why are you calling me at quarter to four in the morning? You are the last person in the world I want to talk to right now. Furthermore, you said you were walking away and you didn't care what happened. You're calling to find out what happened, right?"

"Wrong, as usual. I just wanted to see how you were. I used to wind down about this time every night. It will get easier as time goes on. I think I really called to thank you. I don't suppose that means anything to you. How is Simon taking it?"

Fanny felt her throat constrict. "Simon won't be joining me here in these sumptuous surroundings which really aren't so sumptuous right now. I smashed up the place last night, Ash. Then I turned the power off."

"Way to go, Fanny."

"Tonight some guy from the Harem Lounge tossed me over his shoulder and stood me up in one of the pools because my feet hurt. Someone took pictures. I'll probably make the morning papers, so be advised."

"Did you have a good time?"

"Sure. My feet feel better, too. No one knows how to work the generators. Perhaps you should tell me how to start them."

"There's an On/Off switch. You turn On and *voilà*. You got light. I would have thought you could figure that out. When the generators are working, they only juice the first three floors."

"I didn't try. Your people made it sound mysterious. They said you were the only person who knew how they worked."

"I didn't want anyone messing around with them. One klutz, and three million bucks would have been shot to hell. Run that business about Simon by me again."

"I said he wants no part of this. He won't be joining me."

"So what's the big deal? You can go up there weekends or he can come down to Vegas. Constant togetherness in a marriage causes it to erode. I'm glad you made it through the first day."

"Oh, yeah. I even called a meeting. Do you want to know how it turned out?"

"No. Listen, I hear Polly whimpering. I want to get to her before Sunny wakes up. She had an elevator put in for the two of us. Is that something or what?"

"Yes. That's something. Take care of your granddaughter, Ash."

"She takes six ounces. You should hear her burp!"

"Good-bye, Ash." There was no response.

Fanny buried her head in the pillow and sobbed. "You're dying, and you're finally happy. How am I ever going to understand something like that? I don't wish you ill, Ash, truly I don't. Just take good care of Sunny and the kids. When you can't to do it anymore, I'll step in if she lets me."

Damn, she was wide-awake now.

Fanny picked her way through the debris in the living room on her way to the kitchen, where she brewed a pot of coffee.

What are you doing, Simon? Are you awake? Of course you are. I'm sitting here thinking of you and I know you're sitting on the glider thinking of me. If it wasn't so tragic, it would be funny. Change your mind, Simon. Maybe this won't be forever. If we love each other, we should be able to make it work. I cannot desert my family no matter how much I love you. I just can't. A man flirted with me tonight, Simon. I enjoyed his attention. Oh, Simon, what's going to happen to us?

Careful not to make any noise, Fanny made toast. She really didn't want or need the coffee. She was already one big jangling nerve.

Fanny leaned her head into the palm of her hand. She stared at the stark white refrigerator. She thought about her husband and her family. She wished she was young again, back in Shamrock, Pennsylvania, knowing what she knew now. Such a foolish thought. She thought about Sallie; she always thought about her mother-in-law when she reminisced. No matter how hard she tried, no matter what she did or didn't to do, Sallie's life paralleled her own.

Fanny's thoughts took her backward in time to the day her father-in-law had his stroke and Sallie went to Devin Rollins to break off their twenty-year-long affair. Devin had pleaded with Sallie to no avail. With his love lost to him he'd committed suicide that very evening. Sallie gave up her life to take care of Philip, and, in the end, her guilty, sick devotion to a man she didn't love had killed her. Now, Fanny thought, she was doing the exact same thing, following in Sallie's footsteps. She screamed her despair, banging her head on the glass-topped table.

Bess and Billie leaped from their beds to race to the kitchen. "What happened?" they asked in unison. They listened to Fanny babble incoherently, their eyes wide with disbelief.

"Don't you see, no matter what I do, no matter how hard I try, it always comes back to Sallie and me. It's almost as if she cloned me when I wasn't looking. I don't know how to break the chain. Just look at the similarities. I'm taking over for Ash, doing something I absolutely hate, because he's dying. Sallie gave up Devin to devote her life to Philip, out of guilt. We all know I'm giving up Simon for the same reason. It's never going to end. Never!"

Billie and Bess dropped to their knees. "It isn't the same thing, Fanny," Billie said gently.

"Oh, Fanny, please listen, Billie is right. Sallie wasn't divorced. You are. Sallie didn't remarry. You did. Sallie didn't have a daughter with a progressive disease. Devin committed suicide because he was a weak man. There is nothing about Ash that is weak. Ash has taken the horns of his bull and he's dealing with it the only way he knows how. All he asked of you was to take over his job. It's totally different, Fanny."

"This is a new time, a new place. You hate this business, Sallie loved it. That alone should tell you something. Sallie was locked into a situation of her own making. She wasn't smart enough to climb out of the trap. She gave up. We all loved her, but that doesn't make what she did right. You haven't given up on Simon. He has to be man enough to recognize the sacrifice you're making for your family, recognize that he loves you. If he chooses, and choose is the right word, Fanny, and does not accept it, then he isn't the man you thought he was. Do you agree, Bess?"

"One hundred percent," Bess said.

"How can a person exist twenty-four hours a day doing something he or she hates with a passion? It can't be emotionally healthy. What's going to become of me?"

"If you go into something with a negative attitude, everything you do will be negative. When things are at their worst, they have to get better. Jump into it, embrace it, and remember our goal. Think of this as opening-night jitters. Bess and I are here for you. I'm staying for a full month because my wonderful guy recognizes that I need a separate life. Bess is going to be right here with you all the time. If you falter, we'll pick you up. It's up to you to do the rest, and you can do it. Right now you're still smarting over Simon's attitude, and the way your marriage was the past two years. You've committed, but you haven't committed one hundred percent. When you do that, you don't look back. It will be whatever it's meant to be. Let's go back to bed now," Billie said.

Fanny allowed herself to be led back to bed. "What would I do without you two?"

"You'd do just fine. We're just moral support." Bess smiled. "Do you want us to tell you a story or sing you a bedtime song?"

"Only if it has a happy ending," Fanny said, punching at her pillow.

"No guarantees, Fanny," Billie said softly. She turned out the light and closed the door.

Fanny drifted into sleep. Her dreams weren't of her ex-husband or of her husband. They were of a dark-haired, dark-eyed man splashing water on her as goldfish tickled her feet.

In the room down the hall, Billie kicked off her slippers. "I don't see a happy ending to this chapter in Fanny's life. What do you see, Bess?" Billie's voice was so fretful-sounding, Bess punched at her pillow as though she was pummeling dough in preparation for making bread.

Bess nodded. "Who was that man in the pool? I saw the way he looked at Fanny. You wait and see, he's coming back. Fanny's vulnerable right now." She punched the pillow again, so hard that feathers sailed upward. "I would have thought Ash Thornton was a foam-rubber man."

Billie reached out for one of the feathers. "Maybe it's an omen of some kind. I believe in stuff like that. Do you, Bess? I can't sleep. I'm too wide-awake now."

"Me too. Billie, all that stuff we told Fanny before . . . did we lie? It's getting downright spooky. Fanny's life really does parallel Sallie Thornton's. Sometimes I think Sallie choreographed the whole thing and she's . . . up there saying, yes, no, this is wrong, this is right, do this, don't do that. Am I nuts?"

"Well, if you are, then I am too, because I feel the same way. What we have to do is convince Fanny it isn't so."

"That makes us traitors," Bess murmured.

"I prefer the word friends looking out for another friend. We need to get some sleep. Tomorrow, today really, isn't going to be much better than yesterday. Our first order of the day should be getting that living room cleaned up. Maybe Fanny will let us decorate this place. If I had free rein here, I could turn this penthouse into something Fanny would never want to leave. Maybe that's not good, though."

"For now, it's wonderful. Billie, who *was* that man? He was no ordinary customer, was he?"

Billie was quiet for so long, Bess repeated her question.

"I think he's Fanny's true destiny. If that sounds corny, I'm sorry. When I saw the way he looked at her I got goose bumps. Look at my arms, just talking about him gives me the chills. We need to go to sleep. Fanny's private life is not our business. I'm already spooked, so let's not talk about it anymore, okay?"

"Okay. He had a sense of humor. I like that in a man. Simon takes life too seriously. Ash doesn't take life seriously enough. In my opinion the Thornton men are misfits. I always said that."

Billie snorted. "It's in the genes. The two Coleman men I knew were misfits, too. It's Fanny's and my infusion of blood that made our kids the people they are. *Good night, Bess.*"

"Night, Billie."

Simon stroked Daisy's head as he rocked back and forth. "I'm going to miss you, little girl. Tootsie and Slick are going to miss you, too. All your gear is packed up," he said, a catch in his voice. He stared off into space as the little dog snuggled in his arms.

Off in the distance he heard the sound of a car. Simon's head jerked upright. His shoulders slumped when he saw the military style jeep being driven by the mailman.

"Special Delivery, Mr. Thornton. You have to sign for it or I would have stuck it in the box at the end of the road."

"Thanks, Clyde," Simon said as he signed his name with a flourish.

"Looks like another nice day. How's Mrs. Thornton?"

"Fine, Clyde." *Go already so I can see if this is from Fanny. Please, let it be from Fanny.* Simon tortured himself for another five minutes before he looked down at the address on the heavy manila envelope.

It was addressed to Mr. and Mrs. Simon Thornton. The sender's name stood out starkly in heavy black lettering. THE APEX INVESTIGATIVE AGENCY.

Simon tossed the envelope on the floor of the porch. Like he really wanted to know more about his weird family. Colemans, Thorntons, they were all the same. Finding his mother's brother Josh didn't seem important in the scheme of things. Let Fanny deal with it.

Things seemed to be coming full circle these days. Fanny had at long last found her mother. It hadn't made her any happier. If anything, it had made her more unhappy, because she'd been denied the magical moment she'd always dreamed of. Ash and his decision to leave Las Vegas and turn over the casino to Fanny was something he had always known would happen. And now this envelope. More family. More family meant more troubles, more unhappiness.

Simon leaned over to pick up the envelope. He put it in the dog crate. "Time to go, Daisy. Fanny's waiting for you."

Simon loaded the kennel and a taped box full of Daisy's toys, blanket, and leashes in the back of the heavy-duty utility truck, then walked inside the house to call his wife. He wasn't surprised when the answering machine clicked on. He left his name, the flight number, and the time of Daisy's arrival. He paused a moment, wondering if he should say something else. He decided there was nothing to add and hung up the phone.

"Let's go, Daisy."

13

Fanny slipped onto a thickly padded barstool in the Harem Lounge. Billie and Bess joined her five minutes later. "I won two hundred dollars," Bess said, sitting down next to Fanny.

"And I lost fifty dollars," Billie lamented.

"Tea, ladies?" the bartender queried. The women nodded.

"How do your feet feel, Fanny?" Bess asked.

"They're numb, but the lower heels help. Wow! Would you look at that? I wonder who the lucky recipient is?" Fanny said as three uniformed young men walked past the bar carrying vases of yellow roses.

"Somebody must have won big tonight and they're paying off their good luck charm. Probably one of the showgirls kissed the dice or something equally stupid," Billie said.

The women watched as the uniforms turned about and reentered the Harem Lounge. "Mrs. Thornton, these are for you," one of the young men said, setting the flowers down on the teakwood bar.

"For me! Are you sure?"

Billie unobtrusively looked at the watch on her wrist and gave a slight nod to Bess as Fanny removed the small card from the holder nestled in one of the arrangements.

"Can you imagine Simon doing something so sweet? He knows I adore yellow roses. There must be six dozen of them. On the other hand, maybe they're from Ash, you know, that good-luck thing. Should we make a bet? I think they're from Simon. He left a message you know. I'm just so glad he sent Daisy. That shows he's thinking about me. Billie, who do you think sent them?"

"Simon or the kids."

"Bess?"

"I agree with Billie. Will you open the card already before we die of curiosity?"

Fanny ripped at the card. *Please let them be from Simon. Please, please, please.* Fanny stared at the card. Her voice was flat when she said, "We're all wrong. The flowers are from Marcus Reed. The man who put me in the pool last night."

"Is there a message?" Bess asked.

"Yes. It says, 'Thank you for the most enjoyable thirty minutes of my life.' "

Billie's voice was almost as flat as Fanny's when she said, "Isn't this about the same time as it was last evening when you went *wading?*"

Fanny looked at the clock over the bar. "I think so. What should I do with them?"

"What do you want to do with them?" Billie asked.

"If they were from Simon, I'd sit here and stare at them for the rest of the night. However, since they aren't from Simon I guess I'll just leave them here. The bartender can put them on the tables. They're gorgeous, aren't they?"

"Magnificent. Costly, too. That guy must have some bucks," Bess said.

"I'm flattered," Fanny said. "Things seem to be slowing down. Ash always said the casino's busiest time was around midnight. Do you suppose something fantastic is going on at one of the other casinos?"

"You would have heard if there was. Each casino has its spies. Sometime, you just have an off night."

"I had an idea a little while ago," Fanny whispered. "Do you remember when I gave you the tour and we opened that small empty suite next to the Spa Shop? Think about this, ladies. We decorate it to fit our theme and hire a seer. Fortune-teller, whatever you call those people. We might even be able to hire a *real* psychic. We'll give her a mystical-sounding name of some sort. It could be a lot of fun. Women absolutely love that kind of thing. I always read my horoscope, don't you? Tarot card readings and individual astrology charts go for hundreds of dollars. We could try to locate one of those hands-on people who touches something of yours, closes her eyes, and tells you about your life. It would be a tremendous draw and perfectly in keeping with the theme of Babylon. Billie, you could design us some razzle-dazzle outfits to fit the mood. What do you think?"

"Mega advertising," Bess said. "Reservations only, to begin with, because she's booked three months in advance which means you pay her while she does nothing until you generate enough interest. When you have to wait or can't get something, you want it all the more. It can't be shoddy. It has to be a real class act. When it comes right down to it, it is an act," Bess said.

"I just love harem pants, veils, beads, and bangles. My mother always said I was a gypsy in my other life. I'll make you an outfit that will blow your socks off," Billie promised. There was such enthusiasm in Billie's voice, Fanny laughed.

"We're cookin', ladies. Whoever said this was a man's business was wrong."

"My ex-husband said that, Bess. Three more hours and we can call it a night. I want to go upstairs to check on Daisy. I'll be right back."

Fanny's jaw dropped when she stepped from the elevator. Shoe boxes, one on top of the other, were piled every which way outside her door. She knew immediately who they were from. She struggled to count the boxes and finally gave up. She wondered what kind of taste *he* had and how *he* knew her shoe size. Charles Jourdan. *He* must have looked inside her shoes when *he* was holding them for her. Fanny opened several boxes and nodded approvingly. She couldn't accept these shoes. The question was, where and how was she to return them?

Daisy ran to meet her the moment she opened the door. She fondled the little dog as she pressed the play button to hear her messages. Her eyebrows shot upward when she heard Marcus Reed's voice. There was no hi, no hello, no this is Marcus Reed. "I'm just calling to tell you my sister tells me, and she claims to know everything, that if you soak your feet in Epsom salts and liquid peppermint, your feet will heal and feel wonderful. Both ingredients can be purchased at any drugstore. I'd like us to have dinner the next time I'm in Las Vegas. Lunch is good and so is breakfast if your schedule is tight. Good night, Fanny Thornton."

Fanny sat down with a thump, Daisy cradled in her arms. "Didn't he see my wedding ring? He didn't seem like the kind of man who would hit on a married woman. I did notice that he wasn't wearing a ring. Women notice things like that, Daisy. What am I going to do with those shoes? The flowers were a nice gesture. The shoes are something else." Daisy yawned. "Guess I woke you, huh? I'll take you for a long walk tomorrow and find some grass for you. It's a different kind of life here."

Fanny stared at the answering machine. She could call Simon and thank him for sending Daisy. She placed the call and held her breath while she waited for Simon to pick up the phone. "Simon, it's Fanny. Thanks for sending Daisy. I just came upstairs to check on her. It's late, I thought you might be sleeping."

"No. I was sitting on the front porch. I saw the paper today, Fanny."

Fanny sucked in her breath. She hadn't imagined that she would make news in a small California paper. "It was one of those things that just happened. My feet were burning and I could feel a corn starting to form on my little toe."

"You looked like you were having a good time. Who was the man?"

"Somebody in the casino. He left right afterward. I heard him say he had to catch a plane."

"I guess you're starting to like the bright lights and the noise."

"No. I came up with an idea tonight, though." She told him about her plans for the empty suite next to the Spa Shop. When Simon made no comment, Fanny babbled on, not wanting to hang up. "Billie is here for a month and so is Bess. Billie has agreed to decorate

Ash's apartment so I feel comfortable living here. Simon, can you see your way clear to coming here for a long weekend?"

"I can't, Fanny. I'll say good night now."

"Good night," Fanny whispered to the dial tone ringing in her ears. Tears rolled down her cheeks.

Fanny returned to the casino floor in time to hear excited squeals, ringing bells, and shrill whistles. Bess motioned to her. "A grandmother from Edison, New Jersey, just won the hundred-thousand-dollar jackpot on the dollar machine. Here comes the photographer and the floor manager with the IRS forms. Remember how excited we were the night Sallie let us each win a thousand dollars?"

"I remember. I called Simon and he saw today's paper. He cut me off and said good-night. There was a message on the machine from Mr. Reed and fifty boxes of shoes outside my door."

"Oh my God!"

"That's pretty much what I said myself. I can't even return the shoes because I don't know where Mr. Reed lives."

Fanny hugged the grandmother and posed for a photograph before she handed over the check to the speechless blond-haired lady. "If you don't mind me asking, Mrs. O'Leary, what do you plan to do with your winnings? Readers always want to know things like that."

"Call me Tootsie, Mrs. Thornton. Help my children, save some, maybe Daniel and I will take a vacation. I might buy a new lawn mower for Danny."

"What will you get for yourself?"

"I might buy some books. I love to read. I can't believe this. I've been here a whole week and haven't won a thing. My daughter Mary is going to be so surprised."

"Enjoy it, Tootsie. And come back and see us again."

"I will. I absolutely will, and if you ever come to Edison, New Jersey, stop and see us. We're in the phone book."

"I'll be sure to do that."

Fanny turned to Billie. "I think we can call it a night."

"And not a minute too soon," Bess said.

Fanny yawned, her eyes on the calendar. She'd give anything for twelve uninterrupted hours of sleep. Working the floor at night, sleeping for three or four hours in the early dawn, then working in the office for another four or five hours, snatching a catnap when she could, didn't make for an alert individual.

"A penny for your thoughts, Fanny," Bess said. "If it's any consolation to you, I feel as tired as you look."

"I forget what fresh air is. We've been here four months, Bess. Billie's been gone a month and Thanksgiving is only four days away."

"We've made progress though," Bess said. "We've managed to weed out all the deadbeats Ash had on his payroll, we've hired new people, we stopped the skimming, changed suppliers who were giving the deadbeats kickbacks. On top of all that we work the floor at night and Madam Sarika has turned into a class act. If you really want to take a bow, you're entitled. The Foundation is up and running. Billie's made her family's contribution and Madam Sarika's money is flowing into the account. We done real good, Mrs. Thornton."

"I haven't heard from Simon. Ash never calls. I was hoping Sunny would invite me for Thanksgiving. I hoped against hope that Simon would do the same thing. I called Sage this morning and he let it slip that he, Iris, and Billie are going to Sunrise. They were invited. Do you have any idea how terrible I feel, Bess?"

"Have you called Sunrise?"

"Of course. Several times a week. Sunny says hello, says she's fine, says the children are fine, her dad is fine, then she hands the phone to Ash, who basically tells me to stop calling because things are under control. He doesn't want to hear one word about this casino. My daughter and my ex-husband are living in their own world, and it does not include me. Now, what would you do if you were me?"

"I'd stop calling. Fanny, you're killing yourself and for what? You don't have to prove anything to anyone. You can't be all things to all people. My daughter is cooking Thanksgiving dinner and we'd love to have you join us. I know Billie invited you to Washington. That's two offers."

"I appreciate it, Bess. I'm still hoping Simon will call."

"Fanny, it's been four months. It's time to get your ducks in a row. Stop calling him and leaving messages on his machine. You must have left five hundred by now, and not one was returned. What does that tell you?"

"Hope springs eternal. Maybe I'll drive to the ranch over Thanksgiving. I could cook a turkey, fix all the trimmings, and . . ."

"And if he isn't there?"

"I'll call and leave a message first. If Simon doesn't want me to make the trip, he'll call back and tell me. This silence is so unlike

Simon. He's carrying this beyond stubborn. What he's doing is punishing me. He's done it before when I did something he considered stepping out of line."

"I would have blown up three months ago. Men do not have an understanding bone in their bodies. When John starts to act like that I put him in his place right away. He usually thanks me, saying he didn't think of it that way, whatever that way is. It works for us."

"Simon has a point."

"Which is?" Bess said.

"Those first few weeks when we did speak, he didn't understand how I could be doing something like this for my family when that same family turned their backs on me. I ask myself the same question every day. He doesn't understand that I have to earn back Sunny's respect and love."

"Excuse my language, Fanny, but that's bullshit."

"No, it isn't. I wasn't there for her. She doesn't want me anywhere near her or her children. I haven't told anyone in the family about the medical rehab center we're going to build. They aren't interested in anything I do. They'll view it as a ploy to get back into their lives."

"Oh, Fanny, you don't know that."

"Yes, Bess, I do know that. I'm okay with it. Each day it gets a little easier. The anger is starting to dissipate. Simon is a different story. I could make a life for us here if he would agree. I'm more than willing to give us another chance. Why is it women bend where men are concerned and men trench in?"

"It's the way it is. I hope you weren't expecting magical insight."

Fanny's voice was weary yet stubborn. "If Simon truly loved me, we could work something out. He's unwilling even to talk to me. That, Bess, tells me more than I want to know."

"Time will take care of everything. One day at a time. Look on the bright side, Fanny. Every day you get a dozen yellow roses. Four months is a long time for a person to send roses to someone he only met for thirty minutes. It's so mysterious."

"There's nothing mysterious about it at all. Mr. Reed left a standing order at the florist. He probably forgot all about me. As you said, four months is a long time."

"What did you do with the shoes?"

Fanny snorted. "I've been wearing them." Bess laughed.

"It's kind of quiet this afternoon. Go upstairs, get Daisy, and we'll go for a long walk. We'll get an ice cream on the way back. Both of us need some fresh air."

"That sounds like a marvelous idea. I'll meet you by the service elevator."

Fanny took a moment to savor what Bess called her "new digs." With Daisy in her arms, she walked around the spacious, newly decorated apartment. The chrome, glass, mirrors, marble, and leather furniture were all gone. In their place were cream-colored walls, ankle-hugging wheat-colored carpeting, matching draperies, and soft lighting. Low, deep, comfortable sofas in various shades of brown and beige with matching chairs welcomed her. Green plants dotted the corners next to well-stocked bookshelves. The cream-colored walls hosted vibrant watercolors signed by local artists. The electric fireplace was smoky black flanked by two enormous red chairs—duplicates of the chairs in her old studio at Sunrise. "My personal gift to you," Billie had said. "One for you, one for Daisy." A luscious jade plant and small Tiffany lamp sat in the middle of the table that separated the two chairs. All the comforts of home. "It's gender neutral," Billie had said. What that meant to Fanny was if Simon ever changed his mind, he wouldn't object to the decor. Her bedroom and the guest rooms were in various shades of green and beige.

The kitchen that had once been sterile white with touches of black was now homey and fragrant. The new appliances were almond-colored. The glass-and-chrome table and chairs had been replaced with antique oak, the chairs covered with red-and-white-checkered cushions. The pristine white cabinets had been resurfaced and now sported a rich oak veneer. Green plants in apple red crockery stood on the counter and in the center of the oak table. Braided, colorful rugs replaced the cold black-and-white marble floor. A small metal dish with orange peels and cinnamon sticks warmed over the pilot light, sending off a delicious aroma. The kitchen always smelled like she'd just baked an apple pie.

Fanny reached for Daisy's leash. The little dog danced and yipped as she tried to snare the leash to hurry Fanny along.

As she was locking the door behind her, Fanny heard the phone ring. She fumbled inside her pocket for the key. No one called her during the day. Maybe it was Simon or Sunny. The moment she opened the door, the phone stopped ringing. In dismay she listened to Marcus Reed's voice on her answering machine. A chill raced up both her arms. Her eyes wide, Fanny listened to the mesmerizing voice.

"Mrs. Thornton, this is Marcus Reed. Again, I hope I've dialed the right number. I checked with information and was told there were three listings for Thornton. I've left messages on the other two numbers since I wasn't sure which number was yours. I do hope that won't cause a problem. I've been on the other side of the world these past few months. I'll be coming to Las Vegas in the next few days. I'd like to take you to breakfast, lunch, or dinner if you're free. Since it is a holiday weekend, I'll understand if you aren't available. Family comes first. I'm sorry I missed you."

Fanny pressed the save message and didn't know why.

"Something wonderful must have happened while you were up there. I see a very noticeable sparkle in your eye. Did Simon call? Did you call him, or did the kids call about Thanksgiving?" Bess asked.

"No to everything. Mr. Reed left a message. He said he's been leaving messages at two other numbers. I would imagine those numbers are Sage's line and Billie's. Plus Ash. I wish he wouldn't do that. He never leaves a number so I can't return his call to tell him to stop. He has to know I'm married," Fanny said, wiggling her wedding ring finger.

"Maybe he checked you out. Men do that, you know. Who knows what was said. People here in the casino probably wonder where your husband is. You're working seven days a week and there's no sign of Simon. Ash is gone. You've never offered up any kind of explanation, so that means people can put their own spin on whatever story they feel like telling. Maybe he doesn't even know about Simon. Maybe he thinks you're divorced from Ash, which is true. You have to admit marrying your ex-husband's brother isn't really the norm. So, what did he want?"

"To have breakfast, lunch, or dinner. He's rather persistent, don't you think?"

"I'm not exactly the right person to ask. I'd say the man is interested in you."

"Well, that's just too bad. I'm married. At least I think I am. You know, Bess, it only takes a few seconds to make a phone call. I need to do something where Simon is concerned. The anger I'm starting to feel scares me."

"Fanny, why don't you take the rest of the day off and drive up to Sunrise. Sunny is the one you need to talk to. Ash, too, for that matter."

"Not today. If I'm going to do that, I have to work myself into it. I might call Ash later to . . . to talk. I probably shouldn't even bother since he brushes me right off, just the way Sunny does. Let's just enjoy our walk and talk about something else."

"You're the boss," Bess said as she fell into step alongside Fanny and Daisy.

Fanny kicked off her shoes as she flopped down in one of the big red chairs. Would she ever get accustomed to ending her day at three-thirty in the morning? She was too wired to go to bed, there wasn't anyone to call because no one else kept the kind of hours she did. She wasn't hungry, and she wasn't thirsty. There was nothing to watch on television, and her ears were too sensitive at this time of night to listen to music after listening to the sounds of the slots on the floor all evening long. She stared at her feet and then at the shoes she'd worn all evening. Shoes from Marcus Reed.

Who was Marcus Reed? Where did he live? What did he do for a living? She had to admit the man had managed to pique her curiosity. The big question was, what should she do, if anything, when he came to town? Her conscience took over. *What do you want to do, Fanny? I'll tell you what I want. I want my husband, and if I can't have my husband, I want . . . I need . . . What's wrong with breakfast, lunch, or dinner? Nothing. Nothing at all. So what if the man sends me flowers and shoes. So what! My husband should be sending me flowers and shoes. My husband should be calling me. My family should pretend they care if I'm alive or dead. No one is interested in me. This man is.*

Fanny howled her unhappiness into Daisy's soft fur. The little dog whimpered as she snuggled deeper into the crook of Fanny's arm.

Fanny reached for the phone. Ash would be awake. Ash never slept. She dialed the number in Sunrise and wasn't surprised when he picked up after the first ring. There was no greeting. "Fanny, what the hell are you doing calling here at this time of night? You're going to wake the kids. It's a good thing I was awake. What's wrong? Not that I care. I was going to call you later, after breakfast."

"Now that sounds like the Ash I know. I want to know two things. Have you heard from Birch since he went away? The second thing I want to know is why wasn't I invited to Sunrise for Thanksgiving?"

"No, I haven't heard from Birch. I got a postcard from somewhere in England. I had nothing to do with the guest list for Thanksgiving. I don't blame you for being upset. I imagine you'll be more upset when Christmas rolls around. I want you to know I tried to talk some sense into Sunny. She turned a deaf ear. She said she didn't need you taking over her kitchen and her dinner. She said she could mess it up all by herself."

"Whose kitchen?" Fanny's voice was sharper than she intended.

"Look, I know how you feel. Kids can be ungrateful little snots sometimes just the way ex-husbands can be. She's not doing real good, Fanny. I'd ask you to come up, but that would just throw her into a tizzy. She gets these spells when she gets excited and then she's drained for a few days. It's a damn good thing I'm here, I can tell you that."

"I'm grateful that you are there, Ash. I want you to believe that."

"Fanny, she doesn't even want me to bring up your name. She smacked Jake the other day because he wanted to know where Grandma Fanny was. I was telling him about the family earlier and I kind of made a story out of it and the little guy remembered. Don't you have anywhere to go for Thanksgiving?"

"Of course I have somewhere to go. I've had many invitations. I think it's pretty terrible of my own daughter not to invite me for dinner."

"Iris was upset. Everyone's upset. Where's Simon?"

"Everyone's upset but not so upset that they won't attend. You know what, Ash, I'm starting to get that hard-edged shell you used to have. I don't care anymore. All of you have stuck the knife in me so many times my heart is full of holes. As to Simon, I don't know where he is. He doesn't write, and he doesn't call. You ruined my marriage, Ash."

"If I could do that, then it must not have been worth very much. I'm sorry you feel that way. Is there anything I can do?"

"Yes, yes, yes. Sell this damn casino and let me get my life back."

"Anything but that, Fanny. Look, when I'm dead you can do what you want. Until that happens, it's business as usual. I'll call Simon and talk to him."

"I don't want you to do that, Ash. Don't interfere. I'll handle it. How are you feeling?"

"I have good days and I have bad days. I'm outside so much of the time I can actually sleep a few hours at a time. I have to tell you, Sunny can't cook worth a damn. I'm doing the turkey for . . . sorry, I didn't mean to bring that up."

"Ash, if I tell you something will you keep it to yourself?"

"Sure."

"Some guy sent me fifty pairs of shoes. It's that man who put me in the pool that first night. He sends a dozen roses every night. I don't know what to do about it."

"No shit! You mean you don't know what to do about Simon or the guy?" Not bothering to wait for a response, Ash babbled on. "Simon is as much of a bastard in his own way as I am in mine. You just never wanted to see it. Simon is not the knight in shining armor you thought he was. If he was all things to you as you believed, then where is he? He won't bend, Fanny. You need to know that. I hope you aren't the type to buckle under. If you do, I think I'd lose all respect for you. Play hardball with Simon. One way or another Simon always got his way. In everything, Fanny."

"That's what Simon always said about you."

"There you go. It's up to you who you choose to believe. What else can I do for you?"

"Do you know if Sage heard from Birch?"

"He got the same card we all did. Fanny, do you know Iris is pregnant?"

"Oh, Ash, no, I didn't know." Fanny started to cry.

"We just found out yesterday. I'm sure they'll tell you today. Iris adores you. Sage is walking on a cloud, or so Iris said. I think it's kind of wonderful. Call her up, Fanny, and invite her to lunch. I think she'd like that."

Fanny dabbed at her eyes. "I can't do that, Ash."

"No, I guess you can't. So, what's that guy's name?"

"Marcus Reed."

"Never heard of him. Dangle him under Simon's nose and see if he reacts."

"Ash, I'm not interested in the man."

"Sure you are. If you weren't interested, you wouldn't have brought up his name in the first place. He's intriguing you. Women love that. I am an authority on that subject as you well know. I bet the roses are yellow or pink. Not red, right?"

"What's that supposed to mean?"

"He's setting the scene for a seduction. Same thing as the spider and the web. Don't say I didn't warn you. I played that game hundreds of times."

"You really had to tell me that, didn't you?"

"I care about you, Fanny. I don't want to see some guy sucker my ex-wife. How's that make me look?"

"Like the ass you are," Fanny said. "Why were you going to call me?"

"I want you to go to Atlantic City and buy some property. I have a map and the lots are marked. Pay whatever you have to. You need to do it right away. Atlantic City is going to turn into a mini Vegas. We'll get your brothers to build Babylon II. Swear you won't drag your feet on this. I want it for the grandchildren. I want your promise, Fanny. One for Mom and Dad and one for the kids. It makes sense, Fanny. Before you know it they'll be all grown-up. Will you tell them I did it for them?"

Fanny's head buzzed. She knew there was no point in arguing. "What does pay whatever it takes mean, Ash?"

"Just buy it, Fanny. We'll worry about building it later. Right now boardwalk land is all that's important. Can you leave in a few days?"

"Do you want me to stop at the moon along the way? What is it about you that you can get me to do these things?"

"My irresistible charm. You'll do it then?"

"I'll do it. There's no money to build a casino though."

"There will be at the right time. I feel it in my gut, Fanny. When we're dead and gone, Jake will take over. That's a hell of a legacy, don't you think?"

"You know what, Ash, you're nuts. I'm nuts, too, because I'll be doing it. I'm hanging up now because you're getting on my nerves."

"I love you, Fanny."

In spite of herself, Fanny smiled as she hung up the phone. One more cockamamie scheme to deal with. And she would deal with it. She'd given her promise.

Fanny's clenched fists pummeled the arms of the red chair the moment she hung up the phone.

Alone and weary, Fanny finally slept, Daisy nestled at her side.

14

Fanny eyed the plump turkey sitting on her kitchen counter. It was years since she'd prepared a holiday dinner. She'd spent hours in the supermarket picking just the right yams, just the right cranberries, just the right turnip. And, for what? For whom was more like it. "Me and you, Daisy," Fanny muttered.

All day the phone on the kitchen wall beckoned. She'd lost count of the times she'd almost picked up the phone to call Simon. Instead she went back to unpacking her groceries and cleaning the oven in preparation for roasting the turkey. Daisy sat on one of the kitchen chairs, her eyes following Fanny. She yipped softly. "Okay, I'm going to call him. This is the last time, though," Fanny said as she dialed the number at the ranch, Ash's assessment of Simon ringing in her ears. *It's up to you who you choose to believe.* When Simon's voice came over the wire, Fanny's heart started to flutter. "It's Fanny, Simon. How are you? Simon, why haven't you answered any of my calls?"

"Fanny, there's nothing to say. You stated your position, and I stated mine."

Fanny bit down on her lower lip. Her back stiffened as she eyed the turkey. "This is my last phone call to you, Simon. I want to be clear about this. It's almost Thanksgiving. We all have so much to be thankful for. Especially you and me. Can we meet at some halfway point and share dinner? I was going to make a dinner for Daisy and me, but I'll forgo it if you can see your way clear to meet me. I won't beg you, Simon."

Simon's voice was so cold and bitter when he responded that Fanny flinched. He might just as well have slapped her in the face. "Are you saying you turned your back on our marriage for your wonderful family who now won't be joining you or inviting you for dinner?"

I will not cry. I absolutely will not cry. "Where do we go from here, Simon?" Fanny asked, her voice chilly.

"You tell me, Fanny."

"No, Simon, it doesn't work that way for me. Both of us need to agree on a decision. We might as well do it now, so we can get on with it." *It's up to you who you choose to believe. Simon's a bastard in his own way just the way I am. Simon always gets what he wants one way or the other.* "Are we just going to let it all fade away, Simon?"

Fanny heard his indrawn breath. "Unless you come back to the ranch, I don't see any other way for us to go."

"Even though the last two years weren't happy for me? You're giving me an ultimatum, Simon. I would never do that to you. Why are you taking such a stiff-necked position? Ultimatums mean one person will be happy and the other person will be miserable. Why can't we work this out? I'm willing to try. I'm willing to bend. Why are you refusing to understand what my family means to me? I never saw this stubbornness in you, Simon. How could I have been so blind? I know marriage is never easy unless both parties agree together on issues. You work it out, you learn from each other and you go on. You won't even meet me halfway. Ash was right, you're just as big a bastard in your own way as he is in his. My last words to you, Simon, are, you know where I am, you know my phone number. I won't be calling you again. Have a nice Thanksgiving."

Fanny fixed her gaze on Daisy. "It hurts too damn bad to cry. You know what, Daisy? You are my most precious possession. You're always there for me, you love unconditionally, and you're loyal. You'd never, ever desert me, nor would I desert you. That's what love is all about. Why do I understand that, and Simon doesn't? It's over," Fanny said. "Love stinks." She banged her fist down on the oak table. Pain richocheted up her arm as she yelped in frustration.

Fanny continued to talk to the little dog, who appeared to be listening intently. "This is how I see it. I have given myself a two-day holiday. That means I am not going anywhere near the casino floor or office. I'm going to cook, I'm going to watch television, I'm going to take naps, and I'm going to drink wine. In between all of that I'm going to take you for long walks. When it's time to eat, we're going to stuff ourselves because someone said that's what you're supposed to do on Thanksgiving. You and I will break the wishbone after dinner. Come here, Daisy."

Fanny cuddled with the little dog, who tried vainly to lick at the tears dribbling down her cheeks. Despair, unlike anything she'd ever experienced, flooded through her. "All those magazine writers, they're wrong, Daisy. It's not true that you have to be vulnerable before you can fall in love. To fall in love you have to have the hide of a buffalo."

Thanksgiving morning Fanny woke slowly. She felt Daisy inch up closer to her chest from her position at the foot of the bed. Fanny stroked her silky head as she stared at the ceiling. Two marriages down the drain. To brothers, no less. Yesterday she'd cried her tears. Today was a new day, and it was Thanksgiving. Time to get up and prepare the turkey. Time to get on with the day.

Yesterday was gone.

"Time to go out, Daisy. Get your leash and we'll do a quick scoot down the service elevator and out to the back driveway. Maybe we'll do the long walk after breakfast."

Fanny was back in the apartment and in the shower twenty minutes later. She dressed in jeans, an oversize sweatshirt that said WEST CHESTER and once belonged to either Birch or Sage. She stuffed her bare feet into ratty-looking sneakers with a hole in the big toe. She pulled her hair back into a ponytail with a rubber band, dusted her hands together, and marched out to the kitchen, stopping to turn on the stereo on the way. Soft music flooded the apartment.

Fanny prepared scrambled eggs for herself and fed Daisy as she contemplated the menu for her solitary dinner. The turkey was large enough to feed her entire family with leftovers for at least three days. She would be eating it for at least a month. She must have been out of her mind when she was shopping. She had too many yams, too many marshmallows, too many cranberries, and just the right amount of wine—three exquisite bottles of the best the French had to offer. She'd baked a pumpkin pie, a mince pie, and an apple pie along with some apple dumplings the day before. The aroma was still in the kitchen.

Fanny thought about other times then, other holidays when her family all gathered together. She'd been happy then, her children had been happy. Now, all that was gone. Now she was alone with only a dog for company. "I couldn't ask for more, Daisy," Fanny said, fondling the little dog's ears. "If this is all I'm going to get, we'll make the most of it."

Fanny worked diligently, doing all the things necessary to preparing a holiday dinner. She used her finest linen tablecloth, her china, her sterling, and her crystal. Daisy's place was set on the floor next to her chair on a lace-edged linen place mat. Her bowl was Bavarian crystal, her napkin linen as was Fanny's own. Daisy liked to clean her whiskers after eating.

Candles in silver holders graced each end of the table. The daily delivery of yellow roses sat in the center of the table, festive but lonely-looking. When the candles were burning, when the table was filled with platters and bowls, it wouldn't look so forlorn.

"I used to like to cook," Fanny muttered. "This is a chore." The moment she slid the heavy bird into the oven, Fanny uncorked the first bottle of wine. She poured a generous amount into a crystal flute and sipped appreciatively. She read the paper, smoked, and sipped.

By two o'clock, when she checked on the turkey to baste it, she had consumed one whole bottle of the exquisite wine. She carried the second bottle into the living room and turned on the television.

When the movie ended at four o'clock Fanny decided to check on the turkey, whose instructions said would cook itself. "Good thing," she mumbled as she tried to focus on the browning bird. "I think it's okay." She placed the second empty bottle next to the first one. "We're having a good time, aren't we, Daisy?" Daisy yipped, either in approval or denial. Fanny wasn't sure.

The phone rang as she was tottering back to the living room, the third bottle clutched to her breast. She debated whether she should answer it or not. "You gotta do what you gotta do."

"Hello."

"Fanny, it's Ash. I'm calling to wish you a happy Thanksgiving."

Fanny heard laughter and Jake's voice on the other end of the line. "Isn't that above and beyond the call of duty, Ash? I wasn't going to call you, so why should you call me? Personally I couldn't care less what you're doing there with *my* family."

"You sound funny. Have you been crying?"

Fanny's eyebrows shot upward. "Absolutely not! You aren't worth crying over, and neither is that brother of yours. So there, Ash."

"Fanny, are you drinking?"

"So what if I am. I'm cooking. So there again."

"I see."

"I see, I see. You don't see at all, Ash. You're too stupid to see just like your brother is too stupid to see. So there again and again."

"How much have you had to drink?"

"Is it important for you to know that?"

"Fanny, turn off the stove and lie down. Take a nap. Will you do that?"

"No. Why should I? I'm sick and tired of doing what you want me to do. The answer is no."

"Then I'll have to call Neal to shut off your stove. You sound sloshed."

"Well, you should know. I won't let him in. I changed the locks. Go away, Ash. Go back to my family and pretend everything is fine. I don't want to talk to you anymore. I don't want to talk to Simon either. So there."

"What happened, Fanny? Tell me, maybe I can help."

"Help! You want to *help*? You ruined my life, and now you want to help me! Drop dead, get out of my life! Wait, wait, I'm sorry. I didn't mean that."

"I know you didn't."

"You were right, Ash," Fanny hiccuped.

"About what?"

"About Simon is what. You said he was a bastard just like you are. He won't listen. He won't bend. Life is full of comp-ro-mises," Fanny said, enunciating the word for Ash's benefit. "I'm damn sick and tired of doing all the comp-ro-mis-ing. So there."

"Fanny, I'm coming down there. I'm going to leave right now."

"You better not. If you come here, I'll tell Daisy to bite you. She will, you know, because she loves me."

"Will you turn the oven off and will you stop drinking?"

"I'll turn the oven off, but I still have some wine left. This is the last time I'm going to do what you tell me. I hate your guts, Ash Thornton."

"Everyone in the world hates my guts. I'm going to hold on while you turn off the stove. After you do that, come back to the phone."

"I'm not stupid, Ash. Did you hear me? I hate your guts."

Fanny trotted out to the kitchen, opened the oven door, stared at the turkey for a few seconds before she turned off the oven. "I hate Simon's guts, too."

"Did you hear that, Ash, I hate Simon's guts, too? So there."

"I'll make it right, Fanny. I'll call Simon. He might listen to me."

"You're *toooooo* late. He gave me an . . . ultimatum. Go away, Ash. I don't want to talk to you anymore. You make me crazy. Did I tell you I hate your guts?"

"Numerous times. I wish you were here, Fanny, I really do. This little reunion is fizzling. No one is comfortable. I mean it, Fanny, I wish you were here."

"I wish I was too. Good-bye, Ash."

Fanny stared at the hole in her sneaker. She wiggled her big toe until it worked through the worn canvas. "Did ya see that, Daisy? I can accomplish whatever I set my mind to." She looked around for her wineglass. *Damn, I must have left it in the kitchen.* She swigged from the bottle.

The doorbell rang.

"Shit!" Ash must have called Neal to come up and turn off the stove. "Go away!" she bellowed. The bell rang again. Daisy barked and wouldn't stop.

"All right, all right!"

Fanny opened the door with a wide flourish, waving the wine bottle as she did so.

"Mrs. Thornton."

"Yep, that's me, two times. Soon to be ex for the second time. And you are . . . the shoemaker . . . the shoe man . . . the man with the shoes . . . Roses. They're on the table. I guess you came to see for yourself. Or did you come to see if I turned off the oven? Who cares? Do you want your shoes back? Look!" Fanny said, wiggling her foot with her toe sticking out of the sneaker. "It was hard to do that, but I did it." She took a long pull from the wine bottle as she stood aside for Marcus Reed to enter the apartment.

"Did I invite you for dinner?"

Marcus smiled. "No, I invited you."

"Oh. Ash made me turn the oven off. Dinner's going to be late. Maybe there won't be any dinner. Daisy is hungry."

"I'm a very good cook. Do you want me to finish your dinner for you?"

"Why would you want to do that?" Fanny asked suspiciously.

"Because you're in no shape to do it. There are a lot of starving people in the world, and it's a shame to waste food."

"You're absolutely right," Fanny said smartly.

"If I make some coffee, will you drink it?"

"I love coffee. I drink coffee all day. I hate Ash's guts. I hate Simon's, too."

"Tomorrow you'll feel different."

"Oh no I won't. What are you doing here? Do you know I'm married?"

"I know now. Are you happily married? Marriage is a wonderful institution."

"Yes. No. I don't think so. You have to turn the oven on to make it work. It was almost done when Ash made me turn it off. I used to like to cook. I hate cooking. I hate everything."

"That's not good, Mrs. Thornton."

"Why not? You can call me Fanny. I wear those shoes all the time. That was very clever of you. Did you see what I did with the roses and the wine bottles?"

"Yes, I did. You have to put water in the bottles or the bloom will die."

"That's sad. I don't like it when things and people die. Do you?"

"Of course not. Why are you alone today, Fanny? Don't you have a family?"

"I have a family all right. They didn't invite me. Do you believe that? I love them all so much. I was a good mother. I know I was. I never had a mother, so I made sure I was the best mother I could be. I make one mistake and . . . it's none of your business, Mr. Reed."

"That's true. It isn't."

Fanny did her best to focus on the man standing in her kitchen. "Sallie would never have let it get this far. I'm like Sallie sometimes. For a long time I wanted her to be perfect. She wasn't. I'm not either. That's a perfect-looking turkey. Do you think this coffee will make me sick? I only got drunk once in my life. Me and Sallie."

Marcus Reed chuckled. "What was the question again?"

"I don't know. Can't you remember?"

"No. Did you make these pies?"

"Every last one," Fanny said proudly.

"I think things are under control. What time would you and Miss Daisy like to dine?"

Fanny tossed her hands in the air. "Are you joining us?"

"If you would like me to, then I'd be honored."

"What should we do now?" Fanny asked.

"I think you should take a nap. I'll watch the football game and the turkey."

"That doesn't . . . seem . . . proper. I hardly know you," Fanny sniffed.

"Isn't that strange? I feel like I've known you forever."

Fanny could feel the bile swishing around in her stomach. "You shouldn't be around me. My family doesn't like anyone I . . . never mind. It isn't important."

"Would you like to talk about it, Fanny? I'm a good listener."

"No. Everyone says that, then they judge you. No thanks. I think I will take a nap. Do you promise to watch the turkey?"

"I promise," Marcus said solemnly.

Fanny's voice turned crafty. "Why should I believe you?"

"Because I'm a man of my word."

"Oh. You have lovely taste in shoes, Marcus. Will you call me when dinner is ready?"

"Absolutely. Do you want me to answer the phone if it rings and if so, what should I say?"

Fanny teetered over to where Marcus stood. "Do you want to hear something sad, Marcus? No one calls me anymore. I do all the calling. All my life I tried to live by the Golden Rule. I always put everyone else first. Myself last. This is what it got me. I live with a little dog. I have two friends. That's it. That's the story of my life. It's sad, isn't it?"

Marcus smiled. "Yes. But things will change. When things look the darkest, a light suddenly appears."

"I think you're wrong."

"Why don't we talk about it after you've had a nap?"

"If anyone calls and their names are Ash or Simon tell them . . . tell them—"

"Yes?"

"Tell them to go to hell."

"Yes, ma'am, I can do that." Marcus turned to hide his smile.

"I love these sneakers."

Marcus threw back his head and roared with laughter. Fanny sniffed as she tottered down the hall to her bedroom, Daisy behind her. Inside her bedroom, she locked the door. She looked across the room to where the bed was. It was much too far. "Get me a pillow, Daisy." A moment later she was sound asleep.

"Simon, Ash here. I called to wish you a happy Thanksgiving and to ask you what in the goddamn hell you're doing to Fanny. She's spending Thanksgiving alone with her dog. Even I have to admit that's pretty sad. I talked to her today, and she told me you gave her an ultimatum. You don't ever give Fanny an ultimatum. Are you just going to write her off because she won't do what you want when you want it done? That's how you train a dog, not a wife."

"Mind your own business, Ash. This is all your doing, you and that fucking casino. If it wasn't for you, Fanny would be here with me now."

"I didn't twist her arm, Simon. Fanny has loyalty, something you and I don't have. Yes, I traded on that loyalty. Let me tell you, she's doing a hell of a job."

"For what? So you can die happy?"

"That's a low blow, even from you. I like to think it's my legacy. I wanted Mom to be proud of me the way you wanted Pop to be proud of you. Don't give me that shit that you saw a shrink and came to terms with things. You didn't any more than I did. Face it, Simon, we're both misfits, you in your way and me in mine. The only difference between us is you wore a three-piece suit. At least I look it in the face and admit to my screwups. Fanny told me she loved you so much she ached. That's a hell of a testimonial, little brother. I personally don't give a shit what you do. What I do give a shit about is Fanny's happiness. She deserves better. I know she's going to sell the casino when I'm gone. You must know it, too. Couldn't you have given her the year? Even two if I make it that long. Oh, no, that interfered with that new life of yours. You blew it. That fucking silence of yours, that withdrawal you use as a weapon won't play with Fanny. One last thing, don't come to my funeral. I'm leaving instructions with the kids if you show up they're to boot your ass all the way down the mountain. In other words, Simon, kiss my ass. It's beyond me what Fanny ever saw in you. Enjoy the rest of the day."

Okay, Fanny, that's all I can do. The rest is up to him.

"I guess my dinner was a bit of a disaster," Sunny said.

"It wasn't that bad," Iris said generously.

"Mom always made a great Thanksgiving turkey," Billie said. "Remember how we'd eat off the leftovers for days and days? The stuffing was almost better than the turkey. You should have invited her, Sunny."

"No, I shouldn't have. Why didn't you cook dinner and invite her? Or you, Iris?"

"I was going to, but you invited us first. Sage and I thought you were inviting your mother. It was a slap in the face, Sunny. Does anyone know where Fanny was having dinner today?"

"She was home by herself," Ash said. "She told me she was cooking dinner for her and Daisy. She said she had invitations but elected to stay home."

"Oh my God," Billie said. "Mom was always the first one to invite people so they wouldn't be alone on Thanksgiving. Grandma Sallie used to do the same thing."

"So now it's all my fault," Sunny cried.

"Since it was your dinner and your invitation list, I'd say so. What kind of family dinner did you expect with Birch and Mom missing from the table?" Sage grated.

"This was supposed to be a family dinner where everyone smiles and gets along. At least I tried."

"You aren't Mom, so don't try and pretend you are. Mom is what holidays are all about. Don't even think about asking me for Christmas," Billie said as she started to clear the table.

"Me either," Sage said. "Iris and I are going to her sister's house."

"So go," Sunny yelled as she stumbled from the table.

Ash stared at his son and daughter. "This isn't good for her."

"She's stupid. Did she really think this was going to be a fun day?" Sage growled.

"Yes, she did."

"Guess she was wrong. You know what, I feel like shit," Sage said.

"Me too," Billie said. "I was hoping Birch would call. I guess he won't since it's later in England if he's still there. Maybe he called Mom. Birch was always good about the holidays. I'm going to help with the dishes, and I'm leaving."

"I'll help," Iris said.

"Don't bother. Dad and I will clear up. Jake likes to carry in the plates. If you have someplace to go, feel free to leave. I'm sorry this wasn't what you all expected."

"You need to get those marbles out of your head and grow up. This is the real world we're walking around in," Sage said.

"That's enough, Sage," Ash said, reaching for his arm.

"Now why did I know you were going to say that? It might be a good idea to get Sunny some counseling or a shrink. Get her something, for God's sake, before she goes off the deep end. My advice is stop babying her." Sage turned on his heel, scooped Jake onto his shoulder pretending to be a horse shouting, "Giddy-up, pardner." The little boy squealed in delight.

"You're leaving?" Sunny said, her face full of outrage.

"Under the circumstances . . ." Iris said.

"I thought we'd play some cards or something."

Sage set Jake on his father's lap. "No, we're leaving. Maybe we'll stop and see Mom and wish her a happy Thanksgiving."

"That's an idea," Billie said, shrugging into her coat.

"I think that's a good idea. I want to tell her about the baby," Iris beamed.

"Say hello for me," Ash said.

"Little shits," Sunny said when the door closed behind her guests.

"Little shits," Jake mimed her.

Ash flinched at the sound of the slap the little boy took to his bottom. He reached for him and held him close. "Sunny, if you strike this child again, I will personally call Tyler and tell him you're being abusive. Do we understand each other?"

Sunny fled the room as Ash crooned to the little boy, stroking his head. "It's okay, it's okay, Jake. Let's take a ride in the elevator and guess who gets to push the button. But first we have to check on Polly."

"Hers sleeping."

"I know. We're going to check to see if she's sucking her thumb."

"I loves you, Pop Pop."

"I love you too, Jake." *Now I know what Fanny means when she says she loves so much it hurts. Now I know. Now, when it's too late.*

Marcus Reed wandered around the comfortable living room. He stopped to look at family pictures, touching a knickknack, leafed through a book. This place might be an apartment but it was a home in every sense of the word. He tried on Fanny's reading glasses and winced. They smelled powdery.

He wandered back to the kitchen. He sniffed appreciatively. If he ever got this dinner on the table, it would be a miracle. The clock said 7:10. He was trying to decide if he should wake his hostess when the phone rang. He picked it up after the second ring.

"I'd like to speak to Fanny."

"Fanny isn't available at the moment. Would you care to leave a message?"

"Who is this?"

"Who are you?"

"This is Simon Thornton, and I asked you who you were."

"I'm Marcus Reed, a friend of Fanny's. If you care to hold on, I'll wake her."

"You'll wake her. Why is she sleeping? It's only seven o'clock."

"Earlier, Fanny wasn't feeling all that well. Please, hold on."

Marcus walked down the hall to Fanny's room. He assumed it was her room because the other bedroom doors stood open. He rapped sharply. "Fanny, you have a telephone call. It's Simon Thornton." When there was no response he rapped again, this time louder. Daisy barked furiously. "Fanny, can you hear me? You have a telephone call."

"Yes. Yes, thank you. I'll take it in here."

Marcus walked back to the kitchen. As much as he wanted to hear the conversation, he replaced the receiver in the cradle. He turned knobs on the stove. Dinner was finally under way. He sat down at the table with a cup of coffee to wait for his hostess.

Fanny picked up the phone, her tongue thick in her mouth. "What is it, Simon?"

"I thought I might drive down to Vegas tonight."

"Thanksgiving is over, Simon."

"I guess we need to talk."

"No, I don't think we do. I have a job to do here, Simon, and I cannot leave. You rejected all my overtures these past four months. Now all of a sudden you want to grace me with your presence. I don't think so."

"Who answered the phone? He said you weren't feeling well."

"Actually, Simon, that was a polite way of saying I was drunk and sleeping it off. Mr. Reed is a . . . friend of mine. He stopped by to finish cooking dinner for me and Daisy because I was too drunk to do it. Is there anything else you want to know?"

"Now you're telling me you don't want me to come there after begging me for four months."

"I don't take kindly to ultimatums. Look, I think we both need to cool down a little. We'll talk another time."

"When?"

"When? When I decide, Simon. You've managed to keep me on a string for four months. Don't expect me to rush to any quick decisions. I'm going to hang up now."

"Maybe you shouldn't bother calling me at all."

"Maybe I shouldn't."

"Ash said you would do this."

"What does Ash have to do with this?"

"He called me today and told me off. He also told me not to attend his funeral."

"Well guess what, Simon, Ash told me a lot of things about you, too. I'm thinking about those things right now, and the more I think about them, the more I'm starting to believe them. Good-bye, Simon." Fanny broke the connection. She waited a moment before she picked up the phone again. When she heard the dial tone, she stuffed the receiver under her pillow.

Fanny stared at herself in the bathroom mirror. Holy Mother of God! Who was this person staring at her? She clenched her teeth until she realized she had to pry them apart in order to brush. She gargled, washed her face, slapped on some powder, and brushed her hair.

She was halfway down the hallway when the doorbell rang. Thinking it was Bess, she didn't bother to hurry, since each step she took thumped its way to her head. When she entered the living room, she saw Marcus Reed open the front door.

Fanny shrank back against the wall.

She almost fainted when Marcus came up to her and said, "Your children are here. Look, I don't know what's going on. You look as miserable as they do. If I may make a suggestion, invite them to dinner. Don't make apologies, and smile even if it kills you. Can you do that, Fanny?"

"Yes. Yes, I can do that. Thank you. Thank you very much."

"Okay, stiffen those legs and forget the headache hammering behind your eyes. You have lovely eyes you know. Your children are lucky to have someone like you. Sometimes young people don't see what's right under their noses. Just be their mother and everything will be fine. Trust me, okay?"

"Okay."

15

〜

Fanny did her best to turn an awkward situation into one of comfort. She managed to smile, to hug her children and say kind things while the sledgehammer inside her head pounded away at her temples. "Marcus, I'd like you to meet my daughter Billie, my daughter-in-law Iris, and my son Sage. This is Marcus Reed. Of course you all know Daisy. Please, come in and tell me what you think of my . . . new digs."

"It's hard to believe," Billie said, her face registering awe. "Did Aunt Billie do it?" Fanny nodded.

"Would anyone like a drink?"

"I'd like a beer," Sage said. He tried not to stare at the tall, handsome man who seemed so at ease in his mother's apartment.

"Nothing for me," Iris said.

"Coke," Billie said.

"Entertain your children, Fanny. I'll get the drinks." Fanny nodded, amused at the curiosity in her children's eyes.

"Would you like to stay for dinner?"

"I sure would," Billie said. "I was hoping for leftovers. A full dinner sounds wonderful. Aren't you eating rather late?"

Fanny was about to confess to her afternoon folly when Marcus returned and said smoothly, "I'm afraid it's my fault. My plane was late getting in."

"They're staying for dinner, Marcus."

"That's wonderful. Now you won't have to eat turkey for the next thirty days. You visit, Fanny, and I'll get the food on the table. I hope you all brought your appetites."

Not wanting a lapse in the conversation, Fanny said, "Did any of you hear from Birch?"

"Tomorrow he'll realize it's Thanksgiving and he'll call. He's fine, Mom, trust me on this. Birch just needs to get things in perspective. Near-death experiences affect people differently. He'll be home before you know it. Mom, Iris and I have something to tell you. We stopped by twice yesterday, but you were out. It's not the kind of thing you announce on the phone, and we didn't want to leave a note. Iris is pregnant."

"Oh, Sage, how wonderful!" Fanny said, pretending not to know the good news. "Iris, you must be so happy. Will you allow me to make the layette?"

"Of course. I got some experience today holding Polly. She's a very good baby. Would you like to see a picture of her? We took some Polaroids today."

"Yes, yes I would." Fanny's eyes burned as she stared at the pictures of her grandchildren. "They're beautiful. I'm sure every grandmother says that."

"Jake is a piece of work. He's all boy. He's got Dad wrapped. Dad says Jake gets out of bed at night and sleeps with him. I don't know how long that will last because Jake wets the bed. Dad thought it was funny." Fanny smiled.

Fanny handed back the pictures.

"If you like, you can keep them," Iris said.

"Thank you. Yes, I would like that very much."

"You could go up there, Mom. You might want to think about it before Sunny gets it into her head to put those gates back up. She mumbled something about it today."

"I can't do that. Where I'm concerned, it's by invitation only. I understand her feelings, and I have to respect them. Sunny will do what she feels she has to do. Is she all right?"

"Hell, no, she's not all right. I don't want to talk about Sunny, Mom. How's Uncle Simon?" Sage asked.

"I'm afraid I can't answer that, Sage. I haven't seen him in four months. He did call today though. Just a little while ago, as a matter of fact."

"Dinner's ready," Marcus said from the dining-room doorway.

He looks like he belongs here. Evidently her children were of the same opinion.

"God, real food," Sage said, folding his hands. He said grace, his eyes on the turkey.

"I'd say we made a serious dent in this bird," Marcus said an hour later, pushing back his chair. "Would anyone like food to go? I saw some aluminum trays that would be perfect for one more complete meal for each of you."

"I'm your man," Sage said.

"I'm your girl," Billie smiled.

"I'm eating for two now, so fill my tray," Iris said.

"You ladies sit here and Mr. Reed and I will clear up," Sage said. "I'll wash. You dry. This is Mom's good stuff, so be careful. It all belonged to my grandmother Sallie."

"I'll keep that in mind," Marcus said. Fanny noticed the twinkle in his eyes. For some reason she felt flustered

"Who *is* he, Mom?" Billie asked.

"A friend. A friend who got me through a very bad day."

"Mom, we didn't know for certain that you weren't invited until we got to Sunrise. It was awful. I couldn't wait to leave. Sage and Iris felt the same way."

"Sunny's going through a bad time. You need to be tolerant."

"Mom, it has nothing to do with her condition. It's that thing with you and her. She *will* put the gates up."

"Then she puts the gates up. It won't be the end of the world."

"How is the casino business?" Iris asked. "Later on I'll think about making an appointment with Madam Sarika to tell me if I'm going to have a boy or a girl."

"You don't *really* want to know, do you, honey? That's one of the best things about giving birth, the surprise at the end. At least I always thought so. You're married to a twin so there's a good possibility you might have twins."

"I would love to have twins," Iris gushed. "I'd like to have a little boy that looks like Sage and a little girl that looks like me."

Fanny smiled. "Will you go back to work?"

Iris shrugged.

"Ah, December, the most wonderful time of the year. I have to start thinking about decorations for the casino. I have meetings scheduled all week with decorators who specialize in such things. I didn't even know there were companies like that. Running this casino is an education in itself."

"Mom, do you remember that play village I made when I was ten or so?" Billie asked. Fanny nodded. "What if we shut down Rainbow Babies and Sunny's Togs for a week and make one like it, life-size. We could set it up outside in the hanging gardens. Chue can take the plants out, store them, and after New Year's he can replant them. Sage is great with a hammer and nails."

"I can sew," Iris said. "I can do the elves. Children will love it. Since I'm on a leave of absence I have a lot of free time and I would love to work on this."

"We could have it ready for the first of December," Billie said.

"Honey, that's only a week away."

"We can do it, Mom. We need a Christmas tree, a really big one like they have in New York."

"I went to school with a girl whose father owns a Christmas tree farm in Oregon. I'll call her when we get home. Oh, this is so exciting! I just love this family. You're all so interesting," Iris trilled.

Fanny laughed.

"We need to get on our sticks. Sage!" Billie bellowed. "Let's go. We have business to take care of. *NOW!*"

Sage and Marcus came on the run.

Fanny watched Marcus's face as her children started talking all at once. His head bobbed from side to side as Billie and Iris chattered like runaway trains.

"Are you honest to God saying I finally get to use my carpentry skills after all these years? Yahoo!" Sage boomed. "One week is cutting it pretty close. We can do it. Jesus, I wish Birch was here. He'd get a kick out of this. Marcus, do you know anything about carpentry?"

"I worked summers in construction to put myself through college. Are you requesting my help?"

"Well, hell yes. Do you think you can handle it?"

"Sage . . . Marcus . . . where are your manners, Sage?"

"At the table, Mom. You always said to leave them there. Where are we going to do this?"

"How about calling Red Ruby and asking her if we can do it at the ranch. She's got all those barns and stuff. It won't interfere with her . . . ah, business."

"Are you referring to the famous"—Marcus cleared his throat—"establishment?"

"Yeah, that's the one." Sage grinned. "My grandmother set her up out there. She always gives us a Christmas present. She was in love with my grandfather."

"Sage! How do you know that?" Fanny demanded.

"She told me. She loved Grandma Sallie, so she never, ah, you know."

"Good Lord," Fanny muttered.

"It's settled then. Mom's going to take care of the inside, with those companies she's meeting with, and we're going to do the outside. Are you helping, Mr. Reed?" Billie asked.

"What time should I report for work?" Marcus asked smartly as he slapped the dish towel over his shoulder. "I'm afraid I didn't bring the proper attire with me."

Fanny grew light-headed when Marcus winked at her.

"We can outfit you right now, right here. I'll call downstairs and have them send up some stuff. Is that okay with you?"

Marcus shrugged.

"Mom, there's no dial tone."

"Oh. The receiver's under the pillow in my room."

"I'll put it back on the hook," Iris said.

"I don't suppose you want to tell us why the receiver is under your pillow," Sage said.

"That's right. I don't. Marcus, you don't have to do this."

"I would like to do it. I can take care of my business in the evening. Most of it is entertaining anyway."

"I'm afraid not. This project will be around the clock. You can back out now if you want to," Sage said.

"I'm a man of my word. It won't be a problem. The more I think about it, the more the idea appeals to me."

"Okay, we're out of here. I'll pick you up by the front door at six-thirty. Are you staying here?"

"No. I'll be ready."

"Night, Mom, the dinner was swell."

"Don't forget your leftovers," Fanny said, hugging her children.

When the door closed behind her children, Fanny stared helplessly at Marcus. "I don't know what to say. They really did put you on the spot. How do I thank you for all you did today?"

"I enjoyed every minute of it. How do you feel?"

"I have a monster headache."

Marcus handed Fanny the dish towel. He shrugged into his jacket, straightened his tie just as the doorbell rang. Fanny smiled as he inspected his new working attire, right down to the yellowish brown boots.

"I'll say good night. I would say thank you for inviting me, but then I invited myself. It was a wonderful day. You have very nice children, Fanny. I think I envy you."

"What you see isn't always the way things are, Marcus." Her voice was so sad Marcus stared at her longer than he intended. He nodded to show he understood.

"If your children give me a dinner hour, would you join me?"

Fanny laughed. "Forget the dinner hour. When they get immersed in a project, they gobble donuts on the run. I'll bring out some food around six o'clock. We can have a picnic. You realize you aren't getting paid for this, don't you?" She could hear Marcus laughing all the way to the elevator.

For the first time in months, Fanny looked forward to waking in the morning. She hurried through her duties in the office, tidied the apartment, cooked, and made two trips a day to Red Ruby's with baskets laden with food. She knew she was in the way, but she didn't care. She loved watching her children create things, loved watching Marcus Reed's rippling muscles as he worked alongside her son.

On the third day, Marcus groaned when he saw Fanny approach with the heavy basket. "If it's turkey again, I quit."

"It's not turkey. It's pastrami on rye with real deli pickles and lots of mustard."

"In that case, I'll stay. Sage and I were just talking about opening our own construction business. He only banged his thumb thirty times."

"I don't think either one of you should quit your day jobs." Fanny laughed.

"I'm of the same opinion. I never would have believed this if I wasn't right here on the scene. That little-bitty matchstick thing stuck on a piece of cardboard is now something to take notice of. I'm anxious to see what it looks like when it gets painted with all the Christmas colors. You must be very proud of your daughter, Fanny. I was married once but never had children. I suppose it was a good thing because the marriage didn't last."

"I'm sorry. When all else fails, when things don't go right, you can always count on family to get over the trouble spots. It isn't always a constant in one's life, but it should be."

"Where will you be this Christmas, Fanny?"

"At the casino. Would you like to join us? Don't feel you have to, just to be polite. It will probably be just me and Daisy. The kids might stop by. I can't be sure about anything these days."

"I can't think of anything I'd like more. Of course. Do you do the tree, sing carols, drink eggnog, open gifts?"

"The whole nine yards. We do it Christmas Eve. We have a big as in very big dinner first. Sallie always did it that way. It was wonderful. She invited everyone she thought might be alone. Sallie was the kindest, gentlest, most wonderful person I've ever met. I don't think she was ever truly happy. Are you happy, Marcus?"

"Define the word happy, Fanny. This is a tremendous sandwich."

"Well, it's a wonderful feeling. You can't wait to get up in the morning and you hate going to sleep at night. It's that contented feeling that all is right with your world. It's caring about people who care about you. The sun is brighter, the stars shinier, that kind of thing."

"Then I guess I'm sort of happy. I like crunchy apples. I'd like to stay and talk, Fanny, but your son cracks a mean whip. He doesn't much care for cigarette breaks either. He puffs as he works. Thanks for lunch."

"Isn't it great, Mom? The tree's coming late this afternoon. The delivery people are going to set it up. Mom, would it be impossible to shut down Babylon so we can do all this without interruption? I know we'll lose money, but this stuff is going to bring in people by the drove. How long did the company you hired say their work will take?"

"A day and a half. Sure, we can close down. I'm the boss, remember."

"We have to cover the front doors and windows. We want this to be an in-your-face, blow-your-socks-off opening. By the way, what's it costing for the casino?"

"You don't want to know. We'll recoup. I'll have Neal put up signs, and we'll announce it hourly over the loudspeaker. I have to get back."

"He's got a nice tush. For a man his age. Did you notice, Mom?"

"No, I did not notice." Flustered at her daughter's comment, Fanny packed up her picnic basket.

"C'mon, Mom, he's a groovy-looking guy. For his age. He's nice.

I like him. Sage does, too. The truth is, he's a better carpenter than Sage is. They're both having the time of their lives. I think you are, too; but you won't admit it. He's nothing like Dad or Uncle Simon."

Fanny changed the subject. "How's that twenty-foot-high Santa coming?"

"I'm doing the beard this afternoon. It's one silky strand at a time, and it takes time. The ladder isn't all that steady. The guys are making me a scaffold. I stitch as I go along. Where are we going to store this stuff after Christmas?"

"Right here in Red's barns. The bigger question is, how are you going to transport this to Babylon?"

"In eighteen wheelers. It's all taken care of, Mom."

"All right. Don't fall off the ladder, Billie. I'll see you this evening."

Fanny turned to risk a quick glance in Marcus Reed's direction. There was something about a man in jeans and hard hat. Billie was right. He did have a nice tush. For someone his age.

Back at the casino, Fanny tracked down Ash's business manager and Security chief. She hated going toe to toe with people when they wore the stubborn look Neal was wearing. "It is good business, Neal. We aren't going to fold because we close our doors for two days. I'm not asking you. I'm *telling* you what we're going to do. Post notices at all the entrances and announce it hourly. We'll be open for business Saturday evening at six o'clock. I would suggest you hire extra security. The media will be here in full force. Starting tonight on the six o'clock news, ads will begin to air. They'll run until Saturday. Full-page ads will be in the papers starting tomorrow. Your staff won't be able to handle the crush of people so you should bring in all your people who are off for the weekend. Santa arrives promptly at seven. Do whatever you have to do so there are no glitches. I want this to run smoothly. Oh, one other thing. Mr. Thornton will be in attendance. Ah, I rather thought that would get your attention."

Fanny beelined to her office and immediately dialed the number at Sunrise. Ash answered, laughter in his voice. "It's Fanny, Ash. Is everything okay?"

"Yep. Jake is tickling my feet. What's up, Fanny?"

Fanny told him. "I'd like you to come, Ash. I'd like it even more if you'd bring Jake. Polly's too young. Will you do it? I think I just want to hear you say you're proud of me. The kids are really doing a job on this. It's going to be the most wonderful fairyland. I'm sure

Jake knows about the North Pole, Santa, and the elves. You read him stories, don't you?"

"I can come of course. I'm not sure if Sunny will allow me to take Jake though."

"Ash, Sunny is invited. I wasn't excluding her. Do your best, okay? The kids did everything with Jake in mind. You are absolutely going to be blown away. The kids stopped by on Thanksgiving. Did you tell them to do that? If you did, then I need to thank you."

"It was their own idea. It was miserable when they were here. There's some problems here, but we can talk about them when I come down. I need your clear head on some stuff."

"I'll be here, Ash."

Ash sat for a long time, his thoughts whirling chaotically. He eyed the little boy sleeping on the sofa. His features softened and he smiled. They were going fishing later. Chue had a small natural pond he stocked with plastic goldfish for his grandchildren along with a basket of ten-cent prizes in case one of the children was lucky enough to snare one of the plastic fish. Regardless, they always came home with a prize and a fortune cookie.

Ash steered his way to the closed-in garden room, where Sunny reclined in the last patch of afternoon sun. "How's it going?" he asked.

"Hi. I was sitting here thinking about Tyler. He called earlier and wanted to know if he could take Jake to New York the day after Christmas. He said he'd take him ice-skating and do some father-son things. I didn't say yes and I didn't say no. I wanted to talk to you first. It's just for two days. Jake would like going on a plane."

"By himself!" Ash said, horror written all over his face. "He's only three, Sunny. If someone was to take him, it would be different. I don't think it's a good idea, but it's your decision."

"I always make the wrong decisions. That's why I wanted to talk to you. Jake does miss Tyler. He didn't even ask about Polly. I did send a picture of her that we took on Thanksgiving. He didn't mention it at all. He also said he's dating someone. 'Seeing someone' is the way he put it. I thought that would bother me, but it doesn't. I wonder why that is. Is Jake still sleeping?"

"On the sofa. He climbed up, and he was asleep as soon as his head touched the pillow. This is just a little catnap. He's too excited about going fishing."

"That's so silly, fishing for plastic fish."

Ash bristled. "He loves doing it. I'd like to take him down the mountain on Saturday if you have no objections. Santa is coming to Babylon and it's going to be decorated. A monster tree came in from Oregon, and they're going to turn on the lights. Why don't you come with us?"

"Are you going to see Mom?"

"I imagine so if she's around." Ash wondered if his vague, bland attitude was working. "I thought it would be a good time to pick up my old train set, so we can put it around the tree. It's the only toy I saved from my childhood. I think Simon still has his. The engine belches smoke, there's a real whistle, and the cars have little people in them. Jake will love it. I think you should come with us, though."

"No. I'll stay here. If you take Jake, that will give me time to wrap some of his Christmas presents. He's so curious and already he's poking in the closets."

"Would you object if we stayed overnight? I don't like driving at night with Jake in the car."

"Are you going to stay at Mom's?"

"I could get a room. It would be better if we stayed with your mother."

"No, it wouldn't. If you promise me you'll stay in the hotel, it's okay. Staying with Mom is not okay."

"You're carrying this too far, Sunny."

"You're entitled to your opinion, Dad. I want your word. Jake will tell at some point if you stay with Mom. Please don't make him lie to me."

"All right, Sunny. We'll take a room. Are you sure you don't want to come with us?"

"I'm sure. I think I'll call the people who installed those awful gates for Mom and have them put up again."

"Sunny, for God's sake, why? Your mother doesn't come here. No one comes here unless you invite them, and if you keep on the way you're going, even invited guests won't come. This is your mother's house. It isn't yours. Please remember that. She could put you out tomorrow if she wanted to, and it would be perfectly legal."

"She would never do that," Sunny blustered.

"Don't be so sure. Fanny is a constant surprise. Just when I think I have her down pat, she throws a curve. It's my personal opinion that you've pushed her as far as she will allow. It won't be pleasant if she decides to push back. Leave the gates alone. They don't belong to you."

"I can move back to town," Sunny continued to bluster.

"Yes, you could. The question is, would you and the children be happy there. For the record, I have no intention of moving. I was born here, and I plan to die here." At Sunny's stricken look he added hastily, "At some point in the far future. Sunny, don't you have any friends? We've been here more than four months and no one comes up, no one calls."

"I did. They have lives of their own with families. Two of my best friends moved away. We write once in a while. It's okay. You see how busy I am. Jake and Polly take a lot of time. I'm not devastated about Tyler. It's what it is. Maybe someday things will change."

"They aren't going to change unless you open your mind and heart."

His training pants around his knees, fishing pole over his shoulder, Jake entered the garden room. "Time to fish, Pop Pop."

"Oh, Jake, you peed on your socks. Run in your room and bring me a clean pair. Tell me if Polly is awake."

Jake returned with his socks. "Hers awake. Hers playing with her toes. Mitzi said . . ."

"What did Mitzi say?"

"Hers giving her her bottle."

"Okay. Go with Pop Pop and catch me a big fish."

Sunny watched her father and son until they rounded the bend that would take them to Chue's house. What would she do when her father was no longer here? What would she do if Tyler took the kids? She knuckled her eyes as she shuffled back to the house.

"I've never seen anything so magnificent in my life," Fanny said breathlessly as she walked around Babylon. In every corner, in every aisle, golden Christmas trees complete with gaily wrapped packages graced the casino. Overhead, red velvet swags with golden angels carrying golden trumpets moved in the air from the ventilation system. Bouquets of holly and mistletoe tied with red velvet ribbons could be seen everywhere. Exquisite miniature sleighs, Santas, and elves hung from the tinsel-wrapped chandeliers. Red-and-green signs, their arrows pointing in the direction of the hanging gardens, were in every aisle and by all the exit signs. In the central entrance, a wire arrangement in the shape of a Christmas tree was transformed into a thirty-foot-high poinsettia. Empty boxes wrapped in gold and silver with large red velvet bows sat at the base. In the middle of the casino, above the wide center aisle, suspended from wires, was a real sleigh, with a life-size stuffed Santa, complete with a sack of presents, a small evergreen nestled in the sleigh, and eight prancing reindeer. Every five minutes the Santa offered up a roughish wink and a jolly, Ho-Ho-Ho. Fanny clapped her hands in glee.

Her children and Marcus Reed behind her, Fanny followed one of the red arrows leading to the hanging gardens, where all she could do was stare in amazement. The North Pole complete with swirling snow. "It isn't really snow," Sage whispered.

"I know," Fanny whispered in return. "It's wonderful. You actually built an entire village. Where did the mechanical elves come from?"

"Santa," Marcus quipped. "How do you like Santa's workshop?"

"It isn't a real fire in the fireplace, Mom," Sage whispered.

"I know. It takes my breath away. It's so real. The buckets of paint look real too."

"They're colored pudding with preservatives added. We have to change it once a week," Billie volunteered.

"You actually created an entire village as well as Santa's workshop. I feel like I'm peeking into the magical man's private world. That scroll must be a mile long. Every little boy and girl's Christmas list. And the barn with the reindeer. Oh, my, there's Rudolph. Jake is going to love this. What's in all those baskets?"

Everyone laughed. "Reindeer treats. They're giveaways. Jake asked me what he could leave for Santa's reindeer. They're little bags filled with hay and glitter and tied with a red ribbon. A small instruction slip says, 'Leave outside the front door.' I hired some kids from the university and they made up ten thousand packets."

"It's mind-boggling is what it is. When does the giant Santa go up?" Fanny asked.

"As we speak. I had to polyurethane him. I wanted to make sure he dried. He's under the canopy with his own twenty-four-hour guard. Okay, time to shower and be on hand when the door opens. See you guys later," Billie said with a wave of her hand.

"We're off, too," Iris and Birch said in unison. "See you later."

Marcus Reed held out his hand. "I don't think I ever worked so hard for zero pay. I also didn't think it was possible to enjoy myself as much as I did. I want to thank you, Fanny, for allowing me to be a part of this. I'll say my good-bye now, too."

"You're leaving! You aren't staying for the opening?"

"Business calls. I hate crowds. I hope tonight is everything you want it to be."

Fanny watched Marcus walk away. Suddenly everything seemed off-color and out of focus. The urge to run after him, to ask him to stay, was so strong, Fanny forced herself to dig her heels into the soft artificial snow.

"I'm alone again."

"Did you say something, Mrs. Thornton?" Neal asked

"No. I guess I was thinking out loud. Tell me, what do you think?"

"I never would have believed it. When you said decorate I thought you meant a wreath, a tree, and some red bows. I've never seen anything like this. I think your assessment was on target. We'll recoup our money. Do you mind me asking who that man was in the red plaid shirt?"

"Mr. Reed. He helped build this stuff. Do you know him?"

"No. I think I've seen him somewhere, though, or else he reminds me of someone. It will come to me at some point. You only have ninety minutes, Mrs. Thornton, before the doors open."

"I guess I better hurry then."

Fanny pressed the play button on her answering machine. Ash's voice pealed into the room. "Fanny, I have the okay to bring Jake down. We'll be there for Santa's arrival. I'll book a room. The kid is so excited he's going to make himself sick. He's bringing you a present, so act like you've been waiting all your life for it, okay. We'll see you in a couple of hours."

Fanny sat down on the floor and tussled with Daisy. "Wait till you see who's coming to see us. Actually, we'll be going to see him. I think you might like him since he's a little person. Ah, that's it, give me kisses." Fanny rolled over and over, Daisy yipping and yapping as she tried to snuggle against Fanny. "Okay, okay, you win, two cookies. Roll the can over here." Fanny fumbled with the lid as the phone rang. She burst out laughing when Daisy knocked the can out of her hand, cookies scattering everywhere. "Hello," she gasped.

"Fanny, it's Simon."

The laughter died in Fanny's throat. Her voice went flat. "Hello, Simon."

"I thought I'd drive down tomorrow."

"Why?"

"Why? To see you."

"Why?"

"We need to talk."

"Don't you mean you need to talk, Simon? I said everything I had to say."

"Are you saying you don't want me to come?"

"You can do whatever you please, Simon. I'm a person, Simon, with feelings, with needs. I'm not a possession you can pull out on a whim and then store away again. This weekend is the opening of the Christmas season for us. I won't have any time to spend with you. Ash is bringing Jake down."

"Let me make sure I understand what you're saying. You are too busy to see me and talk to me but you have time to spend with Ash and Jake."

"That's about it, Simon. Ash will be taking care of Jake. I just get to see him. That little boy is very important to me."

"When will you have time? Do I need an appointment?"

"Sometime after the first of the year. Do you realize, Simon, you did the same thing to me your brother did? I will not tolerate that."

"What about Christmas?"

"What about it?"

"Do you want me to come for Christmas?"

Did she? "No, Simon, I do not. I'm sorry to cut you short, but I have to get dressed and be downstairs when the doors open. Have a nice evening."

"Fanny, I'm sorry."

"Sorry is just a word. I've heard it so much in my life it doesn't mean anything. Good-bye, Simon."

Fanny scooped Daisy up into her arms. "Four months ago I thought I was going to die if Simon didn't call me. I thought I couldn't live without him. Guess what, I did . . . I am. Whatever. What's even more amazing is I'm starting to like what I'm doing. Okay, go finish those cookies while I get ready."

What was it Sallie used to say when something was after the fact? Too much, too little, too late.

The story of my life, Fanny thought as she stepped into the shower.

16

Simon Thornton knew his eyes were as wild-looking as he felt. For one crazy moment he debated putting his booted foot through the television screen. He looked around the oversize cabin he and Fanny had called home for three years. Everything he was seeing shrieked Fanny, Fanny, Fanny.

In his gut he knew she was never coming back. In Fanny's eyes he'd done the ultimate, the most unforgivable thing possible; he'd ignored her. He'd given her an ultimatum. *You're doing to me what Ash did, and I will not tolerate it.* He wasn't Ash. Hell, he hated his brother's guts. Whatever Ash did Simon always made sure he did just the opposite. Where in the hell did Fanny get off saying something like that?

Four months of silence. On his part. He regretted that silence now. If he'd just given a little, bent a little—

Simon threw more clothes in his bag. If he put the pedal to the metal he could make John Wayne Airport and be in Vegas before midnight. His shoulders tensed when he heard the snap of the locks on his suitcase. The sound was an ending sound, if there was such a thing. Perhaps, he thought, the word he was looking for was terminal. Suddenly he felt sick to his stomach.

Simon carried his bag down to the kitchen. He looked around. In the beginning the kitchen had been his and Fanny's sanctuary. They'd sit for hours at the old scarred table, talking, drinking coffee or tea, the dogs at their feet. The kitchen had always sparkled. Now it was dreary and grimy. The braided rugs in front of the stove and sink were dirty and stained. The green plants were limp and yellowish-looking. Piles of dirty dishes were everywhere. The copper-bottomed pots hanging from hooks on the rafters had lost their luster. The stove was full of grease and dirty fry pans. The magnets Fanny collected for the refrigerator had shifted to the bottom because he constantly slammed the door. He knew there were bugs in the sink and ants on the floor. He didn't care. He didn't much care about anything these days.

He pressed the intercom and spoke to his kennel manager. "I'll be gone for a few days. Take care of Tootsie and Slick till I get back. If you know of anyone who does housecleaning, will you call them to clean up after me. Pay them out of petty cash. The key to the back door is under the mat. I'll see you when I get back."

Simon looked at his watch. By midnight he'd be face-to-face with Fanny.

Fanny slipped into her red velvet gown. She smiled when she stroked the faux ermine trim. She'd made the dress herself, and one for Bess, just this week. She grinned when she settled the furry white cap with the red tassel onto her head. She couldn't remember the last time she was this excited. Was her excitement due to Ash's arrival with little Jake, the anticipation of seeing the crowd's reaction to the holiday decorations, or was her elation due to a man named Marcus Reed? All of the above.

Whatever it was, it was heady indeed. Something tugged at her memory, something she meant to do. It concerned Ash, but what was it? Ah, Daisy's kennel. She wanted Ash to take it back to Sunrise so she could use the space to line up all her shoe boxes. Fifty pairs of shoes, as she'd found out, took up a lot of room. Well, she might as well drag it out now and put it by the front door so she didn't forget again.

Daisy sniffed and barked as Fanny dragged the huge crate to the foyer. "Take out everything, Daisy. You aren't going anywhere, so relax."

The little dog pawed at the small quilt and a stuffed toy that had been left behind. "What's that?" Fanny asked as she bent down to pick up a manila envelope. She stared at the return address, at hers and Simon's name and then at the date. The thick package was four months old. "Damn you, Simon, you could have told me you put this in the kennel," she muttered. She didn't have time to look at it now. She'd do it later when she was in bed. Five minutes to go.

The private penthouse elevator whisked Fanny to the lobby. "It's wonderful!" she shouted as she looked around at her employees. All the girls wore short skating-style red velvet outfits and caps trimmed in the same faux ermine as her own gown. The men wore red velvet Santa suits and shiny black boots.

"Bess! You look gorgeous."

"Then it must be true. John said the same thing. You look beautiful, Fanny. The outfit is very becoming. My thick waist doesn't do this gown justice the way your twenty-six-inch waist does. Remember now, get under the sleigh, and when the doors open you yell, Merry Christmas!"

"Bess, that's pretty corny."

"Your patrons expect it. One minute to go!"

"Open the doors, Neal!"

The police and security guards held their arms out to allow the first four guests through the front doors; Ash in his wheelchair, Jake on his lap. Billie Coleman Kingsley was on his right, Thad on his left.

Fanny ran to the front of the casino. She kissed Ash's cheek, hugged Jake, whose eyes were so wide they almost popped from his head. "Thank you for coming," she said to Billie and Thad.

"We wouldn't have missed this for the world. You made the news in Washington, D.C. It was one of those television channels that gives a little synopsis of what's going on around the country. Thad gassed up his plane the minute we saw it, and here we are."

"We have to get out of the way."

"Fanny, I don't know what to say," Ash said.

"Don't say anything until you see the village. Take Jake to the hanging gardens, and I'll join you as soon as we fill up."

"The Strip's empty, Fanny. I think everyone in the world is outside. I think there are more people here than we had for the grand opening. This is your grandma Fanny, Jake."

Jake stared at the red gown, his little hand reaching out to touch the fur. "You get me Santy Claus hat, Pop Pop?"

Fanny removed her hat in the blink of an eye. She handed it to Ash, her eyes filling with tears. "He's so beautiful, Ash."

"Yeah, I know," Ash said gruffly as he settled the white fur cap on his grandson's head. "It's a red snowball, sport." The little boy giggled as he tickled his grandfather under the nose with the red snowball.

"We'll see you later, Granny," Ash laughed. "We're in room 2311. He had two naps, so he can probably hold out till midnight. You might want to tuck him in."

"Oh, Ash, yes I would. Let's meet at the entrance to the village say around ten-thirty and see how he's holding up. I sent some presents up to the room earlier. Big red bows and all that. Our kids used to like the paper and bows better than the presents. The empty boxes, too. They used to play with empty boxes by the hour."

Ash stared at Fanny, his face blank. "I never knew that, Fanny."

"I know, Ash. It's all right. It wasn't something important. It was a memory. You better get to the village before the crowds become too dense. Besides, I think that little guy is about to explode. Get his picture taken with the Santa. Be sure to get one for me."

"Okay. You ready, sport? There's a big guy in there in a red suit who is just waiting to ask you what you want for Christmas. You got your list ready?"

Jake fished in his pocket and pulled out a piece of paper. He waved it triumphantly in Ash's face.

"It's almost like a miracle, isn't it, Fanny?" Billie whispered.

"That's strange, Billie, I was thinking the same thing. That man is not the man I was married to. I like the man I was just talking to. Am I crazy?"

"Not at all. I'm glad for you and for Ash. You had so much bitterness for so long. Jake looks like one of the cherubs on a Christmas card."

"Ash said I can go up to their room and tuck him in later."

"I hope this visit is everything you want it to be. I don't suppose Simon is coming, is he?"

"That's right up there with the Pope coming to Vegas, Billy. He did call earlier, and it wasn't a nice conversation. I'm not discounting the fact that he made an overture, but he made it in anger. I could hear it in his voice. I don't feel the same way about Simon anymore, Billie. I want to, but something in me died. It's the same feeling I had when Ash and I split up. Simon asked me if I wanted him to come for Christmas, and I said no. I said no because I'm sick and tired of stress and strain. That's what holidays are, you know. I refuse to put myself through that ever again. Daisy and I can manage just fine. I think I'll get her a playmate."

"I hear something in your voice, Fanny, and there's a strange look in your eyes. I want a full accounting."

"Later, when things quiet down, okay?"

"Okay. Now I better find Thad. He's got money from his colleagues, a dollar each, to play. Big spenders. I wish they'd be that frugal with our tax dollars."

Fanny laughed as her eyes searched the crowd. It wasn't until a long time later that she realized she was looking for Marcus Reed. The realization made her warm all over.

The room looked the same. The men seated around the huge table looked the same. The sterling service was the same. The orchid flower arrangement had been replaced with festive greenery and poinsettias in deference to the approaching holidays.

"The Emperor is back."

"Just to visit. He brought his grandson with him."

"Our customers deserted us. Everyone is outside, waiting to get into Babylon. Who the hell thought Christmas decorations were important. Women!"

"Babylon is one of the seven wonders of the world. The Christmas decor is worthy of the establishment. It's time you all gave some serious thought to hiring a few women. Women have ideas. Women know what other women want. Most women are mothers and, consequently, anything geared toward children will hold a great deal of appeal. Women do not, I repeat, do not want to see tough-looking men in dark suits, cigars, and smelly rooms. They want flowers, bright colors, and an air of gentility. I told you repeatedly your old ways no longer work. Tell me, how many of you here made your way across the street this evening? A show of hands will do nicely." Every hand in the room went up. "Since money is no object, what seems to be your problem?"

"Who can compete with the Thornton name?"

The man at the head of the table shrugged. "You asked me to assess the situation and to come up with a remedy. What do you do when you have an out-of-control fire?"

"Fire, shmire, what the hell does a fire have to do with the gambling business?"

"You dig a trench. Then you build a second fire so they slap at each other, at which time both fires are extinguished."

"You want us to burn down Babylon!" someone asked in amazement.

"*NO.*" The single word was a thunderbolt of sound. "Does the word copycat mean anything to any of you?"

"You want we should make our establishments look like Babylon? *They* won't agree to that."

"All of you here told me money was no object. Are you saying you lied to me?"

"No. We aren't saying that at all."

"If you don't wish to fight fire with fire, then you will have to come up with some other remedy. Short of torching the building."

"We'll offer to buy her out. Things happen all the time."

"Those things will come back to haunt you. How many times do I have to tell you, your old ways no longer work?"

"Women don't know anything about operating a business. She'll run it into the ground in a year. We'll pick up the pieces."

"Let me show you gentlemen something," the man at the head of the table said. "These are P & L sheets for Mrs. Thornton's two companies, Sunny's Togs and Rainbow Babies. It's not important how they came to be in my possession. Look at them carefully and tell me this lady doesn't know what she's doing. All you have to do is look to your own businesses and then look across the street."

"She's stealing our business."

"*NO.* Mrs. Thornton is *generating* business by using her head. A detailed report of my findings will be in your superior's hands by the close of business tomorrow. Good-bye, gentlemen, and good luck."

"That's it! We paid you a million dollars for *this!*" someone shouted.

"You paid me a million dollars to show you what you were doing wrong. I showed you. I still contend Mrs. Thornton is no threat to any of you. She's running her business the only way she knows how, successfully. She has no interest in this side of the street. My original opinion stands: Mrs. Thornton affords you respectability."

"What's she building out there in the desert?" someone sneered.

"A state-of-the-art medical and rehabilitation facility for her daughter and others like her who suffer from muscle and nerve diseases. At our last meeting I suggested you might want to anonymously donate some monies to such a worthy cause. I'm sure Mrs. Thornton will be astute enough to figure out where the money came from and give credit where credit is due. Good day, gentlemen."

"How can we reach you if things change?"

"Your employers know how to reach me. Have a nice holiday."

It was almost midnight when Marcus Reed crossed the street to Babylon. He walked up to the plate glass window and stared inside. He felt like he was a kid again with his nose pressed close to the bakery window. His eyes searched the crowds and then he saw her. She was smiling at someone and talking animatedly. "Well-done, Fanny," he whispered, before he walked away.

Fanny turned when she felt someone was staring at her. Her gaze swept the room and then moved to the front of the casino. Her heart lurched when she thought she saw Marcus Reed. It must have been a trick of the lighting. She moved off toward the elevators. She crossed her fingers, hoping Jake was still up.

"Fanny. Jake and I have been waiting. He's so full of piss and vinegar he's never going to go to sleep. He loves those toys you bought him."

"Ash, if you want to go downstairs, I can stay with Jake."

"Tomorrow is soon enough. I realized I don't miss this place at all. You did real good, Fanny. I'm proud of you."

"Really, Ash. Did Jake love it?"

"Do birds fly? The kid ate it up. He asked more questions. He ate so much junk he's got to be high on sugar. Sunny would take a fit if she knew. He never gets candy, and once in a while she gives him a cherry Popsicle. She pumps him full of all kinds of vitamins and stuff."

Fanny nodded. "Hi, Jake."

"Hi."

"Did you have a good time tonight?"

"Yep. Santy Claus give me this."

"A net. What's it for?"

"Fishing. Where's the present, Pop Pop?"

"Right here."

The little boy ran over to his grandfather, reached for the present and handed it over shyly. "Is for you."

"For me?"

"Merry . . . merry . . ."

"Christmas," Ash said.

"Yep, Christmas."

Fanny unwrapped the small gift that had more cellophane tape than paper on it. "Oh, my goodness, a plastic goldfish."

"Me and Pop Pop caught it. Is a present."

"And a lovely one it is. Thank you very much."

"Do you want to play?"

"Sure." Fanny kicked off her shoes and hiked up her gown before she sat down cross-legged on the floor. "Let's build a castle with the blocks. You'll be the prince and Pop Pop will be the king. Polly will be a princess."

"What's Mommy?"

"Mommy's the queen."

"What's you?"

Fanny's throat closed tight. She struggled to swallow. Her eyes implored Ash.

"Who do you think she is, Jake?"

"Santy Claus's mommy."

Fanny started to giggle. "Okay, that's who I am."

At one o'clock Fanny called a halt to the castle building. "I think it's time to brush your teeth and get ready for bed."

"No."

"No? Are you telling Santy Claus's mommy no? Tsk tsk," Fanny said, clucking her tongue.

"C'mon, sport, let's hop to it. I want to see if there's any fairy dust on those back teeth."

"Okay, Pop Pop. I got it all out the last time."

"Yeah, I know, but it grows back really quick. Stand on the stool and do a really good job."

"Fairy dust! Ash, you never cease to amaze me. He's wonderful. I can see why this place lost its hold on you."

"It works every time. The kid is just dying for me to find some in his teeth. He makes me laugh like hell."

"I guess you're good for each other. Is Sunny doing okay?"

"It depends on what you mean by okay. In my opinion she's doing lousy. She does her exercises, she eats right, she sleeps a lot, and her patience is at the low end of the scale. Tyler wants to take Jake to New York. She's considering it. He told her he was dating someone. She seems okay with it."

Jake returned to the living room half-dressed, his mouth open for inspection. "I think you got it all, Jake."

"Goody. Wanna see?" he said to Fanny, opening wide.

Fanny plucked a sparkling sequin from the cuff of her sleeve. "Oops, looks like you missed one. Hold still. There, I got it."

"Wow! Did you see that, Pop Pop?"

"Boy are you lucky Grandma Fanny found that last little bit of fairy dust. Next time try to remember to brush harder." The little boy nodded solemnly as he hopped up on the couch. He curled into Fanny's arms.

"Tell me a story."

"All right. Once upon a time there was a . . ."

"Out like a light. That's usually how far I get. Then he wakes up around three or four and wants to know what comes next."

"I envy you, Ash," Fanny said softly.

"Don't ever envy me, Fanny."

"You know what I mean. What did you want to talk to me about?"

"Sunny's been hitting Jake. I don't mean a tap on his tush either. She gives him some pretty heavy-handed wallops. I told her if she did it again, I was going to call Tyler. I've suggested everything under the sun. She closes her ears. Her big thing right now is putting those gates back up. She thinks if she does that, it will keep you out. What she's trying to do is lock herself in. Or maybe she wants you to drive up and smash through them the way she did. Aside from that we have some good days. We watch television together sometimes. We cook together. We usually take a walk every day. Like I said, she sleeps a lot. Jake is with me all the time."

"And Polly?"

"Mitzi takes care of her. She's a good baby. There are days when Sunny doesn't see her at all. It's almost like she's forgotten she has a baby."

"Ash, I'm building a facility for her, and others like her, out in the desert. It's like the one you described to me in Texas. Billie Coleman is funding half of it. It's so high-tech it spooks me. We're building an adjacent building for families, so when they come to visit they can stay close, and those patients with children won't feel so separated from their families. It's going to be wonderful. I think, Ash, when it's completed, you might want to talk Sunny into going in for a while. We'll have the best doctors, the best therapists, and round-the-clock care."

"You're really doing it for Sunny, aren't you?"

Fanny nodded.

"I hope she appreciates it."

"That part doesn't matter. Getting her help is what counts. It will be up to you, Ash. I can build it, but I can't make her want to go. If you think I should go to Sunrise and smash through the gates, if she puts them up, and let her get in my face, you know I'll do it. But, if it doesn't resolve anything, what's the point? I apologized, I admitted I was wrong. Now, all I can do is give her the space she says she wants and hope she can work through it. Damn it, I never said I was perfect. I never pretended to be perfect."

"I know, I know. Listen, tomorrow is another day. I'm tired of beating at this particular horse. Let's call it a night."

"I'll stay a little while. He feels so warm and cuddly. I'll try not to wake you when I leave."

"Stay all night, be my guest," Ash said wearily.

Fanny closed her eyes. She was asleep in five minutes.

Ash undressed and lurched onto the bed, his face grimacing in pain. He stared at his ex-wife and grandson for a long time. He picked up the phone and called the desk. "Myrna, this is Ash Thornton. Yes, I'm glad to be back. How's your family? That's wonderful.

Listen, do me a favor. Don't put any calls through. I have my grandson with me, and I don't want to be disturbed. If the president calls, tell him he has to wait till tomorrow at noon. You got that, Myrna? Thanks, sweetie."

Ash continued to watch Fanny and his grandson. When his eyes started to burn, he turned off the light. He, too, was asleep within minutes.

Simon rode the elevator to the penthouse. He rang the bell again and again. All he could hear inside was Daisy's sharp barking. He let his bag thump to the floor. He was more than annoyed that he didn't have a key to the apartment.

His shoulders stiff, his eyes cold, Simon rode the elevator back to the lobby. He headed for the registration desk. He worked a smile he didn't feel onto his face. "I'm Simon Thornton. Can you tell me if my brother is registered in the hotel?"

"Yes, sir, he is."

"Would you ring his room please?"

"I'm sorry, sir, I can't do that. Mr. Thornton left instructions that he wasn't to be disturbed."

The smile left Simon's face. "I'm his brother for God's sake."

"I'm sorry, sir."

"All right. Give me the key to the penthouse."

"I beg your pardon!"

"Fanny Thornton is my wife. She lives in the penthouse. I've come to visit. Will you give me the key?"

"Sir, if you want a key, you'll have to get it from Mrs. Thornton. We do not give out keys to guests' rooms, much less the owner's apartment. There are privacy laws, Mr. Thornton."

"Have you seen my brother or my wife recently?"

"Mrs. Thornton was on the floor all evening. I saw her from time to time. I personally did not see your brother, but I did speak to him."

"I'd like a room, please."

"I'm sorry, sir, we're sold out."

Simon expressed his disgust with a four-letter word. He marched across the lobby to the casino, his eyes seeking and searching. When he saw Bess, he shouldered his way through the crowds, shouting her name.

"Simon! How nice to see you. So, what do you think?" she asked, waving her hands around.

"Very colorful. Where's Fanny?"

"I have no idea. It's been so busy all night, we kind of lost track of each other. Billie and Thad were over by the first row of slots a few minutes ago. She might know. Did Fanny know you were coming?"

"No. I wanted to surprise her."

"I see anger written all over you, Simon. That can't be good for either one of you."

"Have you seen Ash?"

"The last time I saw him was the last time I saw Fanny. Ash brought Jake down from the mountain today."

"Do you know what room he's in?"

"Simon, how would I know that?"

"Jesus Christ! Do you have a key to the penthouse?"

"I don't believe you're asking me that. I do not have a key. If I did have one, I wouldn't give it to you. You should have called ahead. You're very selfish, Simon. Walk around, maybe you'll spot Fanny. She usually stays until around three. Check with Billie and Thad. I'm off. It was nice seeing you again, Simon."

Simon headed for the bar. Bartenders had their fingers on the pulse of everything. He fought his way through the throngs and ordered a scotch and soda. Any idea of talking to the bartender was out of the question. The decibel level in the bar was so high he was surprised the glasses weren't shattering.

He paid for his drink and headed for the bank of elevators. Maybe he could pick the lock on the penthouse. He sure as hell wasn't going to stand around in a bar all damn night.

Simon rang the bell four times before he pulled out the pen knife that was guaranteed to help him survive in the wilderness for a full year. Fanny had given it to him last Christmas as a joke. He picked at the miniature attachments that weren't really all that little. He picked, prodded, and gouged. In the movies a credit card always worked. He tried his. The door held fast. Daisy barked furiously. Simon stared at the door. The he-men in the movies used their shoulders. His eyes almost bugged out of his head as pain shot up his neck and then down his arm.

Simon wasn't about to give up. "Get away from the door, Daisy." He backed up, then ran, his booted foot straight in front of him. The door broke from the jamb. He used his good shoulder to push it in. Daisy cowered against one of the red chairs. Simon ignored the little dog as he stomped his way through the penthouse. He walked back to the door and picked up his bag. The door hung drunkenly on its hinges He carried his bag into the bedroom where he threw it on the bed, then went back to the living room, eyed the two red chairs and the small bar against the wall. He poured himself a drink, gulped at it, then poured a double. He looked at his watch. Three o'-clock.

The scotch bottle was almost empty at five o'clock. Simon drained it. At six he opened a second bottle. At six-ten he raised his bleary eyes to see Fanny towering over him, her gown wrinkled and mussed, the ermine trim hanging askew from the neckline.

"It's about time you showed up. Where the hell have you been? I've been waiting all goddamn night."

"You broke down my door."

"I didn't have a key."

"The reason you don't have a key is because you don't live here. I want you to leave. Where's Daisy?"

"Hiding under the bed. I tried to get her to come out, but she wouldn't listen to me. I asked you a question, where were you?"

"That's none of your business. I want you to leave, Simon."

"I'm not going anywhere until we talk. I can't leave. There aren't any rooms."

"Then go across the street. When you sober up I'll talk to you. Not one minute before. Where are your things?"

"I'm staying here with you. I'm your husband. Where were you, Fanny? You were with Ash, weren't you?"

Fanny walked into the bedroom. She yanked at the bag on the bed and carried it to the front door, where she pitched it into the hall. She didn't know the man sitting in her living room.

"I haven't seen or heard from you in four months. To me, Simon, that takes away any of your rights to question me. Please leave."

"Look at you!" Simon sneered. "You were shacking up with Ash. It's written all over your face. Come here, Fanny."

"If you believe that, then why do you even want me near you? Why are you in my apartment?" Fanny picked up the house phone on the wall at the side of the door. She pressed nine for Security. "Neal, I know it's early, but could you send someone up here to repair my door and two guards to escort an unwelcome visitor downstairs."

"All right, all right, I'm going. I always knew you weren't over Ash. It was always Ash. I was a poor second rebound choice. Go to Ash, see if I care. I'm out of here, and I'll file for divorce first thing Monday morning."

Fanny sat down, her head dropping into her hands. "That's not true. I loved you so much, Simon. You made my world right side up. I gave all of my heart to you. I'm too tired to fight. I don't want us to say things we'll regret later on."

"They've already been said."

"By you, Simon, not by me." Fanny's voice was weary, choked with tears. She fled to the bathroom just as the head of Security arrived.

"Mrs. Thornton, are you all right?"

"I'm fine. Show the gentleman the door and don't admit him to the casino again unless I give the order to do so."

"I want to see Ash. Where is he, Fanny? I'll go, and I won't come back, but I want to see Ash before I go."

"Neal, take him to Ash's room. He's awake. Make sure you wait, though, and escort Mr. Thornton to the door."

Fanny walked over to her husband. "You have no idea, Simon, how sorry I am that this incident is taking place. I never wanted this for either of us. I understand that you will do whatever you have to do." She stood on her toes to kiss his cheek. Simon raised his arm to backhand her, but Neal was too quick. The two burly security guards each cupped one of Simon's elbows and escorted him to the elevator. Simon kicked at his bag as the guards dragged him forward.

In the bedroom, Fanny slammed the door and locked it. She raced over to the bed and dropped to her knees. "It's okay, Daisy, you can come out now. Come here, sweet love." Fanny held the little dog until she stopped shaking.

"That man is just someone we used to know, Daisy. I told you. It's just me and you. Why did I ever think it could be different?"

17

Showered, shaved, and dressed for the day, Ash yelled, "Come in," when he heard the sharp rap on the door. Thinking it was Fanny, he whispered in Jake's ear. His stomach muscles started to tighten when he saw his brother's stormy face.

"Up and about early, aren't you, Simon?"

"Unlike you, I haven't been to bed."

Ash correctly interpreted his brother's dark features. He motioned for Neal to wait outside. "You look like this might lead to something so let me get Jake out of here." Simon nodded curtly.

Ash rang Housekeeping. "Mrs. Gonzales, I'd like you to do me a favor. Could you come up to 2311 and take my grandson out for breakfast? He's ready now. I'll have Neal bring him down. Yes, I miss being here. I'll stop by and see all of you before I leave."

Ash bellowed for Neal and explained the situation. He knew his own eyes were as wary as Neal's when he escorted the little boy from the room.

"Did somebody steal your lollipop, Simon?"

"Cut the crap, Ash, this isn't a social call."

"What the hell is it? If you think I'm going to discuss Fanny with you, you're wrong. Whatever is going on between the two of you stays with the two of you. Don't involve me."

"That's pretty hard to do, Ash, since your face is in everything that goes on between Fanny and me."

"That's because you make it that way. I have a lot on my plate, and I'm trying to deal with it the best way I can. Walk away from here, Simon, and let things be."

Simon advanced, one step, then another step, his fists clenched at his sides, until his knees touched Ash's knees. Ash saw his brother's arm pull back, saw the clenched fist but was powerless to move his chair. He took the full blow to his left eye and cheekbone. He felt the skin rip as the chair moved with the force of the blow. He catapulted out of the chair to land facedown on the sofa.

Ash feel his eye swelling. "I guess you felt you had to do that," he managed to say as he struggled to his knees. Simon's fist shot out a second time. Ash landed backwards, blood spurting from his mouth. He wiped at the trickling blood with his shirtsleeve, his good eye focused on his brother. He made no move to get up. "Who are you going to blame this on, Simon? What the hell do you want? I don't have anything left for you to take. You have an insidious, black, ugly mind, Simon. You're a sneak, you work behind the scenes with that wide-open innocent smile. Pop and I saw through you early on. He tried to tell Mom what a Jekyll and Hyde you were, but she wouldn't listen. You knew how to play the game to get what you wanted. It's so fucking sick it scares the shit out of me. You need help, Simon. You needed help from the time you were five years old."

"You're crazy. You were the one who drove Mom out of her mind."

"Because I was stupid. I refused to believe a mother could or would turn her back on one son to the exclusion of the other. I was a kid, I didn't know how to make her understand what you were. Pop took over to protect me from you. You know, Simon, I don't have much to do these days but think. I started writing stuff down, and then I saw the pattern. You were never happy unless you got what I had. You just waited until the time was right, then you'd strike like a snake. You always had to be first, the best. You even managed to snare someone else's identity just to beat me. It must have really galled your ass that I made Ace. You couldn't steal that from me though, could you? You switched gears then, you went off, supposedly to make it on your own. It wasn't your own, though. Pop told me Mom gave you a bundle with no strings. Self-made, my ass," Ash sneered.

"What the hell are *you?*" Simon sneered in return, his face ugly with his rage.

"For a long time I was the biggest fuck-up going. I never denied it. Nor did I ever hide it. I took my lumps and did the same thing all over again. I thought I was entitled. I used to watch, and yes, I even marveled at how easy it was for you to just take. So I started doing the same thing. You were a hell of a teacher, Simon. It's no excuse. It's the way it was."

"You're full of shit, Ash. You're the taker. You've never given anything in your life to anyone."

"You're right about that. It's funny how we never see our faults until it's too late. Get out of here, Simon. You make me sick just looking at you."

"I'll go when I'm fucking ready to go and not one minute before. I'm going to smash that face of yours until there's nothing left."

"Cut to the chase, Simon. It's Fanny and Babylon that's sticking in your craw. Babylon is mine, and there was no way for you to get it. When Fanny's family stepped in to finish up things, you were wild. For the second time you couldn't steal my thunder. Babylon was my red lollipop. Remember, Simon, when Mom was handing out those suckers you always threw a fit if I got the red one. Then Mom would take it back and give it to you and give me a yellow one. I hate lemon. I had to pretend to love lemon and we both know what you did then. You wanted lemon. It's Fanny, too. You waited and waited, until just the right moment, then you stepped in. Compared to me you really were the White Knight. Fanny fell for it. Mom pimped for you. She set it all up, and you walked right into it. You don't have one ounce of guts."

"Shut your lying mouth, Ash."

"We aren't kids anymore, Simon. I don't have to take your crap. I can say whatever I damn well please and it pleases me to say Fanny has finally seen you for who you are. You know what, she's doing a hell of a job here. Believe it or not, this is where she belongs. She's starting to see it, too. You saw it right away. That's why you did that silence thing you're so good at. You couldn't come here because this is mine. You want it so damn bad you can taste it. Why don't you just admit it? Even when I die, Simon, it can never be yours. Fanny will see to that. There's a bond between Fanny and me that you can never break no matter what you do. You tried. There's that one part of Fanny that will always belong to me. I don't deserve it, but that's the way it is." Ash struggled to his knees. His head high, his shoulders back he looked his brother in the eye. "Take your best shot, you asshole."

"She was here all night, wasn't she? I didn't know you could still get it up. Guess she'll take it any which way she can. She's still my wife."

Ash tottered forward, his hand grappling with the arm of the wheelchair. "I don't care what you say about me, but you leave Fanny out of this. Fanny slept on the couch with Jake all night. Just to keep the record straight, I can still get it up. Now get your fucking ass out of my building and don't ever let me see you again in this lifetime."

Ash brought the wheelchair around so he could lever himself into it but Simon's fists shot forward in a one-two shot that left Ash crumpled on the floor. He managed to let out one bull roar before he lost consciousness.

The door burst open as Neal arrived, two security guards and Fanny in their wake.

"My God, Simon, what did you do?" Fanny dropped to her knees at Ash's side just as he started to come around. "Call an ambulance."

"I don't need an ambulance, Fanny. It's okay. I'll be okay if my teeth don't fall out. Get him out of here, Neal."

Ash struggled to get into his chair. Fanny cringed at Ash's bloody, swollen face. Secure in the knowledge that Simon was in the firm grip of the two security guards, she started to pummel her husband with her fists. "God in heaven, what kind of man are you? How could you hit your own brother like this? How could you beat a man in a wheelchair? Who are you, Simon? More to the point, *what* are you?"

"He's my brother, Fanny, and he's your husband. Let it go and be damned glad this happened now, while I'm still around."

Ash waved the men out the door. "Fix me up, Fanny, before Mrs. Gonzales brings Jake back. How bad is it?"

Fanny dithered. "Don't you know? You were on the receiving end of things. I have to go upstairs to get my first-aid box. I'll be right back. You should see a doctor, Ash."

"I've seen enough doctors to last me a lifetime. Hey, I'm the guy who has a pill for everything, remember? Hurry up. I don't want Jake seeing me like this."

Fanny was back in five minutes. She talked as she wiped and swabbed. "You can't hide this from Jake. Your left eye looks like an open peanut butter and jelly sandwich. Your jaw is swelling, and you look lopsided. Are your teeth loose? Ash, what happened. Did you provoke Simon?"

Ash tried for a smile. He didn't succeed. "Simon is not a happy person these days. I don't know if Simon was ever happy. He has demons. Maybe we should talk later on in the day, Fanny, when Jake is napping. I need a little time to rebound. Do you have any makeup you can plaster on the worst of my bruises? Ditch this shirt. It's all bloody."

"I don't think it will help, Ash. I'll get you an ice bag. You could have a concussion. Ash, who was that person?"

"Fanny, look at me. That person is someone you used to know. He's someone I've known all my life. I have an idea of how you must feel and I want you to know I'm truly sorry. I want to thank you for being the one constant in my life. Now, you would do me the biggest favor if you would take Jake for the day."

"Ash, truly? Are you sure it's all right? What about Sunny? How will you explain it to her?"

"I'll tell her the truth. I'm on a truth kick these days. You know what, Fanny, when you tell the truth it's okay, everyone deals with it and goes on from there. Only a fool denies the truth. If we're lucky, Simon will admit to his truths and go on from there. At least I hope so. Here comes the kid, so don't say anything."

Jake ran to Ash, skidding to a stop in front of his chair. "You look funny, Pop Pop."

"Boo!" Ash said. The little boy giggled. "Grandma Fanny is going to take you out today. Get your sweater and I want a promise from you."

"Whazat, whatzat?"

"Promise me you'll have a good time."

"Promise, promise, promise."

Jake's hand in hers, her face radiant, Fanny turned at the door. "Can I get you anything before we leave?"

"Have them send up some coffee and a bottle of brandy."

"How about some blueberry pancakes and sausage?"

"That too. Don't worry about me, Fanny. I'm okay."

"Keep the ice pack on, twenty minutes on, twenty minutes off."

"Yes, Mother," Ash drawled. It brought the required smile to Fanny's face.

When the door closed behind Fanny, Ash wheeled himself to the couch. He eased himself onto it gingerly. His body started to tremble as tears burned his eyes. "How come you never saw it, Mom? Why wasn't I good enough for you to love? If there was a way for me to help Simon, I would. I don't know how. I didn't put up a fight. I let him beat the hell out of me because I thought . . . hell, I don't know what I thought. I wish you had told me just once that you loved me. Maybe if you'd done that I wouldn't be in this position now, and neither would Simon.

"Guess that's enough for now. We'll be seeing each other soon enough and when that day comes, I want some answers."

"What would you like to do, Jake?"

The little boy trotted alongside Fanny, his chubby legs pumping in his hurry to get outside the door. "Feed birds. Buy peanuts. Eat ice cream."

"I think we can do all those things. Do you know how to skip to My Lou?"

"Uh-huh. Watch me."

"Wonderful!" Together, grandmother and grandson skipped down the street with onlookers smiling their approval. *I need to do this because I want to do it. I don't want to think about what transpired earlier. I want to enjoy every single minute that I can with this little boy.*

It was three o'clock when Fanny led her weary grandchild back to Babylon. In one hand he held a red balloon and in the other a stuffed panda bear. His chin was streaked with chocolate ice cream, his hands sticky. He wore a happy smile as he tried valiantly to keep his eyes open.

"You're lookin' good, sport," Ash said, his swollen lips barely moving. "Are you ready for a nap?"

Jake nodded.

Fanny smiled. "I'll clean him up. We used up all my tissues with the first half of the ice-cream cone. I think I'd like some coffee, Ash. Would you mind calling Room Service?"

Fanny joined Ash just as the coffee arrived. "It's been a day, Ash. I probably would have gone out of my mind if you hadn't asked me to take Jake out. I wish . . . oh, God, I wish so many things. I know it's difficult for you to talk and even painful, but you have to tell me what happened. I need to know. I need to understand. I thought I had a good marriage with a good man. At least for the first year. Was I blind, Ash? What was I supposed to see that I didn't see? I don't know what I'm supposed to feel. Talk to me, Ash, I need to make sense of all of this."

Ash talked. Fanny listened. Then both were silent for a long time.

"Wouldn't it be nice, Ash, if we could turn the clocks backward in time? I know the time I would pick. You go first."

"I think I must have been four or almost four. Simon was trailing me in the yard and I fell and skinned my knee. It started to bleed and I was yelling at the top of my lungs. Simon stumbled and got his suit dirty. Mom picked him up to take him into the house to change his clothes. She didn't even look at my knee. I sat there and cried like a baby. I kept saying, look at my leg, fix my leg. I guess I either whispered the words or was just thinking them to myself. I wish I'd screamed the words so she would have noticed me. I wish that. You know what, you play the hand you're dealt. That's the bottom line."

Fanny's eyes smarted. "I don't have a particular time in mind. What should I do, Ash?"

"Don't do anything, Fanny. Simon will file for divorce. You'll be served papers, and then you'll be a free agent. I'm really sorry. If there's one person in the world who should be married, it's you."

Fanny smiled. "That was the old Fanny. This new Fanny is someone who . . . oh, never mind."

"Is your heart shattered? Are you wounded to your soul by all of this?" Ash queried.

"Strangely enough, no. I almost bolted that first month. I was one miserable human being. Like you, Ash, I had a lot of time to think. Twice divorced. That's not good."

"Sez who?"

"Sez me. Sunny will have a field day. How do you plan to explain your condition to her when you get back?"

"I hadn't thought that far ahead. I'll be leaving in the morning. Would you mind driving me up, Fanny? Bess or Neal can follow behind and bring you back. I'd chance it if it was just me, but Jake changes things. Wanna have dinner tonight?"

"Yes and yes. You should come up and see what I did with your place. You'll hate it."

"Okay, but I have to call downstairs to get someone to come up and sit here while Jake is asleep. You go ahead and I'll be up in a few minutes."

While she waited for Ash, Fanny washed her face and brushed her hair. She stared at herself in the mirror. "I look like I'm seventy years old," she muttered to her reflection. She turned around so she wouldn't have to view her reflection and sat down on the edge of the tub. She thought about all the things Ash had said. She wasn't sure why, but she believed him implicitly. She couldn't help but wonder why her heart wasn't shattered, why she wasn't wounded to her soul. At what point had she fallen out of love with her husband? "Maybe I'll never know," she muttered.

"You here?" Ash shouted.

"Coming. So, what do you think?"

"Jesus, Fanny, this place looks like a hunting cabin in the mountains. This is supposed to be glass and chrome, black and white. Modern . . ."

"Shitful." Fanny giggled. "You know me. I'm a nester. I had to redo it because I smashed all your stuff. It felt great. Come on, I'll show you the rest of the place. By the way, don't let me forget to take Daisy's kennel tomorrow. When you go back down you can take Daisy for Jake to play with if you want. She loves little kids."

"I suppose you got rid of all my black and white towels, huh?" Ash said opening the closet door. "For God's sake, Fanny, do you have some kind of shoe fetish? You never had this many shoes in your life."

Fanny leaned against the wall, her arms crossed over her chest. "You know that guy I told you about, the one who put me in the pool? Well, he sent them to me. He's got good taste in shoes, I can tell you that. He sends me a dozen yellow roses every single day."

"No shit!"

Fanny started to laugh and couldn't stop. "You should see yourself, Ash. I know you want to raise your eyebrows but . . ."

"Don't make me laugh, Fanny, it hurts too bad."

Fanny slid to the floor, still laughing. "I think he has the hots for me," she managed to gasp.

"Yeah?"

"Yeah. He came here on Thanksgiving, and I was drunk as a skunk. He's the one who finally cooked dinner for the kids when they showed up. He even did the dishes."

"Snatch that sucker right up, Fanny."

"Nah. You know what I think my problem is, Ash? I think I'm a one-man woman."

"Don't say that to me, Fanny."

"Okay. Forget I said it."

"You know what I mean."

"Yeah, I know, Ash."

"You know what I want to do, Fanny? I want to sit in one of those red chairs. By the way, where is Daisy?"

"At the groomers getting gussied up for Jake. She's getting her nails cut and her coat trimmed. She loves the blow dryer."

"I'd love it too if somebody blew warm air all over my body."

"Really," Fanny drawled.

"Yeah, really."

"I'm fresh out of warm air." Fanny giggled.

"Now how did I know you were going to say that?"

"That doesn't mean I won't have some later . . . say maybe around midnight when I take my break."

"Wait a minute here. Are you saying what I think you're saying?"

"What do you think I'm saying?"

"That you and me . . . me and you . . . like . . . you know . . . when we had our good times?"

"Uh-huh."

"What are the conditions?" Ash asked, his tongue thick in his mouth.

"No conditions. No strings."

"I'd be a fool to turn that down."

"I'd say so."

"You sound pretty sure of yourself," Ash said. Fanny loved the uncomfortable look on his face. "Is this going to be a performance kind of thing?"

"Whatever you want it to be. I think, Ash, I can sizzle the socks

right off your feet. You think about that, okay? You have to put a
towel over your head though; otherwise, I'll laugh and it won't be
good."

"Jesus, Fanny, what kind of talk is that?"

Fanny giggled. "Do you remember how you used to want me to
talk dirty to you? Well, guess what, I learned a *whole* new language."

"Goddamn it, Fanny," Ash blustered.

"Your face is red, Ash. I think Daisy's home."

"Thank God," Ash muttered. He needed time to think about this
conversation.

Fanny laughed as she sashayed her way to the front door, her buttocks jiggling.

Daisy raced into the room and leaped onto Ash's lap, licking his
face and neck and woofing softly.

"You can take her down with you if you want. You won't let Jake
squeeze her or anything like that, will you?"

"He's good with animals. He's a gentle little boy, Fanny."

"Okay. Call me when you want me to pick her up. What time do
you want to have dinner?"

"How does eight sound?"

"It sounds good."

"The place looks homey, Fanny. You're comfortable here, aren't
you?"

"Yes and no. I miss the yard and the flowers. When that happens
I go down to the hanging gardens and walk around. It's okay for
now."

"And later?"

"We'll deal with later when later comes. We can have dinner here
in the penthouse if you're uncomfortable with people seeing you. Or
we could do the private dining room. You decide and let me know
when I pick Daisy up. Ash Thornton, you're afraid of me, aren't
you?"

"Where'd you get a cockamamie idea like that?" Ash said, his face
reddening again.

"I just have to look at you to know." A devil perched itself on
Fanny's shoulder. "I'll go easy on you."

"That'll be the day," Ash snorted, his neck as red as his face.

"Uh-huh," Fanny grinned.

The intercom in the foyer buzzed. Fanny raced from the bathroom, spritzing perfume as she went along. "Yes?"

"Mrs. Thornton, we have a delivery for you."

"Send it up, Martin."

Fanny's jaw dropped minutes later when a parade of young men carrying poinsettias marched into the room. "Good lord, how many are there?" she gasped.

"One hundred. They were sent in their own delivery truck from San Diego. They have a large poinsettia farm there," one of the young men said.

"Is there a card or message?"

"Not that I know of, Mrs. Thornton. I signed for them. It sure looks like Christmas."

"Yes, it does. Who in the world is going to water them?"

"Call down to the florist. I'm sure they'll be glad to oblige."

"Hey, anybody home?" Bess called out from the doorway. "Oohhh, are they from you know who? I like his style. I love multiples of anything. John's romantic leanings are one rose, one donut, one of whatever. Although, sometimes less is more if you know what I mean. I heard some stories on the floor. Want to talk about it?"

"I'm so sorry, Fanny. Are you okay with all of this?" Bess asked when Fanny wound down. "You look kind of peculiar."

"That's because I propositioned my ex-husband. For the first time in his life he was flabbergasted. I can't believe I did it. I don't even know why I did it. It seemed like the thing to do at the moment."

"The question is, are you going to follow through?"

"What would you do if you were in my place?"

"Oh, sweetie, I'd go for it. All the way. This is a whole new ball game, and the playing field is yours. It is what it is."

"I'm actually tingling at the thought. Just at the thought. I must be out of my mind. Stop and think about it, Bess. I'm divorced from Ash, I married his brother who turns out to be some . . . someone I didn't know . . . and I'm just walking away from that person and hitting on my ex. What does that make me?"

"Horny?"

"It's been a while." Fanny grinned.

"Probably longer for Ash." Bess's face was so blank, Fanny poked her on the arm. She burst into laughter.

"He's worried. He used the word performance. I don't think he ever used that word in his entire life, much less thought about it. He's thinking about it now though."

"Marcus Reed?"

"A friend. For now."

"Later?"

"I try not to think about later. I've been hearing that question too much of late. Sallie told me once that later never comes." Fanny paused. "Do you believe that, Bess?"

"Yes. When later comes it's the here and now. You never really get to later if you know what I mean."

"I want to feel something where Simon is concerned. A sense of loss. Grief, something. I shouldn't be feeling anger and relief."

"Why not?" Bess asked. "They're both honest emotions. You always say it is what it is. One day at a time."

"I loved him, Bess. I never saw what Ash saw. There were little things at times that didn't compute, but I negated them. Then there were bigger things I pretended not to see. It was easier that way. It all died in me when he refused to understand my feelings where Sunny and Jake were concerned, but even then I didn't see what I'd been blind to. Listen, let's talk about something else. Can you follow me in your car to Sunrise tomorrow? Ash is nervous about driving with Jake after . . . the beating Simon gave him."

"Sunny?"

Fanny shook her head. "I won't even go in. We'll just drop them off and turn around and come back. She'll understand my presence on the mountain when she sees her father."

"Maybe the holidays . . ."

Fanny shook her head. "No one has heard from Birch. I'm hoping he comes home or calls. I keep getting this sick feeling in my stomach when I think about my children. I want so badly for things to go right for them, but I realize I can't live their lives for them. We learn from our mistakes. Strange coming from me, eh?"

Bess hugged her friend. "C'mon, it's time to go downstairs and do what you do best, charm the customers."

"That's what Sallie used to do."

"You aren't Sallie. You don't sing. You socialize. Remember that lady from Edison, New Jersey? I rest my case."

"Ash, is it my imagination or are you just picking at your food? You love prime rib, and this is done to perfection. The baked potato has everything you like, cheese, butter, sour cream, chives, bacon bits."

"It's hard to chew, Fanny. It's even harder to open my mouth to get the food in."

"Ash, I'm sorry. I didn't think. Would you like some coffee or a milkshake?"

"No thanks. Fanny . . ."

"You're having second thoughts about . . . later?" It was a question more than a statement.

"If you were in my place, wouldn't you?"

"I don't think so. Are you trying to let me down easy?"

"Of course not. Why would you say something like that, Fanny?"

"You seem so jittery. It has been a long time for us."

"I have a good memory."

"So do I, Ash. Let's do this. Have Mrs. Gonzales baby-sit in your suite. I'll leave the door of the penthouse open. Go up and wait for me. We can have a drink and talk or we can . . . do other things. And, Ash, take the word performance out of your vocabulary. Think in terms of an old shoe and an old sock."

"Jesus, Fanny, that's not very romantic."

Fanny laughed. "Here sits a man who has been called a legend in his own time, a man whose sexual prowess is legendary. And then there's me, the ex-wife who never quite had it all together where you were concerned, intimidating you. Gotta go, Ash, duty calls. If you change your mind, leave a note on my door."

"You're enjoying this, aren't you, Fanny?"

"Uh-huh." Fanny tweaked Ash's ear. She laughed when she heard him groan.

She was still laughing when she walked out onto the casino floor.

Heading straight for her was Marcus Reed.

18

Fanny felt a head rush. Her step faltered. "Marcus!"

"Good evening, Fanny. You look lovely. Was your opening last night everything you wanted it to be?"

"And more. My grandson loved everything. He fell asleep on his feet twice. Did I misunderstand you? I thought you said you were leaving?"

"I was supposed to, but there were some loose ends to tie up. I did manage to get close to the front windows. I'm not much for crowds, so I contented myself by pressing my nose to the glass and staring. I'm glad things worked out. You can't buy the kind of media coverage you received last night. It will continue for the rest of the month."

"You worked like a Trojan, Marcus. It's a shame you didn't get your share of billing."

Marcus shrugged. "That's not important to me. I did it because I wanted to do it. I was wondering if you'd like to have a drink with me."

"I'd love to have a drink with you. Your poinsettias arrived a little while ago. My goodness, Marcus, they must have cost a fortune. You shouldn't do things like that."

"Why?"

"Why . . . because it's so extravagant."

"Do they make your apartment festive? Do you like the colors? Does it make everything very Christmasy?"

Fanny laughed. "Yes. Yes. Yes. I adore the holidays. Everyone seems so real at this time of the year. They're kinder, nicer, that kind of thing. Are you fond of the holidays?"

"Very much so."

"How long are you staying, Marcus?"

"Another hour or so. I wanted to say good-bye. I left rather abruptly the other day. If your invitation is still open, I'll be back for Christmas."

"Of course. I'll just have coffee. I have a long night ahead of me. My friend Billie and her husband are here, and I want to spend some time with them before they leave tomorrow."

"Coffee it is. Fanny, there's a rumor on the street. I heard it this afternoon. Are you aware of it?"

"If it's what I think it is, yes. I try never to discuss my family with . . . other people. I don't mean to offend you."

"Not at all. Is Mr. Thornton all right?"

"The elder Mr. Thornton is . . . okay. The younger Mr. Thornton . . . the best answer I can give you is I don't know. Where are you headed this time, Marcus?"

"Back to Chicago."

"What do you do, Marcus? You never said."

"In some circles I'm referred to as a hired gun. In other circles they call me an advance man or a troubleshooter. My services are for hire.

People call on me when things go wrong with their businesses. I assess the situation, make suggestions, offer remedies that I feel will work. It's interesting, but I never know where I'll be from one day to the next. It doesn't make for a very stable lifestyle. I get tired of hotel rooms, living out of suitcases and eating in restaurants. Sometimes I wake up in the middle of the night craving a peanut butter and jelly sandwich with a tall glass of cold milk. Sometimes I yearn to cook a hot dog and load it with everything. One of these days I might retire and do all those things."

Fanny smiled. "Somehow I can't see you in slippers reading the evening paper while a dog poops on the carpet. You are so . . . bankerish. Is there such a word?"

Marcus threw his head back and laughed till tears gathered in his eyes. "You could be right. You've given me food for thought. Tell me, have you heard from your son?"

"No. I'm hoping he calls or writes soon. If we're lucky, he might come home for Christmas. The boys always loved the holidays. I say a prayer every night."

"How are the rest of your children?"

"If you mean Sunny, I can't answer that. I hope she's well. Sage and Billie are fine."

"And how are you, Fanny? I'm asking because I am genuinely concerned about you. You can't be all things to all people. You need to be your own person."

"I tried that, Marcus. I wasn't very successful. Sometimes I don't think there is a Fanny Thornton. I'm somebody's mother, somebody's ex-wife, somebody's wife, somebody's friend. My husband is divorcing me. That makes two bad marriages. It doesn't say much for me. I have to think about that."

"That's where you're wrong, Fanny. Maybe it wasn't you, maybe it was the two men you were married to. Don't be so quick to shoulder all the blame, and don't listen to other people when they feel compelled to blame you. Until they walk in your shoes, they have no right to pass judgment."

"Thank you for saying that, Marcus. Life is never easy, is it?"

"Life finds a way of interfering in everyone's life. That's why it's called life, I guess. We are philosophical this evening. Whatever it is that's troubling you, Fanny, will pass. Time is a wondrous healer in all things."

"I'll remember that."

"I enjoyed the coffee, Fanny, and your company." Marcus smiled as he brought Fanny's hand to his lips. She flushed. "Fanny, are you going to have a Christmas tree?"

"Of course."

"A real one or a plastic one?"

"Bite your tongue. Real of course."

"Would you be amenable to going with me to the mountains to pick one out? I haven't done that in years. My childhood must be catching up with me. I could come early unless you want to decorate ahead of time."

"I'd like that. Let's say the day before Christmas Eve."

"It's a date."

Fanny felt flustered. "Do you mean it's the date, meaning the day on the calendar, or it's a date as in . . . date?"

"Both."

"Oh. I haven't had a date in years," Fanny confessed.

"Me either. I'm sure there's a book on it somewhere."

"I'm sure."

"Good-bye, Fanny."

"Good-bye, Marcus. Have a safe trip."

"Tell me, how much did you win?" Fanny asked, a lilt in her voice.

"Two bucks," Thad said. "Billie won eighty dollars about an hour ago, and she has five dollars left."

"I love it when a customer loses money. It's going to be a long month. We're jammed to capacity. The hotel is booked solid through January 3. We're taking in a record amount of money."

"Fanny, what's wrong? Don't tell me nothing. I know you too well, and I can see that all is not right with your world." Billie's voice was gentle as she led Fanny away from the crowds.

"Here, Thad, play my last five dollars, and if you lose it, we're going home."

Fanny rattled off the day's happenings. "How is it possible I didn't see, didn't hear, didn't know or even suspect, Billie? I blocked it out, didn't I?"

"You were in love in the beginning. Yes, Fanny, you blocked it out. You didn't want to believe what was going on. How much longer do you think you would have let things go on before you woke up and did something?"

"I think I had already made my decision on our anniversary. Yes,

I loved Simon, but that sick love, and it was sick love, cost me my daughter. I've had it with love and marriage. I'm going to grow old by myself."

"Fanny, you said you had one good year. Some people never even get that. It happened, it didn't work and you don't look back."

"I feel like such a fool."

"We've all been down that road. I don't know a single woman who hasn't felt that way at one time in her life. It's behind you. Are you sure Ash is okay?"

"He said he was. He looks awful. He's concerned about Jake. I'll be driving them home in the morning. When are you leaving?"

"Around noon. We could delay takeoff and have lunch. That's so I can brag about my wonderful Japanese-American grandson."

"Okay, sounds good to me."

"Didn't you leave something out of our conversation, Fanny?"

"You mean Marcus?"

"Yes, Marcus."

"I don't know how to talk about him. I know that must sound strange to you. He's a very nice person. He sent me a hundred poinsettias earlier. He does everything in such high numbers. I think he overwhelms me. He's a friend."

"Relationships are always best when they start out with friendships. Thad and I are the living proof. I didn't know love could be like this. It's what I wish for you, my friend."

"I think, Billie, my life is destined to turn out like Sallie's. Don't pooh-pooh this away. I'll live with that, too. I'm tired of fighting the tide. If something is meant to happen, it's going to happen. Ahhh, see that crowd! I think your husband just won one of our jackpots!"

"Are you kidding? Where! Do you do those bells and whistles every time someone wins?"

"Yep. That's to give the other customers hope that they, too, can win. Let's see how much he took the house for."

"Five thousand dollars!" Thad said hoarsely.

"Darling, that's wonderful! Now you can buy me a present from one of these exquisite shops."

Fanny posed for the obligatory pictures before she walked away to meet Bess.

"Fanny, wait a minute. I need to ask you something. I must be getting senile because each time I see you, it's on my mind, then I lose my train of thought. I want to close the books, and we never did reconcile that money Ash paid out once a month under cash. Five thousand a month is sixty thousand a year. That's a large sum of money. What should I charge it against? Did you ever ask him?"

"No, I never asked him. I will tonight."

"He's still writing the checks."

"Still?"

"Yes. He doesn't fill out the memo part. The signature on the back is just a scrawl. I suppose I could call the bank, but I didn't want to do that without talking to you first."

"I'm seeing Ash later, and I'll ask him. He shouldn't be writing checks on the business account. We'll talk about it in the morning. I'm off at twelve."

"Why don't you go up now? I can handle things down here. Jake might still be awake, and you can tuck him in."

"I just love that little boy. He reminds me so much of Birch and Sage when they were little. He asks a million questions and expects an answer. If the answer isn't something he likes, he asks again and expects a different response. Ash is so good with him, and Jake adores him. Okay, Bess, it's all yours."

Fanny stepped from the elevator, her eyes squeezed shut. She opened them expecting to see a note stuck to her door. Her breath exploded in a loud sigh when she saw that her door was bare. "This is good."

The blaze of red that greeted her made her blink. She really needed to disperse the plants, position them better so they weren't such an eye-blinder. She shed the red velvet gown and pulled on a silky hostess gown. Her high heels were replaced with feathery slippers that matched the gown. The word assignation rippled through her mind. She smiled.

It took her all of thirty minutes to arrange the poinsettias in every room of the penthouse. "Gorgeous! Absolutely gorgeous," she trilled. She looked at her watch; 11:15. Time to sit down and go through the contents of the manila folder. She read the nine-page report slowly as she tried to digest the contents. Now, after all these years, the agency had finally located Josh Coleman, Sallie's older brother.

Fanny read and reread the report. Josh was a widower with three children, two daughters and a son. He had three grandchildren, a boy and two girls. He lived on a five-hundred-acre farm in Mc Lean, Virginia, and raised Thoroughbred horses. The report said he was seventy-nine years old and in robust health. The summary at the end of the report read: Subject appears to be an upstanding citizen. His colleagues and friends have honored him many times for his contributions to the equestrian world. The Coleman farm is prime real estate. Subject's bank balance is not robust. His children are hardworking, upstanding citizens. Grandchildren are also hardworking. One grandchild (a boy) is mentally retarded. The elder Mr. Coleman is said to be devastated that the Coleman name is lost to the family. End of report. Attached to the last page was the bill for the agency's services.

Tomorrow morning she would make a copy of the report and give it to Billie to take back to Washington. Why was it that sometimes the important things in life only came to light when it was too late? Sallie would have given up her entire fortune to find this brother.

Fanny looked at her watch. Ten minutes to twelve. Almost the witching hour. She felt her heart take on an extra beat when the doorbell rang five minutes later. She swore her blood was singing in her veins as she ran to the door. She took a deep breath and thrust it open.

"Daisy's sleeping with Jake. Is that okay?"

"Sure." *He's nervous and jittery.* "Would you like a drink, Ash?"

"Well sure. Scotch on the rocks. Make it a double."

Fanny's eyebrows shot upward. Her smile was lazy when she walked over to the bar. *He's afraid of me. He needs the scotch to go through with this.*

"I'm not wearing anything under this gown, Ash. It looks to me like you're . . . *bundled* up. How long do you think it will take you to get out of all those clothes?"

"For God's sake, Fanny, I just got here. I need to finish my drink." Scotch dribbled down Ash's chin. Fanny tried not to smile.

"Why don't I help you so we can move things right along here."

"You're taking all the . . . fun out of this," Ash sputtered.

"Do you want me to start talking dirty to you now or as you undress?" Fanny leaned over his chair and whispered in his ear. She felt the hot flush that stained his neck and his ears.

"Where'd you learn . . . stuff like that?" Ash sputtered.

"Just you never mind where I learned it," Fanny drawled. She whispered in his ear again. She swiveled his chair until he was facing the couch. With both hands on his shoulders she propelled him forward. He landed in an undignified heap.

"I'm waiting," Fanny singsonged.

"Stop rushing me."

"Are you sure you can get it up, Ash? I'm going to be really upset if you're leading me on."

"It's up! It's up!" Ash squawked.

"But is it *hard?*"

"Like a steel rod."

"You always used to say that and you lied. I wanna see."

"You'll see it when I'm ready to show it to you."

"You never used to be afraid to show it to me. You used to want me to take *pictures!*"

"I'm not afraid!"

"Then why are you undressing under the afghan?"

"Because it's goddamn cold in here."

"It's 72° in here. That's warm. Very warm. Your face is flushed, the part that isn't black-and-blue." Fanny slithered around the back of the couch and leaned over. "For starters this is how it's going to be . . . are you listening, Ash?" She whispered in his ear.

"You can't possibly do *that.*"

"Really."

"Yeah, really."

"When you're ready, you whistle, okay?" Fanny said sitting down across from the couch. She fired up a cigarette and blew a perfect smoke ring. "Is it going down or staying up?"

"What do you think? How long is it going to take you to get out of that get-up?"

"Blink."

She was on top of him as the afghan flew across the room. "Are you in the spirit of things now?"

"You said something about sizzling my socks off."

"You want sizzle or you want a burn?" Fanny hissed in his ear, her hands everywhere.

"Burn me, baby, burn me."

"First we have to build the fire."

"You need to stoke a fire.

"No, no, that's stroke. Just do it. Ahhh."

"You let me know when you're on fire, sweetie," Fanny said.

"Now! I'm on fire now! This is good. This is *really* good. Ohhh, yeah, yeah, I'm blazing."

"Are you an inferno yet?"

"Almost, oh, yeah. More kindling. Stoke that fire, baby. Do it, do it, do it!"

"Am I dead?" Ash asked, a long time later.

"Probably not, but you look it."

"Where the hell did you learn *stuff* like that? What'd you do, take a seminar or something?"

"Or something," Fanny said. "Aren't you supposed to say, was it as good for you as it was for me?"

"I don't have to ask, I know. Where'd you learn that . . . you know *that?*"

"I don't kiss and tell." Fanny grinned.

"Do you know any other? You know . . . different . . . ah things?"

"Why do you want to know?" Fanny drawled.

"I just want to know. In case . . ."

"In case what?"

"Just in case. That's my answer."

"Nah. That was my best shot," Fanny laughed.

"It was a hell of a shot."

Fanny laughed again. "I thought so. I couldn't do it again if my life depended on it."

"Me either."

"You up for a fried egg sandwich?"

"Hell yes. You got any stray duds I can wear? It's a real struggle to get dressed."

"I still have my old flannel robe."

"It'll do."

"I'll meet you in the kitchen. Do you want a beer or hot cocoa?"

"Hot cocoa. It's almost like old times, isn't it, Fanny?"

"Almost."

Over sandwiches and cocoa, Fanny and Ash talked nonstop. She showed him the report on Josh Coleman.

"You should take Billie and go see the family. Mom would want you to do that. Take pictures, do that whole thing. More family. It's kind of wonderful if you stop and think about it."

"Ash, Bess brought something to my attention tonight. I've been meaning to ask you about it for a long time and like Bess, I keep forgetting. Who do you write a check to every month for five thousand dollars? We need to know what to charge it against, and if you're going to keep on doing it, maybe we should set up another account."

When Ash didn't respond, Fanny asked the question again. "Ash, did you hear me?"

"Fanny, please don't ask me that. Let it be, okay?"

"I can't do that, Ash, and you know why I can't do it. Is it your supplier? Who? Why can't you tell me? I won't tell anyone if it's a secret. You know you can trust me."

"I know that, Fanny. I don't want to hurt you. I don't want to talk about it. Some things are better left alone."

"Now you have me more curious than ever. I want to know, Ash."

"It's for my son."

"Your *what?*"

"You heard me. My son."

"How did that happen? *When* did it happen?"

"In the usual way. I unzipped my pants and she took off her underwear. It never should have happened, but it did, and Jeff is the result. He's finishing up his master's. In May my obligation will be over."

Stunned, Fanny could only stare at Ash as she tried to comprehend what he'd just said. When she did manage to find her tongue she said, "It's not the obligation, it's the act. That means you . . . you fathered a child to someone else while we were married."

"That's what it means, Fanny. I could say I'm sorry from now till the end of time, and it won't change a thing. I didn't tell you because I didn't want to hurt you. I took the responsibility. It was a one-night stand. She was a nice girl, and I took advantage of her. That's it. You and I are the only ones who know. Scratch that, I told Simon in a weak moment. I thought about telling the kids a few times, but our relationship was rocky at best. I provided everything I could for him and his mother. He's not in my will. However, I set up a trust fund some years ago. He won't want for anything. He knows the score. He calls me sir. Some things are better left alone."

"I wish you had told me, Ash. Did you ever spend time with him? Were you ever a father to him?"

"No. His mother wanted it that way. I never forgot his birthday or Christmas."

"Do they . . . did you tell . . . ?"

"No. I'm not someone in their daily lives. I'm a check once a month. Maybe it's a blessing that things worked out the way they did. I was never husband or father material."

"Ash, what about later?"

"Are you asking me if either one of them will make a claim once I'm gone?"

"Yes, that's what I'm asking."

"Everything was taken care of legally. If either the boy or his mother decided to renege on the arrangement, it would be tied up in the courts forever. The trust fund would revert to my estate. They aren't greedy people, Fanny. They're the kind of people you would like. Jeff's mother bakes cookies. She gardens and sews. She works part-time in a gift store. Jeff is bookish, an honor student. I bought him a car for his twentieth birthday. He's a greedy kid. Selfish too. I bought them a little two-bedroom bungalow with a nice backyard. They keep the property up. It's neat as a pin. It's me that's the louse."

"I think I'm in shock. Should I know their names in case?"

"Only if you feel you want to do or say something at some point in time. My lawyers will handle it all. Her name is Margaret Lassiter. They didn't take my name. The lawyers wanted it that way. I took care of it, Fanny."

"What if the kids . . ."

"If that happens, you tell them what I told you."

"Ash, it doesn't seem right."

"It is what it is. For whatever it's worth, Fanny, I am sorry."

"You know what, Ash? I believe you. In my wildest dreams I never thought something like tonight could happen. It almost seems like a dream."

"Some dream, huh?"

Fanny nodded.

"Time to go downstairs and my other responsibility. What time do you want to leave in the morning? By the way, I'm going to Atlantic City day after tomorrow."

"Around nine if that's okay with you. That's good, Fanny. Make the best deal you can. I had a good time tonight, Fanny. I guess there aren't going to be any encores, huh?"

"Nope."

"You sure you didn't take some kind of seminar or go to one of those sex classes?"

"What do you think, Ash?"

"I think I'm getting out of here is what I think. See you in the morning."

Fanny leaned against the door staring at nothing for a long time. She felt like she'd been kicked in the gut. Strangely enough, her stomach had taken the blow and was fine now. Was she numb, dumb, *and* stupid? Why wasn't Ash's declaration bothering her? *Because I've moved beyond all that.* Ash said he'd taken care of it, and she believed him. Ash's son had nothing to do with her or her family. She had to believe that, too.

Just another day in the life of Fanny Thornton.

On the ride up the mountain, Fanny and Ash deferred to Jake and his chattering.

"How bad do you think I look, Fanny? If you were Sunny, would you be upset?"

"Some of the swelling has gone down, but you have more purple and yellow in your face. You probably should have gotten some stitches over your cheekbone. It's an ugly gash."

"It's healing. What's a scar in the scheme of things? What should I tell Sunny?"

"Would the truth upset her?"

Ash shrugged. "It's a day-to-day thing with Sunny. What might be okay yesterday won't be okay today. I'll wing it."

"We go fishing, Pop Pop?"

"Sure. How many fish are you going to catch today?"

"Six."

"Are you going to tell Mommy you had a good time?"

Jake's head bobbed up and down.

"Where's the present you bought for Mommy? Do you have it in your bag?" Fanny asked.

"What did he buy?" Ash whispered.

"Two boxes of crayons and two coloring books. He wrapped them himself. He used three rolls of tape." Ash roared with laughter.

"Ash, listen to me. I think maybe it was a mistake to bring the toys I bought him. Sunny might not like it. Why don't you say you bought them?"

"We brought them with us because you spent a great deal of time and effort trying to find something Jake would like. He loves everything. You are his grandmother."

"In name only, Ash."

"I'm trying to change that."

"Don't jeopardize your relationship with Sunny over me, Ash. Promise me."

"Okay. Hey, sport, we're home. Toot the horn, Fanny."

"Ash, no. Let me get out and into Bess's car. You can toot the horn while we're turning around. I don't want a problem."

"Bullshit!" Ash leaned over and gave the horn two sharp blasts.

"Do it again, Pop Pop."

Ash obliged. Sunny appeared in the driveway. Fanny scrambled out of the seat so that Ash could maneuver his wheelchair onto the lift. She waited until he was on the ground and in control of his wheelchair before she climbed out. She reached for Jake and set him on the ground. "I'll see you guys. Have a nice holiday. Hello, Sunny."

Sunny ignored her. She had eyes only for her father. "What happened to you?"

Ash drew in his breath. "Simon and I got into it. He didn't look so hot when he walked away."

"Did you fight over Mom?"

"No. We fought a battle that's been raging all our lives."

As Sunny struggled to make sense of the words, Jake was straining and tugging to get his new toys out of the van. "Here's a present, Mommy. I wrapped it. Is it pretty?"

"Where did you get the money, Jake? Who bought you all that stuff?"

"Her did," Jake said, pointing to Fanny.

Fanny wished the earth would open up and swallow her whole.

"Give them back. Give her this, too," Sunny said throwing her gift in Fanny's direction. Jake started to wail.

"What did I tell you when you left?"

"For God's sake, Sunny, he's only three," Ash said. "Do you think he remembers that mile-long list of instructions? Hell, I can't remember it."

Sunny reached for her son. He howled. "Want to go fishing with Pop Pop."

"No fishing." Sunny grabbed Jake by the ear and started to drag him up the driveway to the house.

Fanny was a whirlwind of movement. She had the little boy in her arms. She was eyeball-to-eyeball with her daughter. "Our problem has nothing to do with this little boy. I want you to remember that. If you forget it again, you will answer to me. Do you understand me, Sunny?"

Sunny's face turned ugly. "You didn't want him before. Now, when you have nothing else, he's suddenly good enough for you. Wrong. Stay away from my son. Do you understand me, Mrs. Thornton? Don't think you can come up here and threaten me."

"I wasn't threatening you, Sunny. I made a promise to you. You know me. I'm a woman of my word. Remember that.

"Ash, I'm leaving now. This can't be good for you. I wish there was something I could do. Take care of them. Call me if there's anything I can do."

"Don't worry about us, Fanny. Tyler is my ace in the hole if things get bad. Go home and water all those plants."

Fanny bent over and kissed her husband full on the mouth. "That's so you won't forget last night."

Ash laughed.

Sunny stared at her laughing parents through the kitchen window. She almost fainted with the rage rushing through her.

Fanny waved from the car window. "Hurry, Bess, I have to get away from here."

She cried all the way down the mountain.

Fanny sat in the rental car as she contemplated the map that would take her to Cape May. Why was she doing this? Because Ash asked her to do it, and she could deny him nothing even when she didn't fully understand what it was she was doing. If she was lucky, she might be able to wind things down and take an evening plane out of Philadelphia and be home by midnight.

Ash had made it easy for her. The lots were clearly marked and the owner's name, address, and phone number had been penciled in the margin of the map. Ash had told her to go to the owner's home instead of calling. "When people are selling they want to see a face, not some fancy lawyer with a briefcase. Briefcases mean someone is going to get skinned. Just carry your purse and a couple of checks."

It was eleven o'clock when Fanny rang the doorbell of an old, dilapidated, paint-peeling three-story house in Cape May. She was chilled to the bone as she stood on the porch of the old house. She turned the crank on the doorbell and waited, the gusty wind slapping at her back. How barren it looked with the arthritic trees bending and swaying. Fanny shivered inside her warm coat. The door creaked open. "Mr. Scott, I'm Fanny Thornton. I'd like to talk to you if you have the time. May I come in?"

He was old, wizened, the woman behind him just as old and just as wizened. "Do we know you?"

"No. I'm from Nevada. I'm interested in buying some property you own. I believe you spoke to my husband several times."

"Everybody wants my property. They don't want to pay for it though," the old man cackled. "Ain't that right, Mother?"

"That's right. We want millions of dollars."

"Okay," Fanny said, sitting down on a chair full of cat hairs.

"We have conditions."

"What are they?" Fanny said as she did her best to breathe through her mouth. Cats, all shapes and sizes, scurried around her feet. There didn't seem to be a litter box anywhere.

"We want to sell this house, too. It's a package deal. Mother wants to move to Miami."

"All right," Fanny said.

"You'll buy this house, too!"

"I have a large family, Mr. Scott. These are the two lots I want, they're marked in red on the map."

"Got three lots for sale. Want to sell the whole kit and caboodle."

"All right. I'll take all three lots and this house. How much?"

"How much, Mother?"

"Ten million dollars," the old lady said smartly.

"Six," Fanny said.

"Nine," the old man countered. "Whatcha goin' to do with the property?"

"Eight and it's my last offer. My husband wants the property for our grandchildren's futures."

"That sounds all right, doesn't it, Mother?" The old lady nodded. "We'll take your offer." He turned to his wife. "She don't look like one of them gangsters, does she, Mother?" he asked.

"She sure don't, Dad."

The old man held out a gnarled, dry, wrinkled hand. Fanny offered up a gentle handshake. "We had everything sur-veyed, the paperwork is in order. You pay us, file the deed, and the property is yours, Mrs. Thornton. We don't want no check. We want one of them wire transfers down to our bank. That's a condition."

"I'm willing to do that. Would you like me to drive you to the bank? Your bank will have the money in an hour. Do you have a lawyer?" Fanny felt giddy. This was the way Sallie had done business during her day. A handshake, money changed hands, and that was the end of the deal. Obviously Ash had watched his mother conduct business over the years. What was good enough for Sallie was good enough for him.

"Don't need no lawyer. Hate lawyers. All they want is your money. They shuffle papers and charge two hundred dollars an hour. Then when they're done messing everything up they make you go to court in front of some dumb judge who don't know as much as I know. It's sinful."

Outside in the bleak sunshine, Fanny looked down at her

mulberry-colored coat. Clumps of cat hairs were everywhere. She sniffed, knowing the smell of cat urine would stay with her, even in the car. She couldn't help but marvel at how easy the whole thing was. Evidently Ash was right, doing business in person was the way to go.

Two hours later, Fanny ditched her coat in the nearest trash barrel, copies of the deeds to the properties secure in her purse. Jake, Polly, and Sage and Iris's unborn child's futures were secure.

It was two in the morning when Fanny, fresh from her shower, sat down to call Ash. "I did it, Ash. Eight million. I hope you know what you're doing. Eight million dollars is a lot of money. It's so stupid, neither one of us had a lawyer."

"Fanny, I talked to the guy a dozen times. He hates lawyers. I told him what to do, and he did it. Everything is legal. You filed the deeds, didn't you?"

"Of course I did."

"Then stop worrying. Did the guy really have twenty-seven cats?"

"More like 107. I smelled, Ash. I had to throw away my coat. I stood under the shower for an hour, and I can still smell cat. I'm tired and I'm going to bed."

"You did good, Fanny. I thank you. One day your grandchildren will thank you when they realize what we did for them. Sleep tight, Fanny."

"You too, Ash."

The date on the calendar said it was April 1. April Fool's Day. Fanny looked around at her family. Even Ash had come down off the mountain for the special event.

"Everything's ready, Mom," Sage said quietly. "The line to Japan is open, Aunt Billie is standing by. We're hooked up to the satellite. We'll be seeing Moss Coleman's plane take off at the same time they do. Dawn's just beginning to break over there. Aw, Mom, don't cry."

Ash reached for Fanny's hand. "I'm sorry I gave you such a hard time about that plane, Fanny. I want it to fly as much as you do. Honest to God I do."

"I know you do, Ash. I don't know what Billie will do if things go awry. It's been a battle every step of the way. Her children are estranged from her over this plane. It isn't right and it isn't fair."

"The test pilot is on his way," Sage whispered. "There he goes into the cockpit."

"He's Amelia's stepson, Lord Rand Nelson. His father was an RAF pilot during the war. Billie says he can fly the wings off a bird."

"God, this takes me back," Ash said. "There she goes! She's up. C'mon, baby, get that nose up. There you go! Jesus, I feel like I'm seeing history in the making."

"You are, Ash. It's so beautiful. Billie's saying something. No, no, she's just mouthing words, 'Rest easy, Moss. In a few minutes it will be history.' *Fanny, Fanny, we did it! Thank you, thank you. We couldn't have done it without you. Thank your whole family. We did it, Fanny!*"

Tears rolled down Fanny's cheeks. "Now Billie's son's death is not in vain. She did what she set out to do, and if she faltered, she picked herself up and continued. I don't know if I would have had the guts to do what she did."

Ash's voice was a mere whisper when he said, "You would have persevered, too, Fanny. And, you would have prevailed."

"Ash, that's one of the nicest things you've ever said to me. This calls for champagne!"

"I hear you, Mom!" Sage bellowed. "We should sing. Shouldn't we?"

"Whatever feels right, Sage," his father said.

"Off we go into the wild blue yonder . . ." The family joined in. Everyone was off key, but no one cared.

PART THREE

1984–1985

19

~

"A penny for your thoughts, Fanny."

"Right now, Bess, they aren't worth that much. Simon's lawyer served me divorce papers early this morning. It's been ten months since that night when he came here and punched out Ash. Ten months, Bess!"

"Time has been going by so fast of late. My mother said that happens when you get older. She said she woke up one day and she was in her eighties." Bess laughed ruefully.

"I didn't think it would bother me, but it does. As the months went by I more or less assumed that . . . well, I don't know what I assumed. He's not simply filing for divorce; he's charging me with adultery and he wants a percentage share of Babylon. I own fifty-one percent and he's going to go after it."

"You're going to fight it, aren't you? I'm having such a hard time believing all this. Simon was . . . such a wonderful guy."

"Not according to Ash. To answer your question, yes, I'm going to fight him. I have to find a top-notch divorce lawyer. I have twenty days to answer these papers."

"Get a woman lawyer. They understand better than men. I've heard horror stories about women getting screwed in court. Some of them don't even get child support. You need a shark. Or a barracuda. Is there anything you want me to do?"

Fanny shrugged. "Is everything on target for Halloween?"

"Everything's been taken care of. Is Mr. Reed going to attend?"

"Don't look at me like that, Bess. I haven't seen or heard from him in months. He's a friend, nothing more."

"That's because you're still married. Things will change. I think the man really likes you. I think you like him, too. You had stars in your eyes last Christmas."

"It was the holidays. I always get stars in my eyes at Christmas."

"Listen, Fanny, why don't you and Billie want any fanfare when the rehab center opens next week? You know, the mayor, the ribbon cutting, all that stuff?"

"Just family. The center is a serious thing. The medical field has been alerted, Su Li, Sallie's young protégée, is in charge of all the medical stuff. She's got a terrific staff lined up, top-notch therapists, great nurses. We just want to ease into it without any fanfare. We thought it best for the patients. Patients with debilitating diseases don't want people gawking and staring at them and asking for interviews. It's important for the patients that things remain calm and serene. The first patients arrive the day after our dedication. We can accommodate a hundred. Keep your fingers crossed that we don't run out of money and that we can meet our payroll."

"They've been crossed since the day construction started. I drove by yesterday and it's beautiful. You and Billie did a wonderful job. Phone's ringing."

"I'll get it. Fanny Thornton, how can I help you this morning?"

"Mrs. Thornton, do you know who this is?"

Fanny immediately recognized the gruff, deep voice on the other end of the line. "Yes."

"Can you meet me at Sophie's Cafe in thirty minutes?"

"Why . . . yes, of course. I'll leave now."

"Who was that? You look like someone just stepped on your big toe."

"It's not important. I have to go out for a little while. Take over, okay?"

"Sure."

Fanny walked to the café, her thoughts in a turmoil. Her heart was beating too fast. It was broad daylight, what could possibly happen?

The moment Fanny closed the door behind her, the Open sign was switched to Closed and the green shades pulled down. A bowl of chicken noodle soup and a cup of coffee were placed in front of her.

Even sitting, the man dwarfed the room. "It's nice to see you again, Mrs. Thornton."

Fanny nodded. She tasted the soup. It was good. She waited.

"My . . . colleagues and I would like to help you. What you're doing out in the desert is a good thing. My side of the street would like to help. Anonymously of course."

"I don't understand." Fanny placed her soup spoon at the side of the bowl.

The man slid an envelope across the table. Fanny reached for it and opened it. Her gasp could be heard across the room. "This is . . . I don't know what to say."

"Thank you is good enough. If you are amenable, we've decided that we will donate one day's proceeds once a year. Look at it this way, Mrs. Thornton. My side of the street is giving to your side. How and what you do with the money is entirely up to you. We will never interfere. We did our own analysis of the situation and there is no way your center can stay in the black with just you and Mrs. Kingsley funding it. It's a worthwhile endeavor, and we'd like to be part of it. There are no strings of any kind."

"Then I accept. I just don't know how to handle this."

"Let your bankers take care of the details. They can talk to our bankers. We wish you every success."

"We aren't having a grand opening or anything like that," Fanny said, grappling for words. "You wouldn't happen to know a good divorce lawyer who's a woman would you?" God in heaven, did she just say that? Evidently she did because the man seemed to be having difficulty switching his mental gears. He shrugged.

"We understand the reasoning behind your decision. Enjoy your lunch, Mrs. Thornton."

"It's very good soup."

"Take some home."

"I might do that."

Fanny stared at the envelope in front of her. Five million dollars. *Five million dollars.* From the other side of the street. Suddenly she felt giddy, light-headed. She was about to leave when a paper bag was placed on the table. Chicken soup to go. She smiled all the way to the bank. She was still smiling when she returned to Babylon. She immediately placed a call to Billie Kingsley.

"You kept it, didn't you?"

"Billie, I did not walk, I *ran* to the bank. It was a cashier's check so the money is already in the rehab account. They're going to donate every year. Ash is never going to believe this."

"Is he coming for the dedication?"

"Yes, and I believe Sunny is coming, too. The sign is going up today. Chue's standing at the ready with his flowers and shrubbery. As soon as they walk away, he'll be planting and laying sod. When he's done, it will look like it's been there for years. I'm glad we decided on calling the center, The Sunrise Rehabilitation Center for your home in Texas and my mountain. It's like it was meant to be. Gotta go, see you on Sunday."

Fanny felt so good she danced a little jig. Her mood darkened immediately when her gaze dropped to the legal papers on the corner of her desk. "Guess what, Simon Thornton. I'll fight you for Babylon until hell freezes over, and then I'll fight you on the ice!"

Fanny tied the belt of the terry cloth robe. Her wet head swathed in a thick towel, she padded to the kitchen to make coffee and to feed Daisy. The doorbell rang at ten minutes past nine just as she was sitting down with her coffee and the morning paper. Daisy ran to the door, barking.

There was only one word to describe the woman standing in the doorway; spectacular.

"Mrs. Thornton?"

"Yes."

"I'm Clementine Fox. A mutual friend of ours said you were in need of an attorney and suggested I stop by."

Fanny wasn't about to ask which mutual friend. "Are you *the* Clementine Fox, better known as the Silver Fox?"

The woman smiled, each tooth a matched pearl. "That's one of my more flattering names. Everyone thinks my hair is dyed. It isn't. I was born with silver hair."

"Would you like some coffee?"

"I'd love some."

"Is the kitchen okay?"

"I love kitchens. As a child we lived in ours. My mother made the sweetest-smelling bread. I lived for the days she made bread and strawberry jam. You look puzzled. Did I come at a bad time?"

"No, not at all. I guess I'm just marveling at how fast people on the other side of the street do things."

The golden eyes beneath heavy lashes looked amused. "The telephone is a marvelous invention."

She wasn't just spectacular. She was exquisitely spectacular. She was lean and trim; obviously, she worked out. Fanny just knew there wasn't one extra ounce of body fat on this woman. She probably spoke seven foreign languages, too. She absolutely *reeked* of capability. The Chanel suit and purse said her bank account wasn't just healthy, it was robust.

"I have a problem," Fanny said.

Clementine crossed her legs, legs with no end. Fanny felt smug when she recognized the shoes on the attorney's feet. "I have all day. Talk to me."

Fanny talked.

Clementine listened, her pen flying over the yellow legal pad.

The moment Clementine capped her pen, Fanny said, "So, what do you think?"

"I think you married yourself one sorry son of a bitch. There's no way to know that going in, so you're excused. I know how to play the game, and I know the *name* of the game. Let me give it to you in clear, concise terms. The first rule in a divorce: if it looks like it's going to be the knock-down-drag-out kind, you fuck them before they fuck you. I know your husband's lawyer. Jason St. Clare studied law under the Devil."

Fanny winced. "Where did you study, Miss Fox?"

"Call me Clementine. From here on in I'm going to be your best friend. I was St. Clare's protégé."

Fanny smiled. "Not one cent from this casino. I mean that."

"I hear you." The long legs straightened themselves out. "I like what you did with this place. It looks like someone really lives here now."

She didn't mean to ask the question. It just rolled out of her mouth. "You've been here before?"

"Uh-huh. I think I was 960 on Ash's conquest list. That was okay," she trilled, "because he was 961 on my conquest list." Fanny burst into laughter. "You were already separated."

"That was a long time ago."

"You then married the brother! I would have thought you would have learned your lesson the first time around."

"Stupid is as stupid does."

Clementine held out her hand. Fanny shook it vigorously She was in good hands, and she knew it.

"You won't hear from me until I have something concrete to tell you. It takes a while to wade through the bullshit. I don't expect Jason to dick around too much. He'll make a lot of noise for his client's benefit, then he'll lose his voice at just the right moment."

"Don't underestimate Simon the way I did."

"I'm duly warned. I want to be clear on something. Are we talking big bucks, whatever it takes, representation?"

"And more if necessary. Thanks for coming by, Clementine."

Clementine nodded. "Don't worry. You're paying me to do that. I can see myself out."

The moment the door closed behind her guest, Fanny dialed Ash at Sunrise. "Ash, it's Fanny."

"How's it going, Fanny?"

"Simon served divorce papers on me. He's charging me with adultery." Ash's hoot of laughter tickled Fanny. "He also wants a percentage share of Babylon."

"Not in this lifetime, baby."

"You wouldn't happen to know a good lawyer, would you?"

"Hell, I know hundreds of lawyers. All shapes, sizes, and colors. Some are good. Some are lousy."

"Anyone stand out in particular?"

"Can't think of anyone. If I do, I'll call you."

"How about old 960?"

Ash hooted again. "I could call her for you. Guess you already talked to her, huh?"

"Oh, yeah. She said you were 961 on *her* list."

"That's what she said all right. Listen, Fanny, she was good, but that thing you did last Christmas, that was the best."

"Thanks, Ash. That just makes my day. Back to business, Simon engaged an attorney here in Las Vegas, so that must mean he's somewhere close by."

"It wouldn't surprise me. Fanny, don't you let him get his stinking paws on my casino. You watch your back, too."

"Ash, you won't believe what happened yesterday. I feel like those people across the street are watching out for me. I can't shake the feeling."

"What happened? Don't tell me they're coming to your Halloween do?"

"How would I know? It's costume only. Listen to this—"

Ash whistled when Fanny finished her story. "That's great, Fanny."

"Did you convince Sunny to attend the dedication?"

"Yesterday she was planning on going. This morning she isn't. I still have time to work on her. The doctor was here yesterday. He is not pleased with her progress because there is no progress. He suggested she go into your center for two weeks. She said she'd think about it."

"At least she's thinking. How's Jake and Polly?"

"He's ready for preschool. Sunny doesn't want to hear about that. Polly is a treasure. She's starting to talk pretty good. When she doesn't have her thumb in her mouth. This whole situation is not good, Fanny. I think it's time for them to go down off this mountain."

"What about you, Ash?"

"Good days and bad days. There seems to be more bad of late."

"Is there anything I can do?"

"If there was, you know I'd ask. I don't want to leave the mountain, Fanny."

"I know. If you need me, call."

"Okay, Fanny. I'll see you on Sunday."

"Are you bringing the kids?"

"Yeah. Tyler's in town, did you know that?"

"No, I didn't. Where is he staying, do you know?"

"He didn't say. He's getting married over Christmas and he wants to take the kids. Sunny is throwing a fit. I think he plans to attend the dedication. Go easy on him, Fanny."

"Why should I do that, Ash?"

"Because I asked you to."

"Oh. All right."

"What are you dressing up as?"

"The wicked witch of something or other. *Nine hundred and sixty!*"

"It's a hell of a memory," Ash laughed as he hung up the phone.

Nine hundred and sixty. I don't think I had sex nine hundred and sixty times in my *whole* life. "I guess I'm a dud, Daisy."

"Blue skies, cotton-candy clouds, the sweet scent of sagebrush, what more could we want, Billie?"

"Fanny, it looks just like the architect's rendering. It really does look like a large Hansel and Gretel building nestled in the cottonwoods. It was a stroke of genius to use the same prairie pink brick we used to rebuild Sunbridge. It will weather beautifully. It looks so homey, so welcoming. God, Fanny, I hope Sunny feels the same way when she sees it."

"Chue did a magnificent job on the sod and the shrubbery. It looks like it's been here forever. The sign isn't too much is it?"

"Nope. It blends right in. The Sunrise Rehabilitation Center. I apologize for my family's lack of interest."

"Don't apologize. You're here, that's all that counts."

"Fanny, why don't our children have the same sense of family that you and I have?"

"I wish I knew. Time, progress, fast food, not enough money, who knows. It's what it is. I tell myself when they get older they'll feel as we do. Then I say, no, that won't happen because you and I had that feeling from the day we got married. Bess did, too. Perhaps it's our generation."

"Fanny, Thad said he'd fly us to Virginia tomorrow morning. If we get an early start we can visit Josh Coleman and fly back in the evening. I'd like to do it."

"Me too. More family. I wish there was a way for Sallie to know."

"She knows. She trusted you, depended on you to follow through. It took a while, but you found Josh. Too bad you could never find that guy Jake. By the way, do you still have his money?"

"I certainly do. That money has been around the block so many times I've lost count. I used it outright, paid it back, borrowed on it, paid it back at least a dozen different times. I put it all in a mutual fund that pays off handsomely. Here come the kids and Bess."

"Ash is parking. Oh, Fanny, Sunny is with him. I prayed she would come." She squeezed Fanny's hand. "Be cool, don't give her any reason to regret coming."

Fanny's breath exploded in a loud sigh.

Ash came up behind Fanny. "I don't know what to say, Fanny. It looks like it's been there for a hundred years. It's an oasis in the desert."

"Where are the kids, Ash?"

"Tyler came up to the mountain last night and took them back to town. He's coming today and will drop them off. There he is, he's parking the car. Jake didn't want to go with him. He wanted to stay with me. Can you beat that?"

Fanny looked around. "I guess we're all here. We're doing the dedication inside. One of the staff doctors is going to give a mini speech as we take the tour. He'll explain the different methods of therapy. He'll probably tell us more than we want to know. Tomorrow, Ash, all one hundred beds will be full. A month from now, the patients' families can come to visit for three days at a time. It's wonderful, isn't it?"

"Yes, Fanny, it is. Actually, it goes beyond wonderful. Billie's calling you."

Fanny took her place next to Billie, in front of the entire staff. She nudged Billie, who had tears in her eyes. "Fanny and I would like to dedicate this facility to the memory of my son, Riley Coleman, and—"

"And to my daughter, Sunny Thornton," Fanny said. She could barely make out her daughter's face through her tears. Fanny heard her, though, as she stumbled and shuffled forward to fall into her arms.

"We should be drinking this stuff instead of smashing it on the pillar," Ash roared.

"I have another bottle," Thad Kingsley roared back.

"Open it!" Ash said, his eyes on his ex-wife and daughter.

"What made you change your mind? Do you think you're up to the tour, Sunny?"

"I'm checking in, Mom. My bags are in the car. Dad brought me down yesterday, and I had the tour, compliments of Dr. Samuels. He told me all the rooms were booked except one—mine. I'm tired of fighting you, Dad, Tyler, Billie, and Sage, not to mention the kids and I include myself. I'm so tired, Mom. Whatever stamina I had is gone."

"Then we'll get it back."

"Dad needs you, Mom. The kids are too much for him, but he won't admit it. He loves the mountain. It's so strange, once he hated it. Will I ever be able to go back, Mom?"

"I think so, if you work real hard. Let's not think about that right now. Let's think about you getting settled here and what it's all going to mean to you."

"I'm not going to say I'm sorry, Mom."

"That's okay."

"This is some place. It kind of looks like elves and gnomes should live here. It's so *snug* if you know what I mean. It looks like it could be home. I guess it is home. I committed."

"That's the beginning of the battle, honey."

"Hi, Mom," Sage said, coming up behind her. Fanny whispered in his ear. His eyes wide, he marched off.

"What did you think of the pool and the whirlpool? The water exercises are supposed to be very good. Every hour of your day will be used up. You'll make friends here, Sunny."

"I know."

"You're allowed a pet. Actually, they want you to bond with a pet. That will be your one responsibility."

"How do you bond with goldfish?"

"No goldfish. I'm talking about four-legged animals. I guess I should have said it's mandatory. The animal will be with you at all times. It's going to work out just fine, Sunny. The key here is no stress."

"Tyler wants to take the kids to New York. I told him no. I can't do that to Dad. Tyler doesn't really care, and all you have to do is look at his girlfriend to know she doesn't want them. I have custody, Mom. I'm not giving that up. He can come here as often as he wants to see them. He's a doctor, and he's on call. His girlfriend works, so the kids would be with a stranger. Can you handle it for me?"

"If that's what you want."

"Mom, how long does Dad have?"

"I don't know, Sunny."

"You need to help him, Mom. He's like a real father these days. I wish . . . I wish so many things. Dad said you're getting a divorce."

"Yes."

"Too bad. Here comes Tyler. I don't want to talk to him. I'm going to walk to my room. Come say good-bye before you leave."

"I will, Sunny."

"Hello, Tyler."

"How are you, Fanny?"

"I'm well, thank you."

"This is wonderful. You have no idea how badly places like this are needed. I wish . . . They'll help Sunny. It's what it is, Fanny. We can't turn the clocks back."

"If I hear that phrase one more time, I'm going to scream. What happened to 'for better or worse'?"

"I'm not going to get into that, Fanny. It happened, it's over, and Sunny and I are moving on. I could ask you the same question, but I won't."

"You want the children?"

"Yes."

"No. I'll take them. I'll fight you, Tyler. Don't make me do that. The kids need to be here, close to Sunny. She's going to need them more than you. You're young. You'll have other children. They love the mountain. It's their home. I will not allow you to disrupt their lives."

"Is that another way of saying you'll throw the Thornton money in the ring with a slew of high-powered lawyers?"

"That's exactly what it means. We can work out a holiday schedule. I would never, ever, stop you from seeing your children. I think you owe Sunny a little more consideration. You don't have to make a decision today, Tyler."

"I'm not an ogre, Fanny."

"I hope not."

Tyler extended his hand. Fanny brushed it away before she hugged him. "We were family once, Tyler. Sallie adored you, as did

I. It seems like time is changing everything. Have a good life, Tyler."

"You make it sound so . . . terminal."

"That's because it is. You're going back to New York. Sunny is someone you used to know. You'll have other children, and these two little ones will become a memory. Your new life will take hold, and, before you know it, this part of your life will fade completely and it won't even be a memory. It's called life."

"I'll say good-bye, Fanny."

Fanny nodded as she walked away. "He's just someone I used to know, too," she muttered.

"Yo, Mom, wait up!" Sage called. Daisy barked as she raced across the carpeted floor. "Why'd you want all her gear? Oh, Jesus, Mom, you're giving up Daisy. You are, aren't you? You can't do that. You'll die without Daisy. I don't mean literally. How's Sunny going to take care of Daisy?"

"She needs the challenge. Don't make me cry, Sage, this is hard enough as it is. Bring all her stuff."

Sage's voice was gruff when he said. "Daisy only knows the penthouse and the mountain and that place you lived in California."

"See. She adapts. She likes Sunny. I'll come and visit."

Fanny leaned her forehead against the wall outside Sunny's room as she tried to choke back her tears She bit down on her lip until she tasted her own blood. *Love is putting the other person first. Remember that, Fanny Thornton.* She bent down to pick up Daisy.

"Sunny, it's me and Sage. Can we come in? I have something for you."

"You brought Daisy."

"Sort of. I'm giving Daisy to you."

Sunny started to cry as she bent down to pick up the little dog. "I can't take Daisy. You love Daisy. She's yours. Daisy loves you, too," Sunny said as she squeezed Daisy so hard she squealed.

Fanny tried to clear her throat. "She'll love you, too. It's all she knows how to do. Maybe you can teach her some new tricks. She's a tremendous responsibility. She gets her nails clipped every two weeks. She goes to the groomer once a week because she gets matted. You have to brush her every day. Once a week you have to clean her teeth so she doesn't get plaque. Dogs get a plaque buildup just like people. She sleeps with her blanket and her mouse. You have to walk her three or four times a day, and you have to play with her." She burst into tears as Sunny started to wail.

"That's it! That's it!" Sage bellowed as his arms circled his mother and sister. "Okay, that's enough now," he bellowed again. He handed out tissues from the dispenser on the dresser. "Everyone blow."

"What if she doesn't want to stay with me?"

"Daisy loves one-on-one attention. Let her sleep on the bed with you tonight. By morning she'll be fine. Call me if there's a problem." Sunny held on to Daisy, crushing the little dog to her chest. "We should leave now. Take her for a walk and give her a light supper because she's excited."

"Mom . . ."

Fanny kissed her daughter on the cheek. "Don't say anything. It's okay. You be a good girl for Sunny, Daisy. I'll see you next week."

Fanny ran down the hall, sobs choking her. She'd just given away the one being that loved her unconditionally. The one little creature who listened, never criticized, and only wanted to please.

She was outside, the wind in her face, running straight into Marcus Reed's outstretched arms.

20
〜

Marcus Reed held Fanny a moment, aware that other eyes were on him. He drew in his breath moving her at arm's length. "Fanny, what's wrong?"

"Everything. Nothing. I didn't know you were coming today." Fanny blew her nose and wiped at her eyes. "You look terrible."

"That's because I feel terrible. I could lean up against this car, close my eyes and you wouldn't be able to wake me for three days. I don't think I've had six hours' sleep in the last week. Add jet lag on top of that, and it should give you a fairly accurate picture of the shape I'm in."

"Then what are you doing here?"

"I wanted to see the center. I wanted to congratulate you and Mrs. Kingsley. I wasn't sure anyone else would . . ."

"Notice?"

"In a manner of speaking. Now, what's wrong?"

Suddenly voices came from everywhere. Fanny heard snatches and bits of conversation and couldn't make any sense of it until Daisy ran to her and leaped into her arms. "Oh, no, Daisy, you have to stay here," Fanny sobbed.

"Mrs. Thornton, we can't allow Daisy to stay. I'm sorry if we didn't explain that to you. These canines are specially trained to work with our patients. They don't roll over to have their bellies scratched every five minutes the way Daisy does." In a soft whisper he said, "Giving Sunny your dog was the best thing you could have done. She understands your motives were sincere and that's what counts. We already have a dog for Sunny. Look!"

Sunny stood under the portico, a magnificent German shepherd at her side. Her arms flopped in the air. "His name is Zeus!" she shouted. The dog let out a deep belly woof. "The staff is trained to recognize the dog's distress," the attendant told Fanny. "He will not leave her side for any reason. You can take Daisy home, Mrs. Thornton."

Fanny blubbered, "She's all I have that is really mine." Only Marcus Reed heard the tearful words as Fanny cuddled the little dog, who was licking at her tears.

Fanny turned at the sound of Ash's chair approaching. A soft linen handkerchief was suddenly in her hands, compliments of Marcus Reed.

"I'm heading back to the mountain, Fanny. Jake and Polly want to say good-bye."

Fanny set Daisy on the ground so she could hug her grandchildren. "Ash, are you up to this?"

"You bet. Chue is sending up two of his granddaughters to help days. With Mitzi and Nellie, we got all the bases covered. Ash Thornton," Ash said, extending his hand to Marcus Reed.

"Marcus Reed."

Fanny watched both men. She didn't realize she was holding her breath until she saw Ash's imperceptible nod. Ash's opinion of Marcus was important to her.

"I'll walk you to the car. I want your promise, Ash, that you'll call me if there's any problem at all. I can be there in forty minutes."

Ash whispered, "Fanny, watch Jake buckle Polly into her seat. He's the best kid."

"What did you promise him?" Fanny whispered in return.

"That we would go fishing and I'd give him a cherry Popsicle if he caught a fish. I want you to know Chue now has *real* fish in the pond. We catch 'em and throw 'em back."

"Good luck." Fanny waved until the van was out of sight.

"Somehow I didn't think Mr. Thornton was the grandfatherly type," Marcus said.

"I didn't either for a long time. Jake and Polly adore him. Those children are his world right now. They're all he has left. In a way it's sad, and in another way it's quite wonderful. Oh, look, here come Iris and Sage with the baby. This is your chance to meet Lexie."

"I'll drop off Daisy's gear on the way home. It was a close call for a minute. I hate to say this, Mom, but Daisy can't hold a candle to Zeus," Sage said.

Fanny was oblivious to her son's words as she reached for baby Lexie. She rubbed her nose against the baby's nose until she squealed with laughter. "When can I baby-sit?"

"Anytime you want. We're due for a night out. A day out, a week out. I could use a month."

"Just call," Fanny said as she handed the baby over to Iris.

"And now to you, Mr. Reed. Thank you for coming. Tell me, what do you think?"

"I think it's wonderful. More places like this are needed."

"Wait till you hear this, Marcus. Yes, Billie and I funded this place, we built it and got it started. Smart businesswomen that we are, we didn't think beyond opening day. We did, but we just didn't think far enough ahead. And then the most marvelous thing happened. My *friends*, and I call them *friends*, with all due respect, gave me a check for five million dollars and promised more each year. It will cost more than that to keep this place operational, but it can be done. I feel . . . and Billie feels the same way that we are accepting accolades and aren't sharing the glory, for want of a better word. It's not right. It's still their side of the street and my side of the street. If the public knew, perhaps it could simply be called *the* street. I really have to do some serious thinking about this."

"Obviously your friends on the other side did all the thinking and want it to be this way. If they wanted publicity, they would have announced it on the six o'clock news. My advice would be to do nothing. Accept things the way they are. Are there any strings?"

"None."

"Then that's your answer."

"Where are you going now, Marcus?"

"Probably a hotel somewhere. If I knew where there was a secluded place with no telephones, no television sets, no radios, I'd snap it up in a second. I have two weeks off, and don't ask me how that happened. I feel like my head is empty, and I need to fill it back up. It's another way of saying I'm on overload."

"Are you in any condition to drive, Marcus?"

"As long as I don't close my eyes."

"I know where there's a place, Marcus. You can be there in an hour and a half. Here's the key," Fanny said, removing a solid brass key from her key ring. "It's a wonderful place nestled in a grove of cottonwoods. When you see it, you'll recognize the similarities to this center. This will probably sound idiotic to you, but when you drive up to it it's as though it holds out its arms to welcome you. Sallie left it to me as a sanctuary. I think you need it right now. I'll draw you a map. Chue maintains the grounds, and he keeps fresh supplies in the kitchen. I'll make sure he doesn't disturb you. I need to warn you, though, it's out in nowhere land. There are a lot of books on the shelves. Do you think you can handle the solitude?"

"God, yes. I accept. This is very kind of you, Fanny."

"It's a very good place to come to terms with one's life. If you get bored, you can build a tree house, since you're so handy with a hammer."

"Don't count on it, Fanny. Are things all right now between you and your daughter?"

"For now. I'm sure we'll work it out. All we can do is try."

"Have you heard from your son?"

"A postcard here and there. The last card was from Costa Rica. Birch joined the Peace Corps. He'll come back when he's ready."

Marcus settled himself in the car, Fanny's map in his hands. "And you, Fanny, how are you?"

"Last week I wasn't so good. This week . . . I think things are going to work out. I've learned to take it one day at a time. Simon served me with divorce papers last week. I read the papers and knew in my heart it was going to get ugly. I asked my friend from the other side of the street if he knew a good divorce attorney and the next day one showed up at my door. I can't shake this feeling that *they're* watching over me. I know that sounds crazy but it's how I feel. Her name is Clementine Fox."

"The Silver Fox?" Marcus whistled. "In that case, I'd say you're in good hands."

"I liked her."

"That's half the battle."

"You should see her, Marcus. She's gorgeous, and she has this air about her that she can do anything. I felt like a den mother compared to her. Anyway, when she walked out my door, I knew my affairs were in good hands. Go already. Your eyes are starting to close."

"Give me the tour some other day, okay?"

"When you come back from your R & R."

"It's a date. A real one. That means you get dressed up, I get dressed up, I ring your doorbell and I bring you back to your door where I kiss you good night."

"Yes, that's a date. Well . . . I . . ."

"Decide, Fanny, before I fall asleep."

"Okay. We have a date."

"Good-bye, Fanny. I'll see you in two weeks."

"Drive carefully, Marcus."

"The last person to tell me that was my mother. She said it because she cared. I hope you said it for the same reason. It's comforting to know someone worries about you."

"My middle name is worry." At Marcus's questioning look she said, "Yes, I care if you get there in one piece."

"Thank you for saying that, Fanny. Bye."

"Good-bye, Marcus."

Fanny turned around to see her daughter sitting under one of the cottonwoods. She walked over to her and sat down. "Wanna talk?"

"I guess so. Who was that guy?"

"He's a friend. A good friend. He's managed to get me through some tough times."

"Are you in love with him?"

"I don't think so. He's never even kissed me. I think, if the circumstances were right, I might be able to love him. He's a comfortable person to be with."

"Uncle Simon?"

"He served divorce papers on me last week. He wants part of Babylon. I won't give him any part of it."

"That's good. Dad talks to me a lot. He told me how it was, growing up with his brother. Everything isn't all black and all white. I think we all learned that. What I don't understand is, how could Grandma Sallie be so cruel to her firstborn son?"

"We can't change the past, Sunny. What you've done for your dad is remarkable. You gave him a reason to live. I will be forever grateful for that."

"I like it that you two get along these days. How did it happen?"

"There was no grand scheme or plan. Things just fell into place. We're different people today. I guess you could say we came to an understanding."

"Do you have any feelings for Uncle Simon?"

"They died when he refused to understand I had a commitment to my family. At first I tried to overlook it, then I realized it was too important to overlook. My eyes must have truly been full of stars for me not to see the obvious. Now when I think back, all the little signs were there. I chose to ignore them. Simon is a control person. If you're looking for a defense, the only one I can offer up is, I wanted to be loved. I wanted to believe someone could love me for me. Your dad . . . never loved me the way I wanted and needed to be loved. That's not to say he didn't care about me in his own way. He did. Simon gave me what I needed for a little while. Even then I think I must have subconsciously known that something wasn't right. I was afraid to leave his side for fear he wouldn't be there when I got back. That's why I . . . didn't do what you had every right to expect me to do. I was the loser, Sunny. I can never get those three years back again. I'm sorry I wasn't there for you and Jake. One of these days I hope you can forgive me. Not right now. Don't make promises unless you mean them."

"I worry about Tyler trying to take the kids."

"Put that worry right out of your mind. It will never happen. Tyler and I had a talk. He left here with a clear understanding of what would happen if he crosses the line."

"Mom, are you sure?"

"Look at me, Sunny. Do you think, even for one second, I would let someone come between you and your children? It will never happen in this lifetime."

Sunny let loose with a loud sigh. "Mom, Iris said something to me today. We were sort of talking about Dad and . . . the future. She said she would take Jake and Polly if . . . Dad found it to be too much. Sage agreed. Lexie will need a playmate later on when she gets older and Polly . . . Polly would do well with her. For those times when I have to be here. What do you think?"

"I think it's wonderful. Jake needs a male presence in his life, and Sage is the one to fill that spot. I adore Iris."

"Me too. Mom, about Daisy."

"Shhh, there's no need to talk about Daisy. It was my mistake."

"It was the single most wonderful thing you ever did for me. It's something only a mother would do."

"Sunny, there's nothing in this world I wouldn't do for you, for any of my children."

"Then you get Uncle Simon by the balls and when you got them in your hand, you squeeze!"

Fanny burst out laughing. "Clementine Fox will be doing the squeezing."

"The Silver Fox is representing you! Where'd you get her? More to the point, *how* did you get her?"

"The people on the other side of the street arranged it. She showed up at my door."

"No kidding."

"No kidding. I'll be out to see you next weekend."

"Sorry, Mom. Once a month. We both have to live with it. I'm psyched for this. I'm going to give one hundred percent. You aren't allowed to call either."

"Okay. If those are the rules, then those are the rules. Thad is going to fly Billie and me to Virginia tomorrow. We found Sallie's brother Josh. We're going to meet the rest of the family. I'll take pictures and show them to you when I get back. Billie brought the Coleman family albums, and I'm taking the Thornton albums. Your dad brought your albums down with you. I hope you don't mind."

"Are you kidding? I love showing off my kids."

"We'll say good-bye then. I'll be back on visiting day. C'mon, Daisy, we're going home."

Fanny climbed from the rental car, Billie behind her. "Do you think we should have called ahead?" Billie asked.

"No. Surprise is always best. Sallie would have just showed up, like she did when she went to Sunbridge to see Seth the first time. Too late now."

"This place looks as big as Sunbridge. All you can see is miles and miles of split-rail fencing. Raising Thoroughbreds must be big business."

"Oh, Billie, look at the arch! Look what it says."

"SUNSTAR Farm." Billie sucked in her breath. "Guess the Coleman children had a thing about the sun. Sunbridge, Sunrise, and now SunStar."

"I know the answer to that even though it wasn't a question," Fanny said. "Sallie told me there was a crack in the shack's roof and if she squinted really hard, she could see the stars at night. I would imagine Josh must have lain in the same cot in the same spot before Sallie came along."

"Seth told my mother the same story. He said he and Josh used to take turns looking up through the crack, trying to count the stars. It almost breaks your heart, doesn't it?"

"Yes. This is the last of the family. Finally, they're all present and accounted for. Ash will have so much to tell Sallie when he sees her."

"Fanny—"

"I'm just repeating Ash's words. He was real keen on this trip. He said when it's time for him to go, he doesn't want to go empty-handed. He's real worried about the Simon business and how he's going to explain that to his mother. I don't want to talk about this anymore. Do we have everything?"

"Six shopping bags, full to overflowing. In the car, everyone," Thad said.

Josh Coleman himself opened the door. His faded blue eyes were alert and curious. Fanny could see the resemblance to Sallie and Seth immediately. "Mr. Coleman, I'm Fanny Thornton, your sister Sallie's daughter-in-law. This is Billie Coleman Kingsley. Your brother Seth's daughter-in-law, and this is Senator Kingsley, Billie's husband. May we come in?"

His voice was deep, gruff and gentle at the same time. "Seth and Sallie? Lord have mercy. I tried for years to find them. Finally had to give up. Come in, come in."

The old man led them to a comfortable room filled with leather furniture, books, green plants, and four skylights overhead. He motioned for them to sit. He looked pointedly at the shopping bags. The denim-colored eyes were full of questions.

"We brought our family albums so you could see our families. I'd like to ask you something . . . well, actually, I think I want to tell you something. Did you name this farm SunStar because you and Seth used to look at the stars through the crack in the roof?"

"I purely did. Ma was partial to the sun. She loved flowers and couldn't understand why the posies wouldn't grow alongside the shack with all the sun we had. It was a long time ago." He paused. "Seth . . . Sallie . . . ?"

"Seth died in 1970 and Sallie in 1975. Peggy is still alive," Billie said.

"Sallie tried to find you for years and years," Fanny said. "She did find Seth, and our two families have been together ever since. This pretty much makes it complete."

"Did Sallie look like Ma?" the old man asked.

"She said she did. She had a beautiful voice and used to sing a lot."

"Don't have much time these days to do much of anything but think. Tell me about Seth." His eyes turned crafty when he asked, "Just how rich was he?"

Billie could almost feel Fanny start to bristle. "He was rich. He had two children, Amelia and Moss. The sun rose and set on Moss. He was a fighter pilot during the war. That's where he met Ash and Simon Thornton, Sallie's sons. If they hadn't met, we wouldn't be sitting here today talking to you. I'm sorry to say I have no fond recollections of your brother. He was never kind to me while he was alive. I don't think he was kind to his wife Jessica either, and he was absolutely brutal to my sister-in-law Amelia. I never forgave him for that. He thought women were worthless. I can't forgive him for that either. He did dote on my son Riley, but he ignored my two daughters as did Moss. Riley was killed flying a Coleman airplane." Billie's eyes filled with tears. "I wish there was something good and kind I could say about your brother, but there isn't. Like you, Seth did ask Sallie about your mother. She must have been a wonderful woman."

"She was plumb worn-out. She loved us, did her best. I was just a young'un, but I knew she sometimes didn't eat so there would be enough for us. Our pa, he drank and was always liquored-up. Where did Seth's money come from?" The faded eyes were full of greedy questions.

"Cattle ranching, aeronautics. Oil. During the war he *sold* his beef to the government. His sister Sallie *gave* the government chickens. That's another way of saying Seth was a taker and Sallie was a giver. I didn't like your brother, Mr. Coleman, and I never pretended I did. I wish it was otherwise."

"Truth is truth. Did he ever mention my name?"

"Not to me. Toward the end when Sallie came into our lives she told Seth she was searching for you. He didn't seem interested one way or the other. Also, I don't know if you're interested in this, but Sallie bought into Coleman Aviation. She owned fifty-one percent of the company. Sallie talked about you all the time. Fanny's in a better position to tell you about Sallie than I am."

Fanny blinked at the brittleness in Billie's voice. There was something wrong here. She cleared her throat. "I think you would have loved Sallie, Mr. Coleman. I tend to think she was as kind, good, and gentle as your mother. She was a simple person who required little in the way of material things. I heard her say many times all she ever wanted in life was a good dress for church on Sunday, to be warm in the winter and cool in the summer, and to have enough food. She educated herself. She told me when she came to Las Vegas she could barely write her name. She brought a teacher to Nevada to educate her and ended up marrying him. They had two sons. She wanted a daughter desperately, but it wasn't meant to be. She spent years searching for her family. I don't think she ever gave up. I promised her I'd keep looking for you. You have five sisters, Mr. Coleman. I don't know too much about Maggie and the others because they prefer their own quiet lives. Peggy, the oldest after Sallie, is married to the former lieutenant governor of Nevada. Peggy told Sallie that when your mother was dying, all she could talk about was Seth and you. I think that broke Sallie's heart.

"Sallie brought Las Vegas to life. She used her money wisely and built the sewage plant and a private power company. She built a medical center, a college. The list of her good deeds is endless. Your sister, Mr. Coleman, is a legend."

"Where'd she get all that money to begin with?"

Billie's eyes sparked. Fanny nodded imperceptibly. "She worked hard for it, Mr. Coleman. Everything we've told you is in the albums, all the pictures labeled along with dates. When you finish looking through them you'll know Seth and Sallie's families.

"Why don't we let you look through the albums, and we'll walk around outside if you don't mind?"

Thad motioned for Billie and Fanny to go outdoors. The old gentleman was already deeply engrossed in the albums.

"I imagine it must be beautiful here in the spring and summer when things are green. It looks pretty barren right now. Let's go down to the barns. I've never seen a Thoroughbred," Fanny said.

They walked around, shivering with the cold for close to two hours, stopping once in the barn to warm up. Other than several grooms, they didn't see anyone.

"I think we can go back now," Thad said.

They let themselves into the house and walked back to the room where Josh Coleman was just closing the last album. "Would you be of a mind to stay on a few days to meet the rest of my family?"

"We can't, Mr. Coleman, but we can leave the albums for you if you give us yours to show our families. We can visit another time. Your family will always be welcome at our homes anytime you want to visit," Fanny said.

"I can do that. It's good to know you have kin. I'm much obliged you took the time to come here. You'd make me proud if you'd have lunch with me. Got some good Virginia ham."

"We'd be pleased to have lunch with you," Thad said.

The all-too-short lunch was filled with reminiscences, real memories, and regrets.

"You're sure now there's nothing I can do for your families?"

Thad laughed. "Seth owned Coleman Aviation and Sunbridge grazes thousands and thousands of head of cattle. The family is self-sufficient. Sallie owned Las Vegas. She was the richest woman in the state. She searched for you and Seth because she wanted to help you both. It's kind of you to offer, though. Have you ever been to Las Vegas, Mr. Coleman?"

"Last year. Lost a poke, too. Went to that there fancy one that's one of the seven wonders of the world or something like that."

Fanny laughed. "In a manner of speaking, that's Sallie's casino. I'm sorry about your loss."

"We got us one of them Coleman airplanes. Now, don't that beat the dickens out of you?"

"I'd say so," Thad chuckled.

"I'm sorry about your boy, Miss Billie. It's not right a parent should bury a child. God acts in mysterious ways. I'm gettin' religion in my old age." He cackled, slapping his denim-clad leg with the palm of his hand to make his point. "I want to thank you for coming all this way. We'll talk again."

Thad filled the shopping bag with six different albums.

"What do you think of SunStar?" the old man asked. His voice turned crafty again when he said, "Did I do as well as Seth and Sallie?"

"Yes, sir, I think you did. It wouldn't have mattered to Sallie if you dug ditches for a living," Fanny said.

"I'm sorry to say it would have mattered to Seth," Billie said.

The old man cackled. "I knew the answer before I asked the question. I was testing you."

Fanny turned around. "Testing us for what?"

"Just testing. I test people all the time. Most times they don't measure up. You two, you measured up."

Fanny wasn't sure if she should be flattered or insulted. It looked to her like Billie was of the same opinion. In the end, both women shrugged.

There were no hugs, no embraces. Everyone shook hands with a promise to stay in touch.

The plane ride home was spent looking at the albums and speculating about this newest branch of the family.

"I think there's something out of kilter with that family. Don't ask me why I think that because I don't know," Billie said. "I didn't like him, that much I do know."

"I more or less feel the same way. Maybe it was something he said and we both picked up on it but didn't know what it meant. It's one of those things that come to you later on. I walked away with that kind of feeling."

"The people in the photographs look so, what's the word I'm looking for? Maybe austere? I didn't see one smile in any of the pictures. Kids always mug for the cameras at one time or another."

"It's not our problem, Billie. We followed through, we did what we thought we had to do. If there's going to be a next move, they have to make it. Let's agree on that."

"I agree. Now, tell me about Marcus Reed."

Marcus Reed stood back to view his handiwork. It was a tree house worthy of *Architectural Digest*. Maybe he should take pictures and send them to the magazine. Then again, maybe he shouldn't.

He sat down on the stump of an old tree. Two more days to go on his self-imposed vacation. All he'd done for the past twelve days was eat, sleep, read, and take long walks, commune with nature. His biggest accomplishment was the tree house. Using the materials at hand had been his ultimate challenge, but he now had a two-room tree house, completely open in the front, with a deck of sorts and a sturdy ladder leading to his haven in the tree. Tonight he might sit in the tree house and watch the stars. Maybe he could get a fix on the lights he thought he saw in the distance this past week.

Fanny had said no one knew about this place. To see lights, even at a distance, meant someone was close by. Someone who didn't belong here. Several times during the past days he'd thought he heard noises outside the house late at night, after he was in bed and the lights were out. He'd attributed the sounds to animals, but he slept with his revolver under his pillow.

He longed for a telephone, a newspaper. He realized all he had to do was get in his car and drive for ten miles and both would be within his grasp but if he did that, his solitude would be broken. He'd enjoyed every minute he'd spent in this secluded place Fanny called a sanctuary. It was that and more. He realized he was going to hate to leave. Maybe it was time for him to cut back on his workload, time to make a life for himself. He could put down some roots in Vegas, which would allow him to be near Fanny Thornton.

Two more days until his date with Fanny. Just the thought made him feel as giddy as a teenager.

Two more days.

Fanny listened to the message on her machine. "Fanny, it's Marcus. I'm at a gas station on the side of the road. I want to thank you for two of the best weeks of my life. I cleaned the house and locked up. I'll pick you up at eight this evening. We'll do the town, dinner, show, the whole bit."

Fanny looked at her watch. She had time to go to the beauty parlor and get the works. She might even have time for a leisurely bubble bath. What to wear? How did one act on a real date? She supposed it would be awkward at first, Marcus doing his best to put her at ease while she tried to fight off her nervousness. And when the evening ended, what would he expect? The kiss was a given. Nothing more. Kisses led to other things. One kiss should be all right. This wasn't an assignation, for heaven's sake. She could handle this. She enjoyed Marcus's company. They were friends.

Fanny looked at her watch again. Could she possibly be ready in five hours? She felt like she needed *days*. She called downstairs to the beauty shop to make an appointment and was told they could take her in an hour.

Fanny was tossing her wardrobe onto the bed, trying desperately to make a decision, when the phone rang. Her voice was light, cheerful sounding when she said, "Hello."

"It's Simon. I want to talk to you."

"I don't want to talk to you, Simon. If you have something to say, you need to say it to your lawyer, who will then say it to my lawyer. I don't want you calling me here. I'll get an unlisted number if you don't stop calling." Fanny hung up the phone. It rang almost immediately. She let it ring until the answering machine picked up. She quickly pressed the erase button. Then she took the phone off the hook.

The intercom in the foyer buzzed. "Mrs. Thornton, there's a message for you. Mr. Thornton wants you to call him at Sunrise."

Fanny called Ash. "Is Simon there with you?"

"No, why?"

"He just called here and I hung up on him. He called back. I took the phone off the hook. Is something wrong?"

"No. Jake wants to talk to you."

"How nice. Put him on."

"Grandma Fanny, will you take me Christmas shopping?"

"Of course. When would you like to go?"

Fanny waited as Jake negotiated the dates with his grandfather. "Saturday. I have money."

"How much do you have?"

"Seven nickels and two paper monies. Is that enough?"

"I think so."

"Pop Pop says you have plastic."

"He did, did he? Catch any fish lately?"

"One big one like my finger. Wanna talk to Pop Pop?"

"Okay."

"He wants to buy presents for everyone," Ash said. "You better start warming up the plastic, Fanny. How's it going?"

"Great. I have a date tonight. You know the kind, he's going to ring the doorbell and all that. We're doing the town."

"You like that guy, don't you?"

"Yes, I do. What did you think of him?"

"He looked like a worthy successor if we discount Simon."

"Ash!"

"Fanny, you asked me a question, and I gave you an answer. Tell the truth, you liked my answer, didn't you?"

"Sort of. Are you managing okay, Ash? Is there anything I can do?"

"Like what?"

"Like anything. You will call if you need me?"

"Fanny, you'll be the first one I call. What would you do if you didn't worry about everyone?"

"Probably get into some kind of trouble."

"There you go. Get into some trouble tonight. Forget about all of us and enjoy yourself."

"You mean that, don't you, Ash?"

"Hell yes. Hey, I looked through those albums from my new old uncle. You know what I noticed? No one fucking smiles in those pictures. Is that weird or what?"

"Maybe they're a serious family, unlike some families I know."

"I think I might like to meet them one of these days," Ash said.

"I'll see if I can arrange it. They have their own plane. A Coleman. How do you like that? So what are you doing with yourself to pass the time since Sunny's been gone?"

"I daydream. I fantasize. The usual. The kids take a lot of time. I spend a lot of time thinking about *that night.*"

"Oh yeah?"

"Yeah. You really fried my ass that night."

Fanny laughed.

"Listen, Fanny, I want to ask you a question. Billie sent a couple of sets of those dolls up here for Jake and Polly and Chue's kids. Sunny has the originals in glass cases. My question is, should Jake be playing with dolls?"

"Why not, Ash?"

"That's girl stuff. He does seem to like Bernie better than Blossom. He gets such a kick out of seeing the commercials on television. Soon as he sees it he runs for the dolls. You must be paying some big bucks for the airtime."

"What do you think of them, Ash?"

"They're pretty damn clever is what I think."

"Did you tell that to our daughter? If you didn't, maybe you should give some thought to calling her. She works sixteen hours a day, Ash. Compliments go a long way."

"Damn it, Fanny, why are you always right? I'll call her when we hang up. Just out of curiosity, how many did you sell?"

Fanny laughed. "At last count, a little over six million. Billie can give you the count right to the minute. She's on top of everything where those dolls are concerned. I told you, Ash, anything to do with kids sells."

"At forty bucks a pop!"

Fanny laughed. "Uh-huh. Do you know where we sell the most?"

"Where?"

"In the shops at the casino. The other casinos stock them, too, out of courtesy to me. Our customers want to take something home to the kids. We can't keep them on the shelves. Billie delivers twice a week. Right now we can't keep up with the demand."

"I'll be damned. And I thought decadence and opulence was where it was at."

"I keep telling you, Ash, everything comes back to family. People come here to this Fool's Paradise in the hopes of hitting it big. When that doesn't happen, they have to go back to their ordinary lives. The gifts they take back home reflect that wonderful, ordinary life. Say wonderful things to Billie, and if you really are concerned about Jake playing with dolls, ask her opinion. Gotta go."

"Bye, Fanny."

21

"Surprise! Surprise!"

Fanny whirled around, startled to hear Billie Kingsley's voice. "How . . . why . . . ? It doesn't matter. I'm just so glad you're here. What's the occasion as if we need one?"

"The occasion is . . . ta-da! I have here, right next to me, my granddaughter Sawyer, my grandson Riley, and this imperious gentleman is Riley's grandfather Shadaharu Hasegawa."

The old Japanese bowed low, his eyes merry. Uncertain if she was to bow, too, Fanny followed suit, then wrapped the old man in her arms. "It's so wonderful to finally meet you. Billie talks about you all the time. I'm honored that you have come to visit. Your grandson is very handsome," she whispered.

"Yes. A chip off the old rock. Did I say that right, Riley?"

"No, Grandfather, a chip off the old block."

"Such strange sayings. He is handsome like his grandfather. You see. It is better when you say exactly what you mean. You will show me around this magnificent establishment, Fanny-san."

"I would love to show you around just as soon as I kiss this lovely young woman and give your grandson a big hug.

"Sawyer, you look gorgeous. However did you sneak away from that wonderful husband of yours and those adorable twins?"

"It wasn't easy. Grandma said I needed a break, and she was right. Adam is so good with the girls. He dishes out lollipops and Popsicles hourly. You guys go ahead and do whatever you want. I'm going to put some money in the Thornton coffers."

"I do love to hear things like that. We'll meet up later."

"Welcome to Nevada, Riley," Fanny said, hugging the tall young man. "I'm delighted that we finally get to meet. Your grandmother talks about you nonstop."

Riley laughed. "It's good to be here. I think my grandfather is expecting to pull a lever and have a ton of money drop in his lap."

"You know what, that can be arranged," Fanny grinned. "However, it has to be our little secret."

"You got it."

"My wife is fixated with movie stars. Do you have any here?" the old Japanese asked.

"All shapes and sizes. I can get you autographs if you would like to take them to your wife."

"I would be too embarrassed to ask," the old gentleman said.

"I'll do it for you. What brings you to this part of the country, Mr. Hasegawa?"

"My grandson said it was time to visit. The young are always right. I must apologize for not visiting sooner. Thaddeus insisted I return with him from Japan. I find I cannot say no to Thaddeus. This is . . ."

Fanny smiled. "First-time visitors are usually speechless. At first glance it is rather decadent. After a while it becomes just another place, just another business."

"Operating costs must be enormous."

"Yes. How long will you be staying?"

"We will leave tomorrow for Texas, then I must return home. I have many daughters and a wife who depend on me. My grandson, as you must know, lives in Texas now."

"And that makes you sad."

"Very sad. He has been in my heart from the day he was born. It is right that he learns about his father's family and his other homeland. One day if the gods smile on this old man, he will return. Right now he's being torn between our ways, and this new life here in America."

"It's understandable. Young people need to find their own way and make their own mistakes. As parents and grandparents we must step aside. I think I know what you must be feeling."

"I could never live here or work here. How do you stand all the clamor?"

"I tune it out after a while."

"And how is your husband? Your past husband."

"He has good days and he has bad days. We take it one day at a time."

The old Japanese nodded. "And your daughter Sunny? Billie speaks of your family as though we are all entwined. I like that. My sense of family is very strong."

Fanny noticed Neal out of the corner of her eye. She offered a slight nod in his direction. "Would you like to try your luck, Mr. Hasegawa?"

"Is your establishment in the need of funds, Fanny-san?"

"No. No, I just wanted you to . . . try one of the machines. When I first arrived here many, many years ago, Mrs. Thornton gave me a silver dollar to play. She gave one to my friend, too. We each won a thousand dollars. It was a wonderful experience. I always like to give special guests a silver dollar to try their luck. Pick a machine, Mr. Hasegawa."

"If I lose your dollar?"

Fanny laughed. "Then I'll give you another one."

"I cannot refuse such an offer."

Fanny looked around the crowded casino as the old gentleman made his decision. She saw Simon weaving his way toward them. For one brief moment she thought her heart would explode right out of her chest. Like Moss Coleman, Simon held a deep hatred for all Japanese. There was going to be a scene and there was nothing she could do about it. Billie had said Riley's grandfather was a gentle man. He was never going to understand Simon Thornton.

Her heart gave another leap when Mr. Hasegawa made his choice and dropped in his dollar. She watched in slow motion as he pulled the lever. The delight in his eyes made Fanny smile as three sprigs of cherries danced across the front of the slot machine. The bells and whistles went off just as Simon shouldered his way toward the machine. Fanny sucked in her breath.

"Easy does it, Fanny," Thad said quietly.

"Grandfather, you won!" Riley said, pummeling the old man on the back. "Is it a jackpot?"

"Did I win a jackpot, Fanny-san?"

"I think you did, Mr. Hasegawa. Eleven hundred dollars! That's a hundred dollars more than I won that first time."

Fanny saw Simon's mouth open, knew he was going to say something vitriolic, knew he was going to embarrass and shame the old Japanese, and she was powerless to stop him. She worked her way around the small crowd, her hand stretching out to cover her husband's mouth, but she was too late; the ugly words spewed out just as Billie yanked at Simon's arm. Fanny's balled fist shot forward and upward, knocking Simon backward. Thad caught him by the shoulders as Simon shook his head to clear it.

"I saw that but I'm not sure I believe what I saw. Did you see that, Grandfather?" Riley asked. "Don't pay attention to people like that man."

"Yes, my grandson. I saw." To Fanny he said, "A magnificent uppercut. Is that the right expression, Thaddeus? Is the man a disgruntled employee?"

Her eyes burning with tears, Fanny said, "No, Mr. Hasegawa, that was my husband. I am so sorry. Things . . . I am so sorry." She fled then, Billie on her heels. Riley, Thad, and the old Japanese were left to pick up the winnings.

"This is not a good thing, Thaddeus," Mr. Hasegawa said. "The words do not matter. It is that fine woman who matters. We must do something."

"You can make it right, Grandfather," Riley said, his eyes sparkling. To Thad he said, "My grandfather can do *anything*. American women are so . . . forceful. Grandma Billie was going for a hammerlock."

"He sees these things in American films. My wife is as addicted to the films as he is. They truly are exceptional young women, are they not, Thaddeus?"

"They are without a doubt, two of a kind. They're both like tigers where family is concerned. Fanny reacted, and Billie followed suit. You are considered family, Shad."

"And I am honored. Later, you will show me exactly how she did that," the Japanese whispered.

"Trust me when I tell you Simon Thornton deserved that and more. We call it a one-two punch. Follow me, Shad, and I'll show you around. When the tour is completed, we'll head for the bar and one of those cigars you aren't allowed to have. And some sake."

"Aahh."

Fanny woke when Daisy woofed softly from the foot of the bed. She looked at the bedside clock. What would wake her at 4:10 in the morning? She climbed from the bed, slipped into her robe and slippers, and crept down the hall, Daisy at her side. In the moonlight filtering through the blinds, Fanny was able to see the old Japanese sitting in one of the red chairs, his head in his hands. She stood still, not knowing if she should make her presence known.

"Did I wake you, Fanny-san?"

"No, Mr. Hasegawa. Can I do anything for you? Can I make you some tea or coffee?"

"I think I would like some tea if it isn't too much trouble."

"It's no trouble. Would you like it in the kitchen or here in the living room?"

"The kitchen will be fine. My wife and I have our tea at breakfast in the kitchen before the girls can bombard us. My wife's favorite room in the whole house is the kitchen."

"Mine too. My next favorite things are the red chairs. I have two just like them at Sunrise. Mr. Hasegawa, are you awake for the day, or are you going to go back to sleep?"

"I rise early. Why do you ask?"

"Would you like to take a ride to Sunrise? It's only about forty-five minutes from here. I can show it to you as the sun is coming up. We can be back here in time for breakfast with your family."

"Yes. Shall we have the tea to go?"

"Absolutely. Just give me a minute to get dressed and we can be on our way."

"I feel like a conspirator," the old man said as he climbed into the Rover. He laughed when Daisy hopped onto his lap.

Fanny drove steadily, sipping her tea and making light conversation. As they approached Chue's house, she wasn't surprised to see him outdoors with his snowblower. She stopped the car. "Mr. Hasegawa, I'd like you to meet my very good friend, Chue. Chue and his family are part of my family. He's lived on the mountain as long as I have."

The old Japanese inclined his head. Chue bowed low. Fanny smiled as the two men chattered like magpies. Billie had told her the Japanese was fluent in seven languages. Obviously Chinese was one of them. She wondered what they were saying.

"He said you are a saint," Hasegawa said. Fanny burst out laughing. "He says he owes you his life. It's a wonderful thing the first Mrs. Thornton did and more wonderful that you followed in her footsteps. Loyalty today is something young people know little about."

Fanny drove on, her eyes looking toward the horizon. "This is

Sunrise, Mr. Hasegawa. My son Sage and his wife and daughter and my Sunny's two children will be moving here . . . soon. Ash and the children are in town this week. I can make us fresh tea. You need to talk, don't you? I can tell something is wrong. If it's not my business, don't be afraid to tell me. I'm a good listener, and I never betray a confidence."

"I know this, Fanny-san. Yes, we will talk in your kitchen over fresh tea. My grandson has told me of this place. He speaks lovingly, fondly of it because that is how Billie has spoken of it to him. He knows where the crooked path is, knows which cottonwood the birds nest in, the step that creaks, I believe he said it was the fourth one from the bottom. He knows about the fried egg sandwiches at midnight. He knows these same things about Sunbridge." His voice was so sad, Fanny felt like crying.

"There's more, isn't there, Mr. Hasegawa? It isn't just Riley."

"How do you know this?"

"I just know. It seems at times my life moves from one crisis to the next with barely a breath in between. I've gotten quite good at anticipating bad news and things that are going to affect my life in one way or another. I think it's a sixth sense most women have. Are you ill, Mr. Hasegawa?" Fanny felt her stomach muscles tighten with the words she'd just uttered.

"How did you know?" he asked.

"Well . . . for many years I worked with fabrics and designs. Your suit is . . . designed to . . . camouflage your weight loss, I suspect. The tailoring is impeccable. Are you, forgive me for this question, trying to keep your health a secret from your grandson?"

"Yes. I don't want him to feel he must return to Japan with me. I believe in my heart Riley desires to live in America. It was always his dream to come here and live among his father's people. When his mother died it became more important to him. Each of us must find our own way as you said. Riley will find his. I cannot put obstacles in his path for my own selfish desires."

"Will he forgive you when he finds out?"

"I do not know. I must continue on the path I have chosen."

"Is there anything I can do?" How anxious she sounded. As if there were really something she could do for one of the richest men in the world. She knew, though, that if this kind, gentle man asked her for a moonbeam, she'd try to find a way to get it for him.

The old Japanese smiled. "Two things, Fanny-san. When we walk through your gardens, I would like a cigar, and you will follow through on your promise for the film stars' autographs?"

Fanny clapped her hands in delight. "Ash has cigars here in the closet. I don't know where he got Cuban cigars, but he got them. Sometimes I think Ash can do things other people only dream of doing. I'm going to miss him terribly. My children will miss him so very much. I don't know if I'll be strong enough for them."

"You must pray for strength. I will pray for you also." The old man shifted his mental gears and said, "Tea in little bags. It is amazing to me that you do not die from this. Sugar in little packages, rice in bags you boil in water, fast food that gallops when you speak into a clown's mouth." He shook his head, his face full of utter disbelief.

"It's called convenience. That's what people want today. I do it myself if I'm running behind."

"When my grandson returned to Japan the last time, he asked for *flapjacks*. My household did not know what a flapjack was. Such scurrying, so many telephone calls to find this out. It was a mission."

Fanny laughed. "They're pancakes."

"I know that now. Gravy, grits, fried potatoes. My stomach rumbles at the mention of the words."

"So does mine. It's light now, would you like to see the sun come up over the mountain? It's beautiful. I'll get you your cigar. We even have sake, Mr. Hasegawa. After our walk we can have some if you're chilled."

"I will take it if it kills the taste of the tea. I am not allowed these things. I sneak them. Thaddeus brings me wonderful cigars. My daughters pretend not to know I smoke them in my garden. We play a game. They fuss and fret, especially my youngest daughter Sumi."

"Put this shearling jacket on, Mr. Hasegawa." The old man obliged. He puffed contentedly as they walked the perimeters of Sunrise. Fanny chatted nonstop, recalling little scenarios of her life, Sallie's life, her children's. The Japanese smiled indulgently.

"And this is the family cemetery. It's so peaceful and serene when the trees and flowers are in bloom. I used to come here often to rest and think. I always felt so comforted when I walked away. Have you seen the cemetery at Sunbridge?"

"Yes. I found it strange that a man would bury his horse next to where he was to rest in eternity."

"Yes." It was all Fanny could think of to say.

"I, too, have such a cemetery at my home. It is high on a cherry blossom hill. I go there often to think. The petals on the blossoms are so delicate and fragile they appear transparent. I find your mountain interesting. I cannot imagine living on a mountain."

"You're shivering. It's time to go back inside. It's a new day. For a long time I hated new days because I was afraid of what they would bring. Now, these new days are rushing by so fast I barely catch my breath and there's another new day in front of me."

"What can I do for you, Fanny-san?"

"Be my friend."

"That has already been done. My spirit meshed with yours the moment we met."

Fanny stopped on the path. "Do . . . you believe in . . . do you think that . . . sometimes I feel like Sallie is . . . there . . . you know, supervising, watching out for all of us . . . that kind of thing?"

"Do you believe it, Fanny-san?"

"Sometimes. I guess one has to keep an open mind until someone proves that it isn't so."

"A perfect answer."

Inside the warm kitchen Fanny boiled water a second time. She laced the tea generously with sake from Ash's liquor cabinet. She watched as the old man cupped the hot cup in both hands. He pretended to roll his eyes in delight.

They spoke then like old friends, of the past, of the present, of Fanny's dreams for the future.

"Thaddeus has shown me pictures of the center you and Billie-san dedicated to my son-in-law, Moss, and your daughter Sunny. He told me many things of this fine place. We drove by on our way to your casino. It wasn't visitors' day, so we could not go indoors. I will help."

"Oh, no, I can't let you do that. We're okay. We get some nice donations from the street. We have this foundation . . ."

"I know of this foundation. Much money is required. Thaddeus told me Billie-san sometimes loses sleep over expenditures. This is not good."

"It keeps us on our toes. It's more than kind of you to offer."

"Are you rejecting my offer, Fanny-san?"

"No. I just don't want you to feel obligated . . ."

"I feel no such thing. Your American newspapers say I am one of the three richest men in the world. They say my wealth is ninety billion dollars. Riley tells me it is so. It's amazing to me that he wants no part of it. He prefers to round up cattle and drill oil wells. My point, Fanny-san, is this—we are family. I would be honored if you would allow me to be part of your foundation."

"In that case, consider yourself a third party to the foundation."

The old Japanese whipped out a check and a gold pen from the inside pocket of his jacket. He signed it with a flourish and placed it in the center of the table.

"But, it's blank."

"You will fill it in."

"But . . . how much should I fill it in for?"

"How many centers do you wish to build?"

"I'd like to build one or two in every one of the states. Even I know that's unrealistic. It's a dream. Each center costs millions of dollars, Mr. Hasegawa. The upkeep is millions more."

"I understand. One, two, a dozen. Whatever you and Billie-san think is wise."

"But . . . that means the funds are *unlimited*."

The old man nodded. A glorious smoke ring spiraled upward and seemed to circle his head. He puffed and smiled.

Fanny's heart thudded in her chest. How was it possible this man, who she'd only known for a matter of hours, would simply hand her a blank check whose account balance was unlimited?

"I don't know what to say, Mr. Hasegawa. Thank you seems inadequate."

"It is more than adequate. Would you and Billie-san be amenable to naming one of your centers after my daughter Otami?"

"Oh, yes, of course. We can have Riley dedicate it."

"Then our business is concluded. We must leave now. We are to breakfast with my grandson. More *flapjacks*, I suppose."

"What would you like for breakfast, Mr. Hasegawa?"

"Noodle soup."

"Well, you're in luck, sir. I know a place that makes the best chicken soup in Nevada. They give you so many noodles you can't eat them all. It's just a small café, nothing fancy. The truth is, it's a dump. Oilcloth on the tables and paper napkins. Big spoons. They serve crunchy bread with soft yellow butter. Are you interested?"

"I am most interested."

Fanny slipped on her coat. The last thing she did before leaving the kitchen was to take the box of cigars from the cupboard. She presented them with a flourish. "I think Ash would want you to have these. Mr. Hasegawa . . ."

The old man cupped Fanny's chin in his hand. "My family is your family. Your family is my family. Coleman, Thornton, Hasegawa."

"Oh, no, it doesn't work that way. You get top billing, Mr. Hasegawa. I insist. There is one more branch of this family that has just come into being. We'll talk about them on the way down the mountain."

"May I smoke one of these cigars in your vehicle?"

"Absolutely."

"And you won't tell anyone?"

"I absolutely will not tell anyone. You should give some thought to the smoke being on your clothes, though."

"I cannot be blamed if other people's smoke settles on me."

"No, you cannot. You are a fox, Mr. Hasegawa."

"That is a compliment, no?"

"That is a compliment, yes."

"We must stop at your friend's house. Ah, there he is. I wish to do something for Mr. Chue. What do you think he would like?"

"Perhaps a trip to his homeland with his family. Then again, maybe not. He doesn't like to leave the mountain."

"That is because you made him part of your family. I understand his thinking. We will offer it anyway. We must revise the family now. It should be Coleman, Thornton, Chue, and Hasegawa."

Fanny smiled. "Whatever you say."

Fanny watched and listened to the intense, long conversation. There were bows, inclined heads, more chatter, more bows. Hasegawa turned to Fanny. "He now understands we are one family. He says he will be delighted to visit his homeland. You will wait one little minute. He wishes me to meet his family, and he wants to show me his collection of yo-yos. A truly remarkable man. You do not mind, Fanny-san?"

"My time is your time, Mr. Hasegawa."

When the old Japanese returned thirty minutes later, he was laden with packages. "Rice cakes, honey cakes fresh from the oven, egg rolls, and this," he said holding up a sparkling golden yo-yo. "He gave me one lesson on how to work this strange contraption. He said it is very relaxing. I will test it later."

Fanny gasped. "That's Chue's favorite."

"I knew that. I did not wish to take it. He insisted. That is why I must master the technique he showed me. I wish to be worthy of such an important gift. He wishes me to have my picture taken and then sent to him. When I have mastered his technique. Do you think I can do this, Fanny-san?"

"I just happen to know somebody who has it down pat. Chue taught my grandson Jake how to do it. He's a whiz at it."

"I am much relieved. We must hurry now, Fanny-san. Riley grows impatient when I am late."

"When he gets to be our age, he'll be more patient. Why is it youth can't wait? Everything has to be done lickety-split."

"Someday they will ask the same thing of their children." His voice sounded weary to Fanny's ears.

In the underground garage, Fanny helped the old man from the Rover.

"I wish to thank you, Fanny-san, for an enjoyable morning. It is my wish that someday you come to Japan and see my home and my cherry blossom hill."

"The first time there is a lull in my life, I'll hop a plane. I'll ring your bell three long rings and one short one so you'll know it's me."

The Japanese chuckled. "Do not wait too long, Fanny-san."

"No, I won't wait too long. I think I can taste that noodle soup already. I don't think I ever had noodle soup for breakfast."

The Japanese chuckled again as he linked his arm with Fanny's.

"Ah, our family awaits," the old man said as he stepped from the elevator.

Everyone spoke at once. "Where were you? We were worried. We thought something happened."

"Something did happen. Fanny-san took me to the mountain. We had tea and sake and I had two cigars. We are now going out for noodle soup. Fanny-san says she knows a dump that serves the best noodle soup in the state of Nevada. They also have *flapjacks*." Hasegawa wrinkled his nose to show what he thought of that menu item.

Fanny leaned closer to Billie. "You won't believe what I'm going to tell you," she whispered.

"Sure I will. Mr. Hasegawa gave you a blank check for the rehab centers. Unlimited funds. One of the buildings is to be dedicated to Otami. Later, one will bear his name."

"You know?"

"Fanny, how could I not know? He's making such a valiant effort for Riley's sake. Thad has known for some time. I love that old man. I really do. Did he tell you we're all one big family now?"

"Yes, and I think it's wonderful. He has this wonderful sense of family. He has all daughters. If ever a man deserved a son, it's Mr. Hasegawa."

"Riley is his son *and* his grandson. That's why he's so devastated that Riley wants to remain in Texas. He's giving me his grandson, Fanny. *Giving* him to me in every sense of the word. That tells you exactly who Shadaharu Hasegawa is."

"Our lives are richer because of him, and I don't mean monetarily."

"I know, Fanny, I know."

They filed into the elevator. "Noodle soup coming up," Thad said cheerfully. "You need to know, Shad, that I'm a chicken-fried steak man myself."

"Fanny-san said you will love this noodle soup. Afterward we will walk down the street and smoke our cigars like . . . butter and egg men."

Fanny and Billie smiled indulgently.

Their family.

22

Fanny pranced back and forth in front of the long mirror attached to the bathroom door, viewing herself from all angles. Daisy growled playfully as she circled her mistress's feet. "It's sexy, but not too sexy," Fanny said. "I like the slit up the side and I love the way this raw silk feels. No pearls tonight, Daisy. They're so . . . *debutantish* if you know what I mean. My diamond earrings and jewel pin will be just enough." Daisy barked again and started to race around the room, rolling in Fanny's discarded clothing. "I know you're trying to tell me something. You don't like the mess I created, huh? Well, I had to find just the right dress for this evening. None of that stuff on the floor seemed *quite* right."

The plum-colored sheath was a *Billie* original. The three-quarter sleeves were banded in rich heavy satin as was the neckline and the generous slit up the side, in a shade darker than the raw silk. It was an elegant, sophisticated dress, the kind Fanny rarely wore. Billie had dyed the silk shoes to match the satin on the dress to create an even, flowing line. The small evening bag was a creation in itself, made from the plum-colored raw silk attached to an intricate, antique gold chain. Fanny felt as elegant as she looked, and it had only taken five full hours to get to this point.

Fanny sprayed a delicious but naughty scent in the air, jiggling back and forth until she was satisfied the misty spray clung to her like a fine cobweb.

She was ready.

The doorbell chimed as she weaved her way through the piles of discarded clothing. Her heart started to thump in her chest when she saw Marcus's look of approval. It thumped harder when her own gaze registered his lean handsomeness.

Fanny smiled.

Marcus smiled.

Daisy chased her tail in a circle.

"Mrs. Thornton, you look exceptionally lovely this evening."

Fanny inclined her head to acknowledge the compliment. "And you, Mr. Reed, look quite dashing. Do they still use that term today?"

"Probably not, but who cares. I'll take any compliment I can get."

In the elevator, Fanny asked, "Where are we going or is it a surprise?"

"I think, Fanny, it's time for you to cross the street. I thought we'd go down the line—appetizers at one, main course at another, dessert at still another, coffee and after-dinner drinks farther down, and a show at the last casino on the block. I promise to have you home by midnight."

"What a wonderful idea. I should have done it sooner. I'm glad we're doing this, Marcus."

The word on the street spread faster than a brushfire; Fanny Thornton had crossed to the opposite side of the street. If there had been a red carpet, it would have been rolled out for her entrance into the casinos. She smiled, shook hands, and reveled in the attention she was receiving.

"Let's walk home, Marcus," Fanny said as they exited the last casino. "I had such a good time. Everyone was so gracious. They aren't at all like everyone says they are. I don't think it was enough of a thank-you though, do you?"

"More than enough. Tomorrow this whole town will know you crossed the street, if they don't know already. Crossing the street means you gave your seal of approval. In this town that's all important. It's what you feel, isn't it?"

"Yes. The owners have never bothered me. Yes, once they tried to put one over on Ash, but they . . . they reconsidered. I think it all has something to do with Sallie. I'm grateful that there have been no confrontations."

"Businessmen respect other businessmen. Just because you're a woman doesn't mean they won't or can't respect you."

"Do you think that respect has anything to do with light switches and flush handles?"

"To some degree. They know you aren't a flibbertigibbet. Is there such a word?" Marcus laughed.

"I think so, but don't ask me to spell it."

"We should do this again."

Never shy, Fanny said, "When?"

"Soon."

"Soon means different things to different people. I'll need time to get a new dress. I love any excuse to buy a new outfit. I'll require some notice, Marcus."

"Is a week long enough?"

"I'd like two weeks. That gives me two weeks to shop and think about the evening. You know what they say about anticipation."

"No, what do they say?"

"Ask someone else." Fanny felt flustered at his teasing look and proprietary hold on her arm.

"Okay, I will. I should be rewarded. I promised to have you home by midnight. It's a quarter to twelve and it looks like something exciting is happening inside your casino. I don't know if you picked up on it or not, but there seemed to be this same kind of excitement across the street all evening."

"Let's check it out."

"I'd say someone is winning big time," Marcus said.

Fanny was close behind Marcus as he shouldered his way to the blackjack table. Her eyes scanned the crowd for Neal. She waved, a frown building on her face as he made his way over to her. "What's happening?"

"That guy has hit every casino on the Strip tonight. The word went out about two hours ago. He's raked in more than two and a half million bucks up and down the Strip. He's hitting us big. He's no high roller either. I've never seen him before, and the other owners say the same thing. He's got a goddamn system. He hasn't done anything wrong so we can't turn him away."

"Does he have a name? I can't even see him?"

"He's a young guy with glasses, dressed well. I don't know this for a fact but one of the other owners said his name is Jeff Lassiter.

They got the name from his license plate when he parked his car. He's into us for four hundred grand, give or take a few thousand."

Fanny's face drained of all color. "I want to see him."

"He's very ordinary-looking. He reminds me of someone, but I can't think who it is. Follow me if you want a better look."

Fanny stared at the young man at the table. Lassiter's tie was askew, sweat beading his forehead as he looked at the cards in front of him. *Put a pair of navy whites on him and he'd look just like Ash at his age.* Fanny's mouth grew dry as a cheer went up from the crowd. Her gaze locked with Neal's.

"Change dealers, Fanny," Marcus whispered in her ear.

Fanny mouthed the words to Neal. He shook his head.

"We can't. When the shift changes, maybe, but not now. The crowd, not to mention Mr. Lassiter, won't allow it. I wonder what his exact take was at each of the other casinos?"

"Probably half a million at each place. He's into you for that right now. He looks to me like he's just starting to warm up. The guy's on a roll," Marcus said.

"The shift changes in three minutes. We'll know if he has a system when the new dealer comes on."

"I'll make some phone calls, Fanny."

"Thanks, Marcus."

The crowd cheered again when the dealer slid a pile of chips toward Jeff Lassiter.

Precisely at midnight, the new dealer approached the table. The crowd voiced its objections as the dealer made way for the new man to take his place.

"Sorry, ladies and gentlemen, my time is up. My family is waiting for me."

Lassiter squawked his disapproval. Fanny sensed that the young man didn't care one way or the other. He was voicing his opinion for the benefit of the crowd. That told her he indeed had a system.

"The house rules are four hours on and four hours off. The house reserves the right to change tables. We'll do that now."

The crowd once again voiced its displeasure. Lassiter smiled. Fanny felt a rush of fear.

"He took all five houses across the street for a half million each," Marcus said. "This is just my opinion, Fanny, but I think this is the casino he plans to hit really big. Keep watching his face, especially his eyes. He's not gambling. He's playing a game."

"Wait here, Marcus, I'll be right back."

Fanny threaded her way to the offices and called Ash. "Listen to me, Ash, I only have a few minutes. Your son, Jeffrey Lassiter, just hit all the casinos on the other side of the street for a half million each. He is now into us for seven hundred thousand and he's not stopping. The shift changed. Neal is changing tables. Tell me what to do."

"How do you know it's Jeff?"

"It's him, Ash. He looks exactly like you did when you were his age. You could never deny that young man in a court of law. It is your son. What should I do? Neal says he has a system. What the hell does that mean, Ash?"

"It means he has a fucking system is what it means. He's no gambler. He was always good with numbers according to his mother. As good as Simon . . . son of a fucking bitch, that's it!"

"What's *it*, Ash?"

"Simon."

"What does Simon have to do with this? Are you saying Simon knows about this boy?"

"Yeah, remember I told you I confessed to him in a weak moment. Back when things were okay between Simon and me."

"Ash, I don't want to hear this. You told me there was no such thing as a system."

"There isn't. Once in a while some guy comes up with something and it works for a little while. You can't beat the odds, Fanny."

"He's doing it. Maybe you should think about getting in your van and coming down here or else call him on the phone. You need to do something, Ash. It's going to be a very long night. What happens tomorrow night and the night after? Just tell me one thing, Ash. If Simon is behind this, is there any way, any way at all, that we can lose this place?"

"Jesus Christ, Fanny, you were married to the guy. You saw a side of him even I never saw or knew. The side I know says yes. What do you say? I'm coming down. The house rules say we can call a one-hour break. I had that initiated for just such a problem. Neal knows about it. Call the break in fifteen minutes. I'll be there before the time is up."

"Are you in any condition to drive?"

"I can drive, Fanny. I'll take care of this."

Fanny dropped her head into her hands. She felt like crying.

"What is it?" Marcus asked from the doorway.

"Jeffrey Lassiter is Ash's son. Ash thinks Simon and his son are . . . in this together. Simon's a whiz when it comes to numbers. Because you're good at numbers, does that mean you can beat the odds? Ash says no. I don't know. He said we can call a house break of an hour. He wants me to do it in fifteen minutes. He's on his way down the mountain. My God, I can't believe Simon hates us so much he would do this, if indeed he's behind it. This is all my fault."

"No, Fanny, this is not your fault. Your husband is a very troubled man who managed to hide it all these years. Some people can hide things like this all their lives and then some small thing, or sometimes some large event will happen and there's an explosion of emotion."

Fanny's voice was weary. "The young man isn't doing anything illegal. He's doing what everyone does who comes into the casino. He's gambling and he's winning. There's nothing we can do. Changing dealers, calling time out, those are just temporary solutions. He'll keep coming back if he has his own agenda, in this case, Simon's agenda. You should leave, Marcus. You said you had an early-morning flight and it's after midnight now. This isn't your problem."

"I can't leave you like this. Things can get ugly."

"We have security."

Marcus perched himself on the edge of the desk. "I was supposed to drop you off at your door and kiss you good night."

"I know. It was such a perfect, wonderful evening, and now . . ."

"Fanny, did you know about your husband's son?"

"I just found out recently. The kids don't know yet. How far will Simon go if he is behind this?"

"Fanny, I wish I had an answer for you. I don't. This is just a thought, but do you think perhaps your attorney made his attorney realize he has no grounds for a claim on Babylon? As I said, it's a thought. I think your fifteen minutes are up. I shudder to think what the young man has won in the past thirty minutes."

"Me too, Marcus."

He was so close Fanny could smell the scent of wine on his breath. She saw herself mirrored in his eyes and thought it strange. She felt deliciously warm as she felt herself drawn even closer and yet she had no memory of Marcus reaching out to her, had no memory of moving. She was there, in his arms, against his chest. The world as she knew it ceased to exist. She waited, knowing he was going to kiss her. It seemed to her in that one brief moment that she had waited for this moment all her life.

Fanny stepped back into reality when Marcus kissed her lightly on the mouth and murmured words she barely comprehended. "I'm not a man who starts something he can't finish. We have a lot of to-morrows, Fanny. Are we in agreement?"

Fanny nodded. Her tongue felt three sizes too big for her mouth and her lips still tingled from his touch. She felt Marcus's chin drop to the top of her head. He nuzzled her hair, murmuring words she couldn't hear or understand. It didn't matter. She felt his heart or was it her own? When he spoke again, she heard the words and she understood them clearly. "I think I'm falling in love with you, Fanny Thornton."

"Guess what, Marcus Reed, I think I'm already in love with you. I don't know how that happened either," Fanny said bluntly. "I think it was the fifty pairs of shoes."

Marcus threw back his head and laughed. "Our timing is incredible."

"It's the story of my life. You better get used to it. It seems I move from one crisis to another with hardly a breath in between. Right now I have crisis 466 to attend to. That's an arbitrary number I picked out of a hat."

Marcus squeezed her shoulders. "Things have a way of working out. I'm going to give this particular crisis my undivided attention, and I'll call you with any suggestions I come up with. It helps to be objective. You and your ex-husband are too close to the situation and you're dealing with emotions that are alien to you right now. I'm not hampered by such things. Come, Fanny, let's see how much more damage the young man has accomplished in the past twenty minutes. Remember something else, Fanny, you're losing other monies as well. By now I imagine play has stopped at the other tables and the slots. Everyone wants to watch a winner. Look at me, Fanny," Marcus said cupping her face in both his hands. "Nothing is so bad that it can't be fixed."

Once they were on the floor it was impossible to shoulder their way through the crowds of people surrounding the blackjack table. "Wait here, Fanny, I'll get your manager."

Fanny watched as Marcus plowed his way through the crowds, using his elbows and shoulders, smiling in apology as he forced the patrons to stand aside. From her position on the fringe of the crowd, she could hear the grumbles and the moans and groans as Neal called for the house break. Then he was at her side.

"Ash is on his way," she told him.

"That's a relief. Who the hell is that guy? He just walked in off the street, opened his tie, rolled up his sleeves, and started to play. He did the exact same thing at the other five casinos he hit. The kicker is he's playing a straight game. He shows no signs of tiring. He's not drinking either. He's alone, no one is with him. I can't be sure but he looks to me like he's ready to bet the whole bundle at one time. We're talking some serious money here."

"I know, Neal. Let's go into the bar. I think I see Ash. He must have flown down the mountain." She looked up to see Marcus, striding toward her.

"I'll say good-bye, Fanny," he said. "You're in good hands now."

No, I'm not. I want your hands. I want you, only you. She nodded as she watched Marcus walk away.

Ash's chair whirred to a stop. "Where is he?"

"Find the biggest crowd and that's where he'll be," Neal said. "Ash, he's playing a straight game. Don't open yourself to a lawsuit. He hit the whole street. He just likes Babylon the best. It's my opinion he's getting ready to play the wad he's won and call it a night. This guy is going to come back. Again and again."

"We'll see about that," Ash snarled. His chair whipped around as he headed down the center aisle to where a small, dark-haired woman stood waiting, her eyes filled with tears.

"This is how your son repays me? Would you mind telling me what the hell is going on here?"

"I don't know. Jeffrey leads his own life these days. You know he has his own apartment. How could I possibly know what he does every hour of the day. Someone called. I don't know who, and I came . . ."

"I suggest you go over to him and bring him here and I suggest you do it right now."

"Ash—"

"Now, Margaret."

"I'd like an explanation, Jeffrey," Ash said, his voice colder than chipped ice.

"I've been winning all night long. I guess it must be important for you to come down off your mountain."

"It's important. The Gaming Commission and the IRS will want to talk to you shortly. As a matter of fact, both gentlemen are on the way as we speak."

"The IRS?" Margaret Lassiter said in a squeaky voice. "Jeffrey, did you hear what Mr. Thornton just said?"

"Did I do something wrong, *Mister* Thornton?"

"I don't know. Did you? The Gaming Commission will decide. You did make one mistake though. You should have stayed on this side of the street."

"What's that supposed to mean?" Jeffrey blustered.

"My God, Jeffrey, did you win money over there, too?" Margaret Lassiter moaned.

"So what if I did."

"I don't think he'll pay attention to me, Margaret. Maybe you should explain what that means to him, to you, and to your lives. Not mine. Yours."

Margaret Lassiter led her son away as she spoke in low tones. Ash watched them, worms of fear crawling inside his stomach. He hadn't even brought Simon's name into the conversation yet. When they returned, Margaret was wringing her hands in frustration while Jeffrey's face exuded bravado.

Ash jumped right in. "I know that my brother Simon put you up to this. I want you to know it isn't going to work. I want you to tell him that for me. I can bar you from this casino, and I will do that. I'll explain the circumstances to the Gaming Commission and go on from there. Babylon is a privately owned casino. We make our own inside rules. What that means, Jeffrey, is, we answer only to ourselves, not Simon. Simon has no part in this casino."

"Yeah, well, how's it going to look to the other casino owners when you won't let me play here?"

"They're going to think I'm one hell of a smart man. They'd do exactly the same thing. You can't beat the odds. What that means is you are doing something you shouldn't be doing. I'm sure Simon promised you a bundle. What's going to be left of your bundle after the IRS takes theirs and Simon takes his? Less than you would get in the trust fund I set up for you and your mother. That's history now. You can take responsibility for that, too. We're finished. I'd like you to cash out now. They're waiting for you at the payout counter. One last thing. My side of the street, the other side of the street, it doesn't make a difference when something like this happens. We take care of our own and we protect what's ours. If I were you, I'd go back across the street and lose all that money you won. Do what you want. You are not welcome here any longer."

"Ash—"

"I don't want to hear it, Margaret. You and your son are on your own now. If nothing else, I did expect a certain amount of loyalty. I didn't expect my son to be so weak he would betray me for money. I'm sorry it turned out this way."

His shoulders quivering with anger, Ash wheeled his chair over to where Neal and Fanny waited. "Boot his fucking ass out the door. Mr. Lassiter is not welcome in this casino. I doubt if he'll be welcome anywhere else for that matter. He's cashing out. Make sure he leaves the building."

"Ash, this is going to hit the morning papers. It's not going to look very good for us."

"When it hits the morning papers, you won't recognize the scenario they play out. How many times do I have to tell you, this town takes care of its own? Take care of business, Neal," Ash said, jerking his head in the direction of the payout window.

"Ash, I'm sorry," Fanny said. "I didn't know what to do. Maybe I'm not suited for this business after all."

"Of course you are. You were trying to be fair because it was my son. I appreciate that. If it was anyone else, your instincts would have kicked in and you would have reacted to the situation in a forthright business manner. I think Simon thought this was going to be a snap, and he'd come out a winner. He's got to be over the edge, Fanny. For Simon to resort to something like this is so totally out of character I'm having trouble trying to comprehend it. Stay tuned for the next installment."

Fanny cringed at the bitterness in her ex-husband's voice. "Ash, he's young. Simon has . . . Simon can . . . charm the bees out of the trees, we both know that. God only knows what he promised the boy. A big windfall would seem like the pot of gold at the end of the rainbow to that kid. Don't be too hard on him."

"He didn't have to go along with it. I might not expect much in this life, but I damn well expect loyalty. Birch and Sage wouldn't have knuckled under to something like that. That's because *you*, not me, brought them up right, Fanny. I think I made it too easy for Jeff and his mother. This is all hindsight now. I'm going back up the mountain."

"Temptation is a terrible thing, Ash. Neither one of us can be certain Birch or Sage wouldn't have done the same thing. Where kids are concerned, you can't afford to bury your head in the sand. Cool off, assess the situation, call your son tomorrow and have a talk with him. Don't leave it like this, Ash."

"Good night, Fanny. Hey, how'd the big date go?"

Fanny snorted, a very unladylike sound. "You see me, do you see him? I guess you have your answer."

"He must be a hell of a patient man. Maybe you need to be more aggressive."

"Ash?"

"What?"

"Shut up."

"Testy, aren't we?"

"Yes, I am."

"Excitement's over. Call him up. The night's not over."

"I'm not looking for advice, Ash."

"It was for free, Fanny. You should never turn anything down that's free."

"Are you sure you're up to the trip home? It's late."

"If I stay, can we do that thing?"

"No."

"Then I'm leaving. I'll talk to you tomorrow. Call me in the morning and read me the paper."

"Okay. Good night, Ash. Drive carefully."

Ash slapped at his head. "Jesus, Fanny, I almost forgot. I got a letter from Birch today. I left in such a hurry I forgot to bring it with me."

"How is he? Is he all right? What'd he say?"

"I'll read it to you when you call me. It wasn't all that long. He did go on for one whole paragraph about how the chickens scratch on his tin roof at four in the morning. He said he hadn't had a bath in eight days. He sounds like he loves what he's doing."

"All I care about is that he's healthy and happy. Thanks for telling me. The night wasn't so bad after all."

"Do you really like that guy?"

"Yeah, I do, Ash."

"Do you like him better than you liked me and Simon?"

"Don't ask me questions like that, Ash. First of all, it's none of your business."

"I feel responsible for you, Fanny. You were my wife once."

"A fact that you conveniently forgot from time to time," Fanny snapped.

"C'mon, do you?"

"It's different, Ash. I'm not the young, crazy girl who fell in love with you. I'm not that needy woman who swallowed Simon's line.

I'm finally me. This new me sees and feels things differently. You do, too, Ash; you just won't admit it."

"I just don't want you to get snookered again. I'm not always going to be here to look out for you. I do, in my own way. I want you to know that."

"I do know that. I thought you didn't want to talk about stuff like this."

"I don't. You know, Fanny, you bring out the worst and the best in me."

"That's a compliment, isn't it?"

"Damn straight it is. Listen, Fanny, if Simon starts to call you, hang up on him. Don't give him a chance to say anything. If you talk to him, he'll feed on it. Promise me. Get an unlisted number. Do it tomorrow."

"All right, Ash. Give the kids a hug."

"Will do."

Fanny looked around the casino. Her new world.

Things were back to normal.

Good or bad?

Good, she decided as she made her way to the elevator.

23

As Fanny made her way down the grocery aisle, she had the strange feeling someone was watching her. The feeling had been with her from the moment she parked her car in the parking lot. She looked over her shoulder, certain she would see someone staring at her. Nerves. The episode at the blackjack tables last night had left her unnerved and today she was paying for it with the jitters.

Ash had been right. The morning paper had relegated the event to page four and one small paragraph. What it said basically was, young man wins big and loses big. So, Jeffrey had followed Ash's advice and crossed the street to return the money by losing. Babylon had taken the hit and things were back to normal.

Fanny scanned the list in her hand. Most of the items in her grocery cart were for Jake's visit on the weekend. They were going to make raisin-filled cookies, Jake's favorite. Peanut butter, jam, cherry Popsicles, cheese sticks, lollipops, and other goodies. The cart was almost full with her own purchases—vegetables, fruits, and a luscious-looking London broil.

Fanny looked over her shoulder again, then up and down the aisle. She tried to shake the uneasy feeling she'd had since entering the store. She saw him then as she reached for a box of cereal. She almost dropped the box. She swiveled around, her eyes wide, and struggled to take a deep breath and then another. Her knuckles gleamed white on the cart under the fluorescent lighting. Her instincts had been right: Simon had been watching her. How did he know she would go to the grocery store at this particular time of day? He couldn't know unless he'd been following her. *Don't panic, Fanny. Hold on to the cart and walk toward the front of the store, where the cashiers and manager are working.*

She could hear his cart behind her, hear the sound of his shoes on the tile floor. The fresh scent of citrus assailed her nostrils. Simon loved oranges, grapefruit, and lemons. She knew his cart was loaded with fruit. *Don't look over your shoulder. That's what he wants. Go to the checkout line. He won't do or say anything in front of other people. When you finish, ask to use the phone and have Security come to the market.*

She felt his touch on her shoulder. Once his touch had thrilled her. She recoiled and stepped to the side. "Hello, Simon."

"Fanny, imagine meeting you here."

"I wonder what the odds of that happening are." She was right. There were six grapefruit, a bag of oranges, and a bag of lemons in his cart. "I think you've been following me, and I'd like to know why. Don't do it again, or I'll apply for a restraining order."

"Don't flatter yourself, Fanny. I have as much right to shop in this market as you do. What am I doing wrong? Nothing."

He looked so normal in his white dress shirt open at the throat, the sleeves rolled to his elbows. His chinos were crisp and fresh. He was freshly shaven. She could smell his woodsy aftershave, a scent that had once made her dizzy with desire. He looked so damn normal. Until she looked at his eyes. The urge to bolt and run was so strong she yanked at the cart to put more distance between them.

Simon chuckled. "You're afraid of me, aren't you?"

"What do you want from me, Simon? Your plan didn't work last night, did it? That was a low-down dirty thing you did. I knew about Jeffrey. Ash told me. Nothing you do is going to work."

"I want Babylon. Give it to me, and I'll get out of your life. You can go back to sewing baby clothes."

"Not in this lifetime, Simon. Ash will never give it up to you."

"Ash isn't going to live forever."

"That's an ugly thing to say. Ash is your brother. He could very well fool us all and live another twenty years. If that doesn't happen, I'll make sure you never get a foothold."

Simon laughed. He sounded like she'd just told him a joke. She shuddered. Ash had told her not to talk to him, and here she was, babbling like some crazy person.

"You're just spinning your wheels, Fanny. I want it, and I'm going to get it."

"No. I won't let that happen. You just want it because of Ash. You said you hated this town, this casino. That was all a lie. I'm stupid, but Simon, you're even more stupid. If you had come here with me, I probably never would have caught on to you because I loved you so much. You couldn't come though, could you? Ash would have seen through you in the blink of an eye. That was your first mistake. Everything else you've tried has been a mistake, too. Your mother must be having a fit."

"Mom would want me to have Babylon."

"If that's true, Simon, why didn't she make provisions for you to have it?"

"Fanny, you're right, you are stupid. She didn't know I wanted it."

"It's the red and yellow lollipop. The rules changed, Simon. I'm not Sallie and this red lollipop is a billion-dollar industry. The only way you might have a shot at this is over my dead body, and even then the kids inherit, not you."

"Nobody lives forever," Simon said, then added, "I always liked the kids."

"This is going nowhere." Fanny shoved her cart at Simon's cart, making it spin out of the way. She literally ran down the rest of the aisle to the checkout counter. Ragged little puffs of air exploded from her mouth as she tossed her groceries onto the counter. She looked over her shoulder a dozen different times before she made her way to the parking lot. Simon was nowhere in sight.

It wasn't until she was back in the apartment with the door locked that Fanny drew a deep breath. Coffee in hand, she dialed the business office of the telephone company and was issued an unlisted number on the spot. She then called down to the office to tell Bess to call everyone and give them her new number. "It will go into effect at noon. Call the rehab center first. I have to call Ash, so I'll give him the number."

Fanny put away the groceries, her mind racing. Maybe she shouldn't call Ash. Maybe she should go up the mountain. Her sixth sense, the one that always kicked in when trouble loomed, was kicking in now. She didn't know how she knew, but she knew Simon was going to go up the mountain. She yanked the plug from the electric coffeepot, grabbed her purse and ran to the elevator. *Stupid, stupid, stupid. Call Ash, warn him. Have him take the kids to Chue's house.*

Fanny raced back into the apartment, dialed Ash's number, her foot tapping the floor as she waited to hear his voice. "Ash, it's Fanny. Send the kids down to Chue's. I'm on my way up the mountain. I think Simon is on his way as we speak. No, I'm not sure. It's my gut instinct. Just do it, Ash. Then go down to the studio and lock yourself in. I had special locks put on a long time ago. Your brother wants your billion-dollar yellow lollipop."

Fanny's eyes were everywhere as she barreled up the mountain at ninety miles an hour—directly ahead, in the scrub at the side of the road, in the trees, in the rearview mirror. It was all a blur until she reached Chue's house. She slowed, the car fishtailing in the middle of the road. "Block the road, and if Simon shows up, he'll have to make the rest of the way on foot. He'll leave his car. Push it over the mountain, Chue. I mean it, don't think twice. Then pile everyone into your truck and head for Babylon. Do you understand?"

"Yes, Fanny."

"Where's Ash?"

"In the studio."

"Okay." Fanny backed up the car and drove the rest of the way at a sedate eighty miles an hour. She skidded to a halt. She looped her purse around her neck as she ran from the car, the door hanging wide open. She was breathless when she reached the studio. "It's me, Ash. Open the door!"

"Fanny, what in the goddamn hell is going on? You damn near gave me heart failure."

"What do you think you would have felt if I hadn't called you and Simon got here before me? He cornered me in the supermarket. He's been following me, stalking me. Ash, he said . . . he said if Sallie had known he wanted Babylon, she would have given it to him. He *believes* that. He means to get it. Last night was just a game. It didn't mean a thing to him. He just wanted us to spin our wheels to show us what he can do if he wants to really get us going. I looked in his eyes, Ash. I couldn't see anything because there was nothing to see. He's gone."

"What makes you think he's coming here? Why would he come here?"

"For you. Think, Ash, he can't get the yellow lollipop unless you give it up. Sallie isn't here to take it from you. That means he has to step out of character and snatch it himself. Sallie isn't here to approve or disapprove of what he does."

"Fanny, I'm having trouble with this. Do you think he's going to push me off the mountain?"

"Yes, Ash, I do."

"You should have called the police."

"Get real. He hasn't done anything. It's like last night all over again. The police can't do a thing, and you and I both know it."

"Is it your intention for the two of us to hide out here in this studio *forever*? You must realize I have a slight disability here."

"We need to get out of here. I'm taking you back down the mountain. Chue is taking his family, Mitzi, Nellie, and the kids as soon as Simon shows up. He's coming, Ash. I know he is."

"Then why aren't we leaving?"

"Because we'll pass him on the road and he'll just turn around and race us back down. Who do you think is going to go over the side, the car in front or the car in back?"

"You're saying my brother wants to kill me. I don't want to believe that."

"You damn well better believe it, Ash. With me here he gets two for the price of one. He said no one lives forever. The Simon I spoke to in the grocery store is not the Simon either one of us knows. That Simon is gone. He looks so normal. He functions, and that's what boggles my mind. He was clean-shaven, he'd had a haircut, he was creased and pressed. He even *smelled* good. Listen, Ash, I don't want to die. I have things to do and places to go. I want to enjoy my children and grandchildren. I don't have a plan if that's your next question."

"What?"

"I can't anticipate him. You have to do that. You know him. He's in a place I've never been. You've been there. You lived in that place. What will he do? How far will he go to get what he wants? What's his Achilles' heel? Does he have a breaking point? I don't know those things. Look. I might be wrong. Maybe I didn't read him right."

"No, you're not wrong. Simon has no Achilles' heel. He has no breaking point. He's always been totally fearless. He will do whatever it takes to get what he wants. He used to hold his breath until he turned blue and passed out. Mom was scared out of her wits when he'd do that. She'd hold him and rock him and croon to him and then she'd give him what he wanted. It didn't matter what it was. If he'd wanted my skin, she would have ripped the hide right off my body. He has no conscience. I always thought everyone had a conscience of one kind or another. I never met anyone who didn't, except Simon."

"I hear a car, Ash."

Ash's face turned as white as the shirt he was wearing.

"I told Chue to block the road with his vehicles and when Simon got out to walk, he was to push his car over the mountain at which point he'll head for town. It's you and me, Ash."

"It's always been you and me, Fanny."

"To a degree. I'm your legs, tell me what to do. I know this mountain like the back of my hand. I can lure him away from here and that will give you time to get in the van and partway down the mountain. I'll meet you at some point. I'll tell him you went with Chue and the kids. I think he'll believe that. He'll think I came here to get you to safety because I still love you. He wants to believe that."

"Do you, Fanny?"

Fanny made no pretense of not understanding. "A small part of me will always love you, Ash. I would never deny that. If you care about me at all, you'll do what I said."

"All right, Fanny. I'd change my shoes if I were you."

"God, yes. I think I left my mountain boots here. Ah, here they are." Fanny kicked off her heels and pulled on the boots. Just then, there was a tremendous crashing sound.

"Jesus! What the hell was *that?*"

Fanny's face was grim. "*That* was Simon's car going over the mountain."

"Until just this moment I've been thinking this was all a bad dream."

"You aren't going to have much time, Ash. I have to go now."

"Fanny—"

"Shhh," Fanny said, placing her finger on his lips. "Be careful, Ash."

"You too, Fanny."

Fanny closed the door behind her and walked up to the house and then around to the back patio. She climbed on the picnic table so she could see the road leading onto the driveway. The moment she saw Simon set foot on the driveway she shouted. "I'm back here, Simon. What do you want?"

"Where's Ash?"

"The least you could do is say hello." She started to walk away, toward the top of the ravine where her children had played Tarzan light-years ago. She knew he was following her. She could hear the frozen grass crackling under his feet.

"Where's Ash?"

"He left with Chue and the kids. They pushed your car over the side. It exploded. If you stand here, where I am, you can see Chue's truck going down the mountain. You really didn't think I was going to let you get hold of Ash, did you? Simon, Simon, what a fool you are. He's mine, Simon. I love him. You know that though, don't you? I'll never let you hurt him. I only married you to get even with Ash for fooling around with other women. I made a fool out of you. You need to run to Mama, Simon, and tell her what nasty old Fanny did. Mama will make it right, won't she?" Fanny taunted as she inched closer to the edge.

Fanny saw something spark in Simon's eyes. She fumbled in her pocket, brought out one of the lollipops she'd bought for Jake. "I have the yellow one, Simon. I love yellow. Ash loves yellow, too. Here, you can have the red one. Red tastes nasty."

Fanny went over the side, slipping and sliding as Simon bent to pick up the red lollipop. She continued to taunt him as her eyes searched out the overgrown path. The moment she heard the sound of Ash's van engine turning over, her fist shot in the air. "Oh yeah."

Fanny ran along the crest, her boots digging into the slippery pine needles as sweat dripped down her body. She forged ahead. Simon close behind.

Fanny could hear Simon's ripe curses as his leather-soled shoes failed to gain traction on the pine needles. She ran, her breathing ragged, her eyes scanning the terrain for familiar signs. She'd played here with her children hundreds of times, maybe thousands. Where were the markings? She realized they'd been gone for years because of the elements. She had to go on memory now. She had to get away from the crest and the tree line. Go down, go down, and climb back later. He won't be able to follow you, her mind shrieked.

Her lungs ready to burst, Fanny started the climb, slid backward, and rolled down until her back smacked into a scraggly pine tree. The wind knocked out of her, her eyes smarting with pain, Fanny scrambled up the embankment on her hands and knees, only to be driven back by a violent gust of wind. She felt something cold and wet on her face. Snow. It seemed darker now in and among the trees. Where was Simon? She moved then when she heard brush cracking behind her.

Eventually Fanny reached higher ground. The trees were thicker, the old trail overgrown and barely discernible. She weaved her way to the right and then to the left, past small mountains of boulders, through deadfalls and thickets.

Overhead snow clouds were black and ominous. Fanny stared up at the top of the ridge, unsure if she had the strength to make it to the top. The stinging snow slapped her in the face. She was chilled to the bone, yet sweat dripped from her forehead. She scrambled, her hands digging into the tree roots and vines that hampered her climb. She felt a wet stickiness and knew her hands were raw and bleeding. A low branch whacked her across the face, stunning her for a second.

Simon was closer, his curses more distinguishable. *Move!* Her subconscious ordered. *Faster!*

Fanny toiled higher and higher. She felt her strength leaving her as she fought for handholds with her bleeding hands. She felt cold, so very cold. She knew her body heat was leaving her. He was closer and gaining. She stumbled when she saw a break in the trees. Black clouds scudded over the treetops. She stumbled and fell again. She didn't allow herself the luxury of stopping. She climbed on all fours until she saw another break in the line of trees. She had to be near the top. The air felt more fresh and wet. If only she could see through the snow squall.

Flat ground. The shoulder of the road? *Yessss. Thank you, God.* She was on her feet, running, shouting Ash's name. She heard it carried over the mountain to return to her own ears. She ran, the snow pelting her. She heard the horn, saw the lights, heard Ash's voice, and then the van was alongside her, the door sliding open. She used the last of her strength to climb in. The door slid shut.

"Go! Go!" she managed to gasp. "He was right behind me."

"Fanny . . ."

"I'm all right. Just go, Ash."

"I've been up and down this goddamn mountain five times blowing the horn and yelling until I got hoarse. Are you sure you're okay?"

"I'm alive. You're alive. That means we're okay. The kids are okay. When it comes right down to it, that's all that matters."

"You're right, Fanny. You're always right. Now what? Do we go to the police?"

"And what will we tell them? That I lured him down the mountain and he chased me? He's still my husband. You're my ex-husband. Forget it, Ash."

"We have to do something. That was a gutsy thing you did back there."

"Yeah, and it was also stupid. Want a red lollipop?"

"You got some?"

"A whole pocketful. That's how I got him over the edge. I taunted him with the yellow ones. The things I do for you, Ash." Fanny rolled over, the lollipop stuck in her mouth.

"What you have to do with these lollipops is work up a good spit. I guess I owe you my life. If I had a dollar for every time you bailed me out of a jam, I'd be rich, Fanny. Thank you hardly seems to cover it."

Fanny didn't hear him. She was sound asleep.

A fierce protectiveness he'd never experienced before shot through Ash. "I'm going to kill that son of a bitch" he said through clenched teeth, "for what he's done to you."

It was five o'clock before Chue and his family were settled in one of Babylon's luxurious suites. Iris had stopped by, while Fanny slept, to take Jake and Polly home with her. Ash sat in the living room, one ear tuned to Fanny's bedroom in case she woke. His brain whirred faster than the chair he scurried around in. He'd just gotten off the phone with the police chief, who told him the exact same thing Fanny had told him. Now what was he to do? Hire extra security guards to protect his family? Fanny would probably nix that idea the minute he brought it up. He could call Clementine Fox and apprise her of the day's events.

Ash was about to make the call when the phone rang. He picked it up on the first ring. It was Marcus Reed. "Fanny's sleeping, Marcus. She had a rough day. Do you want me to have her call you when she wakes up?"

"Is anything wrong?"

"There's a lot wrong here."

"Is Fanny all right?"

"Yes and no. She's going to be stiff and sore for a while, but she's okay. I might as well tell you what happened. Fanny herself will probably tell you when she calls you back."

"Fanny doesn't discuss her family with me, Ash. I'd like to hear what happened. Perhaps I can help."

Ash told him.

"It sounds to me like your brother views himself as a law unto himself. Sometimes the legal system is slow to act, Ash. My advice, and I realize you didn't ask for it, would be to let Fanny's attorney handle the matter."

"I guess we think alike then. I was going to call her, but your call interrupted me. I'll do it now. Shall I have Fanny return your call?"

"I would appreciate it. Watch over her."

"I guess you haven't realized that it's Fanny who does that watching over thing. I'll do my best."

Ash stared at the phone in his hand so long the operator came on to tell him to hang up. He lowered the receiver onto the cradle.

The clock on the television told him Clementine Fox was gone for the day. Tomorrow morning would be soon enough to make the call.

Fanny slept on. Ash called Iris to check on Jake and Polly and was told they were fine. With nothing to do, he made coffee and laced it liberally with brandy. He spent an hour watching the evening news and another hour watching two game shows. He was about to make himself a sandwich when Fanny limped into the living room.

"Do you feel like you look?"

"Worse."

"How about some coffee and a sandwich?"

"I'd like that."

Fanny lowered herself gingerly onto the couch. "I think I need to start exercising more. Muscles I didn't even know I had hurt. Did you check on the kids, Ash?"

"They're fine. Iris said they were stringing popcorn. I think what she meant was they would string it if there was any left. Jake loves the fluffies that pop first. He knows the difference. Marcus Reed called. He wants you to call him back."

"Did he leave a number?"

"No."

"Then how can I call him back?" Fanny asked wearily.

"I guess he was too upset and forgot to leave it. I told him what happened."

"I wish you hadn't done that, Ash. This is family stuff, and I don't make a habit of talking about family matters to anyone but Bess and Billie."

"I didn't know that, Fanny. I'm sorry."

"It's okay. He'll call back. If he doesn't, he doesn't."

"It doesn't sound to me like you're in love."

"Ash, Marcus Reed is the least of my problems right now. Your brother is front and center, and we need to decide what we're going to do."

"He's going to sulk for a while. He'll fall back and regroup and come up with some other devious scheme to get at me."

"You realize you can't go back to the mountain, don't you?"

"I know that, Fanny. I can get a room if you think I'll cramp your style."

"Don't be ridiculous. I'm glad for the company. We need to stick together. I think we should both get restraining orders in the morning."

"I agree. That won't stop Simon, though. You realize we're just going through motions to make ourselves feel better."

"I don't care. I want a restraining order on the record."

"Then that's what we'll do. More coffee?"

"Sure. Bring some ice cream."

"What are we going to do tonight, Fanny?"

"I don't know about you, but I'm going to soak in a hot tub and then I'm going back to bed. You can make breakfast. Don't worry about Daisy. She has a pad by the front door for emergencies."

"Alone again," Ash grumbled.

"How does it feel, Ash?"

"Pretty damn shitty. Fanny, thanks for today."

Fanny nodded. "You would have done the same for me, wouldn't you?"

"Yeah. Yeah, Fanny, I would have."

"See you in the morning."

"Okay."

Simon Thornton walked around the house, his hands stuffed in his pockets. The wind whistled and howled, sending chills up and down his spine. Ash probably had warm clothes and boots in the house. He knew he needed to change before his wet clothes froze to his back. He was covered with snow from head to toe, his wet hair plastered to his head in frozen layers. A hot shower would be good. He let himself into the house by the back door, turned on the kitchen light. Everything was neat and tidy, like Ash himself. He wandered around, looking at things, touching things, whistling to himself as he did so.

He made his way up the steps to his old room—Jake's room now. Toys were scattered everywhere. He closed the door and entered Ash's room. It was still Ash's room. All his stuff was here. His commendations, his pictures hanging on the wall, Ash's past. A picture of Ash and Fanny sat on the dresser. He looked at it with clinical interest. A picture of Jake holding his fishing pole was on the night table. He studied it for a long time.

Ash had five children and three grandchildren. He had none. Ash had a family. He didn't have one because he'd been sterile all his life. Ash had everything.

Simon opened the dresser drawers. Everything was neatly aligned. The best of everything. He rummaged through everything just the way he had when he was a boy. The closet beckoned. He did the same thing, jerking suits and jackets off the hangers and dropping them on the floor. He kicked at the line of shoes on the floor. He spent an hour going through Ash's personal things he kept on the top shelf. There wasn't one thing in the closet he wanted to take with him. He felt cheated, disappointed that Ash didn't have anything worth taking.

He rummaged some more, found a heavy jacket, some corduroy pants and a sweater. Pushed far back in the closet was a pair of shearling-lined boots. He was in good shape for the walk down the mountain.

He headed for Ash's bathroom where he showered, shaved, and dressed. He dropped his wet towel on the floor. Ash hated a mess.

In the kitchen he made himself a ham sandwich. He peeled an orange and ate it. He left the peels and bread crumbs on the counter. He took one last look around the house before he returned to the living room where he zipped up his jacket. He reached for Ash's knit cap on the hat rack and pulled it down over his wet head.

The last thing he did before leaving the house was to light a cigarette. Before he snapped the lighter shut, he held it to the hem of the lace curtains on the front window.

From time to time on his walk down the mountain he turned to look back at Sunrise, watching the flames dancing high in the sky.

He whistled all the way down the mountain, the wind carrying the sound high and wide.

24

Fanny woke, a feeling of panic squeezing her chest. She felt the puffiness in her face, the skin stretching beyond its boundaries near her right eye. She moved her bruised body to see the clock. Two o'-clock. What was it that woke her? Not Daisy; she was sleeping peace-fully at the bottom of the bed. Ash? Not Ash. Daisy would be prancing around if something was wrong where her ex-husband was concerned. Was the television on? Was Ash having a sleepless night? She listened. The apartment was tomb quiet.

Maybe her body had all the sleep it could handle for one night. She struggled to get up, her muscles protesting each movement, no matter how slight. It was a monumental effort to fit her arms into her robe, but she did it. Her slippers were nowhere in sight. She padded barefoot into the kitchen, Daisy behind her. She was re-lieved to see the blank screen on the television. Ash must be sleep-ing.

Fanny measured coffee into the wire basket, put the lid back on the coffeepot. She pressed the red button. She hated smoking before she brushed her teeth, but she fired up a cigarette anyway. Daisy cir-cled her feet, panting and wagging her tail.

"It's not morning. I'm off schedule." Fanny reached inside the re-frigerator and unwrapped three slices of cheese. She broke it up into pieces and dropped them into the little dog's bowl. "Something's wrong, Daisy. I can feel it in my bones. Everything bad happens in the dark of night," she muttered.

Fanny was on her second cup of coffee when she heard Ash's chair. She looked up. Daisy was sitting in his lap. "Is something wrong, Fanny?"

Fanny poured him a cup of coffee. "I don't know. I feel like there is. I woke up and had this feeling of panic. I suppose I could have been dreaming, but if I was, I don't remember what the dream was about. Maybe my body just had enough sleep. That happens sometimes. If it was the kids, someone would have called."

"Jesus, Fanny, I took the receiver off the hook. I didn't want it ringing all night to wake you. I forgot to hang it back up." His chair backed up, circled and returned a moment later. "I'm sorry, Fanny."

"I do that too, Ash. If something was *really* wrong, there would have been a knock on the door. Daisy would have alerted us." Both Ash and Fanny stared at the phone on the kitchen wall.

"Fanny, call the switchboard. You have an unlisted phone number now."

"I forgot about that." Fanny pressed the zero for operator. "Have there been any calls for Mr. Thornton or me this evening? Thank you." She shook her head. "I told you, Ash, it's just a feeling. After yesterday, I'm entitled to feel a little strange."

"How about some breakfast?"

"Bacon and eggs?"

"Sounds good."

Fanny was placing the bacon strips in the fry pan when a loud knock could be heard. Daisy raced to the door, the hair on the back of her neck on end, her tail between her legs. Fanny turned off the stove, her eyes locked with Ash's. "It's someone strange, someone she doesn't know. Her tail isn't wagging."

"Ask who it is before you open the door," Ash said.

"I'm not an idiot. Who is it?" Fanny called.

"Pete Wilson, Mrs. Thornton. Neal is with me."

Fanny opened the door and stood aside. Ash backed up his chair. "What's wrong?"

"There's a fire on your mountain. Is anyone up there?"

"No, we all came down yesterday. The house is empty. Is it the house or the mountain?"

"Our main concern was that people might be in the house. Three of my men are slogging through the snow as we speak. When the call came in, we sent out a truck, but the roads were too treacherous. They had to turn around and come back. What do you people do when the weather turns bad up there?"

"Chue takes care of it. He's here in town with his family. He sands, salts, and uses the ashes from the fireplaces. Ash, what should we do? How can there be a fire if it's snowing?" Ash shot her a disgusted look.

"Is Birch's Land Rover still in the garage?"

"I think so."

"I'm sorry, Mr. Thornton. We can attempt it again, but I don't hold out much hope. It's been burning for some time now. My guess is it's the house. The trees are wet and covered with snow. The wind is pretty fierce, and for the flames to be as high as they are whatever it is that's burning has a good start on us."

"I'll get dressed," Fanny said, limping her way to her room.

"Thanks, Pete. Do what you can." This last was said over his shoulder as Ash maneuvered his chair down the hallway. Daisy barked until the door closed behind the two men.

Twenty minutes later, Fanny was behind the wheel of the Land Rover, Ash in the passenger seat.

"Don't worry about my chair. There's a spare in the garage. I alternate the chairs. Chue charges the one not in use. The chair isn't important, Fanny."

"*He* wouldn't . . ."

"Yeah he would. Now look, Fanny, take it easy. I know you know the mountain, but snow changes everything."

"I know, Ash. Talk to me."

"You look pretty ugly, Fanny. You're going to have a shiner for about ten days. I wouldn't let Marcus Reed see you right now."

"That's just what I need to hear. If you can't say something nice, shut up."

"I thought you wanted me to talk. It's probably arson. Houses don't just burn for no reason. Simon did this. How are we going to prove it? There was no one on the mountain. He could sue our asses off if we make our feelings known."

"He was there, Ash, we both saw him. All you have to do is look at me to know there was some kind of confrontation."

"Big fucking deal. His car is at the bottom of the mountain. How do we explain that? The son of a bitch is liable to go after Chue. The word 'lie' isn't even in Chue's vocabulary. What you should have done was have Chue push his car to the side and take his keys."

"I should have done a lot of things, Ash. What if he had a spare tucked in his wallet? I never said I was thinking clearly. All I knew was I had to get to you before he did. Should have, could have, would have. What the hell difference does it make now anyway?"

"I'm trying to think ahead," Ash said defensively. "He'll lie low now for a little while. When we were kids and he'd pull one of his more outrageous stunts, he'd hide out in his room for days until everyone calmed down. My mother would coax him to come out on an hourly basis. She'd buy him junk, make sure we had his favorite foods, that kind of thing. She'd just be so damn relieved that he finally came out and smiled at her, she wouldn't do a damn thing except to swat me saying I instigated whatever it was he did."

"Goddammit, Ash, he burned down my house."

"That's not how he sees it, and we aren't sure it's the house. Simon thinks the house is mine now because I've been living there the past few years. Don't you get it, Fanny? He thinks it's *mine*. He's going by what he sees and hears. He's not going by instinct now. I think that's good where we're concerned. He's bound to make a mistake soon."

"Soon?" Fanny screeched. "Soon can translate to a very long time. Soon could be tomorrow."

She concentrated on her driving. It got more and more difficult.

"Chue's house is safe," Ash said as they passed it. "We should be thankful for that."

"Oh, Ash, look, it's gone," Fanny wailed as she brought the Land Rover to a stop at the end of the driveway.

"I need my chair, Fanny."

Fanny motioned to the three firemen. One of them trotted off to return with Ash's spare wheelchair.

"It was too far gone when we got here, ma'am. We couldn't save it."

Fanny nodded, tears trickling down her cheeks. "Take the Rover back to town. Mr. Thornton and I can stay in one of the cottages or the studio. It's the only way you'll get off the mountain."

Fanny watched the Rover back up and start down the mountain.

"It was just a house, Fanny. Pete's right, it can be rebuilt."

"It was more than a house, Ash. It was your mother's home, your home, my home. I raised the kids here. They're going to be devastated. It's so senseless, so *insane*." Fanny's shoulders started to shake. She dropped to the ground in the snow, tears streaming down her cheeks.

All Ash could do was stare at the ruins and at his wife.

"Sallie liked to open the windows and watch the curtains billow. Birch used to hide from Sage in that little cubbyhole under the steps. Sage never caught on, so I guess it really was a secret place. Billie used to line up her paper dolls and that small sewing machine Sallie gave her on the dining-room table. She used to make a regular parade, and she'd talk to the dolls."

"Fanny, don't do this to yourself."

"Sunny would run up and down the steps a hundred times a day. Either she was chasing the twins, or they were chasing her. Now she can barely walk. I must have taken a thousand pictures of the kids on the steps. For some reason they always wanted to pose on the steps. The paint's still on the living-room carpet where Sage spilled it. I don't know why I never replaced it."

"Fanny—"

"The cradles Sallie gave us were in the attic. All the things I saved from our kids that I wanted to give to our grandchildren are gone now. I put everything in boxes and labeled them. Sallie's things were in the attic, too. Even stuff from your dad that Sallie saved. All Jake and Polly's stuff is gone, Ash. We can't ever get it back. It's just a pile of dirty ashes.

"Simon took away my past, Ash. He took away all my memories."

Ash's hand reached out to Fanny. He slid from the chair to sit in the snow next to her. "You still have the memories, Fanny. He can never steal those from you." He put his arm around her shoulder. Fanny leaned her head against him, tears blinding her.

"I loved this place, Ash. Sunny did too. It was so right for her to live here with the kids. This mountain used to rock with sound when their friends came up from town. I can't believe it's gone."

"We'll rebuild it, Fanny."

"It won't be the same. It won't feel the same. It won't smell the same."

"I used to love coming here on the weekends. The house always smelled like cinnamon and spice and celery. It never smelled like that when we were growing up. I think I hated it then. Maybe it was Simon I hated and not the house at all. That goddamn safe is still standing. Part of the second floor looks to be intact. Is there anything in the safe, Fanny?"

"Yeah, all kinds of stuff."

"You'll have to take it out."

"I know. Oh, Ash, Polly and Lexie will never get to know this place." Fanny's shoulders shook with the force of her sobs. "How are we going to tell Jake the house is gone? Losing his mother for months at a time is bad enough. How, Ash?"

"We'll handle it. We're the old guard, Fanny. You can rebuild this for the next generation. It's what you put into it, Fanny, that made Sunrise what it was. The good feelings I have in regard to Sunrise are because of you, not because of my mother and the time I spent here as a kid. Sunrise is you, Fanny. Mom knew that. That's why she left the mountain to you. She knew in her heart you'd make it into what she could never do. She was right to do what she did by leaving it to you. My ass is freezing, Fanny. Let's go down to the studio and get warm. We can come back later. It's going to smolder for days, so there's nothing we can do right now. It's going to be light soon."

"All right, Ash," Fanny said struggling to her feet. She struggled again as she tugged and shoved Ash into his chair. "Do you think, Ash, if it hadn't snowed, the mountain would be gone?"

"Yes. And that you could never rebuild. It would take a hundred years for new trees to grow to this splendor."

"Then we need to be grateful for that."

Three days later, when the steep mountain road was cleared, the fire marshal gave Fanny permission to walk through the rubble. She watched as the arson squad left in their specially equipped van with all their high-tech equipment. She wondered if they would ever be able to prove what had happened.

"Fanny, why are you torturing yourself. We should leave and come back in the spring."

"You're right, Ash. I just want to walk through to see if there's at least one thing that didn't burn. I have to clear out the safe, too. Chue is lending me his pickup truck. I'll need all the space in the back. I just hope it will hold everything."

"Wait, just a minute. What the hell's in that safe that we need the back of the pickup to haul it?"

"Cotton Easter's gold."

"Cotton Easter's gold," Ash said, a stupid look on his face.

"Yeah. He left it to your mother. It scared her. She left it to me. It scared me, too."

"How . . . how much is there?"

"At least a ton. I don't know. The shelves are full of it."

"The shelves are full of it. Fanny, what the hell does that mean?"

"It means I have to move it. Unless you have a better idea."

"Well . . . are you sure you aren't exaggerating?"

"Ash, come see for yourself. You can watch me move it. I'll back up the truck and just throw it in the back. It's in sacks."

"And you never told me?"

"No, I never told anyone. I never considered it mine even though Sallie said it was. For some reason I thought your mother would have told Simon, but she didn't. I was the only one who knew. I think . . .

and this is just my opinion, Ash . . . but I think she knew . . . wanted me to use it for Babylon. It wasn't anything she said in words. It was a feeling she gave me. She told me I would know what to do with it. She was so wrong. We'll have to decide what to do."

Fanny worked the combination. When she heard the desired click, she pulled, shoved and used her backside to move the massive door. Ash stared at the contents, speechless for the first time in his life. Fanny started to lug the sacks to the back of the truck.

At the end of her seventeenth trip, Ash found his voice. "What's all that other stuff?"

"Stocks, bonds, deeds. Sallie's stuff."

"Sallie's stuff."

"Ash, stop repeating everything I say."

"What would you be saying if you were in my place?"

Fanny leaned on the end of the pickup and lit a cigarette. "Ash, I never wanted the responsibility of all this. I told you. I never thought of it as mine. It belongs to you and Simon." She told him about Jake then. "That money wasn't mine either. I borrowed on it a dozen times. Once I outright used it. I always paid it back. It's in a mutual fund collecting something like a 15 percent return per year."

"And you never told me that either?"

"Nope."

"What else haven't you told me?"

"I think that about clears my conscience. I'd give Jake's money back, but I don't know who to give it to."

"Try the boys across the street. I bet you all the gold in that truck if you march across the street and ask any one of those five owners if they remember a Jake and a large amount of money disappearing, they'll own up."

"How will I know if they're telling the truth?"

"Let them tell you the story. It's like fishing, you throw out the line with some good bait and you wait to see if it's snatched up."

"I can do that. It's a princely sum of money."

"I'll just bet it is. Fanny, you never cease to amaze me."

"I'm going to take that as a compliment."

Fanny went back to work. Ash was bug-eyed as he continued to watch her.

"That's the last of it," Fanny said a long time later. "I think my back is breaking. I want to . . . to walk through. It will only take me a few minutes. Do you mind, Ash?"

"Not at all."

"The heater is on in the truck. Get in. I'll take your chair back to the garage."

The fierce protectiveness Ash felt toward Fanny surfaced again. "You look like a tired old dog, Fanny. Let it go."

"I feel like a tired old dog. I can't let it go. I have to . . . I have to do this. There might be something. I want something. I need to . . . walk away knowing there's one small thing left. I don't expect you to understand. I understand, and that's all that is important. I won't be long."

Ash rolled his window up. He rolled it down minutes later when he heard Fanny's joyous shout.

"Ash! Ash! I found Sallie's old desk! One of the legs is burned through. It's burned and scarred all over, but it's here. I can't get it down, though. Her slate board is here too."

Ash could feel his shoulders start to crumple. Great heart-wrenching sobs shook his body. Of all the things in the world to be saved, his mother's desk. The desk where she had toiled to become the woman she was.

Fanny climbed into the truck. "It's okay, Ash. We can rebuild Sunrise now. We have something that belongs here. It's probably the most important thing of all. I'll have Chue get it down, and I'll find the best furniture refinisher there is to restore it. I could still see her initials in the corner where she scratched them. S.C. for Sallie Coleman. I don't feel so bad now."

Ash's voice was choked when he said, "Fanny, what if I don't live long enough to see it finished?"

"Don't even think such a thing, Ash Thornton. I give you my personal word you will not only see it finished, you will live here again. I never broke a promise to you, did I?"

"No, Fanny, you never did. That's good enough for me. I feel like singing. Do you feel like singing, Fanny?"

"I feel like singing, Ash."

"Off we go into the wild blue yonder . . ."

Please God, don't make me a liar. Let me keep my promise. "Climbing high, into the sky . . ."

"I must be getting old, Charlie," Ash said to the bartender. "The noise is really getting to me. I don't think I ever saw so many people in one place in my whole life."

"It's the Christmas season and Mrs. Thornton's decorations. It's going to be like this till after New Year's. Guess that mountain of yours is pretty quiet, eh. Can I get you something to drink, Mr. Thornton?"

"A ginger ale will be fine," Ash said, craning his neck to see his grandson being led off by Billie and Thad Kingsley. He relaxed as he reached out to accept the soft drink.

"There was a lady in here earlier looking for you, Mr. Thornton. A real looker. She reminded me of someone, but I can't put my finger on it. She asked for you specifically. She came in right after the doors opened. Did she find you?"

Ash shrugged. "Did she have a name, Charlie?"

"No. I just told her you were here somewhere. She said she'd find you. The night's still young." Ash shrugged again. He lit a cigarette as he continued to make small talk with the bartender and the customers lined up at the bar.

An hour later when the noise and the smoke started to bother him, Ash steered his chair away from the bar and out to the floor. His eyes raked the crowds for a sign of Fanny and Billie. He turned again when he felt a light touch to his shoulder.

"Mr. Thornton?"

Ash looked up. Charlie was right, she was a looker. If this was the woman asking for him earlier. "I'm Ash Thornton. Is there something I can do for you?"

"Is there someplace we can go where it's a little more quiet?" Her voice was soft, cultured, almost musical.

"Follow me. I think my office might be a little more quiet. Have we met before?"

"No. We should have, but no, we never met."

Charlie was right, she reminded him of someone. He said so. The woman laughed, the sound as musical as her speaking voice. Ash opened the door to his office, the chair whirring through the oversize opening. He turned so that he was facing her. "I'm afraid you have the advantage. You know me, but I don't know you. Can I order you a drink from the bar?"

"No thank you. I'm Ruby Thornton. I'm your sister. Half sister, actually. The shocked look on your face tells me you didn't know about me."

"Whoa," Ash said holding up his hand, palm out. "You can't just waltz in here and drop something like that on me."

"Why not? Because it's Christmas? Because my mother and father kept my birth a secret? I know everything there is to know about you and Simon. You two were the princes living in the castle and I was the scullery maid living in a brothel. My mother kept scrapbooks on you and Simon. My mother was Red Ruby, my father was your father. Does that explain why I look so much like Simon?"

"Now, hold on here," Ash blustered.

"My mother and our father made a deal. I guess it was the same kind of deal you made with Margaret Lassiter. I know about Jeff. My mother was in a position to know everything there is to know about the people in this town. She left a detailed diary when she died. I might publish it someday. Do you find it amusing that your mother and my mother were . . . ladies of the night? As well as friends."

"My father would have told me about you. He never kept anything from me."

"Like you told him about Margaret Lassiter. He knew though. My mother told him. I think he was a little more comfortable with his secret after that."

"Spit it out, what do you want?"

"My share."

"Of what?"

"Everything. I think I'm entitled. A third of your parents' estate. I think that's fair. Your mother knew about me. They sent me to Boston to school. I came home summers when mother closed the . . . business. I was never permitted to come home on the holidays. One year my mother would visit me at Christmas and the next year it would be my father. It was the same with Easter and Thanksgiving. I wanted to know you and Simon so bad. I wanted to tell the world I had two big brothers, but I wasn't allowed to do that. I stayed on in Boston, got my master's and my Ph.D. Your mother didn't like that one little bit. Your mother was so beautiful compared to my own mother. I used to pretend she was my mother. I knew if she'd been my mother, she wouldn't have kept me hidden. I cried myself to sleep for many years."

"How old are you?"

The trilling laughter seemed to tickle the walls. Ash found himself shivering. "Does it matter? Here, this is what you probably want to see. Everything's in it, my birth certificate, your father's will, Mom's will. The contract Dad had with Mom. I inherited Thornton Chickens, did you know that?"

Ash cleared his throat. "No, I didn't know that."

"I want a third of everything in that old iron safe on the mountain."

"I'm afraid that's impossible. My mother left all that, including the mountain, to Fanny, my ex-wife. My father died first, leaving everything to my mother. She in turn made a new will and did what she wanted."

"My father made a later will. There's a copy of it in the envelope."

"Why are you coming forward now? Why do you want to rake up the past? Are you in this . . . scheme with Simon? It would be just like him to pull something like this."

"No, I haven't talked to Simon. I came to you because you were the older brother. My mother died last year. I've spent the year trying to decide what to do. I don't know if you'll understand this or not, but . . . I always wanted a real family. Everyone at school had nice normal families. I made one up. I had two handsome older brothers who were flying aces during the war. My mother was beautiful, warm, and gentle, and my father was a bookish professor who adored me. I told everyone they traveled all over the world and that's why they were never at school on visitors' day. He did, you know. Adore me, I mean. He used to send the most wonderful, creative presents, and he'd always sign the card, Love, Daddy. He was truly proud of my accomplishments. Much the way he was of yours."

Ash scanned the papers in his lap. She appeared to be telling the truth. A chill ran down his spine. Fanny said her life paralleled his mother's in so many ways. Now, here he was, experiencing the exact same thing. The chill seemed to settle around his lower extremities, causing a numb feeling in his legs. The urge to smash something was so great he gripped the arms of the wheelchair, his knuckles as white as the shirt he was wearing.

"Well?"

"Well what? I'll speak to my lawyer. I'm sure something can be worked out. If my mother wanted you to share in Thornton Enterprises, she would have done so. It was her decision, not mine and not Simon's. Dad . . . the lawyers can handle it. I think you'll have a fight on your hands."

"I'm prepared for that. Understand something, all of this"—Ruby said waving her hands about—"is through no fault of mine. Our father, your mother, my mother, they did this. You might not like it, but you are my family. I'd like to get to know my nieces and nephews. I'd like to believe they would want to meet an aunt if they knew they had one. My mother was a whore, your mother was a whore, and yet we shared the same father. This is not about money."

"The hell it isn't. Everything, when it comes down to the bottom line, is about money. I busted my ass for this casino, and I'm not about to give it up to you or anyone else, sister or not. You got Thornton Chickens? You didn't see me showing up on your doorstep making a claim. Another thing, whatever my father had came from my mother. He was a schoolteacher, and he didn't have a pot to piss in. My mother was the one with the money. There's no court in this land that will give you what's ours. And, it is ours, make no mistake. Have your attorney get in touch with Clementine Fox. She represents this family," Ash lied. Clem could find him a lawyer. Since she represented Fanny it would be a conflict of interest for her to step in where Ruby Thornton was concerned. Ash thought he saw a flicker of fear in the gray eyes at the mention of Clem's name. If it was fear, it was gone a second later.

"Oh, there is one other little thing," Ash said. "My mother pulled your mother out of the gutter. She set her up at the ranch. She did right by Red and we can prove it. This town takes care of its own."

"So I've heard. But I have the book. You know the book I'm talking about. All those upstanding citizens from here, there, and yonder. Does that fall under this town taking care of its own?"

"I wouldn't mess with that if I were you. Red was an honorable woman, and she would never have done what you just said. That red book was for her eyes only, and you damn well know it. You could ruin a lot of families if you do something foolish."

"Then those *families* aren't worth much, are they? The key word here is family, is that right?"

"That's right. I wish you had just walked in here and said you were my sister. I always wanted a sister. In his own way I think Simon did, too. This family has always been generous to a fault. We're all givers. I wasn't for a long time. I had to learn how to do that. We don't bow or bend to pressure and intimidation. You don't appear to be a stupid woman."

"I'm not. I just want what's mine."

"Well, lady, you're shit out of luck because you ain't gettin' one cent from this family."

"Ash . . . Mr. Thornton . . . please, I want you to understand where I'm coming from. You're my family. I have a right to be here. I have as much right to all of this," she said, waving her arms about, "as you do. Legally and morally."

"That's where you're wrong. You were right about Jeffrey Lassiter. Yes, he is my son. He doesn't bear my name, but I did take responsibility for him. I will never deny him in a court of law. My father . . . my father rubbed you under my mother's nose. That's the only way he could make up for her not loving him. My father used you. He didn't love your mother any more than I loved Margaret Lassiter. It never should have happened, but it did. I dealt with it. You have to deal with it, too."

"My case is different. Our father loved me. My mother loved him. I don't know if Philip loved her or not. There were times when I thought he did. I do know they were wonderful friends for many, many years. I think a jury and a court of law will make the right decision."

"I doubt it. There's not a person in this town who isn't aware of where my mother's money came from. My father, your father, had nothing to do with it. It was my mother's decision on how to divide her money at the end. She was more than generous in giving your mother a million-dollar company. As long as you own that company, you will never want for anything. It will support you and provide a very luxurious lifestyle. The ranch is yours, too, thanks to my mother. A jury will view you as a greedy bitch trying to put the bite on the Thorntons."

"I'm a Thornton, too."

"In this town you're from the other side of the tracks. I will not allow you to come in here and disturb our lives. For a woman as educated as you say you are, you must realize how foolish this is. What I'm trying to say without being cruel is you don't belong here. We have our lives; you have yours. If it's recognition you want, I'll tell the world I have a sister. That's as far as I'm willing to go."

"That isn't far enough."

"Let me ask you a question. Should you prevail, which you won't, then what? Do you honestly think any one of us will welcome you after a court case like the kind you're talking about? You said it wasn't about money. I guess that was a lie, right?"

"No, it isn't about money. Didn't you hear anything I said? How would you have liked to grow up like I did? If you were me, what would you do? Be honest?"

"Sit down, Miss Thornton, and let me tell you a story. I'm going to be so brutally honest with you you are going to run out of here in tears."

Ash talked and Ruby Thornton listened. When he finally wound down, Ruby offered him a lace-edged hanky. "All right, Mr. Thornton. You made your point."

"I want to know what that means."

"It means I'm going to walk away from here. It means I'm giving up any dream of belonging to a family, my family. It means I'm sorry we never got to know one another. To me you will always be the prince, and I'll always be the scullery maid. Obviously there was a lot my parents didn't share with me. My heart doesn't understand that you aren't the family I always wanted. I'm sorry your time has come. I want to believe we could have been friends had we been allowed to do so. I'm sorry I came here. I really am."

"I'm sorry, too. For the circumstances. I don't know if we could have been friends or not. I wasn't the same person back then that I am today. I'm sorry they messed up your life the same way they messed up mine and Simon's. Do you want me to tell the family about you or do you want to . . . what?"

"Let's pretend I never came here."

"Simon?"

"He doesn't sound like someone I'd ever want to know. You now, you're another story all together. I think I would have given you a run for your money. I'll be at the ranch if you . . . ever . . . you know."

"C'mere," Ash said motioning for her to drop to her knees. "Look at me, Ruby Thornton. You got the best of the deal. You may never believe it, but you did. Your mother and father loved you. They did what they thought was best for you. It was the best, unlike what our parents did to us. All things considered, you're the lucky one. You'll realize that when you think about this night in the days to come."

"Perhaps. Families aren't all black or white. I guess that's what makes them a family. I want you to know I adored Dad. I loved my mother, too. I used to count the hours and the minutes when it was time for them to visit me at school. I should be leaving. It's late and I've taken up enough of your time." Ruby stood and held out her hand.

Ash shook his head as he struggled to get out of his chair. He wrapped his arms around her before he gave her a kiss on the cheek. "Have a good life, Ruby Thornton, and don't have any regrets."

"Ash! I've been looking all over for you. Oh, I'm sorry, I didn't know you had company."

"She isn't company, Fanny. This is my sister, Ruby Thornton. Ruby, this is my ex-wife and my grandson Jake."

Fanny's jaw dropped as she held out her hand. Jake ran to his grandfather and climbed on his lap. "Santy Claus is wunnerful. He gave me this and this and this . . ."

"It's nice to meet you, Fanny. Good night everyone. Have a nice holiday."

When the door closed behind Ruby, Ash said, "She's my father's daughter. Red Ruby was her mother. Mom knew. We won't talk about this again. It's what it is and that's the end of it."

"I see."

Ash smiled. "No, you don't. That's okay, Fanny. She looks like both me and Simon, don't you think?"

"Ah, yes."

"So, is Jake ready to call it a night?"

"I don't know about him but I certainly am. You should take him up, Ash, unless you want me to do it."

"No, I'll do it. He'll probably be asleep before we get out of the elevator."

"Ash . . ."

"There isn't a problem, Fanny. Don't look for one, okay?"

"All right, Ash. I'll be up in a little while."

"Life goes on, Fanny."

"Yes, it does."

"Another year is almost gone," Fanny said to her ex-husband. "Tomorrow will be the first day of the new year. Are you looking forward to spending New Year's Eve with Sage and Iris?"

"I sure am. I wish you could come along."

"Ash, this is the busiest night of the year. I'll come by in the morning. Iris said she's making a brunch. I'm so excited that Sunny has a pass to leave the grounds. And, she's bringing a guest. I was hoping Birch would make it home, but I guess we need to be grateful for all the good things that have happened this past year. It doesn't pay to dwell on the bad."

"I gotta get going. Jake can tell time now, and I promised to be there by six. If he calls, tell him I'm on the way. Happy New Year, Fanny."

"Are you okay, Ash? You look a little flushed to me."

"It's the excitement of seeing Jake. He said he made me a present. That means it's something for him with my name on it. I'll see you tomorrow."

"Give everyone my love and kiss the kids for me."

"Will do."

Fanny rode the elevator down to the main floor. It wasn't her imagination. Ash was flushed, and his eyes were glassy. She called Iris from the phone on the bar to tell her to watch over Ash. Sage came on the phone. "Happy New Year, Mom."

"The same to you, Sage. Listen, I don't think your father is feeling all that well. It could be nothing. Then again, it could be something."

"I'll watch him, Mom. Bess and John are coming for brunch tomorrow, so we can have John give him a once-over."

"I'll see you tomorrow."

"Okay, Mom."

Fanny wandered into the Harem Lounge fifteen minutes before midnight. She sat down at one of the tables with a cup of coffee. Suddenly she wanted to cry. She had spent so many holidays alone. One more shouldn't make a difference, but it was. She could feel her eyes starting to burn.

"I seem to recall you sitting at this same exact table eons ago. Happy New Year, Fanny."

"Marcus! Oh, Marcus, it's so good to see you. I was just sitting here feeling sorry for myself. I was about ready to cry."

"No date of mine cries on New Year's Eve."

Fanny smiled. "Are we having a date? You didn't call."

"I have an excuse. I spent the last two days sitting in an airport in New York. They had a raging blizzard. All the flights were canceled and the phones were down. All I did was eat greasy food."

"I feel sorry for you, Marcus."

"No, you don't. Not even a little bit. I'm sorry I couldn't spend Christmas with you. Someday, Fanny, you and I should go to Australia. By the way, I have a whole week off. What kind of plans do you have and is it possible to break them?"

"I don't really have any plans. I do have one meeting with an architect and a contractor the day after New Year's. I'm free the rest of the week unless Ash gets sick. Would you like to go with me to brunch tomorrow at Sage and Iris's house?"

"I'd love to. Fanny, I am so sorry about your house on the mountain. Have there been any new developments where Simon is concerned?"

"No. The lawyers are still wrangling. Three minutes, Marcus! I have to get out to the floor." Marcus allowed his hand to be taken. They reached the main floor just as the customers started to chant the countdown.

"Three! Two! One! Happy New Year!" the boisterous crowd shouted.

Fanny lost herself in Marcus's arms as he kissed her. When he broke away, Fanny said, "Oh my, do that again."

Marcus pretended to take a great gulp of air before his lips found hers a second time. "I can do better without a crowd watching me."

"How do you think you'd do with just one little tiny dog in attendance?"

"Steam will ooze out from under your door."

"Uh-huh," was all Fanny could think of to say.

"When do you think you'll be going upstairs?" Fanny smiled at the way Marcus's eyes crinkled at the corners when he tried to be serious.

"How about right now?"

"You are a woman after my own heart. Do you remember what I told you about kissing?"

"That it leads to other things?"

"Uh-huh."

"I'm ready for those other things."

"Why are we still standing here then?"

"I thought you wanted to talk it to death."

"I don't, Fanny."

"Neither do I. Follow me, Mr. Reed."

"Lead the way, Miz Thornton."

She did.

Fanny rolled over, her naked body slick with sweat. She leaned up on one elbow. "I want you to know I have never been this satisfied in my entire life."

"Should I consider that a testimonial?"

"If I was in your place, I would." Fanny fell back against the pillows. "I'm surprised Ash never put mirrors on the ceiling. I wonder what that would be like, making love under a ceiling of mirrors. You'd be able to see *everything*. From every angle."

Marcus's fists pounded the mattress as he howled with laughter. "This is just an opinion mind you, but I would think both parties would be too busy to look. Stop and think about it. If you kept risking glances overhead everything would be out of sync."

"That's probably why Ash never did it."

"Do you always talk this much?" Marcus teased.

"Would you rather I did other things?"

"That's a topic worthy of discussion."

"Would you like me to expound on it?"

"Hell no. Show me."

Fanny shifted her body until she was on top of Marcus. Her hungry mouth searched for his, his fiery body heating up her flesh until she thought she would burst into flames.

They tore at each other, each of them seeking that which the other could surrender. There on the satin coverlet, they devoured each other with feverish lips and grasping fingers, just as they had done twice before.

Imperceptibly, Marcus's embrace tightened. Fanny smiled and stared into dark eyes that she later swore mirrored her soul. Once again hungry mouths searched, found, and conquered. He held her close, devouring her with his wet, slick body that glistened in the dim light on the nightstand. Gently he nuzzled her neck before he released her to the softness of the pillows.

"I can't think of anything more pleasurable than sleeping in your arms, Marcus. Why did we wait so long?" Fanny asked sleepily.

Marcus shifted his weight. "I guess we both had our reasons." His voice was as sleepy-sounding as Fanny's.

"Will you be here when I wake up?"

"A bomb couldn't get me out of here. Why do you ask?"

"Everyone leaves me. Sometimes I think I'm not meant to be loved. I don't want to feel that way with you."

"That's one thing you don't ever have to worry about. I want to marry you, Fanny. I want us to grow old together. I want to love you forever and ever and I want you to love me in the same way. Is it possible for that to happen?"

"Oh, yes. Yes, yes, yes. The first moment I'm free."

They slept, their arms wrapped tightly around each other, each secure in the knowledge they would awaken together.

Over coffee and toast in the morning Fanny and Marcus stared at one another, wonder in their eyes. "When will you be free?"

"Soon, I hope. When are you going to settle down here?"

"The exact moment you're free."

Elbows propped on the table, chin in her hands, Fanny said, "I love you, Marcus Reed."

Marcus propped his elbows on the table as he dropped his chin into his hands. "I love you, Fanny Thornton."

"This is a gambling town, so what do you think the odds are of us living happily ever after?"

"Very good."

"And if something goes awry with my divorce?"

"If that happens, we'll deal with it then. I have something for you. Before I give it to you, I want to explain what it means to me."

"Marcus, I'm not a person who expects or requires presents. I'm one of those card people, you know, the message is more important than the present."

"I understood that about you the first time I met you. Wait here. I'll be back in a minute." He was as good as his word, returning with a small box clutched in his hand. "This belonged to my mother. My father worked three jobs to pay for it. That was a long time ago. It cost $12.98. My mother wore it until the day she died. If you look closely, you can *almost* see the diamond. My three sisters didn't want it. They wanted those big solitaires. My father gave it to me. The box is tattered and torn. I don't think it came with the ring, but I'm not sure. When it's time for me to put a ring on your finger, will you be insulted if I gave you this one?"

"Oh, Marcus, not at all. You're wrong though. If I squint, I can see the diamond clearly. I'm honored that you want to give me this. I'll treasure it as much as your mother did."

Marcus stared at Fanny for a long time before he stuck the box back into his jacket pocket. He knew she meant every word she said.

"Happy New Year, Marcus."

"Happy New Year, Fanny."

25

Fanny picked up the phone on the third ring to hear Marcus Reed's excited voice. "I found Jake, Fanny! What I mean is I found out who he is and where he's from. I've been on this damn phone for almost four hours, but I now have substantial information."

"Is he alive? He can't be. Where? Can we go there?"

"His name was Jake Garrety and he died ten years ago. I know the cemetery in California where he's buried. He wasn't married, but he had a lot of female friends. They were all . . . ladies of the evening.

Two are in some kind of retirement village and three are in nursing homes. They're all in their late seventies. I have addresses if you want to visit."

"I do. What about those guys he traveled with?"

"They're all gone, Fanny. He was a courier. He always carried large sums of money and always used public transportation. I guess it was a cover. By the way, how is Ash?"

"He's doing nicely. He leaves the hospital today. It's a good thing we insisted he go in or he'd have pneumonia by now. I wish he wasn't so stubborn sometimes. John and Bess want him to stay a week with them, so John can monitor him hourly. John always takes the first week of the new year off. To get ready for the year ahead is how he explains it. Iris and Sage live around the block, so she can take the kids to see Ash every day. He lives for those kids."

"Any news from the architect or the contractor?"

"They'll be ready to start building in four weeks. They understand the . . . urgency. The contractor assured me everything would be done in four and a half months, maybe three. He has no other projects on hand, so there's every chance it will actually be finished by the middle of June. It has to be, Marcus, I promised Ash. Where are you calling me from?"

"In my car on my mobile phone. I've been looking for a house."

"How wonderful! Any luck?"

"One or two I'd like you to look at. When we get back from California. Any developments where Simon is concerned?"

"No, and I'm starting to get angry. I want it over. I called Clementine this morning, and she said he's holding tight. What he did, Marcus, was lend me money. I insisted on signing a note because I'm an honorable person. When I paid him back, he didn't give me back the notes. He's saying I still owe him millions of dollars. He handled my financial affairs, so I didn't question anything. He pulled some kind of deal with Sunny's Togs. I told him to sell the company and he said he did, but he didn't. Then he gave it back to me as a present. There were millions in that transaction alone. It's my own fault. I was so naively stupid I couldn't see straight where he was concerned. He's willing to forgive the debts if we turn over Babylon. Ash was right, Simon's as slick as they come. Clementine is looking for the paper trail. She'll find it because I paid him back. She said he's getting cocky and overconfident, and that leads to mistakes. He called the hospital several times to check on Ash. I guess he thought this was it. I'm having a hard time with this, Marcus. Let's talk about something else."

"When can you be ready to leave?"

"If we're driving, right now. If we're flying, one hour from now."

"We're driving. We can be in San Diego before dinner. I'll meet you in the front. Bring Daisy."

"She loves going in the car. I'm on my way downstairs right now." Fanny knew she had at least ten minutes. She used the time to call Ash, Bess, and Sage to tell them where she was going. She walked through the doors, Daisy in her arms, just as Marcus pulled his car to the curb.

"Marcus, I am so excited. At long last I can repay Jake's money. That money has been a burden on my back for so long. I have my checkbook with me."

"Fanny, the money didn't belong to Jake."

"Do you know who it did belong to?"

"Not exactly. You know what things were like here back then. It could have been anyone. It was such a large amount my thinking is it would have belonged to a *select* group."

"Can you be more specific?"

"No."

"Then the ladies of the evening get it. I think Jake would approve."

Marcus burst out laughing. "I second the decision. You know, I'm actually looking forward to this little adventure."

There was a lilt in Fanny's voice when she said, "Me too."

"Here it is, Restful Palms. It would be nice if the owners had planted at least one palm tree," Marcus said.

"It's so shabby and dismal-looking," Fanny murmured. Daisy hopped from her arms to run to the door.

"Let's get to it," Marcus said. "According to my notes, Lola, Pearl, and Gertie are in residence. You ready, Fanny?"

"Yes."

The lobby was clean but shabby. The smell of Pine Sol and something Fanny couldn't define, assailed her nostrils. Daisy started to bark. The lobby chairs were covered in orange plastic. Tired-looking plants in need of water stood in the corners. Pictures of movie stars hung on the walls. Marcus marched up to the desk. "We'd like to see Lola, Pearl, and Gertie."

The receptionist allowed her jaw to drop. She recovered and said, "Who should I say is calling?"

"Jake Garrety's friends," Fanny chirped.

"Wait here."

"I'm not sitting in those orange chairs." Marcus guffawed.

"You think this is funny, don't you?" Fanny hissed.

"Yes I do."

Fanny perched on the edge of one of the orange chairs. Thirty minutes later she said, "What's taking them so long?"

"They're probably *getting ready.*" Marcus erupted into laughter again.

"For what?"

"God only knows. I hear footsteps."

Fanny wished for sunglasses. Daisy barked. Marcus sat down on one of the orange chairs.

They looked like triplets. Resplendent in various shades of satin with matching shoes, they teetered forward, their feather boas swinging in the breeze they created. Their sparse hair was frizzed and adorned with gaudy clips. Robin's egg blue eye shadow covered their wrinkly eyelids. Outrageous false eyelashes clung precariously to their own skimpy lashes. It was easy to tell their touch was less than steady with the way their rouge and bright red lipstick had been applied.

Marcus stared at the movie stars on the wall. Daisy continued to bark.

Fanny cleared her throat. "Ah, ladies, I'm Fanny Thornton, and this man is Marcus Reed. This is Daisy. She's my dog."

"We're charmed," Pearl, the one in the middle said.

"We purely are. Charmed," Lola said.

"Ladies, Marcus and I came here today to ask you if you'd . . . we'd like to do something nice for you in Jake's memory. We thought . . . if you aren't happy here we could get you a house with a garden and maybe a pet or two. A housekeeper of course and someone to mow the lawn, that kind of thing. We'd furnish it, too. Do you think you would like something like that?"

"You say you want to do this for us in Jake's memory?"

Fanny nodded. "New clothes, whatever you want."

"Did Jake ask you to do this for us? Did he name us in his will?"

"Ah . . . yes, in a manner of speaking. It . . . was left up to me."

"Forever and ever?" Lola asked, her eyes filling with tears.

Fanny's voice was soft and gentle when she said, "Forever and ever. If you have other friends here who would like to go with you, it's okay. We can get a big house with lots of bedrooms."

"And we won't have to worry about anything ever again?" Tears rolled down Lola's cheeks. "I'd like a yellow cat."

"A yellow cat's good."

"Can you get us a housekeeper who knows how to make corn bread? I love real corn bread. Will she cook what we tell her?"

"Absolutely," Fanny said.

The three women huddled, their whispers loud.

"We'd like a front porch. With screens."

"Okay. Anything else?"

"One of those big television sets so we can watch baseball games. A piano."

"You got it. Make a list. We'll be sure to get you everything you want. Here's my business card and my home phone number. I think this might take a month or so."

"We have a lot of time. Can we join the Literary Guild?"

"I'll enroll you myself. You can order as many books as you want."

"We accept," the three women said in unison.

Fanny held out her hand. The women pumped it vigorously. Everyone smiled, including Marcus. Daisy sniffed at the spike-heeled shoes.

"It was nice meeting you all." Marcus nodded as he too offered his hand.

"Where is Jake buried, do you know?" Pearl asked. "If it isn't too far, we'd like to maybe visit."

"I'll arrange it, ladies," Marcus said.

"We'll be in touch. Work on your lists and if anything else comes to you, call me and we'll take care of it."

The women nodded. "Any friend of Jake's is a friend of ours," the ladies said.

"You'll be hearing from us," Fanny said.

Fanny watched as the women teetered toward the door in their spike-heeled satin shoes. At the door they turned and flicked their boas. Fanny waved.

"We can do this, can't we, Marcus?"

"For you, Fanny, anything."

"It's kind of nice, isn't it? They went to so much effort to dress up for us. You know they don't get any visitors. Everyone's forgotten them. That's not right. They aren't giving up on life. I like that kind of spirit, and I don't care what they did for a living. All they want is recognition and attention. If it's in our power to give it to them, then we should do it. It's Jake's legacy. Marcus, I want to visit at some point in time when they're settled in."

"Anytime you want, Fanny."

"You're sweet to do this with me, Marcus."

"That's because I'm a sweet guy."

"That you are. I wish I had met you thirty years ago."

"Everything happens for a reason."

"I know. Sometimes I just want to know the why of it all."

"Let's finish taking care of business here so I can get you back home. I know you're worried about Ash."

"How do you know that?"

"I know, Fanny."

"And you don't mind? My concern for Ash doesn't bother you?"

"If you weren't concerned, it would bother me. He is the father of your children. Whatever came before, Fanny, isn't my business. Where your family is concerned, I will never interfere. I'll consider it an honor if you allow me to be part of it."

"Someone else said that to me once and it was a lie."

"I'm not Simon, Fanny."

"Thank God for that."

Clementine Fox and Fanny Thornton stepped from the elevator into the foyer of the law offices of St. Clare, Raddison, and Raddison. Subdued lighting, rich paneling, and marble floors greeted them.

The receptionist looked up as Clementine Fox sailed past her circular mahogany desk, Fanny in her wake. She looked like she was about to say something, then changed her mind as the Silver Fox, resplendent in floor-length sable, strode past her. She did manage to press Jason St. Clare's call button with the tip of her long manicured nail.

Both Simon and his attorney were standing when Clementine and Fanny walked into the office. Fanny inclined her head at the introduction. She did her best to avoid looking at Simon, who was smiling affably. Fanny felt her stomach muscles start to flutter. Simon looked like he was holding a straight flush. She wished she knew what kind of hand Clementine held.

This was an unexpected meeting she hadn't planned on. Clementine had called her at five minutes past nine and said the meeting was scheduled for ten-fifteen. "Consider it a belated Christmas present." Fanny took that to mean the Silver Fox held a hand of winning cards.

Fanny accepted a cup of coffee and lit a cigarette as the two attorneys exchanged pleasantries. They moved off to the far end of the table, their voices hushed.

"How are you, *Fanny?*"

"Does it matter, Simon? I don't understand why you're doing this. I was such a fool to think you were someone I wanted to spend the rest of my life with. You're worse than Ash ever was. If your mother is watching over you, she must be beside herself at what you're doing. When this divorce is final, Simon, I'm getting married."

Simon uncrossed his legs. He stared at Fanny for a long moment. "I always knew you'd go back to Ash. That's just like you, Fanny, to marry a dying man." He was agitated now, hunching and unhunching his shoulders.

Let him think what he wants to think. He's nervous now. He didn't expect me to say what I just said.

Clementine and Jason St. Clare sat down. Simon focused his gaze on his attorney's face. Fanny lit another cigarette as both lawyers opened their briefcases.

"I called this meeting, Mr. Thornton, so that we could have some face-to-face dialogue. Before things go any further, either you or Mrs. Thornton might wish to rethink your positions. I would like to say at this time, and Mr. St. Clare agrees with me, that it's very hard to hide things today with all the high-tech equipment at one's disposal. There's always a paper trail to be found. Subpoenas for Internal Revenue tax documents are standard fare these days. I've found, haven't you, Jason, that when a person is willing to pay out large sums of money to buy information that the term 'money talks and losers walk' is more than appropriate, especially in a situation like we have here in front of us. Does anyone have anything to say?"

Simon sat stone-faced. Fanny sipped at her cool coffee. She shrugged.

"Let's see what you got, Fox." St. Clare said.

"Everything I told you I had. My client does not owe your client one red cent. This is the proof. Mr. Thornton's friend and confidant ... I believe his name was Malcolm something or other ... found himself in need of a cabin cruiser which, by the way, sleeps six. He said he would give serious thought to naming his boat the *Silver Fox*. I found him to be a very nice man. Very *chatty*. Your buddy sold you out, Mr. Thornton, for sixty-five grand."

"Simon . . . why don't we go into one of the other offices and . . . *talk*."

When Fanny was alone with her attorney, Clementine said, "How badly do you want this divorce?"

"I don't want to be married to Simon one minute longer than I have to be. Does that answer your question?"

"Your husband wants one half of all your assets *and* Babylon. Those are his conditions to the divorce if we take away the debts he says you owe. That means half of your clothing business, half of everything you have in brokerage houses, and the bank."

"Fine. Not Babylon. Let him build his own damn casino. He has the money. I will not allow him to take Ash's casino."

"Then there's no divorce."

"Okay, no divorce. Draw up whatever papers are necessary and I'll sign them. I'm out of here, Clementine. I can't stand to be in the same room with Simon."

"Fanny, you don't understand. If there's no divorce, you don't pay him anything. Your husband doesn't care if there's a divorce or not. All he wants is the casino."

"I told him I was getting married when the divorce was final. He assumes I'm planning on marrying Ash. I didn't bother correcting him."

"I see," Clementine said. Her voice was thoughtful as she stared at Fanny. "Would you have any objection to my . . . planting a few seeds . . . of discomfort?"

"You can plant a whole garden for all I care. You know where to reach me."

Clementine finished packing her briefcase just as Simon and his attorney walked into the conference room. "No dice, gentlemen. Mrs. Thornton said she doesn't much care one way or the other if the divorce goes through. She's just so happy that her first husband's health has improved to the extent he's prepared to take over his duties at the casino. They're planning on living together in the penthouse. Can you imagine, Jason, being at death's door, staring at the great beyond, and then you get a cold and are hospitalized and boom, you get a clean bill of health? I guess The Emperor is going to reign again. That must make you very happy, Mr. Thornton, Ash being your brother and all."

"Don't answer that, Simon. She's baiting you. Enough, counselor."

"Ah, Jason, did I rain on your parade today? Look at it this way. Today it was just a little-bitty drizzle. Wait for the downpour. It's coming."

"What the hell is that supposed to mean, Clementine?"

"Jason, Jason, Jason, you don't really expect me to answer that now, do you? Wide-eyed wonder does not become you."

Clementine extended her hand in Simon's direction. "No hard feelings, Mr. Thornton, but you are one sorry son of a bitch." Palms flat on the conference table, Clementine leaned over, Jason St. Clare ogling her cleavage. "I'm gonna get you, Mr. Thornton. When I do, it will all be legal. That's a promise. Tell him, Jason, that I've never broken a promise in my life. And tell him what I hate more than anything in this world."

Jason St. Clare's voice was a low monotone when he said, "Miss Fox never broke a promise in her life. The one thing she hates in this life more than anything else is a man who tries to screw over a woman in a divorce case."

"And the bottom line, Jason."

St. Clare's voice dropped to an even more boring tone when he said, "Miss Fox has no scruples and no conscience."

"There you go. I knew you'd get it right. Good day, gentlemen."

The Silver Fox laughed all the way down in the elevator. She made one call on her car phone as she drove away. The message was short, concise: "He refuses to cooperate."

Fanny returned to the penthouse, her thoughts in a turmoil. What was Clementine Fox going to do or say? "You know what, Daisy, I don't even care."

Daisy leaped from her arms and raced to the front door. A second later the bell rang. "Come in," Fanny called.

"Hi, Mom. Long time no see." Billie wrapped her mother in her arms and gave her a great smacking kiss.

"And whose fault is that? You're in Hong Kong, Japan, New York, England. When are you ever here?"

"I call, though."

"Yes, you do. Would you like some coffee?"

"I would love some. How's Sunny doing? Sunday is visitors' day, so I'll be here to visit. Are you going?"

"Of course. She's doing wonderfully. She's made some friends, one in particular. Harry seems like a very nice man. The doctors told me they're good for each other. Why am I telling you this, you met him?"

"I liked him. He doesn't take any crap from Sunny. Dad told me she's really mellow these days. I'm so glad, Mom. I'm going with Iris when she takes the kids to the park in a little while. I brought some presents for the kids. Dad's looking a lot better, too."

"And what about you, Billie. Is there anyone special in your life?"

"Not right now. You know how fickle I am. As soon as some guy starts to get serious I get scared. I like my life just the way it is. That's just another way of saying the right man hasn't come along. How's your life, Mom?"

"Parts of it are good. Other parts aren't so good. That's life."

"When will your divorce be final?"

"Probably never." Fanny told her daughter about the morning events in the lawyer's offices.

"It's just so hard to believe that Uncle Simon could turn like that. Back when we were kids and he'd come to Sunrise, I used to see him stare at Dad when he thought no one was looking. His eyes were so strange. I was a kid, what did I know?"

"Have you heard from Birch?"

"Not since early October. He asked me to send some kid clothes to Costa Rica. I must have sent a ton of stuff. He sent a card saying it all arrived safely. That was the last I heard. We all write, long, wonderful letters. Maybe they make him feel bad and that's why he doesn't write. Sage writes pages and pages and sends pictures of Lexie. He misses Birch the most. He'll be back, Mom."

"I know that. I miss him."

"Well, that's my news. Gotta run or Jake will take a fit. Some fool bought him a kite and he wants to fly it. I was elected. I really love that kid."

"He's a precious little boy. Ash adores him."

"Is that strange or what? He's like Dad's shadow. Polly's a little priss. Lexie is a delight. Sage is so good with all three of them. Don't be surprised, Mom, if Sunny agrees to Iris and Sage adopting Polly and Jake."

"Honey, nothing surprises me these days. Tyler will have something to say. He is their father."

"Nope. He already gave his approval. He's another one that failed the test where I'm concerned. Simon and him. Guess nobody gets it all. I like your new fella, Mom," Billie teased.

"He is kind of nice."

"He's a lot nice. Dad said he was aces. Now, that has to mean something."

Fanny laughed. "They get along well."

"I think it's hilarious that Uncle Simon thinks you want to marry Dad again. This is one weird family."

"Weird but nice. Kiss the children for me."

"I will, Mom. I'll call."

"More than once every month, okay?"

"At least once a week. By the way, the business is going great guns."

"Thanks to you."

"Whatever."

The apartment was so quiet after Billie left that Fanny turned on the stereo. Daisy danced on her hind legs, barking vociferously.

"Okay, you deserve a nice walk in the park. I do too. Get your leash."

An hour later, Fanny unhooked Daisy's leash and sat down on a bench to smoke a cigarette. She watched, a smile on her face as Daisy chased a fat poodle who had no interest in running away. They tussled, barking at each other. Fanny felt like an indulgent mother as she watched the two dogs under the trees.

"Is this seat taken?" a voice behind her said.

Fanny shivered. "As a matter of fact it is, Simon. I'm calling the police. You're in direct violation of the restraining order. Get away from me."

"Fanny, it was so good once. Why can't we get that back? I'd like to try."

"Talk to my lawyer. It wasn't good. It was only good when you got what you wanted, when you wanted it. It took me a while to get my eyes open, but they're open now. I don't want you, and I don't want anything from you. I mean it, get away from me."

Fanny ran toward Daisy, scooped the little dog up in her arms, and ran from the park, her heart pumping faster than her legs.

The owner of the fat little poodle walked toward Simon. "I saw you bothering the lady."

"What's it to you?" Simon snarled.

"This is what it is to me. See this. It's my fist. Now, feel this." The man's fist shot forward into the middle of Simon's stomach. He looked around. Satisfied that no one seemed to be paying any attention, the man's fist shot upward. "Bother the lady or any other lady again and I'll blow out your kneecaps.

"Come to daddy, Cupcake." The fat poodle waddled over to her owner and waited patiently to have her leash hooked onto her collar.

Owner and dog walked away without a backward glance.

Simon rolled over on the ground as he massaged his jaw. He sat down on the bench trying to get his breath. He stared after the man, hatred spewing from his eyes, obscenities rolling off his lips.

26

"Well, Mrs. Thornton, what do you think?" the building contractor asked.

All Fanny could do was stare at her beloved Sunrise. "From this distance I can't tell the difference. It's hard to believe there was ever a fire."

"That man of yours, Chue, he was under our feet every single minute with his grass seed and plants. He worked from a *map!*"

"I know. That's how he was able to make things look the same. I don't know how to thank you, Mr. Wyler. You finished four months to the day."

"We had some unexpected help." Fanny shot him a questioning look, but the contractor didn't expand on his statement. "Are you having a dedication or family party?"

"No. Ash will be moving in tomorrow. The furniture is coming today, and my friends are coming up to help hang the curtains and things like that. I don't know what to say, Mr. Wyler."

"This has to be one of the prettiest spots in the world. My father used to tell me stories about Sallie Coleman and this mountain. I'm happy to have been a part of the restoration. Tell Ash I said hello. We miss him in town."

"I'll be sure to tell him, Mr. Wyler."

Fanny watched the contractor drive off in his pickup. She was alone now with her thoughts, even though Chue stood off in the distance, not wishing to intrude. She walked around the house, marveling at the neatly trimmed shrubbery, the flowers that looked as if they'd just bloomed. The patio furniture was new, the umbrella candy-striped. Clay pots full of geraniums added the final touch. Ash loved flowers. She hadn't known that until last year. There were so many things she hadn't known about Ash until last year. Her eyelids started to burn.

A sudden burst of anger raged through her. She kicked off her heels and ran around the house to the cemetery, where she banged on Sallie's tombstone with clenched fists. "Do you know what you did? Do you have any idea, Sallie?" she screamed. "You backed the wrong horse! Do you hear me, Sallie? Your son, the one you loved above all else burned down this house, and he's trying to steal Babylon! I believed you when you said he was wonderful. I believed all those lies because I couldn't imagine you would ever lie to me. You lied, Sallie! You damn well lied to me! Ash is dying, and you better have some answers when he gets there because he's got a list as long as that mountain road out there. Why did you do that to me, Sallie? You knew what Simon was all about. He wanted me because of Ash, and you set me up for that . . . evil, ugly person."

Fanny dropped to her knees, her hands still pounding the stone. "I'm turning out just like you. I can't marry Marcus because of Simon. It's you and Devin all over again. That's your legacy to me. If you loved me, Sallie, how could you have done that to me? How *dare* you do that to me!"

Chue's gentle hand on her shoulder caused Fanny to sob harder. "How . . . why, Chue? You lived here. You saw everything."

"Yes. I tried not to be involved in Miss Sallie's family. Come, let me clean your hands. We can talk in the kitchen. There is a first-aid kit the contractor left behind in the pantry. We will talk."

"You knew, Chue. Why didn't you say something?"

"It was not my place, Miss Fanny."

"Did Ash tell me the truth, Chue?"

"Ash was never a saint, Miss Fanny. He was a boy whose heart couldn't accept what was being done. He retaliated in the only way he knew how. As I said, he was no saint, nor was he a devil the way his brother was. I watched over Ash, as did Mr. Philip. Miss Sallie was blind to many things. You must let it go."

"Let it go! I would like nothing more, but I can't. We all know Simon burned this house down, but we can't accuse him because we didn't see him do it. He will not give me a divorce unless I turn the casino over to him. Ash is dying, Chue, he's coming home to the mountain to die. There's nothing I can do for him except to be here. How does one handle the fact that one knows one's only brother, one's flesh and blood, is waiting for him to die? How, Chue?"

"You and your God will give him the strength, Miss Fanny."

"Which one did you like the best?"

Chue grinned. "I did not much care for either one of the boys. I understood Ash's pain, so the things he did were understandable. He did not like his brother. I saw many things that wounded my heart. I could not interfere, Miss Fanny."

"I think I hate her, Chue. I really do. I think I hate her as much as I hate Simon."

"Perhaps for now. Later the pain will fade."

"It will never fade, Chue. My whole life is tied to this family, to Sallie and her sons. How can that fade?"

"You must make a new life. Somewhere else. A life free of the Thornton name."

"I'm not free to marry."

"Then you will live in sin," Chue said smartly. "Many people do this today."

"My family is here. The casino is here. Who will take care of things? I can't walk away from my family and my responsibilities. I did that once, and it proved to be a disaster."

"It is a heavy burden. I know you will make the proper decisions when the time is right. I brought a letter for you to read from your son."

"From Birch?"

"He writes to me quite often."

"He does! I never knew that, Chue. I don't think I should read your mail. What does he write about?"

"Everything and nothing. They are long letters. I have many should you want to read them."

"We only get postcards. I think it's wonderful, Chue, that Birch chose you to correspond with. Did you tell him of Ash's condition?"

"Yes. He will be home soon. You did not write, Miss Fanny?"

"I did, but Ash didn't want me to tell him how severe his condition is. He didn't want Birch to feel he had to come home because he's dying. I guess he's remembering when Sallie died and how . . . things were at that time."

"Time heals all wounds, Miss Fanny."

Fanny's voice was sad when she said, "Chue, time is not a magical elixir. All it does is dull the pain. Ash's pain has never gone away, and he's going to die taking it with him. Simon is living with his own demons every minute of the day. It started down below in that town and then carried up here to the mountain. It's as though my hands are tied. I can't change anything."

"Come, Miss Fanny, I hear cars on the road."

Fanny wiped at her eyes. "You've been a wonderful friend all these years, Chue. Your family has been more than kind to all us Thorntons."

"You are my family as much as my own flesh and blood."

"That's one of the nicest things anyone has ever said to me, Chue."

"You are nothing like Miss Sallie, Miss Fanny."

"Thank you for saying that too. Chue . . . do you think Sallie heard me? I wanted a sign. I wanted the earth to tremble, the skies to open. I wanted something."

"Something like *that*," Chue said pointing to the small cemetery where a dark cloud hovered overhead. "From here you can see that it is a gentle rain. Perhaps it is a cleansing rain."

Fanny ran to the cemetery. The huge cottonwood seemed to be bowing, its branches dripping with rain. Chue was right. It was a gentle rain washing her tears from Sallie's stone. She raised her eyes. "It's a start, Sallie, but you aren't off the hook." She was muttering. Something she rarely did. People in white coats locked you up when you talked to yourself or to clouds, the trees, and tombstones.

"Look, Miss Fanny."

Fanny turned to look in the direction Chue was pointing. The dark cloud overhead surged forward and scudded across the yard until it was over the house. She watched the rain pelt downward in a brief downpour. Fanny ran back to the house to stand on the patio. "You're christening it, aren't you?" she shouted. "It's not enough, Sallie! You need to make it right before Ash gets there."

Chue hugged his arms to his chest, his oblique eyes full of shock.

Thunder boomed overhead as a jagged streak of lightning ripped across the sky.

"You need to make it right! It's time. If you don't, I'll do it for you. You won't like that, Sallie. I want to know that you understand what I'm saying."

The rain came down harder, plastering Fanny's clothes to her body. She stared upward, the rain pelting her face. Lightning struck one of the beams from the old house that were piled high in the middle of the backyard. Fanny watched as the old wood smoked and sizzled. Her shoulders slumped. A good sign or a bad sign? Using every ounce of willpower she possessed, Fanny straightened her shoulders. Chue was looking at her as though she'd lost her mind. Maybe she had for a few minutes. What sane person talked to spirits and expected them to make things right in the earthly world?

"This person, that's who," Fanny shouted.

"The rain is over. The cloud is moving on. Very strange," the old Chinese murmured.

"Not at all, Chue." Fanny sloshed ahead of him as she made her way to the front of the house to greet Billie and Bess.

"We get rain squalls like that in Texas all the time. We even get them in Vermont," Billie said.

"That wasn't a squall. That was Sallie. We were having a . . . little discussion."

"I used to have some very intense conversations with Seth. Once or twice he made the earth move when I let him see my strength. I believe in stuff like that. So, Fanny, who won?" Billie asked, her voice upbeat.

"I think I did. I can't be sure."

"I always felt like that, too. We have the edge though. We're *alive!*"

"You're both crazy," Bess said, her eyes going from one to the other.

"Maybe," Billie said.

"There are worse things in life," Fanny said.

"Whatever. Here comes the furniture truck. We have all the curtains, linens, and dishes and stuff in the van that Ash was gracious enough to let us use. I say we get cracking and get this all done today so you can bring Ash up tomorrow. He told me he can't wait to get here. It worked out perfectly, Jake is finished with preschool and he has the summer off. Somebody up there is watching over you guys and it ain't Sallie Thornton."

"Let's not get into *that*," Fanny said. "Was Thad upset that you came, Billie?"

"Not for a minute. Thad understands everything about me. He knows how important family is to all of us. He's so busy right now. He encourages me to do things on my own, separate from *him* and separate from *us*. Thad is one of a kind. I love him so much sometimes my teeth hurt. I clench my teeth and say, I love him, I love him,

I love him. The first thing he always says is, what can I do? That's the kind of person Thad is."

"Whoever would have thought you would marry your husband's best friend. On the flip side of that coin, who would have thought I'd marry my ex-husband's brother? Maybe Bess is right, and we really are crazy."

"I was teasing, Fanny," Bess said.

"I'm going to iron the curtains, Billie is going to nail in the hooks and you, Bess, are going to hang the curtains. Did you bring an ironing board?"

"Yes. This is not a Mickey Mouse operation, Fanny Thornton."

"We need to switch up here. I see the furniture men need me, so someone else has to iron."

Billie and Bess grumbled good-naturedly as they moved off to the kitchen.

When the grandfather clock in the foyer chimed five times, Fanny dusted her hands dramatically. "Done!"

"It looks the same," Billie said, her voice full of awe.

"If you didn't know it wasn't the old house, you would think this place had been here forever. Ash will be so happy. Jake's room came out perfectly."

"It used to be Simon's room," Fanny said.

"Not anymore. There's not one iota of anything that says that was his room," Billie said.

"Do you want to see the schoolroom?"

"What happened to that iron monstrosity that took up a whole room?" Bess asked.

"I had the construction people push it over the mountain. They had to use cranes and bulldozers and all kinds of heavy equipment. We couldn't build the house around it, they couldn't get it down the road, so there was nothing else we could do. It's in a deep ravine. In two hundred years it might rust away to nothing. It's my mountain, so I guess it's okay."

"Ladies, your supper," Chue called from downstairs.

"Let's take our first ride in the elevator," Billie said.

"It works," the three women said in unison as they stepped from the elevator.

"Won ton soup, fried rice, spare ribs, chow mein, egg rolls, and fortune cookies." Chue unpacked the heavy picnic basket. "No cartons. We use bowls. My wife say you wash, give back. My sons and

I will have those old beams carried away by dark, Miss Fanny. There will be no sign of the fire at all. Mr. Ash will be most happy. The pond is stocked for Jake. You will tell him, please, that the fish are waiting for him."

"Thank you, Chue. I'll tell them. We should get here by ten tomorrow morning. Please come up and see Ash."

"I will do that, Miss Fanny. Good night, ladies."

It was seven o'clock when the women climbed into their cars for the ride down the mountain.

The following morning, Fanny drove Billie to the airport. "Fanny . . ."

"Shhh, I know what you're going to say. He's got a month, if he's lucky. He's dealing with it. I'm dealing with it. I'll call you, Billie. Go home to your husband and give him a big hug and kiss for me."

"I will, Fanny. If you need me . . . you know . . . sooner, call. Day or night. Thad can fly me here, so I don't have to mess around with reservations. I want your promise, Fanny."

"You have it."

"Do you really think you won that round up there, when you squared off with Sallie?"

"Yes, I do."

"Good for you. Love you, Fanny."

"Love you too, Billie."

"Are you comfortable, Ash?"

"Fanny, stop fussing. I'm okay. It's not a long ride. I didn't see my black canvas bag. Did you put it in the van?"

"Yes. Ash, you asked me that three times." Fanny slowed the van and pulled to the side of the road. She climbed in back, rummaging between the luggage. "Here it is, do you want to hold it? Do you have your life savings in here or what?" She handed the bag to Ash before she climbed behind the wheel.

"Ash, speaking of savings, we need to make a decision about all the stuff that was in your mother's safe. What do you want me to do with it?"

"Fanny, I don't give a good rat's ass what you do with it. Mom left it to you."

"It belongs to you and your brother."

"I don't want it. I sure as hell hope you aren't planning on giving it to him. You need to think ahead. Simon has no children, so unless he has some kind of airtight will, it will come back to our kids. He's got more money than he can spend in three lifetimes. Just keep it."

"I don't want it, Ash. I'm not feeling very kindly toward your mother's memory these days."

"You said there's a waiting list at the rehab center. Use it to add on or build another one."

"You wouldn't mind?"

"Hell no. Sunny's doing great. We went out to see her yesterday. I wanted to say good-bye. I think she's happier than I've ever seen her. We talked about the adoption. She cried, but she knows it's best. Sage and Iris will make sure the kids know she's their mother. It's going to work out, Fanny."

"I'm so glad you planted that first seed, Ash."

"You know, huh?"

"Of course I know."

"Then you know I don't want her to see me again until . . . it's over."

"Shut up, Ash, I don't want to talk about *that*."

"We have to talk about it."

"No, we don't. I'm here to take care of you. We aren't going to . . . dwell . . . talk about things. We'll pack each day with wonderful things."

"You know, Fanny, you're wonderful. You truly are. What wonderful things are you talking about? Once I start on those pills, it will be all I can do not to jump out of my skin. I'm going to turn mean and nasty because the pain will be unbearable. You'll wish you never signed on for this gig."

"I'm prepared, Ash."

"I think you are. I'm not. Therein lies the difference."

"I want you to remember one thing, Ash. God will never give you more than you can handle."

"Words are so easy to say, aren't they? They just roll off a person's lips and people react to those words. Stop the car for a minute, Fanny. Do you see that blue sky, those snowball clouds, those fragrant pine trees? I'm never going to see them again. I'm never going to ride up and down this mountain again. I'm not going to be able to take Jake fishing. All the things you do every single day of your life and take for granted will be gone for me. I won't be here. My heart will cease to beat. This chair will sit empty in the garage. I won't be able to count the stars with Jake. Most of all, Fanny, I won't be able to spit and snarl at you. I want so damn much to be able to leave this earth a man, so that when you think of me you'll have kind thoughts. I'm sorry for everything. At this point in time I know it probably doesn't mean anything. What it means to me is I finally got the guts to say it out loud. If it wasn't for you, Fanny, I'd probably be in a ditch somewhere. I owe everything to you. I didn't know that for a long time. It's eating at my soul, Fanny. I want to be what you want me to be, and I don't know how. I don't know how, Fanny."

Fanny climbed from her seat and dropped to her knees. She wrapped her arms around Ash. "Let's both cry now and get it over with. I just want you to be who you are. I don't care how you spit and snarl. I'll spit and snarl back. When the pain is bad, Ash, I'll give you enough pills to ease it. I know you have a stockpile. You will always be in my thoughts no matter where you are. You were right, there's a bond between us that can never be severed. I don't want you to worry about being a man now at this particular time. You came through when no one else cared enough or . . . You know what I'm saying. None of us will let Jake forget you. You'll always be a part of his life. I promise you that, Ash. Will you trust me with these last days of your life?"

They cried together, their arms entwined, their bodies shaking with their grief for each other. It was Ash who finally said, "Enough already. Let's get this show on the road. Jake will be up in a couple of hours. I want to get settled in. We're going fishing. Want to come along, Fanny?"

"I'd love to go. Should I pack up a picnic lunch?"

"Potato chips, Popsicles, gumdrops, and mallow cups."

"Ash Thornton! Is that what you give him for a snack?"

"Nah, that's the bait. Chue gives us homemade egg rolls and fortune cookies. You don't know the first thing about fishing, Fanny. Gumdrops are great bait when there's any left."

Fanny laughed.

"God Almighty! You really did do it, Fanny," Ash said thirty minutes later when she steered the van up the driveway. "It's perfect! It looks like it's been sitting here for hundreds of years. Too bad Simon can't see this. He'd piss his jockies."

"Wait till you see the inside. The furniture's the same, it's just not battered and worn. The elevator is a little bigger. The refrigerator is one of those super duper jobs that makes ice cubes. I got us one of those big screen television sets and the satellite dish brings in more channels than before. We get wonderful reception now. I had the men toss that ugly monster safe over the mountain."

"No shit! Bet that was a feat in itself. It's amazing. You'd never know there was a fire. You kept your promise, Fanny. I knew you would."

"How did you know, Ash?"

"Fanny Thornton always keeps her word. Is thanks sufficient?"

"It's sufficient. What do you want to see first?"

"Three green pills. Not one, not two, three. A shot of brandy to wash it down."

"Coming right up."

It took a full twenty minutes for the tightness to leave Ash's face. Fanny used the time to brew a pot of coffee and to carry the bags from the van inside. Ash still had the black canvas bag on his lap.

"Let's do the tour, Fanny."

"Yes, sir," Fanny said, saluting smartly. "Let me load the bags in the elevator first. I'll unpack your stuff as you make the rounds on the second floor."

She found him in the schoolroom, his eyes wet, his shoulders slumped. "I feel like this is where it all started. I actually feel it, Fanny. I wish I had the words to tell you how much I loved my mother and how I missed her when she died. My father, too. I didn't know how to handle it then, and I don't know how to handle it now."

"Let your emotions go, Ash. Say whatever you want. If there are no words, don't worry about it. If you want to cry, cry. Whatever you want to do is all right."

"I have a list. I keep it in my pocket at all times. A pencil, too. I'm taking it with me when I go."

"A list is good," Fanny said. "I'm going to get your room ready and hang up your clothes. You have time for a nap before Jake gets here if you want."

"I don't want to waste the pills. I'm feeling halfway decent now. I'll just sit here for a while."

Fanny busied herself first in Ash's room and then in her own room. She waited a full hour before she called out to Ash. "I'm ready to go downstairs. How about you?"

"Me too. Let's have some more coffee in the garden."

It was a companionable silence broken only by the sound of Iris's horn as she parked the car behind the van. Jake whooped his way to the backyard, shouting at the top of his lungs, "Pop Pop, I'm here. Let's go fishing!"

They all went fishing. Fanny said later that it was one of the nicest days of her life.

When it was time to go, Jake crawled on his grandfather's lap to smother him with hugs and kisses.

"I'll bring him up every morning until . . . and Sage will come up to get him around three," Iris said. "Ash won't be able to keep this up much longer."

"I know. I appreciate it, Iris. If it looks like it might be a bad day, I'll call you in the morning."

"If there's anything you want . . . if there's anything I can do . . . call me."

"Of course."

Three weeks to the day of Ash and Fanny's arrival at Sunrise, Ash took to his bed.

Two more days passed, with Ash slipping in and out of consciousness. The third day he woke, completely alert. "Fanny, I want to ask a favor of you."

"I know, you want me to talk dirty to you," she teased.

"Okay, but do me the favor first. Will you promise before I ask it?"

"Sure, Ash. You're making this sound so mysterious."

"I want you to call Simon and ask him to come up here. I know I don't have long so will you do it?"

"If that's what you want, Ash, of course I'll do it. I'll have to go through his attorney. I don't even know where he lives."

"Try, okay? Will you have the cook bring me some coffee?"

"Tea would be better, Ash."

"Coffee, Fanny."

"Coffee it is. My address book is in the kitchen. I'll make the calls from down there. Are you all right?"

"No, Fanny, I'm not."

"John Noble is coming up this morning."

"He shouldn't waste his time. Go, Fanny."

Her heart pounding, Fanny ran down the steps. "Take some coffee up to Mr. Thornton."

Fanny used up forty minutes until she heard Simon's voice on the other end of the wire. "Simon, it's Fanny. Ash wants you to come to Sunrise. I think he wants to make arrangements about Babylon where you're concerned," Fanny lied. "Can you leave now? I don't think he has much time."

"Really."

"Is that a yes or a no?"

"I'll have to think about it."

"I wouldn't think too long, Simon. The offer is only good as long as Ash is alive."

"What will we all do without Ash in our lives?"

"I don't know about you, Simon, but I'll grieve. What should I tell Ash?"

"Tell him I'm on my way."

"Thank you, Simon."

Fanny ran upstairs. "He said he's coming, Ash. Who knows if he'll actually show up. I lied to him, said you wanted to talk to him about Babylon. How was the coffee?"

"It wasn't a lie, Fanny. I do want to talk to him about Babylon. I spilled the coffee on the rug. I couldn't hold the cup."

"It doesn't matter, Ash. Stuff like that isn't important." Fanny stared at the gaunt-eyed man who had once been her husband. If there were a way to breathe her own life into his wasted body, she wouldn't think twice. She knew he was nearing the end, and he knew she was aware of the little time he had left.

Ash struggled for words. "I want to be cremated, Fanny."

"I know, Ash. Please, don't talk, save your strength. I'll keep telling you what time it is, so don't worry about that. Do you want to hold the clock?"

"No. There seems to be some kind of film over my right eye."

"It's a cataract."

"You aren't going to call everyone, are you? Will you let me die in peace?"

"Absolutely."

"Is he here yet?"

"Soon, Ash. I'll read yesterday's paper to you if you like. Maybe hearing my voice will help you stay awake."

"Read."

Fanny read for thirty minutes. She heard Daisy bark downstairs and knew what the bark meant: Simon Thornton had arrived.

"I think he's here, Ash. Are you sure you want to do this?" She was alarmed at his ashen skin and the perspiration dotting his brow. She knew if she touched his hands or face, they'd be cold and clammy.

"Fanny, can you prop me up just a little or else get me a few more pillows?"

Fanny struggled, her own forehead beading with sweat at the effort she expended to get Ash into a more upright position. She understood perfectly that Ash didn't want to be flat on his back with his brother towering over him.

Simon was debonair and arrogant when he walked up the steps ahead of Fanny. "Aren't you going to say anything about the house, Simon?"

"What is there to say? Did you do something different?"

"Yes, something," Fanny snarled.

"Ash, how's the world treating you. Not too good by the way you look."

"Fanny, close the door," Ash said.

"But, Ash . . ."

"Close the door, Fanny."

"I'll be right outside."

"Simon, stand at the bottom of the bed, right in the middle so I can see you. Among other things I have a cataract."

Simon moved to the foot of the bed. "So what made you change your mind? Guess you figured you were going to be seeing Mom and Dad and you wanted them to know you did the right thing, huh?"

"Yes. I'm going to do the right thing."

"You look like you plan on taking my picture. Wouldn't that be something if you did and you took it with you to show Mom."

"Why don't you smile, Simon? I'd like to remember that smile of yours when I move into eternity."

Ash's hands moved under the cover. The moment Simon threw his head back in laughter, Ash pulled the trigger of the gun he'd brought with him from town. Simon crumpled to the floor as Fanny rushed through the door.

"Ash! Oh my God!"

"Did I kill the son of a bitch?"

Fanny leaned down to feel for a pulse. Simon's wide-open eyes glared at her. She wanted to close the lids, but she couldn't make her hands move.

"He's dead, Ash. Why? Why did you do that?"

Ash grappled with his breathing. "For you, Fanny. He would never give you a moment's peace. In the end he'd do something terrible to you. I'm dying so it doesn't matter. He wanted to be first in everything. He'll get there before me. I gave him an edge, Fanny."

"Oh, Ash."

"You promised not to cry."

"I lied." She reached for his hands and held them tight. She tried not to look at the hole in the bedspread.

"You'll be okay now, Fanny. It was all I could do for you. Mom's going to be pretty mad."

"I don't think so. The day before we came up here Sallie and I had a confrontation. I won. It's going to be . . . it's going to be . . . okay when you get there. I promise, Ash."

"I can see her. Look. There's Pop behind her, and Devin. Where's my list, Fanny? I need my list. Quick, get it for me."

"Where is it, Ash?"

"Find it. I need the list."

Fanny stepped over her husband's body as she searched for the clothes Ash had worn last.

"Mom's holding out her hand, Fanny. She wants the *list*."

"I have it! I found it, Ash!" She crumpled it into his hand. She heard him sigh with relief as she held his right hand.

"Let go, Fanny."

"No. No. I don't want you to go, Ash." She held his hand tighter.

"You have to let go of my hand, Fanny. It's time for me to go. Please, Fanny, let go."

"All right, Ash," Fanny sobbed. "Think about me sometime, okay?"

"Be happy, Fanny."

Fanny threw herself across the bed, her body shaking with sobs. What seemed like a long time later she felt gentle hands pulling her backward.

"John. Oh, John. I didn't think it was going to be like this. I didn't know I would care so much. He killed him for me, John. This is my fault. I swear to God I didn't know he had a gun. He brought this black bag with him from town. He was so concerned about it. It was heavy. I should have known. Somehow I should have known. That's why he asked for the coffee, so the cook could get the bag out of the closet for him. He couldn't ask me. The last thing he said was, be happy, Fanny. Oh, God, John, I feel like I want to lie down here and die, too. What are we going to do? As much as I detested Simon, he didn't deserve to die at his brother's hand."

"Ash must have thought so, Fanny. I know this will sound strange coming from me, since I'm a doctor, but if you stop to think about those two brothers you can understand Ash's thought processes. His condition, his concern for you, Simon's demands. That damn list he talked to me about last week."

"They're both dead, John. Does . . . do we . . . ?"

"I'll take care of it. What's he holding in his hand, Fanny?"

"The list. A list of all the . . . things Simon did and all the things . . . The grievances he planned to present to his mother when . . . *he got there.* I don't know. I never read it. I don't want to read it now. He said . . . he could see his mother and father and Devin. He said his mother was holding out her hand for the list. I know dying people always say things like that. Do you think he did see them?"

"I think Ash thought he saw them. I hope he did."

"He said he gave Simon the edge by letting him go first. Oh, God, John, how am I ever going to live with this?"

"One day at a time. Bess is on her way. I tried to get here sooner, but we had some emergency surgery earlier. Go downstairs, Fanny, and wait for Bess. Send Chue and his sons up."

Fanny did as John asked. There was nothing else for her to do.

Three hours after his death, Simon Thornton was buried in the Thornton cemetery by Chue and his children. Fanny, Bess, John, Chue, and his sons were the only mourners in attendance. John rushed through a prayer, his words garbled. No one seemed to mind. The moment they walked away, Chue and his sons began replacing the dirt. Fanny shuddered at the sound of the clumps of dirt hitting the pine box Chue had nailed together. By sundown the grave would look as though it had been there as long as the others.

John Noble signed Simon Thornton's death certificate under the watchful eye of his wife Bess. The cause of death was listed as cardiac arrest.

The following day, John Noble tendered his resignation to the Thornton Medical Center, citing the need to spend more time with his family as the reason for retiring from the medical profession.

It was the Thornton children, not Fanny, who decided to hold a memorial service for Ash Thornton at the small church called Saint Cotton Easter. It was a candlelight service because a delegation of casino owners had asked that Fanny darken the Big White Way for one hour. She agreed. Ash would have loved the tribute.

There were no stark headlines in the morning paper, out of consideration for the Thornton family. Page two carried a brief article with a small picture of Ash in his navy whites. Simon's obituary was on page seven, halfway down the page. There was no mention of how he died.

It was done. It was over. A large part of Fanny's life was gone forever, but life would go on.

Ash had said, don't be sad at my passing, be happy you still have what you have. She knew he was right.

"I *need* to grieve. Forgive me, Ash, for denying you your last request of me."

Fanny wept for the past.

27

Fanny hugged her children one last time.

"Do you have *any* idea of where you're going, Mom?" Sage asked.

Her voice was choked when she said, "Here, there, yonder. I'll call."

"We'll take good care of things, Fanny," Bess said. "John is just itching to help me at the casino. Think about it, if someone faints because they win too much money, we have a doctor on the premises. Take care of yourself, Fanny," Bess said.

"I will."

Sunny stepped forward. She hugged her mother. "I want to thank you, Mom, for everything. I'm sorry I was such a shit."

"It doesn't matter, honey. I'm so proud of you, Sunny. Promise me you'll keep up the good work."

"I promise, Mom. Jake wants to say something."

"Hi, big guy, catch any fish lately?"

"I got a big one yesterday. Are you going to see Pop Pop?"

"Not this trip, Jake. One of these days . . ."

"Okay. I miss him. I sent him a letter in a balloon."

Fanny cleared her throat. "Pop Pop loves to get letters."

"Don't get into any trouble, Mom," Billie said.

"I'll try not to."

"I'm going to hang around here for a while. I hate traveling."

"That's nice to know, Billie."

"No more hugs, no more kisses, no more *crying*," Sage bellowed. "We'll be here if you need us."

"I'll carry that thought with me. You know I love you all, more than I can ever say."

"Mom, will you go already!" Sage bellowed again. Fanny could see the tears in her son's eyes.

Fanny slipped the 4 by 4 into gear and left the underground garage. The time was 7:20 A.M. At the top of the ramp she was able to see a tall figure outlined in the early-morning sun. She pulled the Rover to the side and lowered the window. "You're up early, Marcus."

"I never went to bed. I've been sitting here on the curb all night. I wanted to say good-bye. Where are you going, Fanny?"

"I don't know."

"Are you coming back?"

"I don't know, Marcus."

"I love you, Fanny."

"I love you, too."

"I'll wait as long as it takes."

"I'll carry that thought with me. Will you watch over my family?"

"Fanny, the whole damn town watches over your family. I'll add my name to the list. Travel safely. Will you call or write?"

"I will when I need you the most."

Marcus nodded.

Fanny drove away. She didn't look back.

She had things to do, places to go.

Her first stop was Sunrise.

Chue watched from the gardens as Fanny climbed from the Rover, the ashes in her hand. He felt his heart thud in his chest when he saw Fanny go to the edge of the mountain. "You're free at last, Ash! You're one with the universe now." In a voice that was cracked and harsh she, who could never carry a tune, broke into song. *"Off we go into the wild blue yonder . . ."*

"Climbing high into the sky . . ." Chue sang, his arm going around her shoulder.

They finished the song, tears dripping down their cheeks.

"I saved a little," Fanny said, handing the urn to Chue. "Put them next to Sallie. Just a cross, Chue, nothing elaborate like what we did for Simon."

"Yes, Miss Fanny."

"Isn't it wonderful that Sage is moving his family here now? The children love the mountain. Everything happens for a reason. Ours not to reason why. Watch over my family. Someone told me earlier that many people watch over them. I didn't know that."

"Have no fear, Miss Fanny."

"I hope you put some real whoppers in that pond. Jake can't wait to get here."

"It is done, Miss Fanny."

"Good-bye, Chue."

"Good-bye, Miss Fanny."

Done.

Over.

Move on, Fanny.

It was eleven o'clock when Fanny parked her car in a neatly bordered driveway. A small box in her hand, she walked up the walkway to the door and rang the bell. Margaret Lassiter opened the door and held it wide for Fanny to enter.

"Mrs. Thornton, I'm so sorry about your husband and his brother. If there's anything Jeffrey or I can do, you only have to ask."

"I saw you and Jeffrey at the memorial service. It was nice of you to attend."

"We didn't want to intrude."

"Is Jeffrey home?"

"He's at work. He won't get home till around six."

"I wonder if you would give him this. It's . . . what it is . . . is Ash's aviator wings. I thought he might like to have them. Ash has . . . other wings now."

"Oh, Mrs. Thornton, I know Jeffrey will be so pleased. You have no idea how he's anguished over that episode at the casino. Are you sure you want to give *my son* his father's wings? You have boys of your own."

"I'm sure, Mrs. Lassiter. I have to go now. Thank you for seeing me."

"Good-bye, Mrs. Thornton."

Done.

Over.

Move on, Fanny.

Fanny looked at her watch the moment she turned off the engine. She'd made good time, the radio blaring for company. She took a long moment to commit the house nestled in the cottonwoods to memory. She looked at her watch again as she climbed from the car. She took one last walk around the property, marveling at the tree house Marcus had built.

A jackrabbit jumped from the bushes. Startled, Fanny backed up to the makeshift ladder leading to the tree house. She sat down on the third rung from the bottom. She stared at nothing, her thoughts whirling inside her head. She looked at her watch again. She had ten minutes. Time to get on with it.

Hands jammed in her pockets, Fanny walked to the center of the backyard, her head raised to the sun. "Hey, Sallie, listen up! In ten minutes this place is just going to be a memory. I'm breaking the chain. I don't want your legacy. Not anymore. This is the last link, Sallie. You hoped I'd bring your precious son Simon here. That was a mistake, Sallie. I will not allow myself to end up like you. Ash took care of that for me. Bet your hair is standing on end over that. All that stuff in your safe is gone. So is the damn safe. The first thing I did after Ash died was to throw your desk and blackboard down the mountain. I've got a regular junkyard down there. If there was a way to get rid of that cemetery, I'd do that, too. Private cemeteries are obscene. When I figure a way to get rid of it I'll do it. For now, it's what it is, a place. Nothing more. This house is the last link. Ooops, gotta go, I hear the machinery out on the road. I don't want any sign from you, Sallie. I don't think rain, thunder, and lightning are going to do it this time. Oh, yeah, one last thing. I'm taking back my maiden name. This is Fanny Logan signing off, Sallie." She offered up a sloppy salute before she walked to the front of the house.

"Mrs. Thornton?"

"Mr. Wyler. It's a beautiful day, isn't it?"

"Yes it is. This is the house?"

"Yes. It's pretty, isn't it?"

"Name your price. I'll buy it from you."

"I can't do that. You brought your wrecking ball. The house is made from quarry stone. Is your machinery strong enough?"

"Yes, Mrs. Thornton, it will do the job. You're sure now?"

"Yes, sir, I am."

"You want all the debris carried away to the quarry."

"Yes. Please, will you rake the grounds so nothing remains. The tree house, too."

"Okay, Mrs. Thornton, you're the boss."

"I'm not Mrs. Thornton anymore. I came here plain old Fanny Logan from Shamrock, Pennsylvania, and that's how I'm leaving. I know you don't understand. It's all right. Send your bill to the casino."

Daisy in her arms, Fanny watched as the heavy piece of machinery backed up, advanced and then backed up again. The massive iron ball swayed in the air. As far as Fanny could tell, there was no breeze anywhere. Her eyes didn't leave the ball for a second.

"Do it!"

The moment the ball hit the roof of the house, Fanny climbed into her car.

She didn't look back.

Done.

Over.

Move on, Fanny.

Fanny was exhausted by the time she drove the Rover down the long road that led to Josh Coleman's farm. It was late, almost eleven o'clock. The lights encouraged her to drive around the horseshoe-shaped driveway. Someone inside must have heard her engine. The front light under the overhang suddenly glowed a warm yellow. "Stay, Daisy, I won't be long."

Fanny walked up the four stone steps to the front door. Before she could ring the bell, the door opened. Josh Coleman stood in front of her, his face puzzled at this late visit. Fanny made no apologies.

"Mrs. Thornton, come in. Has something happened? Is something wrong?"

"I'm returning your family albums. I'd like mine back if you don't mind. I also brought you a letter from your nephew, Ash. He passed away two weeks ago on the same day his brother Simon died. There are only two Thornton men left in the family to carry on the name— my twin sons Birch and Sage."

"Was it important to you to bring these albums back to me at this time of night? I sense a certain anxiety in you."

"I dislike confrontations. I came here to tell you I think it's despicable what you and your brother did to that family you left behind in a tar paper shack. There are no excuses. Even if you had one, I don't want to hear it. A family, Mr. Coleman, is the most precious thing on this earth. When all else is gone, when everything else fails, family is the only thing that counts. I don't believe you looked very hard to find your family. You and Seth were already rich men when Sallie returned to that shack. You could have done the same thing. You could have gone back.

"The hatred she felt for what you did is what brings me here. Because of that deep hatred, she ruined her sons' lives and she tried to ruin mine. Today was the culmination of it all. My albums, please."

"Mrs. Thornton . . ."

"I'm no longer Mrs. Thornton. I'm Fanny Logan. My albums, please."

The old man inclined his head to the right where her albums were stacked neatly. Fanny picked them up and held them close to her chest. A sob tore at her throat. She felt herself being led to a chair. "I think you need to talk, Fanny Logan. I'm a good listener. If you want to cry, I have a whole pile of hankies."

A long time later Fanny stood, her hand extended. "I forgot about my dog. She's still in the car."

"Would you like to spend the night? It's a long drive to town."

"No thank you. It's late. Good night, Mr. Coleman."

"God willing I'll make my way to Nevada and Texas before the cold weather sets in. It's time for my clan to meet the others."

"Consider yourself damn lucky, Mr. Coleman, if any one of them opens their door to you."

"I'm not above begging and pleading," the old man said.

"Those are just words."

"You're wrong, Fanny Logan. Those are promises."

Done.

Over.

Move on, Fanny.

It was two o'clock in the morning when Fanny pulled into an all-night diner. She ordered food and carried it to the car, where she gobbled it down almost as fast as Daisy did. She sat in the parking lot for a long time, sipping her coffee and smoking cigarettes, Daisy cuddled in her lap.

At four-thirty she headed for Washington National Airport. She parked the car in long-term parking, wondering exactly what the words long-term meant. At five-thirty she was the first in line at the Delta checkin counter.

"Where to, ma'am?"

"Home. Shamrock, Pennsylvania. Two first-class tickets, one for me and one for my dog."

"Yes, ma'am. Your flight leaves in forty minutes. Gate Three."

Fanny walked across the concourse, her eyes searching for a phone booth. Daisy woofed softly when she placed her call.

"Marcus?"

"Fanny?"

"Fanny Logan, Marcus. I just wanted to tell you I love you. I also wanted to tell you I know where I'm going."

"Where, Fanny?"

"Home."

"Which home, Fanny?" Marcus asked gently.

"The only one that was ever really mine. Shamrock."

"Would you like some company? I mean besides Daisy."

"I would like that very much."

"Then hang up so I can get it all in gear. I can charter a plane. Will you wait for me at the airport in Pittsburgh?"

"Yes."

"How long will you wait?"

Fanny laughed. "Marcus Reed, me and my dog will wait as long as it takes. Didn't you hear what I said? I love you."

"You better be saying the same thing when I get off the plane. Hang up, Fanny."

"Marcus."

"Yes, Fanny?"

"I did everything I was supposed to do. I broke the last link."

"How do you feel?"

"I feel like I did in 1944 when I left Shamrock."

"Hot damn. Hang up, Fanny."

"Okay."

"You see, Daisy," she whispered, "something good did come of all of this."

She was going home. And when she got to that wonderful place called home, the man she had waited for all her life would join her.

Her world right side up, Fanny strode down the concourse to Gate Three on the last leg of her homeward journey.

Don't miss the other two novels in Fern Michaels's
magnificent Vegas Trilogy!
Read on for a special preview of each book.
New trade paperback editions on sale from
Kensington Publishing Corp.

1

༄

1923

The old attorney stared out his grimy windows and winced. His secretary had cleaned those windows yesterday. He'd watched her swish her soapy rag over them, then polish them until he could see his reflection. Now, less than fifteen hours later, they were dirty and grimy as though they'd never been cleaned. He looked down at his desk and saw the same grainy granules of desert sand. Irritably, he blew at them and wasn't surprised when the offending sand refused to move. He told himself he was in the desert; sand was to be expected.

Alvin Waring, attorney-at-law, worried as he shuffled the two folders—one thick, one thin—from one side of his desk to the other. Waring knew exactly what was in each folder. If he were pressed, he could rattle off the contents without missing a heartbeat.

He saw her then, and he thought about waterfalls, summer blue skies, picnics and wildflowers. He wished, in that single second of time, for his youth. The two folders on his desk made perfect sense now. He stood, his old bones creaking as he walked around the side of his desk, held out his hand and touched hers, softer than any flower petal. She smiled, her summer blue eyes crinkling at the corners.

"Mr. Waring, I'm Sallie Coleman. I received your letter several days ago. I would have come yesterday, but I . . . I had to . . . sort through some things. I don't have much money, Mr. Waring. I used all my available cash to pay for Cotton's funeral. I do have this," Sallie said as she withdrew a small burlap sack from her purse. "Cotton gave it to me the first day I started to work at the bingo palace. He said it was to be my nest egg if things didn't work out. I'm not sure how much it's worth. Cotton said it was seven ounces of pure gold."

"Nest eggs should not be touched. They're for the future." The attorney cleared his throat as he handed back the sack of gold. He wondered what it would be like to walk with this young woman through a green meadow filled with daisies. In his bare feet. Holding her hand.

Sallie backed up a step, but didn't reach for the little sack. The summer blue eyes were questioning. "I don't understand. It could take me years to pay off . . . The gold would help me get to the end quicker. Did I say that right?"

"It makes no mind. There is no need for you to assume payment for Cotton Easter's bills. First, he didn't leave any bills. His estate would have paid for his funeral. There was . . . is . . . no need for you to assume the responsibility."

"Yes, Mr. Waring, there was a pure need for me to be doing that. Cotton was my friend. It was hard for me here in the desert when I first got here. He helped me. He watched out for me. Cotton didn't let anyone bother me. He was a kind man, a good man. Sometimes . . . most times, he was down on his luck, but when he had money he always shared with me and a few others who were less fortunate. I don't regret paying for his funeral. If he didn't leave any bills, and you don't want my nest egg, why did you write me that letter asking me to come here?"

"Sit, Miss Coleman. I have some things to explain to you. I'm going to read you Cotton's last will and testament."

"Mercy, Mr. Waring, isn't a person's will a private thing? I don't know if Cotton would like you to be telling me his secret thoughts. Cotton always told me a man's life and his past belonged to him alone. He said that and a man's good name were all God gave him when he came into the world, and when he left this world, his name on his marker would be all that was left. Now that I told you that, Mr. Waring, I'll be getting back to work. I'm having his marker erected next Sunday afternoon. The preacher agreed to say a few words. I'm going to serve a meal at the palace for anyone who wants to come."

Alvin Waring couldn't believe what he was hearing. She was almost to the door when he barked at her to come back and sit. He gentled his tone and smiled when she perched herself on the edge of the hard wooden chair. The summer blue eyes were frightened.

"Now, little lady, you just sit there and listen to me read you Cotton Easter's last will and testament. Before I do that, I want to tell you about Cotton. If I don't, you won't understand the will. Cotton came here to the desert with his daddy many years ago. He was just a small child at the time. His daddy was an educated man whose wife died before her time. With a small boy to raise, he de-

cided to come here to seek his fortune the way his own father had
done. He was very successful, almost as successful as his father. He
sent Cotton back to Boston to get educated, and the minute the boy
finished his studies, he hightailed it right back here and took his
place next to his daddy. The main reason his daddy came here was
because his father had mined the Comstock Lode. That would be
Cotton's granddaddy. The old gentleman left all he held dear to
Cotton's father. And, there was a lot that he held dear. Cotton's
daddy sold all the shares to the Comstock that his father left him at
just the right time, and banked a fortune. Sold high, $22,000 a
share, and he owned thousands of shares. Cotton's daddy was a
gambler and won acres and acres of land in poker games. He never
touched that money. He struck it rich time and again. He had a big,
old ugly Wells Fargo safe made special, and he kept his fortune in
it. Didn't trust banks or the stock market. A wise man. He bought
up half the desert for fifty cents an acre. He grubstaked many a
man who later paid back double for the stake. In some cases the
veins and mines found their way back to Cotton's daddy. When he
died, his estate went to Cotton, who didn't give a whit about the
money. Cotton wanted his own strike. He amassed his own fortune, and it all went into the Wells Fargo safe along with his daddy's
money, and his granddaddy's money. Make no mistake, Miss Coleman, Cotton knew exactly what was his, what was his granddaddy's, and what was his daddy's. I don't think he knew or even
cared about the amount. I tried to tell him, but he simply wasn't interested. He wanted to be like all the other miners—spinning yarns
and drinking rotgut, loving women on the run, gambling, and hitting the mother lode. He craved respect, and you were the only
person who gave it to him, Miss Coleman. He said you nursed him
when he came down with pneumonia, and that you fed him when
he was hungry. He said you washed his clothes once or twice and
said you were—ah, what he said was . . . you were, forgive me, a
lusty bed partner."

Sallie blushed, but the summer blue eyes didn't waver.

"Cotton left all of his holdings to you, Miss Coleman."

"Me! Now, why would he do a thing like that, Mr. Waring?"

"Because you accepted him for who he was, and he said you respected him and asked his advice. He said nobody else, man or
woman, ever asked for his advice. You followed it, too. That was
important to Cotton."

"But . . . but—"

"You're a very rich woman, Miss Coleman. It's a short will. I'll read it to you, and you can ask me questions, if you want, when I'm finished."

Sallie listened to the old attorney's quivering voice, understanding only one word: rich. Other people were rich. People like herself were never rich. If she were rich, she could go back to Texas and help her family. She would have to ask how much money that would take. She wished then that her life had been different. She wished she could read and write well. Cotton had helped her a little, but she'd been too ashamed and embarrassed to let him know how ignorant she was.

The attorney's voice trailed off. He was finished. She needed to pay attention. He had said she should ask questions. He was staring at her expectantly. "Mr. Waring, I'd like to help my parents out if that's possible. These past few years I've sent little bits of money back home, but there are quite a few young ones to take care of. How much do you think that will cost? If there's enough I'd like to maybe move my family to a little house with a yard for the children. Maybe buy a toy or two and a new outfit. Schooling too. My pa, he . . . how much will all that take?"

"Compared to what you have, what you're asking is a spit in the bucket. You're rich, Miss Coleman. Let me put it to you another way. Do you know how much a million dollars is?" Sallie's head bobbed up and down. In her life she'd never seen more than fifty dollars at a time. A million had to be a lot more than that. She wished she'd paid more attention to Cotton when he was doing numbers with her. All she wanted was to be able to count the money at the end of the day and know it was accurate.

"Then you multiply that by about fifty and that's what you're worth, possibly more, thanks to Cotton Easter. That doesn't count the property. Right now it's not worth much. Possibly someday it will be worth a fortune. Cotton's daddy thought so, and so did Cotton. My best advice to you is to take some of that money and buy up the rest of the desert and sit on it until the time is right to sell it. It's going for about sixty-five cents an acre. I can arrange all that for you if you want me to handle your affairs. If you have another attorney in mind, that's all right, too. I'll be sending you monthly reports on your finances, which pretty much stay the same since everything is locked up. Later, I'd like us to sit down and talk about the stock market. Will you be wanting to move into the Easter house? They gave it a name when Cotton was just a tad. His daddy called it Sunrise. You own the mountain it's sitting on." He dangled a set of clanking keys to make his point.

"What house is that, Mr. Waring?" Sallie gasped.

"Cotton's daddy's house up on Sunrise Mountain. A fine house it is, too. Cotton's granddaddy had everything sent here from Boston. The finest furnishings money could buy. Real plumbing. There's a well and an automobile. There's a couple who look after the place. You can live there if you like. It's yours."

A house called Sunrise. Sallie wondered if she was dreaming. "How many rooms does it have?"

"Eleven. Four complete bathrooms. Beautiful gardens. Do you like flowers, Miss Coleman?"

"Oh, yes, Mr. Waring, I love flowers. Do you?"

"Wildflowers especially. Bluebells, and those little upside-down bells, the yellow ones. My mother used to have a beautiful flower garden. Where do you live now, Miss Coleman?"

"In a boardinghouse. I have a big room. It has pretty wallpaper and white curtains on the windows. I can't open the windows, though, because of the grit and sand. I'd like to see those curtains move in the early morning breeze. Window screens are frightfully expensive."

"You don't have to worry about things being expensive anymore. If you don't mind me asking, Miss Coleman, what will you do? If you have a mind to tell me a little about your background, I might be able to help you. Plan your future, so to speak. Cotton trusted me. I'd like it if you would trust me, too."

Sallie sat back in the hard wooden chair and stared directly at the old attorney. She spoke haltingly at first, and then, as she grew more comfortable with the truth and shame, the words rushed out. "I'm one of eight children. I'm the oldest girl. The boys, they took off as soon as they could. My pa, he drank too much. My mother took in washing and ironing. I helped. There was never enough food. I was never warm enough. I left when I was thirteen. I made my way here and sang for my supper. Cotton said I sang like an angel. He loved to hear me sing. The miners gave me tips sometimes. Cotton was always generous. He didn't care that sometimes, when there was no money, that I would . . . take money for doing things that would shame my mother. That's just another way of saying I was . . . am . . . a whore. You didn't expect me to say that, did you, Mr. Waring?"

"No, I didn't. I'm not going to judge you, Miss Coleman."

"That's good, Mr. Waring. I won't judge you either. Now we can start out fair. I can read and write a little. Maybe I can get someone to teach me now. There was no time for school and no nice clothes back in Texas. The good ladies in town called us white trash. Nobody cared about us. I wanted better, the way my brothers wanted better. Someday I'm going to find them, and help them if I can. I'll be taking you up on the offer to move into that fine house. Do you know if the windows open?"

The old attorney smiled. "I'll make sure they do. Miss Coleman, I have an idea. Do you think you could find someone to take your place at the bingo palace, for say, six months? Maybe a year. I know a lady in California who operates a finishing school for young ladies. If you're amenable, I can make arrangements for her to . . . to—"

"Polish me up?" Her tinkling laugh sent goose bumps up and down the attorney's arms. "I suppose so. But first I have to go back to Texas. Family needs to come first, Mr. Waring. When I get back, we can talk again. Where's that safe you spoke about? Do you give me the money or do I just open the safe and take it? Do I have to write everything down?"

"Miss Coleman, you can do whatever you want. When would you like to visit the house?"

"Today."

"It's a two-day trip on horseback. I can make arrangements to have you taken up tomorrow if that's all right with you. Here is the combination to the safe and the keys to the house. These past few years a lot of the funds were put in banks once I felt it was safe. This box sitting here has all the bankbooks. They're yours now. All you have to do is walk into any one of them, sign your name, and take as much money as you want. You're agreeable, then, to my purchasing more desert acreage?"

"If you feel it's a wise thing to do."

"I do."

"Then you have my permission, Mr. Waring."

"How do you feel now, Miss Coleman? I'm curious."

"Sad. Cotton was such a good friend to me. I cannot believe that he would leave me all this money. Is there something in particular he wants me to do? I guess what I'm saying is, why? Why me? He had friends. There must be family in Boston. Are you sure it is meant for me?"

"I'm sure." Waring rose, walked around the desk, and held out his hand. He held her delicate hand a moment longer than necessary. "Enjoy your new fortune, Miss Coleman."

"I'll try, Mr. Waring."

Sallie held out her hands for the small wooden box containing the bankbooks.

* * *

Outside in the late morning sunshine, Sallie stared up and down the street. She wondered how things could look the same as they had looked an hour ago when she first walked up the steps to the attorney's office.

Sallie's eye traveled to the line of stores whose owners she knew by name. Toolie Simmons owned The Arcade where beer on draft was sold, The Rye & Thackery run by Russ Malloy, the Red Onion Club, The Gem Counter with the letter N backwards on the rough sign, and on to the Arizona Club, whose sign proudly proclaimed its whiskey was fully matured and reimported. Men sat in the small pools of shade on spindly chairs, tilted back at alarming angles, talking, smoking their cigars and pipes as they waited for the saloons to open at noon. Those men would work if there were work to be had. Maybe she could do something about that. Some of them waved to her, others tilted their straw hats in recognition.

"Gonna sing us a pretty song tonight, Miss Sallie?" one of the hard rock miners shouted.

"Not tonight, Zeke, I'm heading for Texas to see my family, and I have a lot to do. Soon, though. You just tell me what you want me to sing, and I'll do it just for you."

"Heard the Mercantile got some canned peaches yesterday, Miss Sallie."

"Thanks for telling me, Billy. Would you like some?"

"I purely would, Miss Sallie."

"I'll get some on my way back and drop them off. You gonna be at the Arizona Club?"

"Nope. Don't got a lick of money in my poke today. I'll be waiting right here for you."

Sallie nodded as she skirted the barrels of hardware and produce outside the Mercantile Company. She smiled at Hiram Webster as he stopped sweeping the sand from in front of his doorstep to let her pass. "Good morning, Mr. Webster. It's a fine day, isn't it?"

" 'Tis that, Miss Sallie. Lots of blue sky today."

Sallie was convinced no one knew about her good fortune. As she walked along she remembered the tents and the smell of frying onions that permeated the air the day she'd first arrived. The tents were all gone now, replaced with newer wooden buildings. It was still a rough town, a shoddy town, a *man's* town. She realized she could fancy up the town now if she wanted to. She could buy up whatever she wanted. She could knock down all the shabby buildings and start over. Cotton said if the price was right, a person could buy anything.

Sallie stepped aside as three ladies walking abreast passed her, straw baskets on their arms. They didn't acknowledge her in any way. Sallie smiled anyway, and said, "Good morning, ladies." The scent of sagebrush seemed to be all about her as she walked along, past the bakery, the icehouse, the pharmacy, and the milliner. A gust of sand swirled past her. She tried to dance away from the circular swirl that spiraled upward, but her shoes were covered with sand. She stomped her feet and shook the hem of her skirt.

"Mornin', Miss Sallie. What brings you to this end of town? Can we do anything for you here at the Chamber of Commerce?"

"Yes, you can, Eli. How much do you think it would cost to plant cottonwoods up and down this fine street, on both sides?"

"Why do you ask?"

"I'd like to donate them and pay for the labor to plant them in memory of my friend Cotton Easter. Maybe some benches under the trees for the ladies to sit on. I think they'll make the street real pretty."

"That they will, Miss Sallie. The town's coming back to life a little at a time. I like that."

"I do, too, Eli."

Sallie fought the urge to dance her way down the street. It was a dream—but if it was a dream, what was she doing with the box in her hands? Well, there was one way to find out for certain. She stopped in a shop doorway, stuck her hand into the box, and withdrew one of the bankbooks. She looked at the name of the bank embossed in gold leaf on the front. Sallie retraced her steps, walked around the corner, and continued walking until she came to the bank. She entered, walked up to the bank teller and handed him the small blue book. "I'd like . . . five hundred dollars, please."

Five minutes later, Sallie walked out of the bank in a daze, the five hundred dollars safe in her purse. It was real, it wasn't a dream. She tripped down the street, giddy with the knowledge that everything Alvin Waring had said was true.

The money secure in her purse and loose bills in the pocket of her dress, Sallie stopped first at the Mercantile Company for a bag of canned peaches that she immediately handed over to Billy along with ten dollars. She handed out money to all the hard rock miners, admonishing them to eat some good food and to take a bath before they spent the rest in the Red Onion.

Sallie opened the door to the bingo palace with her own key. In the bright sun filtering into the large room, it looked like a sleazy, smoky, rinky-dink parlor with rough furniture, a rickety bar, bare windows, a cashier's cage, and a small stage that doubled as the bingo stand, where the bingo numbers were called, and where she sang at the beginning and end of the evening. She walked around, touching the felt-covered poker tables at the far end of the room, sitting down and then getting up from the bingo benches. She straightened the stack of bingo cards into a neater pile. Maybe she should throw everything out and start from scratch. She sat down again and closed her eyes. How best to pretty things up? A real stage, small, with a red velvet curtain that opened and closed. Matching draperies on the windows that could be closed in the winter. Chandeliers over the tables for better lighting. Perhaps a spotlight for the stage. A new bar, the kind the Arizona Club had, shiny mahogany with a brass railing. Leather stools with brass trim to match the bar. A new floor with some sections of it carpeted. No more spittoons. Definitely a new front door with glass panels, maybe even colored glass. She'd have some trees planted around the building, flowers if they would grow. She walked over to the farthest corner of the room, where she sat when things were slow or when she just wanted time by herself. She sat down on a wobbly chair and leaned her arms on a table whose legs didn't match. She smiled when the table rocked back and forth the same way her chair did. Cotton said the man who made the chair and table had a crooked eye. She wondered if she would miss things the way they were now. Old things were comfortable. New things took some getting used to.

Sallie stared at the small stage where she called out the bingo numbers hour after hour. She was always happy when a grizzly miner won his four bits and whooped in delight, his dirty boots stomping on the floor, the other miners cheering him on.

The bingo palace didn't make a lot of money, barely enough to pay the winners and herself. The doors opened at noon for her regular customers. By paying close attention she was able to tell which customers were hungry, which customers came to gamble, and which ones just wanted to hear her sing. The hungry ones were her biggest problem. Jeb, the owner of the steak house, allowed her to run a tab for hard-boiled eggs and pickles that she handed out on a daily basis. Most days if she had thirty customers she was lucky. The three poker tables covered in green felt had dust all over them. Most of her customers didn't have enough money to start up a poker hand, and those that did had to extend credit and write IOUs. The bingo cards were safer. Often she sat at one of the tables with her customers, playing poker for dry beans. She always lost. On rare occasions when one of the miners had a little extra in his poke, he'd lay money on the bar for her. Right before she closed at midnight she'd slip that same money under Jeb's door to pay off her marker.

What she really loved about her customers was the fact that they did their best to act like gentlemen when they came into the palace. They'd spruce up by slicking their hair back, shaking the dust from their clothes and boots. Most times they washed their hands even though they didn't have enough money for a room and a hot tub. She could always tell when they trimmed their whiskers, and she'd always compliment them and tell them they looked like fashionable Boston gentlemen. They'd cackle with glee and then she would laugh, too, when she was forced to admit she'd never seen a proper Boston gentleman.

Things were going to change now. For the first time in her young life, Sallie felt fear of the unknown. If only she weren't so ignorant of the world. There wasn't much she could do about the fear of the unknown. She could get some learning, though. She wished again for her brothers, Seth and Josh. If only she knew where they were. All in good time or, as Cotton said, Rome wasn't built in one day, whatever that meant.

In her room at the boardinghouse, with the door closed and locked, Sallie opened the wooden box. Sitting cross-legged in the middle of the bed, she looked at all the bankbooks—red ones, blue ones, green ones, two brown ones. So many numbers. She tried to comprehend the number of zeros. Mr. Waring made it sound like she could buy the world. The world! She wept then at her ignorance.

When there were no more tears to shed, Sallie's thoughts turned to Cotton Easter, her benefactor. *I don't understand, Cotton, if you had all that money, why did you live like you did? There were times when you were hungry and didn't have the money to rent a room. You didn't have a dollar for a bath. Life could have been so much easier for you.*

I wish you had let me know what you were planning. What should I do with all your money, Cotton? I never knew there was so much money in the world. You must want me to do something. What? She looked around, half-expecting to hear Cotton's voice. She flopped back against the ruffled pillows, the wooden box toppling over. She saw it then, the crinkled piece of white paper. A letter. Maybe it was for her, from Cotton. She crossed her fingers and then blessed herself. *Please let it be printed letters. Please, God, let me be able to read the words. Don't let me be ignorant now. I need to know why Cotton was so good and kind to me. Please, God. I'll build a church. I swear to You I will. I'll call it St. Cotton Easter. Cotton was a religious man. He prayed every day. He taught me a prayer. I promise I'll say it every day.*

Sallie squeezed her eyes shut as her fingers played with the folds of the crinkled letter. When she was calm, she spread the single sheet on her lap. The block letters and simple language brought tears to her eyes.

DEAR SALLIE,

IF YOU HAVE THIS LETTER IN HAND THEN YOU KNOW I DIED. I'M LEAVING YOU ALL I HAVE. I DON'T CARE WHAT YOU DO WITH IT. I MEAN THE MONEY. IT NEVER BROUGHT ME ANY HAPPINESS, BUT IT WILL ALLOW YOU TO BECOME A FINE LADY. ALVIN WILL HELP YOU. HE'S A GOOD MAN AND YOU CAN TRUST HIM. SALLIE, YOU WILL BE THE RICHEST WOMAN IN THE STATE OF NEVADA. YOU JUST BE CAREFUL WHO YOU TRUST. DON'T EVER TELL ANYONE THE WAY INTO THE SAFE. NOW YOU CAN STOP SLIDING INTO OTHER MEN'S BEDS. THERE'S NO NEED FOR YOU TO TELL ANYONE YOU DID THAT. REMEMBER WHAT I TOLD YOU. DON'T SHARE YOUR BUSINESS WITH OTHER PEOPLE. SOME THINGS NEED TO BE KEPT SECRET. I LOVE YOU, SALLIE. DON'T GO LAUGHING ON ME NOW. I KNOW I'M OLD ENOUGH TO BE YOUR PA OR YOUR GRANDDADDY. A MAN CAN'T HARDLY STOP WHAT HIS HEART FEELS. I DIDN'T EVEN WANT TO TRY. I WANT YOU TO BE HAPPY, SALLIE. YOU HAVE A GOOD, KIND HEART. SOMETIMES YOU ARE TOO GOOD. YOU TAKE CARE OF YOURSELF AND WHEN YOU HAVE TIME, VISIT MY GRAVE AND TALK TO ME. I WON'T BE ABLE TO ANSWER YOU, BUT I'LL BE ABLE TO HEAR YOU. THAT'S ALL I ASK OF YOU, SALLIE. I HOPE YOU FIND A GOOD MAN WHO WILL GIVE YOU CHILDREN AND WHO WILL LOVE YOU THE WAY YOU DESERVE TO BE LOVED. DON'T SHARE YOUR PAST, SALLIE, OR IT

WILL COME BACK TO HAUNT YOU. I LOVE YOU,
SALLIE.

YOUR FRIEND,
COTTON EASTER

Sallie rolled over on the bed and burst into tears. "I never got a
letter before," she whispered into her pillow. "I'll keep this letter
forever and ever. I'll read it every day and I'll do what you say. I'll
visit and we'll talk. I'll talk and you listen. That's what you said,
Cotton. You have my promise that I won't . . . you know, do what
you said." A moment later she was off the bed and out the door.
She ran, skidding around the corners, not caring who saw her or
what they thought. She had something to do. Something important. Later she could worry about acting like a lady.

When she arrived at the cemetery she was breathless and di-
sheveled. Her eyes were frantic as she searched out the mound of
dark earth that waited for the marker. When she saw the dried
flower petals she knew she had the right grave. She'd spent the last
of her money on the small bouquet. Now she could bring fresh
flowers every day if she wanted to.

Sallie sat down on the hard ground. She brought her knees up to
her chin and hugged them with her arms. "Cotton, it's me, Sallie. I
got your letter today. It was in the box with all the bankbooks. It
was real nice of you to leave me all your money. I'm going to take
the train to Texas and visit my family. I took some of the money out
of the bank. I'm going to buy my mama a nice little house and a
new dress. I'll get things for the young ones, too, and maybe see
about getting them some learning. I can't wait to see my mother's
face when I walk in the door. She always said Seth would be the
one to make a lot of money. Seth was the oldest. I never knew him
because he lit out before I was born. So did Josh. Ma was so proud
of her two oldest sons. Every day she'd say they're coming back
and will bring presents for everyone. They never did. Then Ma
stopped talking about them. I don't even know what they look like,
Cotton. Ma said they were the spittin' image of Pa. Maybe someday I can find them and help them out. It don't seem right that I
don't know what my own brothers look like. All I can see, Cotton,
is Ma's face. I know she was pretty when she was a young girl, but
Pa, he drained the life out of her. I used to hear her cry at night, but
she always had a smile on her face in the morning.

"I haven't seen that house up in the hills yet. It must be a beautiful place to be called Sunrise. Maybe Mama will want to come here and live with me. That would be okay, wouldn't it, Cotton? I'll get her a fancy chair so she can just sit and do nothing. I'll bring her flowers and give her steak to eat every day. I'm going to get her the prettiest dress in the whole world. Fancy shoes, too, and stockings. A pearl necklace, Cotton. I'll rub glycerine on her hands, file her fingernails, and maybe put some polish on them. I don't know what I'll do about Pa. Maybe I'll just let him drink hisself to death. That seems to be the only thing that makes him happy.

"I'm going to buy a new dress, Cotton, for the trip. I want Ma to be proud of me when she sees me. I want to thank you for all this good. I promised God I was going to build a church and call it St. Cotton Easter. Maybe the preacher will let me sing on Sunday. I'd like that. I'll sing for you, Cotton. You look down on me, you hear. Do you have wings, Cotton? Jeb McGuire said angels have wings and they ring little bells. 'Course he was drunk when he said that. I like the way it sounds. I have so much to learn, Cotton. I don't hardly know nothing. I'm going to be twenty years old and I'm ignorant as some of them miners who never had any schoolin' at all.

"I know you wanted to be planted here, Cotton, but I been thinking. If I move into that house up in the hills, I won't be able to come here too much. I don't want you gettin' lonely here all by yourself. I'd be willing to dig you up and take you up there. Mr. Waring said there's all kinds of flowers and gardens. I could make you a cemetery and talk to you every day. I want you to think about that, Cotton, and when I come back the next time, I want a sign that you think it's okay. If Jeb is right, ring your little bell. It's going to be a couple of weeks till I can come back here. I'll tell you all about my trip to Texas on the train. Maybe I'll have my whole family with me when I come to visit next time. My mama will want to thank you personal like. She has manners, my mama does.

"I need to be going home now. I'll be here on Sunday when they put up your marker. I want you to know, Cotton, I paid for that with my own money, not yours. I don't like to say good-bye so I'll just say I'll be back. The sagebrush smells real sweet today. There aren't any clouds in the sky. It's dusty and dry." There was genuine concern in her voice when she said, "If there aren't any clouds in the sky, what are you resting on?"

Sallie stood, smoothed down her dress, and did her best to tuck her flyaway blond curls back into place. She sniffed at the sagebrush-scented air before she waved her arm in a jaunty little salute of happiness.

Sallie climbed down from the wagon that was loaded with her personal possessions. She savored the moment by squeezing her eyes shut and then opening them slowly, drinking in the sight of her new home. In her life she had never dreamed such a place existed. The flower borders surrounding the house were every color of the rainbow. She bent down to touch the dark soil. It was moist to the touch, and from somewhere she could hear water dripping. The lawn was springy underfoot and damp, greener than a carpet of emeralds. She looked to the left and then to the right. "Now I know why Cotton's granddaddy called this place Sunrise," she murmured.

She backed up until she was standing between a row of tall stately-looking trees that afforded her a better look at the house, which was now hers. Pristine white columns glistened in the sun. She thought about the tar paper shack she'd lived in with her family back in Texas, a shanty with no windows and a door that had to be nailed shut and stuffed with rags in the winter. The door on this house was stout and beautiful, with tiny diamond-shaped panes of colored glass at the top. A heavy brass handle was just as shiny as the windows. But it was the heavy quarry stone in muted shades of gray and brown that brought a smile to her face. There would be no drafts in this house in the winter.

Sallie meandered around the grounds. Benches circled trees, and stone ornaments of different animals dotted the little path that led nowhere. It was cool and dim, green and lush. She tried to imagine herself sitting in the gazebo with a frosty glass of lemonade, dressed in a frilly pink afternoon dress, with a book in her hand she couldn't read. She giggled. "Oh, Cotton, you should see me now."

She was at the front door now. Should she lift the heavy brass knocker? Should she fit the huge brass key into the lock? She was saved from making a decision when the heavy door creaked open. A plump woman, wearing a white apron and a braid of hair that circled her head like a halo, smiled. "Please, miss, come in. Joseph will see to your bags. I am Anna. I cook and clean. My husband tends the gardens and takes care of the animals. Come, come, let me show you your new home."

"Can you open the windows?" Sallie asked.

"But of course. Would you like me to open them for you?"

"Oh, yes. Yes, yes, I would. I want to see the curtains flutter in the breeze. Do all the windows have screens?"

"Yes. I do not open them because Joseph and I don't use the house. We live in one of the cottages in the back. Is there anything you'd like me to do for you now?"

"I'd like to see my room and maybe take a bath. If you don't mind, I'd like to walk through the house myself and look at things."

"It is your house, Miss Coleman. Do you have anything in particular that you'd like me to make for your dinner?"

"It doesn't matter. I do like pie, though. Sweet pie. Very sweet." She smiled wickedly and patted her hips. "I like gravy and potatoes. I like most anything."

"Joseph has a garden he tends. I can the vegetables for the winter. We have a wonderful cold cellar. The special room is in the back. Joseph has a key. He'll turn it over to you at supper. Is there anything else I can do for you? Would you like me to draw your bath?"

"No, thank you. I want to do all that myself. Later on we can discuss your . . . duties."

Lordy, Lordy, Lordy, she was acting like a grand mistress. How wonderful it felt! She sobered almost immediately when she thought about how her mother waited on other people and wore herself down to nothing more than skin and bones. Sallie made a promise to herself that she would never take advantage of anyone who worked for her. Cotton always said you should treat people the way you yourself wanted to be treated. He was right. She'd learned so much from Cotton.

Sallie walked from room to room, her lips pursed in a round circle of approval. She didn't know how she knew, but she was sure that this house looked like houses in Boston. All of the shiny dark furniture must have belonged to Cotton's grandmother or mother. The rugs were thin, colorful, with fringes around the edge. Some were round, most of them square. There were big ones and little ones. Her mother was purely going to smile and smile when she described the brilliant bird in the center of one particular rug. But always, in each room, her gaze settled on the windows and the lace curtains.

She chose a room at the end of the long hallway that overlooked the lush green gardens. The small balcony leading off the dressing room made her squeal in delight. She loved the French doors and the fine wooden floors. The high four-poster with the three-step stool with its canopy of lace made her grin from ear to ear. "I can't hardly believe this," she whispered to herself. Two giant closets rested side by side on one wall. Plenty of room for her ricky-ticky saloon gowns and feather boas. A dresser with flowered marble drawer pulls on all nine drawers caused her to suck in her breath. She didn't have enough underwear to fill the deep cavities. She walked around the room, finally sitting down on a sky-blue satin chaise longue that looked like no one had ever sat in it. Well, she was going to sit in it every day.

Now it was time to open the windows. She pushed the lace curtains aside, stretched her arms to push and tug at the window, and reached down for the wooden screen. She waited for the lace curtains to billow inward. When nothing happened, Sallie rustled the curtains. Still they didn't move inward. She was so disappointed she wanted to cry. She marched over to the bed and climbed up. She sat, determined to wait as long as she had to, until the curtains moved.

Maybe she should lie down and rest her eyes. Within minutes she was sound asleep. The afternoon passed quietly, and she woke when she felt a warm movement of air. She wiped the sleep from her eyes, uncertain if she was truly awake or not. A smile that rivaled the afternoon sunshine stretched across her face when she saw the lace curtains dance in the breeze. "Ohhhh," was all she could think of to say. "This is the happiest day of my life," she said aloud. "Thank you, Cotton, thank you from the bottom of my heart."

Sallie forgot about the step stool and slid off the bed, landing on her backside. She laughed then, peals of joy, as she kicked out with her legs, banging the heels of her shoes on the carpeted floor.

Time for her bath. She looked around for the doorway and saw her bags and boxes stacked neatly to the side. Anna must have unpacked while she slept. The door to one of the closets was slightly ajar. The garish saloon dresses looked out of place. The feathered hair ornaments she wore with her colored boas rested on the top shelf. They, too, looked out of place. A warm flush crept up to her neck and cheeks. She checked the dresser and wasn't surprised to see that her worn underwear and stockings filled only half of one of the drawers. She wished she had been the one to unpack her belongings. The flush of shame and embarrassment that someone else had seen her threadbare underwear deepened. Her shoulders stiffened. Everything was clean and mended. There was no need for shame.

* * *

In the huge, galvanized tub full of bubbles, Sallie leaned back, one long soapy leg extended. She eyed the red polish on the tip of her toes. Decadent! "Who cares!" She scrubbed and rubbed with a cloth that was softer than feathers until her skin was red. The length of toweling was just as soft, and long and wide enough to wrap completely around herself. She loved the way it made her feel. She stared at her reflection in the mirror. Her blond hair curled in ringlets around her ears and neck. She smoothed it back until it was slick against her head. When she wore her hair pulled back like this she looked older, more experienced. When her curls tumbled about her face she looked fifteen.

She thought about her mother again as she dressed. Her mother's hair was like her own, but dull and usually greasy. She wore it pulled back from her sweet face with a string. Sallie was going to buy her a pearl necklace and some earrings. She'd take some of the soap that smelled like roses and wash her mother's hair and fix it the way the ladies in town wore their hair. She knew how to do these things now. Her mother was going to be a queen, and her little sisters would be princesses. She could make it happen now that she had all the money in the world.

Tomorrow she was going back to town. Tonight, when she got ready to sleep in the high bed, she was going to make a list of things to do when she got there. She wasn't going to wait one minute longer than necessary before she returned to Texas to see her family.

Sallie felt every inch the grand lady when Anna served her supper in the dining room at the long table with the huge centerpiece of fresh flowers. The meal was hearty and heavy—thick steak, fried potatoes, gravy, sliced tomatoes, and bread spread with real butter. She thought about the thin gruel and the hard bread spread with lard that she'd eaten when she lived in Texas. Well, that was never going to happen again. Never, ever. She dug into her rhubarb pie with a vengeance and asked for a second helping. When she was finished with her meal she asked for Joseph.

"Ma'am, how can I help you?" he asked respectfully.

"I want to go back to town tomorrow, early, before the sun comes up. I plan on . . . going to Texas. I'm not sure when I'll be back."

"Would you like me to take you in the automobile, ma'am?"

"Why, yes, I would purely love that. Where did Mr. Easter get an automobile?"

"Won it fair and square in a poker game. I learned to drive it all by myself. Mr. Easter didn't want no part of something on four wheels with an engine. He said it was the devil's own machine. I'll be ready at sunup."

"So will I," Sallie responded smartly. "How hard was it to learn, Joseph?"

"Not hard at all, ma'am. I could teach you when you get back. You need to practice so's you don't run into no trees and scrub along the way."

"You need to wear a hat, miss," Anna said. "Your hair will look like the end of a broom if you don't. Dust and sand get in your eyes. Joseph wears special spectacles when he drives that machine."

"Will you be wanting to see the secret room now?" The old man held out a key ring with a large brass key dangling from the end.

"Yes, I would, Joseph. Thank you for supper, Anna. It was real good, specially that pie. Who pays you your wages, Anna?"

"Mr. Waring. He comes up here on the first of every month. In the winter he pays us for three or four months at a time. Will you be thinking of changing that, ma'am?"

"No. But, maybe he should be paying you more now that I'm going to live here and you will have more duties. I'll speak to him. If you want someone else to help you, I can ask in town."

"I would have no objection to someone helping out. Joseph and me, we ain't young'uns anymore. Our bones creak a bit. Whatever you think best, ma'am." Sallie nodded, and followed Joseph out of the dining room.

"This be the room, miss." Joseph held out the key and withdrew discreetly. Sallie waited until the old man was out of sight before she fit the key into the lock. The door swung open. She stepped into a huge, bare room with no windows. Sallie held the lamp high in order to see better. Against the wall was the largest safe she'd ever seen. It went from floor to ceiling, an iron monster, shiny black with a huge silver eye in the middle and a thick iron handle.

It took Sallie six tries before she managed to open the safe. When she heard the final click on the dial, she yanked at the handle. The heavy door refused to budge. She dug her heels into the carpeted floor and pulled backward until she thought her head was going to explode right off her neck. The door creaked open. With her back against the inside of the door, she shoved with her backside until there was enough room to look inside. For the first time in her life she grew faint. Six long shelves, maybe six feet long, were filled with small burlap sacks. Each appeared to be the same size and weight. She opened three of the sacks. Gold. A wooden box full of papers sat square in the middle of the third shelf. Directly underneath was a second wooden box, this one with a lid. Sallie removed the lid and stared down at thick stacks of money.

Sallie sat down on the floor and hugged her knees. She stared at the contents of the safe, wondering what she was meant to do with this fortune.

A long time later, when the lamp started to smoke, Sallie pushed the massive door closed, twirled the knob, and backed out of the room. Her footsteps were sluggish as she made her way back to her room. Her shoulders slumped as she undressed and pulled on her nightgown. She wished suddenly that she could turn time backwards. She wished she'd never gone to Alvin Waring's office, wished Cotton were still alive, wished she were back at the bingo palace singing for her customers. In just three short days her life had been turned upside down. "I don't know what to do," she whispered into her pillow. "I understand, Cotton, this was a load on your shoulders, and that's why you didn't want it all. Maybe if I get more learning, it will be different. I don't think so, though. Is this what you meant when you said money was the root of all evil? Will I turn evil? I don't want to be evil. I just want to be me. The Lord, He must want me to be here. He must have placed His hand on your shoulder and told you to do this. I don't know why. Maybe I'll never know."

Sallie wept then, like the child she was. Eventually she slept, her pillow stained with tears.

The next four days passed like a whirlwind. Sallie shopped for new clothes, then purchased two valises and packed them with gifts for her family. She spent hours with Alvin Waring signing papers, making arrangements for the church to be built. She carried her plans one step farther and asked to have a town house built for herself so she wouldn't have to go back and forth to the house on the mountain. The last order of business was instructing Alvin Waring to buy the bingo palace and remodel it.

Sunday found her at the cemetery along with Cotton's friends. The preacher said his few words, she said hers, and Alvin Waring made a small speech that dealt with life and death, the Lord, and anyone else whose name he could remember. The preacher blessed the marker as Sallie placed her bouquet of flowers at its base.

The bingo palace was opened for the luncheon spread that Sallie paid her old landlady to prepare. Sallie sang song after song until her throat was hoarse. When it was over she helped clear away the debris. Then she closed the door and didn't look back. In two hours time she was going to step onto the train that would take her to Texas and the family she'd left behind.

The last thing she said to Alvin Waring was, "I would appreciate it if you would increase Anna and Joseph's wages. I'd like it very much if you could find someone else to help out. There's a young Chinese girl at the laundry house who might be interested in the job. Her name is Su Li. She has a sister and a brother. If I bring my family back here, I'm going to need lots of help. They work very hard at the laundry. Children shouldn't have to work that hard. If they're interested, tell them I'll pay them good wages and they won't have to work on Sundays."

"I'll speak with them, Miss Coleman. Have a safe trip. I hope everything turns out the way you want it to. Call on me when you return; I'm at your service."

"Thank you, Mr. Waring, for everything. I'd like it if you'd call me Sallie. You won't forget to call the Pinkertons and have them start a search for my brothers Seth and Josh. It's mighty important for me to find them so I can share my . . . just share."

"I'll take care of it . . . Sallie. You take care of yourself."

"I will." The child in her bubbled over. "I can't wait to see my mother. I bought her all these fine things. I hope she likes them. She will, won't she, Mr. Waring?"

"Of course she will, child. I think, though, more than anything, she's going to be so happy to see you, she won't be thinking of fine presents. Your love and the fact that you're going back to help will be all she wants. Mark my word."

"What does that mean, Mr. Waring, mark my word?"

"It means what I said is almost certainly true."

"Oh. Good-bye, Mr. Waring." She reached up on her toes to kiss the dry, withered cheek.

Alvin Waring stood for a long time watching the train chuff out of sight. If he'd been younger, he would have run after the train. He sighed. He had a long list of things to do for Sallie, and there was no time like the present to get started. It would be a labor of love.

Tears of happiness dripped down Sallie's cheeks. She didn't care. *I'm coming, Mama. I'm going to make everything better for you. I'm coming, Mama.*

She was going home.

1

At three-thirty in the afternoon, the loudspeaker in the offices of Babylon crackled to life. The decibel level remained high; customers continued to gamble. "This is a reminder, ladies and gentlemen, that Babylon will close its doors promptly at 6:00 P.M. and will not reopen until one minute past midnight. This announcement will be repeated six times during the next three hours."

"Oh, Marcus, do you really think it's going to be a surprise?" Fanny asked her husband. "What I mean is, Bess and John are smart, don't you think they'll see through that little ruse we conjured up to get them out of the casino?"

"No, I do not. Bess knows you never ask her to do anything unless it's important. She thinks she's going to the chicken ranch to coax Ruby Thornton, your—what is she, Fanny, your half sister-in-law—to come to the casino? I think it's wonderful of you to want to include her in the family."

"She's part of this family even though Ash said she came in through the back door. She has Thornton blood, and that's good enough for me and the kids. The same goes for Ash's son. It's not right to deny either Ruby or Jeff Lassiter their rightful place. They're both wonderful people. I know it and so do my children."

"I hope it works out, Fanny."

"Of course it will work out. Why wouldn't it? Don't rain on my parade, Marcus."

"As if I would ever do that. Did the boy really agree to come in here and take over for Bess and John? I find that . . . amazing."

"I had to do some fast talking. His mother helped convince him. He's worked in the casino summers and holidays while he was in college. He knows the business and what he doesn't know, he'll learn. We signed a three-year contract with him two days ago. It has to work, Marcus, because I had no other options. If Birch was here, it would be different. He isn't here, so I did what I had to do. It's settled, so let's not talk about it. What am I going to do if Bess and John balk at their retirement present? Just because I think a year-long trip around the world is wonderful doesn't mean she and John will think the same way. Her children packed their bags and brought them over earlier. The limo is coming for them at midnight to take them to the airport. Everything is set unless she balks." Fanny clenched and unclenched her hands as she paced around the office. "She won't, will she, Marcus?"

"Not a chance." Marcus's voice was airy, offhand. "She's going to love it. Stop fretting, Fanny. Let's check the dining room to see if your decorations are finished."

"Billie did it all. She even planned the menu, all of Bess and John's favorite foods. For five hundred people. She didn't even blink, Marcus. My daughter never ceases to amaze me. She said Bess and John weren't the only ones who were going to be surprised tonight. What do you think she meant by that?"

Marcus chuckled. "It's probably one of those inside Thornton family jokes. You love surprises. Guess you'll have to wait." He steered her into the dining hall, then watched as she darted across the room to embrace Billie.

"Oh, honey, it's beautiful. We have to take pictures." Fanny hugged her daughter.

"The ice sculpture goes in the middle of the main table," Billie explained. "There's a gizmo under the table that keeps it from melting. Sage hooked up the fountain. Chue brought the orchids earlier this afternoon. Aren't they gorgeous?"

"Only half as gorgeous as these tablecloths. Seed pearls sewn on linen, Billie?"

"I'm going to use them at our next trade show. I have a machine that does it. I wanted this to be really special. They're bringing the balloons at five o'clock. When Bess and John walk through the front door they'll drop. From there on, it's fun, fun, fun. Our own private night. Bess's family and friends, the Colemans, all our workers and their families. Josh Coleman is about to arrive from Virginia with his family. He called last night. We're going to have a full house. Think about it, Mom. Our blood family and our working family."

"It's like a dream. I just hope Bess and John love it all. Marcus and I are going upstairs. We'll be down at five-thirty. Call me when Aunt Billie and Thad get here."

"I don't miss this place at all," Fanny said as she unlocked the door to the penthouse. "It's a shame it sits here empty. I offered Jeffrey the use of it, but he said he prefers to live at home. I don't think his mother is well, and he likes to look after her. I respect that in a son. Ash was proud of the boy even though he wouldn't admit it. I think he's going to do very well."

"Does that mean you like our little house better than these sumptuous surroundings?"

"Marcus, I love our house. What I really love is seeing you cook in that state-of-the-art kitchen. It's cozy. I love cozy things. I guess I'm just a snuggler. It reminds me so much of our old house back in Sunrise. We have a front porch, a back porch, a garden for flowers and vegetables, a dog run, a gorgeous fireplace, a Jacuzzi. You to share it with. I couldn't ask for more. Retirement is so blissful. Being able to wake up and decide at a moment's notice to take a trip is . . . what is it, Marcus?"

"It's wonderful. I have an idea, let's take a shower together."

"Mr. Reed, you do come up with delicious ideas from time to time."

"I do, don't I? Last one in has to wash the other one's back."

Sage Thornton stood at the end of the jetway, his stomach muscles churning. He wondered if he was going to get sick.

He would have known his twin anywhere even though he was seeing him in profile. And then Birch turned. Air hissed from between Sage's lips. He stared at his father's image. Somewhere during his life, he'd seen this exact same scene. Probably sometime during his teens when he picked up his father from the airport.

Even from this distance Birch looked lean and fit, with a bronze tint to his skin. A baseball cap that said Thornton Chickens was pushed back on his head. It was worn and frayed. A tee shirt with "Babylon" across the middle, equally worn and frayed, faded blue jeans, and scuffed hiking boots completed his outfit. A canvas carryall was slung over his shoulder. His eyes were bluer than sapphires against his tan. His teeth pearl white. At six-two, Birch could see over the heads of his fellow passengers. The moment he spotted Sage he dropped his bag and shouldered his way through the crowd of deplaning passengers.

They stood eyeball to eyeball as passengers milled about them. Sage's voice was choked when he said, "It's been a long time, Birch."

"Too long. The only thing I missed was you and Mom. C'mere,

you big lug. Jesus, it's good to see you, Sage." His voice was just as choked as his brother's. "I knew you'd be the one to get married first and have a family. I want you to meet my wife."

Sage's jaw dropped. "You're married!"

"Yep, to the most wonderful girl in the world. We lived in a tent for three years so that should give you some kind of an idea of what she's like. She's simple and earthy like Mom. She's standing over there because she wanted to give us a few minutes alone. You're gonna love her." Birch motioned for his wife to join them.

She was tall like a showgirl, thin but well proportioned, with blond hair faded white from the sun. Her eyes were dove gray, almost translucent against her honeyed tan. An eerie feeling washed through Sage when he met Celia's gaze. Somewhere within him an alarm sounded. He backed off a step and held out his hand once the introductions were made. He saw the puzzled look on Birch's face. His brother had expected him to hug his wife and welcome her into the family. Later he was going to have to think about this scene.

Celia's voice was sweet, almost honeyed when she reached for Sage's hand. "I feel like I know you. Birch spoke about you every single day."

Sage forced a laugh. "I hope it was good."

"Only wonderful things. I'm looking forward to meeting your family. We hung the pictures of you and your family in our tent. We used safety pins. Those pictures were the first thing we saw in the morning and the last thing we saw at night."

"I'm flattered. You could have written more, Birch."

"You know me. I was never a letter writer. You aren't either. Who's kidding who?"

"Okay, I'll give you that one. Do you have a lot of luggage?"

Birch and Celia burst out laughing. They pointed to their duffel bags. "This is it. We lived very frugally. I'm going to have to borrow some clothes or else show up at the party in this attire. I'm assuming it's black tie."

"You assumed right. Big doings. Mom and Billie have been planning this for weeks. Probably months. Is this just a visit or are you staying? You didn't say."

"We're here to stay. When you wrote that Bess and John were retiring I knew it was time to come back and run the casino. That's why I'm here. It's time."

Sage thought his stomach was going to lurch right out of his body.

"I figured we'd live in the penthouse if no one objected," Birch went on. "How do you like living at Sunrise, Mr. Family Man?"

"I love it. Iris and the kids don't even want to come to town anymore. She says we're hermits. Maybe we are." He could feel the translucent gray eyes boring into his back.

"We have to buy something to wear, Birch. I didn't realize how awful we looked until I saw all these people so dressed up. Living in a Third World country is not conducive to fashion."

"It's not a problem, honey. We'll just go to one of the boutiques in the casino and get whatever we need."

"Just like that!"

"Uh-huh."

Sage concentrated on positioning the bags in the trunk of his car.

"God, I can't wait to take a shower. I'm going to stand under it until the water runs cold," Birch said.

"Sweetie, we have to shop. We don't want to embarrass your family."

"No, Celia, we don't have to shop. We call downstairs and they send the stuff up. We pick and choose and they take the rest back. You can do that while I'm standing under that nice hot shower."

Sage scrunched his big frame into the driver's seat. "Mom and Marcus are in the penthouse. I got you a room."

"A *room?*" Celia said.

"Actually it's a suite," Sage said. He wondered why his voice sounded so defensive.

Birch's voice was cheerful when he said, "Guess you're going to have to wait a while to move into that fancy penthouse, honey."

"It doesn't look the same, Birch. Mom redid it when she moved in. She hated all those mirrors, chrome and glass. She smashed the place up one day. It kind of looks like Sunrise now. She's got a set of those red chairs."

"What does Sunrise look like?" Celia asked from the backseat.

"Comfortable and worn. Green plants, bright colors. Home," Birch said.

"Oh," Celia said.

"You're gonna love it, honey."

"I'm sure I will."

"So, tell me about this party tonight. No, on second thought, tell me about the family. How's Mom?"

"Mom's great. She's happier now than she's ever been. She has a wonderful life with Marcus. They live on the outskirts of town in a small house. They garden, they travel, they take the kids for days at a time. She really is happy. She and Dad made peace the last few years. There at the end he turned out to be quite a guy."

"If you call pumping a bullet into your brother quite a guy, I guess so."

"You weren't here, Birch. It was wrong, but it was right, too, in a cockamamie way. It's over, and I don't want to talk about it."

"Sure. I want you to know, Sage, I tried to get a plane out but it was the rainy season and I couldn't. I was sick over it. Hell, we couldn't even get to a phone for ten days. I figured it was just better to stay where I was at that point. I did grieve, Sage."

"We all did." Jesus, what was wrong with him. Why was he acting so . . . so stupid? This was Birch. This was his twin. This was his best friend sitting next to him, and he was acting like he had a burr in his Jockeys. He struggled with his emotions. "Sunny's doing great. She's in a remission state right now, and she's living permanently at the center. She has a whole new life. There aren't any words to tell you how I admire our sister. She's good with the kids, too, considering her limitations."

"I don't think I could ever give up my children for adoption," Celia said from the backseat.

Loyalty ringing in his voice, Birch said, "If Sage was your brother, you could. I bet Iris is a wonderful mother to Sunny's kids. She's like Mom, isn't she?"

"Yeah. Yeah, she is. Mom gave her all her recipes. She taught her to sew and do all those mother things. She helped a lot with Dad at the end. Iris gets along with everyone. When the kids are older, she might want to go back to teaching at the university but then again, maybe she won't. Wait till you taste her strawberry-rhubarb pie. You can't tell the difference between hers and Mom's."

"Billie?"

"She's on top of the world. Three years in a row she was voted Woman of the Year by the textile industry. She managed to sell sixty-five million Bernie and Blossom dolls. They're still going strong. She's thinking of creating little brothers and sisters now. She's working on the prototypes. We'll test-market them in a few months."

"Guess that means the Thornton coffers are full, eh?"

Sage took that moment to look in the rearview mirror to check on an eighteen-wheeler behind him that wanted to pass. He felt his shoulders stiffen at the sight of Celia's glittering eyes.

A devil perched itself on Sage's shoulder. "You know Mom. She siphons the money out as soon as it comes in. It goes right to the rehab centers."

"How is the casino doing? The last letter I had from Mom said it was bigger and better than ever. She even sent me a clipping from one of the newspapers. The article said Vegas expects to host 33,000,000 visitors this year. It went on to say each visitor is expected to gamble $154.00. That's some very heavy money."

"You never showed me that article, Birch," Celia said.

"I didn't think you'd be interested, honey. I threw it away."

Sage risked a second glance in the rearview mirror. The glittering eyes looked hard and cold to him. He knew in his gut Celia was trying to calculate the amount of money in her head. He could feel a nerve start to twitch under his eye.

Birch, oblivious to his wife's petulant face, continued to ask questions. "Can we stop and see Sunny?"

"She's at the casino, Birch. Mom brought her and her friend over early this morning. It was almost like old times except you were missing."

Celia leaned over the front seat. "In a wheelchair? Doesn't that create a problem?"

"No, honey. Dad was in a wheelchair. The whole casino is wheelchair accessible. My grandfather made sure of that so Dad wouldn't have any problems."

The devil on Sage's shoulder bounced back. "She has her dog with her. So does Harry."

"In the casino! That's so . . . unsanitary," Celia said.

"They're trained," Sage said tightly. He didn't like this girl leaning over the seat, didn't like her warm breath wafting into his right ear, didn't like the soap and water smell of her. He didn't like her, *period*. Talk about instant reactions.

"Will you relax, Celia. Mom is closing the casino tonight—so it will be just friends and family. The dogs are special. The dogs enable Sunny to get out and about more. I think it's great."

Celia flopped back against the seat cushion. Sage knew her eyes were glued to the back of Birch's head.

"Where are you from, Celia?"

"A small town in Alabama. Population twelve hundred or so."

"Are you going back for a visit?"

"No."

"Celia's family is gone. There's nothing to go home to. In a manner of speaking she's an orphan. Was an orphan. Now she has me and our family. Right, honey?"

"I know I'm going to love your family, Birch. We never talked about anything else but your family. Morning, noon, and night. I feel like I know every single one of you, even the children."

The devil on Sage's shoulder moved slightly. "Didn't you *ever* talk about your family, Celia?"

"There wasn't anything to talk about. Your family is so interesting."

And rich, Sage thought. "Do you want to go in the front door or up through the garage?"

"The garage. Neal would boot our asses right off the floor looking the way we look. What room are we in?"

"Dad's favorite room, 2711."

"What time should we be downstairs? Do you want me to hide and make a grand entrance? What's the drill here?"

"The party starts at six-thirty. Bess and John are coming in through the front door and everyone is going to yell, SURPRISE! Balloons will drop. Billie said you should weave your way around the crap tables and then we'll all yell SURPRISE again, at which point Mom will faint so be prepared to catch her. Nice meeting you, Celia. Oh, by the way, we all kicked in to get Bess and John a year's trip around the world. Tap that trust fund, big brother."

"A year's trip around the world. That probably cost more than I could earn in a lifetime. What trust fund? Do you have a trust fund, Birch? Shame on you for not telling me. It was nice meeting you, too, Sage."

Sage leaned against the wall. "This is not good," he muttered. He sat on the trunk of his car, his thoughts chaotic as he smoked three cigarettes, one after the other. Maybe he was having an off day. Maybe he didn't see what he thought he saw in the new Mrs. Thornton's eyes. *Keep your thoughts to yourself. Don't look for trouble,* an inner voice warned.

Sage walked over to the elevator. He shivered and didn't know why.

"Here they come! Here they come! Get ready!" Fanny cried, excitement ringing in her voice.

The great doors opened. Bess and John Noble walked onto the casino floor to the shouts of "SURPRISE!" Colored balloons rained downward.

Fanny ran to her friends of forty years and swept them into her arms. "Don't cry, Bess, I don't have any tissues. We wanted to do this for you. It hardly seems enough for all you've done for our family." She couldn't hold the news back for one more instant. "We are giving you a trip around the world! A whole year, Bess, to do nothing but spend time with your husband. Please say you want it."

"I'm saying it for both of us," John said. "We were just talking about taking a trip last week. Nothing as grand as a trip around the world. We accept, don't we, Bess."

"*Yes.* But Fanny . . ."

"Shhh, it's our pleasure. All the kids chipped in. Your kids packed your bags. I know they packed all the wrong things so if you play the third machine from the left in aisle two you'll have enough money for a new wardrobe."

"Oh, Fanny . . . what a good, kind friend you are."

"Hey, I'm taking up too much time. The line behind me is getting longer and longer. Everyone wants to give you a kiss and a hug. Tonight you're Cinderella and your limo will be by the front door exactly at midnight. I'm going to miss you so. . . ."

"Mom, look over there by the crap tables," Sage whispered in her ear.

"Is that Birch? No! It is!"

Sage stepped aside as his brother swept his mother into his arms, twirling her around and around until she was dizzy. "Oh, Birch, it's so good to see you. You look so handsome. Actually you look just the way your father looked when he wore his tux. This is such a wonderful surprise!"

"Mom, this is Celia, my wife."

"You're married, and you didn't tell anyone!"

"Mom, she's special. I didn't think I'd ever meet anyone like her. She's so gorgeous she takes my breath away. We're here to stay. I'd like to start to work on Monday if that's okay with you."

Sage, his wife Iris next to him, watched as Birch drew Celia forward. He was in a perfect position to see his mother's raised eyebrows at the young woman's attire. He didn't think it was his imagination when he saw her shoulders tense.

Celia was wearing a strapless, backless black sequined sheath of a dress with a slit up the side. As she stepped forward, Fanny reached for her hands but didn't kiss or hug her. "I'm so pleased to meet you, Celia. Welcome to the family. How do you like Babylon?"

"It's . . . fantastic. I shopped all afternoon. Living in a tent and taking a shower under a waterfall is . . . this is just wonderful. I can't believe you *own* all of this."

"It is a bit startling at first. After a while, it's just a place of business."

Iris turned away to stare at the people surrounding Bess and John. "What would you do if I dressed like that, Sage? I feel like a Girl Scout leader compared to her. For someone who lived in a tent and showered under a waterfall she looks pretty good in those diamonds. I thought you said they only had raggedy stuff."

"She went shopping," Sage hissed. "Mom didn't hug her or kiss her the way she did you when she first met you."

"She's taking a wait-and-see attitude. Birch was shock enough. Coupling that with a new bride who looks like she belongs in the chorus line should give you your answer. What do you think of her?"

Sage evaded the question. "Birch is in love with her. It doesn't matter what anyone else thinks. She just got here. She's probably nervous, and by now she's aware that she isn't dressed right."

"Oh, she's dressed right. Those shoes she's wearing cost $800. I saw them in the shop last week. What you're seeing is who that young woman is. She's a lot younger than Birch, too. She was pleasant enough, but I don't think I'm going to like her."

Sage's sigh of relief was so loud, Iris shook his arm. "You don't like her either, do you? You were waiting for me to say it first. We need to give her a chance. First impressions are not always what they seem. Let's agree, Sage, to stand back and be fair. Okay?"

"Sure, honey. You don't look like a Girl Scout leader to me. That's a nifty dress you're wearing, and you look great."

"Aunt Billie made it for me. She made one for Sunny and Billie, too. Sunny's looking better than I've seen her look in a long time. I guess it's because she's happy."

"Guess so. I'm going to check on the kids. Lexie's probably wading in one of the pools by now."

"Marcus is watching them. They were picking flowers for Sunny in one of the hanging gardens."

"I'll check it out. It's my turn to kiss Bess and John. I'll see you later by the banquet table."

Sunny waved from across the room. Iris weaved her way toward her. She bent over to kiss her and Harry, whose chair was parked next to Sunny's, their dogs next to their respective chairs.

"There she is, one of my two favorite people in the whole world.

Here comes the other one," Birch said, as Billie came up behind Sunny's chair. Iris watched as Birch kissed and hugged both his sisters before he introduced his new wife. She didn't know if she should laugh or cry at the expressions on Sunny's and Billie's faces. The expression of distaste on her sister-in-law's face was so fleeting she thought she imagined it until Sunny, in her own inimitable way, let her know she'd seen it, too.

"Harry and I were wondering if we dare head for the banquet table. We forgot our bibs." She looked pointedly at Celia when she said, "We drool and dribble our food at times. What would happen if you did that wearing such a fancy dress?" she asked Celia.

"I guess I'd have to get it cleaned." Celia looked pointedly at her husband, who was talking to Harry, Sunny's companion.

"The cleaners would ruin it," Billie said.

Celia made a little face. "I think I made the wrong choice when I picked out this dress. Birch has always said this was such a glittery, shimmering place, I thought it would be appropriate. I was wrong. I just itched to buy it. I lived in cutoff jeans and raggedy tee shirts for so long. I just didn't think. I hope I didn't offend anyone."

"Just my mother and me," Sunny said. Billie cleared her throat. Iris looked away.

"Did I miss something?" Birch asked.

"No. Sunny was just agreeing with me that I'm dressed all wrong. She said I probably offended your mother."

"See, I told you, but you wouldn't listen." Birch tweaked Celia's cheek before he walked over to Bess and John Noble.

"Are those diamonds real?" Sunny asked.

"The jeweler said they were. Birch insisted I get them. He said he wanted me to sparkle tonight."

Sunny's voice was prim when she said, "We're not a showy family. Actually, we're all rather modest. Mom always said less is more if you know what I mean."

"Yes. Thank you for pointing it out to me."

"My pleasure," Sunny said.

"Excuse me. Birch is motioning for me to join him."

"Sunny, that was uncalled for," Billie said.

"Damn straight it was. I saw the expression on her face when she looked at me and Harry. It was distaste. Ask Iris if you don't believe me." Iris nodded, her face miserable.

"She's in a new environment. We're all strangers to her. So she dressed wrong, so what. All of us at one time or another either overdressed or underdressed. Don't create a problem, Sunny, where none exists. She's Birch's wife," Billie said.

Harry, silent until now said, "I used to paint portraits. I was pretty good, too. The critics always said my eyes were the best. That's because they're the mirror of one's soul. That young woman has no soul. That's strictly my own opinion. Let's try the banquet table, Sunny. My hands are more steady than yours are today, so I'll hand you the food. We'll come back here to eat it out of the way, okay?"

"Sure. Will you guys watch our dogs?"

"Sure," Billie said.

"I admire Sunny so," Iris said, a catch in her voice.

Billie's voice was soft when she said, "Me too."

"Birch's timing was off. I think that's what this is all about. It would have been nice if he'd waited and made it a family thing where Celia could be the center of attention. However, I understand where he's coming from. Sage said he expects to start work on Monday. Did anyone tell him about Jeffrey? Sage said it wasn't his place to tell him. He also said Birch doesn't know how to play second banana. Does that mean there's going to be a problem, Billie?"

"Off the top of my head, I'd say yes. Let's not worry about that tonight. We're here to have a good time, so let's have a good time."

"Do I look dowdy and frumpy, Billie?"

"Absolutely not."

"Then why do I feel that way?"

"Because your quiet, peaceful world has been invaded by a smashing blond bombshell. I feel a little dowdy myself. I thought I looked pretty good when I left the house."

"So we're jealous is what you're saying."

"No, that's not what I'm saying. We're who we are, and Celia is who she is."

"Sage sees something we aren't seeing. He was so hyped about going to the airport to pick up Birch. He hasn't slept for three nights, that's how excited he was. He wanted to take the kids to the airport to show them off. He wanted his brother to see his kids. When he got back, it was . . . sad. I felt so bad I wanted to cry for him. He had these wonderful plans, these great expectations, and suddenly a new wife on the scene wiped all those plans away. He knows there's going to be some kind of blowup when Birch finds out Jeff signed on to run Babylon."

"Everything will work itself out, Iris. Mom will step in and do what she always does, bring order and sense to everything."

"Not this time, Billie. Birch has a wife now, and she's going to have a voice in everything he says and does."

"There's Jeff now. He does look a lot like your dad. Ruby's really nice. I like her a lot. I'm glad your mom welcomed her into the family. She belongs. Right off she wanted to know what she could do. She pitched right in. She looks so damn normal compared to . . . Celia. I thought you were bringing your boyfriend tonight."

"He had duty. Detectives are on call twenty-four hours a day. He might stop by later. It's not serious, Iris. We're good friends. I like him. He likes me. He doesn't just listen to me, Iris, he actually *hears* what I say. I like that in a man. I'm not about to get serious. I like being my own person, making my own decisions. It works for me the way being married and having kids works for you."

"What do you think works for Celia Thornton?"

"The Thornton money."

"I'm of the same opinion."

"Sunny's dribbling. Let's go clean her up."

"Billie, earlier Jake . . . what happened was Sunny was drinking a soda pop and she let the bottle slip. Jake . . . that little kid was so good about it. He wiped it up and said, 'Heck, Mom, I do that all the time.' Sunny's eyes filled up, and Jake wiped away her tears. He whispered to her for a long time. I guess he was giving her a pep talk because she started to laugh. He was grinning from ear to ear. He's really good with Harry, too. Ash made sure Jake understood his mother's limitations. He really understands, Billie. Do you think as he gets older that will stay with him? Every day I do my best to reinforce all that your dad taught him."

"That boy idolized his grandfather. Trust me, his teachings will stay with Jake. I appreciate you telling me this, Iris."

* * *